Praise for bestselling author
Tori Carrington

"Tori Carrington is an unparalleled storyteller
with an imagination that is absolutely matchless.
These authors are extraordinary and have
a true gift for putting their own special brand
on anything they touch."
—*Rendezvous* on *Private Investigations*

"Tori Carrington's books are noted for being sexy,
with excellent characterization and plotlines that
keep you enthralled 'til the very end."
—*Romance Reviews Today*

"Carrington delivers an intense, very sensual book."
—*RT Book Reviews* on *Branded*

"One of the category's most talented authors."
—*EscapetoRomance.com*

"One of the genre's most beloved authors."
—*Rendezvous*

TORI CARRINGTON

Bestselling husband-and-wife duo Lori and Tony Karayianni are the power behind the pen name Tori Carrington. They've won an *RT Book Reviews* Career Achievement Award and published forty novels, including numerous Harlequin Blaze miniseries, as well as the ongoing Sofie Metropolis, PI, comedic mystery series with another publisher. Visit www.toricarrington.net and www.sofiemetro.com for more information on the couple and their titles.

TORI CARRINGTON

Indecent

Wicked

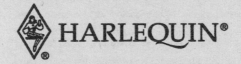

HARLEQUIN®

TORONTO • NEW YORK • LONDON
AMSTERDAM • PARIS • SYDNEY • HAMBURG
STOCKHOLM • ATHENS • TOKYO • MILAN • MADRID
PRAGUE • WARSAW • BUDAPEST • AUCKLAND

Recycling programs
for this product may
not exist in your area.

ISBN-13: 978-0-373-68809-8

INDECENT & WICKED

Copyright © 2010 by Harlequin Books S.A.

The publisher acknowledges the copyright holder of the individual works as follows:

INDECENT
Copyright © 2004 by Lori & Tony Karayianni

WICKED
Copyright © 2004 by Lori & Tony Karayianni

CONTENTS

INDECENT   7

WICKED   251

We wholeheartedly dedicate this book to Susan Till,
who read between the lines and knew
what we wanted to say even when we didn't.
Thanks for making us look so good!

INDECENT

CHAPTER ONE

GOING WITHOUT sex wasn't Colin McKenna's idea of a good time. Which meant he'd had a pretty lousy time of it for the past three months.

His athletic shoes clapped against the cement walkway paralleling the Maumee River, his cadence even, the sound of his breathing filling his ears. To his right, the sun was just beginning to break the horizon causing the temperature to rise on the clear June day. He'd run this route along the river ever since buying his downtown penthouse condo last year. But in the past three months the route had lengthened and lengthened along with his rising level of sexual frustration.

Another man might take things into hand, literally.

Colin preferred running.

His lungs began burning, protesting the pressure he was putting on them. He grudgingly slowed his paced then came to a stop, panting as he turned toward the sun's rays and squinted out over the river to the East Side and International Park. He'd grown up here in Toledo, Ohio, though a long way from downtown in the suburb of Sylvania. But he hadn't hesitated when a block of newly renovated condos had gone up for sale in an old department store building, putting him in the heart of the mid-size city that was an intriguing mix of old and new.

He took several deep breaths, each slower than the one before, as he brought his pulse rate under control. As a psychiatrist, he knew the power of mind over body. It was of some interest, then, that his body was increasingly overruling his mind's need for control.

He'd never paid much attention to the importance of sex in his life until he'd been falsely accused of indecent behavior by one of his patients three months ago. That was when his attorney had suggested he go without until the case was either dropped or settled in order to create a picture of himself as a model, upstanding citizen. Not that he hadn't been that before, but he realized he had been a serial dater.

The case was also the reason why he no longer counseled patients one-on-one but rather took only group and couples sessions.

Three hours, a shower and two such therapy sessions later, Colin sat back in his office chair, listening as the married couple before him bickered about the price of their last meal out. Actually it didn't matter what the topic was, the couple would argue about it. How they'd managed to keep from killing each other much less stay married for the past ten years was beyond him.

Give up and head for divorce court now, he wanted to say, but didn't.

He glanced at his watch. Only five more minutes in the session to go.

Colin didn't think he'd last two.

He absently rubbed the back of his neck. There were times when being a couples therapist was just as bad as going without sex, if only because his experiences over the past ninety days seriously undermined his belief in the institution of marriage. There were two types of couples—married and unmarried—that came to counseling. With the first type, the union was beyond repair and they were looking for him to work miracles on it and with the second type the participants were genuinely interested in putting their individual needs aside for the greater good of the union.

More often than not he saw the former. And the extent of his job was to play referee. One of his three partners at the Sylvania Mental Wellness

Clinic had offered to get him scorecards for sessions like the one he was currently in the middle of or, better yet, a scoreboard and a buzzer to indicate when one of the spouses had entered foul territory.

In the case of the Hansens he would have ruled a TKO three sessions ago. Significant, considering this was their fourth session.

"Jocelyn," Colin said quietly, watching as the woman's face grew redder and spittle formed at the corners of her mouth. Normally an attractive woman, she looked like evil incarnate as she lit into her husband with all the finesse of a pro.

"...and if you think I'm just going to roll over and play patsy, you've got another think coming. I already have three kids. I don't need another. I work a full-time job, same as you, and if I'm too tired for sex every now and again..."

"Jocelyn," Colin said again, never having had to raise his voice during a session before but afraid this time might prove the exception.

Her husband, Larry, was shaking his head, his own color growing darker. "Shut up, Jos."

The room fell silent.

Colin blinked. It was the first time Larry had said something of that nature before. Normally quiet, he nodded and probably didn't pay attention to half of what was being said by either his wife or Colin. Not that Colin could blame him. Jocelyn didn't so much as speak with you as she spoke at you.

Colin took in Jocelyn's shocked appearance, spotting all the signs of a major outburst on the rise. He rubbed his thumb and forefinger against his closed eyelids. That was it. He was never getting married.

A brief knock on the door, then it opened. Colin frowned. The temporary receptionist that an employment agency had provided to fill in for their regular receptionist was not the brightest bulb in the string.

He squinted at the female figure that had come to a halt just inside his door. Definitely not the mousy temp he'd expected to see. Long, long legs encased in sheer black stockings. A short, short skirt that hugged her curvy hips in all the right places. A tight, tight white tank top that looked small enough to fit a six-year-old. Flame-red hair fell to the middle of her back and would no doubt tickle the dimples at the curve of her bottom when she was stripped down to her bare, creamy skin.

Mary Magdalene and the Virgin Mary all wrapped up in one provocative package.

His body was making it all too clear it didn't like his self-imposed temporary celibacy.

His mind told him to hold up on the decision never to marry.

"Ooops. Sorry," the walking advertisement for everything a man ever wanted in a woman said, then twisted her full lips. "Wrong room."

Colin lifted his pencil and pointed over his shoulder. "Rest rooms are the next door up."

She seemed to take her time as she sized him up, then smiled. "Thanks."

Such a simple word.

Such an unexpected reaction as his groin and his throat tightened farther.

The door closed and Colin reluctantly returned his attention to Jocelyn and Larry. Only Larry was still looking at the closed door, his tongue nearly lolling out of the side of his mouth. Meanwhile Jocelyn looked an inch away from smacking her hand against his chin and shearing his tongue in half with the help of his own teeth.

"My, look at that," Colin said before round ten of the Hansens' weekly boxing match could begin. "Our time is up."

He rose to his feet and put his notepad on the chair behind him. "I think we've made some good progress today," he lied. "Same time next week?"

Jocelyn was still glaring at her husband while Larry shook Colin's hand and thanked him. Before they were even through the exit door on the other side of the office, Jocelyn had already begun her next verbal attack. Colin closed the door, hoping they didn't get into an accident on the way home. Not that he was particularly concerned about their well-being. Rather he was more worried about the unsuspecting drivers around them. Never mind the three children that waited at home.

As an only child of older parents, his upbringing differed greatly from what he guessed the Hansen children endured. Discussions at the McKenna dinner table had tended to evolve around page three of *The Wall Street Journal* or a novel one of them had recently read rather than whether his father's inappropriate appreciation of a woman's physical assets had been a shade beyond decent.

He edged around his desk and sat down. He wasn't cut out for this couples-counseling gig. He fared a little better at group therapy sessions—like the addictive personality disorder one that was on tap next, and the monthly sessions he sat in on at a local runaway shelter—but still he preferred the one-on-one approach that allowed him to make significant progress in a patient's psychological development.

He made notes on the Hansens, put the file aside, then pulled the five other files for the group he was due to meet in ten minutes. He fingered through them. He was familiar with four of the members, but the fifth was new. He opened the file on one Lucky Clayborn and sat back in his chair. Court-ordered therapy for two D.U.I.'s in a year and a half.

He pinched the bridge of his nose, silently praying that Lucky Clayborn wasn't the woman who had walked in during his previous session.

Unfortunately, the way his luck was running he fully expected that the sexpot and the drunk driver were one and the same.

FEW THINGS were hotter than a gorgeous guy who had no idea how appealing he was.

Lucky Clayborn sat back in the soft leather chair, her gaze focused on sexy Dr. Colin McKenna while he listened to one of the other group members.

As accidental as it may have appeared, her walking into his office during his previous session had been anything but. After getting no farther than Step Two in the Twelve Step Program on three previous occasions, she'd been curious as to what the court-approved Dr. Colin McKenna was all about. She wasn't an alcoholic, her court-appointed attorney had pointed out to the court during her last time in front of the judge. And while her word against the arresting officer's the second time around hadn't held much sway, she hadn't been drinking when she'd been charged with the last count—she'd been on cold medication. But it seemed ever since the lowering of the legal intoxication limit, a generous tablespoon of cold medicine before you got behind the wheel was enough to set off the Breathalyzer.

And if every now and again she liked to blur the edges of her life with alcohol, that was between her and the vodka bottle.

The problem was she hadn't gotten through the Twelve Step Program because she had, admittedly, been uncooperative. So the judge had restricted her driving privileges for six months and ordered her to six weeks of counseling (as an aside she'd also suggested Lucky stay away from any cold medications that contained alcohol).

So Lucky had wanted to get a look at the guy who had the power to have her license taken away altogether.

And she'd liked what she'd seen.

She slowly recrossed her legs, watching the sexy doc's gaze slide to watch the movement even as he focused on the other patient's progress report.

"Miss Clayborn?" he said a moment later, startling her. "Would you like to go next?"

Go where? She almost asked.

Then she realized she was being asked to introduce herself.

She glanced over the four other group members—two men and two women—who had all shared their stories. Two admitted alcohol was their stimulent of choice while the other two claimed prescription drugs were to blame for their addictions.

She quietly cleared her throat then crossed her legs again. "I'm Lucky Clayborn and I'm here to get help for my habit of taking cold medication when I'm sick then getting behind the wheel of a car and going to work."

There was a heartbeat of silence, then one of the women laughed, the other three members smiled and Dr. Colin merely continued gazing at her with those rich dark-brown eyes without blinking.

"Cold medication was to blame for both counts?" he asked without consulting notes or a file or even looking away from her.

For the first time in a long time, Lucky broke a challenging gaze. "You've done your homework," she said quietly. "I'm impressed."

"And you're avoiding my question."

She folded her hands in her lap, trying to ignore how damp her palms were. "No. No, cold medication wasn't to blame for both counts."

She looked for something else to focus on rather than his face and found his hands an intriguing substitute. They were large and thick and it was all too easy to imagine them covering her breasts, her taut nipples between his thumbs and index fingers. Her gaze wandered up his perfectly starched white shirt and boring tie, resting briefly on the enticing, cleanly shaven stretch of his neck before lingering on his mouth.

After his bedroom eyes and thick, dark-blond hair, his mouth was by far his most appealing feature. She enjoyed watching his well-defined lips move when he said something in his deep baritone, then smiled. And he would undoubtedly know just what to do with his mouth when words were no longer the order of the day. Yes…Dr. Colin McKenna would definitely know how to kiss a woman. A man as attractive as he was not wearing a wedding ring—if she were married to him she'd probably solder it to his finger—didn't get far without tasting his share of women. And though she wasn't getting exactly the response she wanted from him with her leg-crossing, she did recognize the flare of attraction in his eyes before he covered it up and moved on to the next topic.

The problem was, he wasn't moving the topic anywhere at the moment. He'd stayed silent after her last comment, obviously expecting her to go on.

Lucky swallowed hard and shrugged. "That's it."

He squinted, as if trying to get a handle on her.

She could have told him not to waste his time. There was no handle to find. If there was, she would have found it a long, long time ago and maybe wouldn't have to depend on that vodka bottle to help her get by every now and again when the shadows of the past grew long and her ability to battle them short.

Finally, Colin turned his attention to the man to his right.

Lucky shifted, though this time it had nothing to do with getting the sexy doc's attention. Rather she was slightly relieved that she no longer drew his attention. Of course she couldn't be sure if the tension filling her stomach had to do with his question or her insane attraction to him.

But she was sure she was going to find out....

CHAPTER TWO

COLIN COULDN'T REMEMBER a time when his tie had felt tighter.

"Thank you, Dr. McKenna," Doris Borgdoff said as she passed him on her way out the door. Forty-five years old, mother of two grown boys, secretary at Owen-Illinois, he found it interesting that she still had trouble meeting his eyes when she spoke. "I got a lot out of today's session."

Colin forced a smile and said something he hoped was acceptable as his gaze shifted to the final member of the group. The reason for the peculiar tightness of his throat. The sole participant who had not participated, but who had accomplished what she'd set out to do, which was to drive him to distraction.

Sexy Lucky Clayborn glided, rather than walked, to stand in front of him and he was aware of every inch of her shapely legs, her lithe body, her full breasts under her thin shirt.

She smiled up at him, a seductive mixture of fearless feline and mesmerizing minx. He wasn't even aware that she'd slid her hand against the door to close it until he heard the soft click of the catch hit home, essentially leaving them alone in his office.

"I was hoping to have a word…alone with you for a minute," she said quietly, her deep-green-eyed gaze trapping his.

Colin's tie was no longer tight, it was choking him. Everything that was male in him responded to everything that was female in her. A kind of primal reaction that elevated his heart rate and made him all too aware of how long he'd gone without sex.

And how much he wanted to have sex with her.

During the session he'd been overly aware of every move Lucky had made, the sound of her bare thighs sliding together as she crossed and recrossed her legs seeming to grow louder until he'd sworn he could smell the musk of her sex and had imagined what kind of underwear she had or didn't have on. His gaze dropped to her plump lips, devoid of anything but a hint of gloss and moisture from where she'd just licked them.

Dear God, she was a patient. And he'd had

attractive patients before. Even attractive patients that had come on to him.

But no one had made his groin ache the way Lucky Clayborn did.

He broke eye contact and moved to stand behind his desk. The more distance between them the better. "What is it, Miss Clayborn?" he asked, pleased that his voice still sounded like his voice.

She stood still for a long moment, apparently considering his movements, then she crossed to the desk—behind, not in front—and smoothly sat on top of it, giving him a peek of hot-pink panties under the short black skirt.

"You call all the other patients by their first name," she didn't say so much as purr. "Why not me?"

She sat not a foot away from where he stood and he was certain now that he could smell her unique musk. An intriguing mix of ginger and one-hundred-percent turned-on woman.

"You're new," he managed to push past his tight throat. "I generally address new patients by their proper names until a doctor-patient relationship has had a chance to develop."

"Mmm." She slowly scooted over until she sat in front of him.

Despite his best intentions, Colin's gaze dropped to her sleek thighs, watching as her skirt hitched up a little farther. His mouth watered with the desire to put his tongue right there where a lone mole sat an inch or so away from the pink edge of her panties.

"Miss Clayborn," he said, trying to keep things light though he felt anything but. He met her gaze, noting the widening of her pupils, the unmistakable desire to be kissed tinting her alluring features. "It's my duty to remind you that as long as you're my patient, there can be nothing of a personal nature between us."

The way she was sitting directly in front of him, with her legs slightly spread, it would be all too easy to slide between those supple thighs, put his arms around her curvy body, then claim that decadent mouth of hers with a kiss that he knew would lead to so much more.

And boy did he want that. He wanted that bad.

She gave him a sexy half smile that suggested she knew exactly what he was thinking. "Shame," she whispered, though she stayed right where she was.

"Mmm," he admitted.

He forced his gaze away from her face, and his thoughts away from the voice that urged him to kiss her. Just once. Just touch his tongue to hers to see if she tasted as good as she looked. Slide his fingers up to see if her panties were damp.

"You didn't participate in the session much," he said, focusing on his Medical College of Ohio degree and his Ohio license to practice which hung in customized frames on the far wall. He'd worked hard to obtain both and wasn't about to throw them away because of one electrifying temptress. "I can't force you to, but you understand that I'm to submit progress reports to the court."

That seemed to urge her into action. She slowly slid from the desk, putting her luscious body flush up against his.

Making her all the more irresistible.

Colin froze, trying not to notice the way her hips pressed against his, the graze of her hardened nipples against his chest through her shirt and his. His erection pulsed and twitched. There was no doubt she was aware of his aroused state. Their physical closeness allowed for few secrets.

He didn't dare move. To do so would be to tip his hand, to let her know she had control. And he couldn't give that to her. To do so would be to undermine their professional affiliation.

To do so would be to lose control, period. Not just over his desires, but over his entire life. Because to kiss Lucky, with those false charges hanging over his head, would be akin to kissing his career goodbye.

"Well, we all do what we have to in the end, don't we?" she finally said.

She stepped away, but not before brushing against him in a way that made him grit his back teeth to keep from shuddering with need.

She smiled at him, picked up her purse from the desk, then let herself out the exit door.

Colin swallowed hard, and he was pretty sure sweat dotted his brow as he collapsed into his desk chair and made a mental note to himself never again to be alone in a room with Miss Lucky Clayborn.

LUCKY WAS LATE for work. Again.

Of course, it hadn't helped that she'd lingered at Dr. Colin McKenna's office after the group session, acting on an explosive attraction she hadn't felt in a long, long time.

She knew enough about men to know that not many of them had the strength to do what the sexy doc had. Oh, yes, involvement with her would very surely put his career in jeopardy. But she'd seen the fiery attraction in his eyes. Had felt his erection, long and thick, pressing against her sex. And she'd known he had read her own signals clearly. Not that she'd been subtle about it. No, subtle would have been easy to ignore for a man like Colin McKenna. So she'd laid it out there for him...literally.

And he'd had the strength to refuse her when another guy would have shoved up her skirt and taken her right then and there on the desk.

A shiver ran the length of her spine as she rushed inside Harry's Sports Bar.

Lucky waved a quick hello to the head cashier as she hurried back to the employee lockers just to the right of the kitchen and then shoved her purse inside the one marked with her name. She was aware that a couple of the male waiters stood in the corner watching her strip down to her bra and shimmy into her Harry's T-shirt and apron. She barely glanced their way as she closed her tank inside the locker then twirled the attached combination lock.

"You're late."

The manager's name was Harry, although he wasn't the Harry on the sign, no matter how much he liked to pretend he was, especially when introducing himself to customers. "Hi, I'm Harry. Are you enjoying your meal?" he would say, leaving them to think he was the Harry of note.

He was somewhere in his mid-forties, was at least that many pounds overweight, and more often than not could do with a shower.

Lucky caught the way he stared at her breasts

under the tight T-shirt and put her hand on her hip. "I told you I had an appointment."

"You also told me you'd make it here on time," he said to her breasts.

Since she'd landed the job four months ago, Harry had come on to her no fewer than ten times, usually when she worked closing and after all the staff had shared a wind-down beer. Now she usually opted for the earlier shifts even though the tips were better later, her patience for his unwanted attention wearing thin.

As she looked at him now, she suspected the same could be said for Harry. He looked a broken plate away from firing her and hiring another waitress that might be more open to his advances, despite the wedding ring on his left hand that he tried to hide with his class ring.

"I'm sorry. The session ran over," Lucky said then reached around him to pick up a tray so she could bus a table in her station nearby.

He caught her arm when she tried to pass. "Consider this your second warning, Lucky." He smiled at her in a way that made her skin crawl. "I don't think I need to tell you there won't be a third."

"Understood," she said as Connie, another waitress, came up on Harry from behind. Since Connie had been there over a year, she was apparently more open to Harry's attentions.

She was glad when Harry moved his gaze from her breasts to Connie's, and she left to go clear the table and take an order from a couple of guys who were sliding into a booth near one of the big-screen televisions on the back wall.

Lucky had been waitressing since she was seventeen and the job was second nature to her. She liked the noisy atmosphere, the nonstop movement, the odd hours. If every now and again her feet felt swollen a point beyond pain and her back ached, she just treated herself to a long, hot bath and a day spent reading then rushed right back into the fray. She'd never given much consideration to doing anything else. She liked her life the way it was. Uncomplicated. Routine. Familiar. With a little spice like the delectable Dr. Colin McKenna thrown in to liven things up from time to time.

Just thinking of him made her smile.

"What'll it be?" she asked the next table as she straightened the condiment caddy and took out her order pad.

She was doing pretty much the same thing an hour later when two men walked in and took a booth in the next station. She usually gave customers only a cursory glance, but one of the two warranted a double take. Simply because he was one unmistakable Dr. Colin McKenna.

Lucky stood staring in his direction. Of all the

gin joints in all the towns in the world…of course, he would have chosen Connie's station to sit in.

"Are you going to take our order or not?" the guy in the booth next to her asked.

"Not," she said, walking away.

COLIN ACCEPTED a menu from the girl who had seated him and his best friend, Will Sexton, then stared at the five big-screen televisions on the walls tuned in to different sporting events. He raised a brow at an archery competition then settled his gaze on Will.

"Come here a lot?" he asked.

Will and he had roomed together in college and had remained best friends ever since. While he'd gone the psychiatric route, Will was now a surgeon at St. Vincent-Mercy's Trauma I Center.

"Don't you?" Will asked in his thick British accent, cocking a grin at him. "Reminds me of the pubs back home."

Colin highly doubted that, but didn't say anything. Mirroring their choice in careers, Colin liked things quiet and subdued while Will's motto was the more chaotic the better. At least in most things. When it came to their sex lives Colin usually liked things a little more wild, while Will had always chosen the sorority girls with the pink ribbons in their hair. Even now he was dating a sweet little resident who planned to go into pediatrics.

Of course, Colin's preference had made turning down Lucky Clayborn in his office earlier all the more difficult.

Merely thinking of the hot, seductive woman made him tug at his collar, something he was free to do now that she was no longer in front of him.

"Welcome to Harry's, gentlemen. Can I get you something from the bar?"

Colin looked up and nearly choked for the second time that day when he found himself staring at none other than the woman in question.

As soon as he had verified that not only wasn't she a figment of his imagination, but that she was a waitress, he noticed that Lucky didn't look anywhere near surprised. In fact, her predatory smile told him she'd probably spotted him the moment he'd walked in.

"Hello, Dr. McKenna," she said with that sexy, throaty voice of hers. "Or may I call you Colin now that we're no longer in the office?"

Will raised a brow at him. "Friends, are we? And here I thought you'd avoid a place like this like the plague."

Colin dropped his hand from his tie. "Actually, we met elsewhere. Will, this is Lucky Clayborn."

Will briefly offered his hand to Lucky. "Such an auspicious name. Nice. Very nice."

Lucky stared at Will's hand for a long moment then finally put her own into it and gave a brief shake, apparently not used to the greeting. "Nice to meet you," she said, her gaze immediately returning to Colin.

He tried not to notice the way her T-shirt hugged her just as tightly as her tank had earlier, the green fabric making her eyes look huge in her pale face.

"Can I bring you a draft?" she asked. "Harry brews his own."

Colin swallowed hard and forced his gaze to his menu. "I'll have bottled water."

Will winked at her good-naturedly. "I'll take a draft. Unlike the stuffed shirt here, I'm just knocking off work."

Another waitress neared the table and stopped next to Lucky. Her whisper was none too subtle. "What are you doing? This is my table."

Lucky shrugged her away. "Would you guys like to order now or would you like a few more minutes to go over the menu?"

Colin got the definite impression that if he so wanted, he could order her up with no problem.

His tie wasn't the only item of clothing that suddenly felt tight.

The other waitress strode away toward the back of the restaurant. Colin looked around Lucky to watch the other woman strike up a conversation with a man he guessed was the manager or the owner.

"We'll order now," he said, thinking the less interaction with Lucky the better.

"Are you in some sort of trouble?" he asked after he and Will had made their choices.

Lucky glanced back to where the manager was staring at her while the waitress pointed in her direction.

She smiled as she accepted their menus. "Nothing I can't handle."

She walked away. As soon as she was out of earshot, Will pulled at his own collar. "Did the temperature just get a little hotter in here or is it my imagination?"

Colin grimaced as he straightened his silverware. "It's your imagination."

"Well, I certainly hope so because I'm guessing she's a patient of yours. And you don't want to be taking any chances right now. Not with everything that's hanging in the balance." His gaze trailed back to Lucky. "That's one hot number, though. I don't know what I would do if a patient of her caliber came on to me the way she's coming on to you. A package like that has a way of making you forget about medical degrees. Pass her on to one of your colleagues quick, mate."

Colin had considered and discarded the option earlier. To pass her on to one of his partners wouldn't look good. And right now he couldn't afford even a hint of impropriety. "So why did you pass Miss Clayborn onto your partner?" he could hear himself being asked during a legal deposition. What would he say? "I wanted to screw her so bad my balls ached, that's why."

The sound of raised voices caught his attention. He looked over to where Lucky was facing off with the manager, the other waitress standing nearby with her arms crossed under her impressive chest. Colin couldn't make out what was being said, but given the man's stern expression he didn't think it was good.

And when Lucky took off her apron and then peeled off her T-shirt and draped both over the manager's head, he knew he'd guessed correctly.

There were hoots and hollers as Lucky strode, as casual as you please, toward the kitchen where she disappeared behind the doors.

"Whoa," Will said, his eyes wide. "Something tells me I won't be getting that ale any time soon."

Colin watched as Lucky came back out of the kitchen wearing the same tank she'd had on earlier.

She ignored the manager as she walked through the place then out the front door.

He started to push from the table.

Will caught his arm, his expression stern. "I wouldn't if I were you, Col."

Colin considered him. "I know. But you're not me."

And then he went out after Lucky.

CHAPTER THREE

IT WAS raining.

Figured. Lucky kept her chin high and her shoulders back. It was raining in her professional life, so why shouldn't it be in reality?

She squelched a groan. She'd really needed that job. Aside from the good tips, the flexibility had allowed her to work around her morning job at the pancake house within walking distance of the bar. And considering that the pancake house didn't have an item on the menu that cost more than five dollars and ninety cents, her tips were minimal, by no means enough to live on.

And she'd thrown the job away for a man....

She tripped over her own feet, missing a puddle by millimeters. Had she ever done something so spontaneously irresponsible before? Not when it came to the opposite sex. Sure, she might like to shake things up a bit wherever she was, and she didn't take well to leering bosses, but a few un-wanted stares at her breasts had never been enough for her to walk away from a well-paying job. And in this case, she had not only walked away from it, she'd gone to Colin's table knowing full well she'd be fired.

Of course, at the time it had seemed more than worth the unguarded expression on his face when he'd looked up to see her.

Now? Well, now she wondered which errant hormones had made her act so impulsively and how she might go about getting them back under control.

Sure, the shrink was thigh-quiveringly sexy. But no man was sexier than a good night's worth of tips. Not when she had bills to pay.

She opened the door of her twenty-five-year-old Chevy and slid onto the well-maintained leather driver's seat, breathing in the scent of old car and raspberry air freshener as she fished her keys from her purse. The ping of rain against the roof was the only sound…even after she turned the ignition key.

Not even a sputter, a whine or a crank from the old vehicle. Nothing.

Lucky tried starting the car again with the same results.

She rested her forehead against the cracked

leather steering wheel and closed her eyes. Great. Just what she needed considering she'd just lost her main source of income.

There was a light tap on her window. She leaned back to stare at the blurry image through the rain-spattered glass. Was that…

Colin.

"Are you all right?" she read his lips rather than heard the muffled words.

Lucky blinked at him. Was the doc really standing out in the rain with no protection, his hands tucked into his slacks pockets as he bent to look inside her car? Yes, he was. And in that one moment everything that had transpired in the past ten minutes had been worth it.

She yanked open the door and climbed out of the car to stand in front of him. He straightened, seeming to squint at her in the gloomy light.

"What was that you said?" she asked.

"I asked if you were all right."

Lucky twisted her lips, giving his tall, lean body a full once-over before returning her gaze to his eyes. "Considering I just got fired five minutes ago, my car won't start, and the lack of an umbrella has made my tank top transparent? I'm just peachy."

His gaze dropped down to her breasts. Lucky didn't have to look. It didn't take a physics professor to know that white cotton and steady rain made her look like a wet T-shirt contestant.

Only she was unprepared for the warm shiver that slaked through her at Colin's slow perusal.

She rounded him to stand at the front of her car. After sliding her fingers in between the grill slats, she tugged on the release then braced herself as she hauled open the old car's hood.

"You wouldn't happen to know anything about cars, would you, Dr. McKenna?" she asked.

He came to stand next to her, staring at the grease-covered engine. "I know enough."

"And would any of that knowledge help me out with what's happening now?"

He looked at her, his mind appearing to be on everything but the status of her car. "It's my guess your battery's dead."

He walked to the driver's door, opened it, then pushed in the button that turned off the headlights. When she'd gotten into her car, Lucky hadn't even been aware they were on. Then again, why would she? If the headlights had drained her sorry excuse for a battery, then there wouldn't be any juice left to illuminate them now, would there?

Great.

Colin closed the door then reached to close the hood.

Lucky turned to face him. The fact that they

stood without a raincoat or an umbrella in the pouring rain didn't matter to her. Nor did it appear to matter to him as they stood just staring at each other.

"Well," she said slowly, feeling oddly turned on by the attention. Attention she had wanted only a few hours earlier in his office but that now seemed somehow…very intimate to her. "I guess you won't have to worry about running into me again here."

He nodded. "Fired?"

"Very."

His mouth turned up into a small smile. "How do you feel about that?"

Lucky narrowed her eyes. "Dr. McKenna, are you trying to psychoanalyze me in a parking lot in the middle of a thunderstorm?"

He looked up. "It would have to be thundering in order for it to be a thunderstorm."

Lucky could have sworn she'd heard a few cracks and felt the ground shake, but she wasn't going to say anything in case the sensations had nothing to do with the weather and everything to do with Colin McKenna.

"And you're avoiding my question," she said just as he had in his office earlier.

The very handsome Colin McKenna looked even more delectable mussed up and wet. "Sorry. Hazard of the trade, I guess."

"What is? That you always end up sounding like a doctor?"

He nodded. "Especially when talking to a patient."

That's right. They still were doctor and patient, weren't they? Despite all that had happened in her own life in the past half hour, their connection remained the same. A connection that prevented the more sexual one she wanted more in that minute than she had at any other point during the day.

"Mmm."

His smile widened. "Can I give you a lift?"

"What would your lunch companion have to say about your disappearance?"

He glanced back toward the sports bar.

Lucky reached into her car, took her keys from the ignition, and grabbed her purse. "That's all right, Dr. McKenna. I wouldn't want to ask you to do something that might appear inappropriate."

Actually, she wanted to ask him to do something very inappropriate. She wanted to ask him to kiss her. To brand her skin with his hands. To show her what she'd only felt earlier in the office when she'd provocatively brushed up against him.

"How will you get home?"

She took a card out of her purse and waved it at him. "It's called the bus."

Lucky began to round Colin to start toward

Secor Road and the bus stop across the street, then stopped parallel to him. Despite the weather, she made out the warm scent of his cologne. Or was it aftershave? Whichever it was, the smell made her want to press her tongue to his skin to see if he tasted as good as he smelled.

And before she knew it, she turned to do exactly that.

COLIN HAD KNOWN a moment of disappointed relief when Lucky turned down his offer of a ride. He wasn't sure what he was thinking when he'd made the offer, but he knew it was linked to whatever had compelled him to come outside to see if she was all right.

And he needed to get a handle on it before he and the sexy waitress…patient crossed paths again.

He was pretty sure he exhaled when she began walking toward the road.

After a few steps, she stopped and turned. "Actually, there's one thing you can do for me real quick, Doc," Lucky said lightly grasping his arm. "You can kiss me."

Colin opened his mouth to protest. The problem was the movement allowed her better access as she took his bottom lip between her teeth, then kissed him like a woman who could teach classes on the subject.

He felt a groan grumble up from his chest. It had been a long, long time since he'd so thoroughly enjoyed a kiss. More than three months, though he'd gone without sex that long.

He stood still, reveling in the soft, uneven texture of her lips. The rasp of her tongue as she took full advantage and slid it past his teeth.

"Mmm."

Lucky made that sound again that tugged on something within him. Something deep and elemental and undeniable.

He reached out to pull her closer when she pulled away.

Raindrops clung to her lashes, making them look longer and thicker and giving her cat-green eyes an even more vivid appearance. Whatever makeup she may have had on had long since been washed away by the rain, revealing a light smattering of freckles over her pale skin. And her red hair shone almost black with wetness.

"That was even better than I imagined," she said softly. "And I have quite an imagination."

Then she was walking away from him, her hips swaying, seeming completely oblivious to the rain and to him as she made her way toward the road some hundred yards away.

Colin absently rubbed his chin, then held out his hand, absently watching the rain pelt his skin then run off to accumulate in a puddle at his feet. He was soaked and somehow couldn't remember how he'd gotten that way. He glanced up toward the battle-gray sky then back to the street, only Lucky was long gone.

FOR AN ENTIRE WEEK Colin both dreaded and anticipated the moment when Lucky would walk through the door to his office and either prove or disprove his attraction toward her. A case of raging hormones, he'd tried telling himself over and over again. An instance of temporary insanity. But no matter how many times he tried to apply reason to the erotic kiss he'd shared with Lucky in that parking lot seven days ago, he fell well short of the mark.

Then the moment he'd been waiting seven long days for never came.

Colin sat back in his chair, tapping his pencil against the incoming mail and files the practice secretary had placed on his desk after the group he'd finished with had vacated the room. The group that should have included Lucky.

He leaned forward, browsing through the files, looking for hers. Normal procedure dictated he contact the court, let them know the terms of their

orders were being violated. But he was reluctant
to do that. Maybe she'd got caught up at work.
Perhaps she hadn't repaired her car.

He couldn't find her file.

Grimacing, he went through the pile again with
the same results. A pink envelope fluttered from
the files in his hands and landed squarely in the
middle of his lap.

That's odd. It looked like expensive personal sta-
tionary. Definitely not the type of thing he would
think of Lucky possessing. He slit open the side
with his opener and took out the single sheet of
pink paper.

She's pretty.
I could have been pretty for you.

Colin's blood ran cold.

While the handwriting wasn't familiar, the
words—or rather the taunt in them—was.

Jamie Polson.

He pushed from his chair and didn't stop moving
until he stood in front of his secretary's desk.

Having been out with the flu the week before,
Annette looked the worse for wear.

"Where did this come from?" he asked, flashing
her the envelope that simply said Colin across it.

Annette blinked at him. "I don't know. I don't

remember seeing it when I sorted through your things a little while ago." She took the envelope and turned it over. "This I definitely would have remembered." She smiled as she handed it back. "Love letter?"

Far from it, he wanted to say.

"Hi," the breathless greeting sounded behind him.

Colin turned to find Lucky Clayborn smiling at him sexily. He nearly crumpled the letter and envelope in his grip. Someone had gained access to his office to put Jamie's card there. And the card itself bore an unspoken threat of sorts that upped the level of tension. He'd hoped time would allow Jamie the space to move on. To drop the case.

Instead Jamie appeared even more determined to keep him on the run, both in court and out. And he couldn't help wondering at the coincidence of Lucky's presence at the same time he'd discovered the card.

Colin discovered he was staring at Lucky's full mouth and allowed his gaze to linger there before lifting it to her eyes. "You're late," he told her. "The session's over." He stared at his secretary. "Where's Miss Clayborn's file?"

Annette appeared puzzled as she answered the phone then put someone on hold. "In with Dr. Szymanski's files, of course. Miss Clayborn called and asked to be transferred last week."

Lucky had moved to Morgan Szymanski, one of his partners?

Colin's pulse rate leapt at the knowledge that Lucky was no longer his patient.

"Do you have a few minutes?"

Lucky had asked the question from behind him, but Colin didn't trust himself to look at her. Without the doctor-patient wall standing between them, there was no longer any reason to resist her. He stared at the note in his hands then glanced at her.

"Why don't we talk in my office?" he suggested.

CHAPTER FOUR

BEING INSIDE Colin's office with him, alone, was exactly what Lucky had had in mind.

She followed the handsome doc through the door to the right of the secretary's desk, waiting until he closed the thick wood before she did what she'd been yearning to do all week.

She stepped within breathing distance and kissed him fully on the mouth.

Incredible…

Lucky had just spent the past hour getting to know her new therapist and her three new group mates. She'd volunteered more than during last week's session, though Dr. Szymanski had been even less impressed with her participation than Colin had. But, with the simple touch of her lips against Colin's, she forgot all about the fact that she was to begin keeping a daily journal. Gone was her agitation at her inability to find a job. A distant memory was the dent to her savings made by the money she'd had to pay to replace her car battery.

And long forgotten was her fear that Colin would refuse to see her even though she was no longer his patient.

Instead she just…well, she merely allowed herself to feel.

As she lifted her hands to thread her sensitized fingers through his velvet hair and intensify the kiss, sizzling heat spread across her skin, then went deeper, igniting her nerve endings in a flash fire. Want pooled in her belly, tension coiling even though her muscles relaxed.

There was something about this one moment in time that made the world look different to her somehow, the instant when she gave herself over to attraction and allowed her body to lead instead of her mind. There was something primal in the action, something freeing.

Something that freed her from her past, if only for a short while.

Kissing Dr. Colin McKenna did all that and much, much more.

By now Lucky should have dived for the waist of his pants, seeking even greater release. Strangely she seemed to be satisfied merely kissing the handsome doc. She couldn't remember feeling that way before—happy simply feeling the firmness of a man's lips against hers. Usually her mind had already moved ahead a step and her hands and body quickly followed. Now it seemed to take every ounce of concentration to kiss him.

Colin groaned and backed her toward the leather couch positioned against the wall under a print of downtown Toledo. The same couch Lucky had fantasized about taking him on a week ago. Regaining some control over her actions, she turned him around so she could push him down against the rich, fragrant leather. The instant he was prone she climbed on top of him, mindless of the way her miniskirt hiked up her thighs, focused only on the red-hot sensations flowing through her.

It felt so good, so right, so natural to be doing what she was. Colin cupped her breasts and she gasped, surprised by the shock of his touch. He broke the kiss and gazed down at her chest as he stroked her through her cotton top. But she could do him one better. She reached for the hem and hauled the material up and over her head, leaving only her red lace demi-cup bra behind.

She hungrily licked her lips as she watched the brown of Colin's eyes nearly disappear under his dilating pupils. She began to bend to kiss him again, but the feel of his fingertip burrowing into the top of her bra then rasping against her distended nipple stopped her. She watched, trembling, as he peeled the lace back from her breast then lifted his head to suckle her deep into his mouth.

Lucky stiffened, her womanhood pulsing between her thighs, her heart thudding against the wall of her chest. She'd rarely experienced such a burning need to have sex with someone before. Oh, she'd always loved sex. But the hungry heat accumulating low in her belly took her breath away.

She wriggled her hips, happy when the thick ridge of his hard-on fell between the sides of her fleshy valley. She stretched her neck, riding out the waves of sheer pleasure at the meeting, despite the obstacle of their clothes.

Colin took advantage of the momentary lowering of her barriers to reverse their positions so that her back was against the soft leather and he pressed against her front. Lucky stared up at him in part surprise, part wonder, but most of all need.

When he leaned to kiss her, he did so with animal abandon. He bit and sucked and plucked, his breathing ragged, his hips cradled hard between her thighs. Lucky blindly pulled at his shirt, tugging it from his pants, then flattened her hands against the solid plane of his abdomen. He was rock-hard and lean and so hot she nearly singed her palms. She pinched his flat nipples, listening to the low growl in his chest, then dove for his pants, the sound of his zipper opening loud in the otherwise quiet room. She knew such an urgency to have him inside her that when she felt his finger edge inside the elastic of her panties and flutter against her clit, she nearly came on the spot.

Finally Colin's throbbing erection filled her hand. Lucky pulled back from their kiss so she could see the thick width and length of him. Her doing so seemed to turn him on even further, his hips bucking involuntarily. She gently squeezed, then moved her hand up the shaft without releasing her grip, watching moisture gather on the tip.

Colin shuddered against her at the same time he thrust two fingers deep inside her dripping wetness. The move was so unexpected that Lucky reached orgasm, bearing down on his hand and gyrating as sensation after sensation crashed over her.

Then the hand was gone from between her legs and was instead clutching her jaw. She blinked open her eyes. But rather than see the man who had given her the best orgasm she'd had in a very long time, she saw Colin's angry face.

"Did Jamie put you up to this?" he ground out.

ONE MOMENT Colin had been on the verge of spilling his seed all over Lucky's hand, the next he was seeing her as the enemy, a modern-day Mata Hari bent on destroying him.

He glimpsed the fear in Lucky's eyes before she quickly blinked it away.

Colin cursed loudly and rolled off her luscious body to stand. He slipped his painfully erect penis into his pants, then tucked his shirt in and did up his pants.

"How much did Jamie pay you?" he said after long moments.

Lucky was right where he'd left her, her fingers gingerly tracing the line of her jaw where he'd gripped her, perhaps a little too hard.

She swung her legs over the side of the couch, and tucked her breasts back into her bra. Her golden-red hair was sexily tousled, her color high. And Colin had no idea how he'd found the strength to deny his need to have sex with her.

"What in the hell are you talking about?" she finally asked, pulling her top back over her head then removing her long hair from the back. "And who in the hell is Jamie?"

Colin rounded his desk. A good fifteen feet separated him from the woman he'd nearly ravished mere minutes ago, but it might as well have been nothing. His nose was still filled with her musky scent. His body still ached with the desire to claim her. "Come off it. A guy doesn't get this lucky unless he's going to pay for it later."

She flicked him a fiery smile. "Yes, well, this Lucky doesn't do it for money."

She got up from the couch and straightened her short skirt.

Colin crossed his arms. "The timing of your being assigned to me…your coming on to me so hard…switching doctors then showing up here… it has to be more than coincidence."

She stepped toward his desk, making his pulse leap. "Whoever this Jamie is, she really screwed you up, huh?"

Colin found it more than a bit odd that he was standing in his office with a patient—ex-patient— and she was the one doing the analyzing.

"I consider myself a little on the suspicious side, but you," she was standing in front of him now and poked her finger into his chest, "you really take the cake, Dr. McKenna."

Colin stared into her flushed face for long moments. Could he be wrong? Could everything that had happened between him and Lucky have been just a natural progression of events?

Even as he asked himself the question, he knew there was nothing natural about his wanting to claim her in a way he'd never claimed another woman before. Or perhaps it was purely natural, some kind of primal instinct to overpower his enemy.

She tsked as she ran her fingertip down over his buttons. "It's a shame."

She turned around and walked toward the exit door.

"What is?" Colin couldn't resist asking.

"That I won't be seeing you again." She opened the door, then stood leaning against it. "You see, I make it a habit not to get involved with anyone more screwed up than I am. And you, Colin, have demons not even I can compete with."

He squinted at her as she gave him a once-over.

"It really is a shame. I have the feeling you're very good in the sack. And I definitely was interested in finding out how good."

Colin winced at the quiet click of the door closing.

FIVE DAYS LATER Colin was no closer to finding out the truth behind what had happened than he had been when he'd been cushioned between Lucky's sweet thighs, literally an inch away from having sex with her.

"Come on, Mac, get your game on!"

Colin absently twirled the tennis racket in his hand and stared across the tennis court at Will who had just taken the first set and was two points into winning the next game.

The ball hit the center line then whizzed right by his left ear.

He'd agreed to meet his friend at his condo complex for tennis hoping some exercise and Will's company would help him forget about what had transpired in his office. Instead all he could think about was that it was Saturday morning and he had two whole days to fill before he could go back to work on Monday morning. Two yawning spring days that he usually looked forward to but now dreaded.

Twenty minutes later Will called the second set and tossed him a clean towel as they left the courts.

Will grinned at him. "Well, that was certainly a nice change of events. You usually beat the crap out of me at tennis."

Colin used the towel to wipe his face, though he didn't need it, then draped the terry cloth around his neck. "Yeah, well, I took pity on you this morning."

Will nudged him in the arm with his covered racket. "No, mate, you're distracted. And I don't think it's one of your whackos behind this one."

Colin grimaced at his friend. "For a doctor you can be very insensitive."

"Me? What would make you say that?"

"Whackos?"

"I'd never call them that to their faces."

"Your referring to them that way at all makes you insensitive."

Will chuckled. "I'll let you have that one. If only because I'm concerned about your mental welfare after this morning's match."

They walked in silence, winding around the three buildings that separated the tennis courts from the Victorian block that held Will's condo. Will made some comments about the quality of the women sunbathing at the pool then turned his attention back to Colin.

"So, are you going to share who she is or not?"

"Who?"

"The wily female who's stolen your brain straight out of your head."

"There's no one in my life right now. You know that."

"I know that's what your attorney advised."

Colin slanted him a wary look.

"Good, then. You wouldn't mind doubling with me and Janet then tonight."

"What?"

"You heard me." Will feigned a couple of tennis moves then continued walking next to him again.

"The pretty resident has finally agreed to go out with me, but only on the condition that I bring someone along for her girlfriend."

"No way. If you'll remember correctly, my attorney advised me not to date anyone."

"This won't be a date. This will be two pals getting together and running into a couple of girls while they're out."

"Mmm."

"You wouldn't deny a guy a chance to take the pretty pink ribbon out of Janet's hair now, would you?"

That's how Will always referred to the women he dated. And quite accurately at that. While it was highly unlikely Janet wore an actual pink ribbon, she was the type that would have done so in high school. While she was the head varsity cheerleader.

"I would and I am."

Will took his keys out of his pocket as they neared his building. "Why? Has something happened on the Jamie front I don't know about?"

Colin ran his hand over his face, not really up to talking about it just then. "Yeah, a couple things. But nothing to be worried about."

Will held open the door for him, but when Colin would have entered, two young women bounded out, looking as if the only thing they would do with pink ribbons was tie them around their body piercings. Short, tight T-shirts and even shorter denim cutoffs revealed bodies buff enough for the cover of *Playboy* without the need for airbrushing.

"Hi, Willy," the short brunette said, stopping in front of Will and smiling at him in open suggestion. "So when are we going to hook up? How about tonight?"

Colin covered his grin with a none-too-discreet cough while Will squirmed under the sex kitten's attentions. "Another time, perhaps?"

"Mmm. Another time. I'm going to hold you to that, Willy."

The woman gave Will a loud kiss then followed after her friend who was a good twenty feet down the walk.

"Friend of yours?" Colin asked.

"Neighbors." Colin followed Will's line of sight. Yes. Despite his preference for young and innocent, Will's gaze was definitely glued to the brunette's pert backside.

And what a backside it was, too.

"And she's gay."

"Is not," Colin objected.

"Is, too. That's her girlfriend. And when I say girlfriend, I don't mean they're both girls and they're friends. I mean they share the same bed at night and they do more than sleep in it. Come on. Maybe it will be quiet now without the two of them playing their music so loudly."

Colin led the way inside and climbed the steps to the first floor where Will's condo was located. Halfway up, Will stopped and said, "Don't tell me it's the girl from the bar that's got you all worked up."

Colin turned to stare at his friend. "What?"

Where in the hell had that come from?

Will jabbed a thumb over his shoulder. "It's just that I was thinking about how those two were just your type—well, if they went in for that sort of thing, anyway—when I remembered that girl, that redhead that got fired from the bar."

Colin looked away.

"All this, your distracted state, it is about her, isn't it?"

Colin cleared his throat. "Are we going to catch a shower and get going to that lunch at the club or not?"

Will slowly ascended the stairs to stand next to him. "Oh my God. I'm right, aren't I? You're preoccupied with thoughts of banging a patient. An out-and-out whacko."

"She's no longer my patient. And she's not a whacko."

"Oh? Cured that fast, hey?"

Colin stared at him, then at what Will was staring at. Namely, the fist Colin had raised.

Colin blinked. He'd never been a scrapper. Had never even gotten into a fistfight. Not in elementary school. Not in junior high. Never.

So what did it mean that he had a fist raised against his best friend?

"Whoa. This is worse than even I feared," Will said quietly as Colin regained control of his hands and his thoughts. "I have some advice for you, mate," Will said as he unlocked his condo door then led the way inside.

Colin tensed at the blast of cold air that hit him. He hadn't turned on the air conditioner in his own apartment, although they'd had it on at the office for a few weeks now.

"And that is?"

Will put his tennis gear away in the hall closet then turned to grin at him. "Come out with me tonight. I bet Janet's friend will be able to make you forget what's-her-name."

That's what *he* thought.

"Or else…"

Colin sat down on the white leather couch. Everything in Will's place was either white or off-white. Well, there was no accounting for taste. He and Will didn't share the same taste in furniture or women.

"Or else what?" he prompted when Will didn't immediately offer.

"Or else screw the woman's head off and get her the hell out of your system."

CHAPTER FIVE

"ANNETTE, could you please bring me Miss Clayborn's contact information?"

Two days later Colin sat tensely in his office chair. It was five before five and the staff was about to go home. But the lateness of the day and his own uncomfortable interest in the sexy siren wasn't what prompted his request for Lucky's file. Rather, his partner Morgan Szymanski had just left his office after consulting with him on what to do about Lucky's not showing for her group session that afternoon.

A brief knock then the door opened and Annette handed him a paper. "Just put it on my desk when I'm done, okay? I'm on my way out."

Colin thanked her and wished her a good night as he stared at the sheet sitting in the middle of his desk.

So innocuous.

So dangerous.

He'd managed to talk Morgan out of contacting the court, although even now he couldn't be sure why. He supposed after what he'd done last week, he owed Lucky at least the benefit of the doubt. After all, she had shown up for her previous two sessions.

And, after all, he had practically bruised her jaw when he'd accused her of being sent by Jamie.

He blew out a deep breath then leaned back in his chair and picked up the paper. Home phone, address, the works. Colin eyed it, familiar with the northwest Toledo area near the Michigan line, though he'd never been there.

He picked up the phone, then put it back down, cursing under his breath.

In the two weeks since he'd met Lucky Clayborn nothing about his life had seemed right. If he wasn't thinking about her, he was ordering himself not to think about her. And when he did allow himself the luxury of remembering her, he got hard as a rock, recalling how she'd opened her thighs to him, and how her pale fingers had squeezed his erection.

Colin clamped his eyes closed, trying to banish the thoughts.

He'd met with his attorney yesterday, but his father's old friend Don Maddox was no closer to settling the fraudulent case against Colin than he'd been three months ago.

Meanwhile Jamie was making it clear that Colin's life was an open book.

From notes left on his car, to curious answering machine messages, whenever Colin began to forget about Jamie's presence, he was reminded again that out there somewhere someone had it in for him.

He'd taken the notes and made copies for his attorney, but at this point there was no solid way to connect Jamie to the goings-on. Besides, the police likely wouldn't be interested unless and until a real physical threat was made.

Colin ran his hand through his hair several times. Wasn't the threat to his career enough?

He grabbed a yellow legal pad, scribbled Lucky's home address near the bottom, then ripped the slip off and stuffed it into his pants pocket. No matter what was happening with the case with Jamie, he was worried about Lucky. There was…something about her that called to him on a level he had yet to understand. Despite her ballsy behavior and saucy smiles, he was concerned about her in a way that had nothing to do with sex and everything to do with her.

But to initiate contact with her outside the office to inquire about office matters was like inviting the devil to come out to play.

He grabbed his jacket, then locked his office door after himself.

Devil or not, he needed to see that she was okay.

Screw the woman's head off and get her the hell out of your system.

Will's direct words of advice ran through his mind. He put Lucky's contact info on Annette's desk, leafed through his phone messages, then headed for the parking lot. As crude as it seemed, his best friend might have had a point. Colin was all too aware that the more you made an object off limits, the more appealing it became. Was that what was happening with him and his growing obsession with Lucky? First she'd been inaccessible to him because she'd been a patient. Second... well, second, he'd allowed paranoia to get the better of him, although if he'd been thinking clearly he would never have allowed things to go as far as they had last week. When he'd invited her into his office to talk about her having switched doctors, he'd been fool enough to believe he could control his sexual impulses. What he hadn't anticipated was Lucky taking the initiative and kissing him, putting him at a very definite disadvantage.

He pressed the button on his key chain to unlock his Lincoln Navigator SUV then climbed inside the sleek black-and-tan vehicle. And what made him think he'd be any better at controlling what happened if he showed up unannounced at her house?

He caught sight of his reflection in the rearview mirror and grimaced. He looked tired even to himself. And this constant obsessing about Lucky wasn't getting him anywhere. Whatever the outcome of this visit, he needed to attain some kind of mental closure. If he and Lucky had sex…a long, hot shudder ran through his body. If he and Lucky had sex, well, they were adults and consenting.

If they didn't, he hoped that whatever transpired would be enough to stop her from haunting his dreams at night. From interfering with his work during the day when thoughts of her crossing and uncrossing her shapely legs intruded. From compelling him to seek her out outside office hours on a Monday night.

He pointed his car in the direction of her apartment and pushed the button to roll down the window rather than switching on the air-conditioning. All around him were the unmistakable signs of summer. Convertibles roared by, stereos pumping out thick, bass-heavy music. Kids played on neighborhood streets. The ice-cream parlors were open for business and full of Little League teams sitting at picnic tables eating cones either as a reward for winning or as consolation for losing.

The scenery was familiar, yet it seemed odd to Colin that while he wasn't looking the season had changed. Though it had been rainy and chilly only two weeks ago when Lucky had first walked through his door, now summer was in full swing, as were the colorful activities that went along with it. And the sensory input was almost overwhelming. When he ran early in the morning, just before dawn, most of the city was still asleep, the warming temperatures and changing vegetation the only reminders of the time of year. There were no children learning how to ride a bike for the first time. No young women in cut-off shorts. No cars cruising by blaring rap music. There was only him and the river and the odd jogger or two.

He rolled the window back up then switched on his own state-of-the-art radio to an oldies station. The song "Summertime" filled the interior of the SUV. He immediately changed the station to classical, looking for something to drown out the sounds of summer around him, but mostly hoping for something to calm his growing anticipation of seeing Lucky again.

He pulled his collar away from his throat, surprised to find he was lightly sweating, although it was relatively cool in the car. And if he checked his pulse, he was sure it would be a couple of beats above par for him.

He'd been engaged once. A long time ago. He'd just graduated from medical school and had completed his residency at the Medical College of Ohio, and he'd figured what the heck? He'd been dating Amanda on and off—but mostly on—for the past three years. The next logical step was marriage, right?

Wrong. Oh, she'd accepted the two-carat engagement ring. And they'd picked out wedding invitations and shopped around for houses together. They'd seemed perfectly matched. He was a psychiatrist. She was a lawyer. They would easily gross well into six figures annually. Enough to start a family, live anywhere they chose. They weren't limited by resources in any way.

But their sex life…

Colin absently rubbed the back of his neck.

His sex life with Amanda had been perfunctory at best right from the beginning. While they'd matched up in every other area of their lives—they traveled in the same circles, laughed at the same jokes, were both early risers and joggers, enjoyed going to the same restaurants and films and exhibitions—in bed she stopped short of staring at the clock on the night table, and he always felt rushed to finish. Afterward as she snuggled close to him, seeming to prefer his embrace more than his love-making, he'd felt oddly…empty. Unsatisfied.

And the closer the wedding got, the more unsatisfied he'd become.

Then one night, after a particularly aggravating sigh of impatience from Amanda during sex, he'd rolled off her without climaxing and asked her what was wrong. She'd assured him nothing was the matter, that she enjoyed making love with him and then she'd tried to coax him into continuing. But he'd put the brakes on and after a long, awkward silence had suggested they postpone their wedding plans and consult a therapist.

Amanda had been horrified and suggested that maybe they shouldn't marry at all.

He'd agreed and the next day life had gone on as if she'd never been a part of it.

After seven years of higher education and another seven of work experience, Colin still mentally debated what had happened between him and Amanda. He'd thought he'd loved her. To this day he still cared about what happened to her, and he'd even attended her wedding five years ago to an old classmate of his from way back. They have two children now. Surely if he had loved her he would feel something other than happiness for her? Wouldn't jealousy be mixed in there somewhere? Pain? Or had his love for her been the same kind one sibling would have for another?

Was romantic love really love without strong sexual chemistry between the two participants?

And was great sex without love enough to see a couple through the years ahead?

He supposed his experience with Amanda was one reason he was attracted to more sexually available women. Not to say that every woman who wore her blouse buttoned to the neck was asexual. But in his experience over the past few years, most women who wore clingy miniskirts and tight shirts that sexily displayed their physical assets were strongly sexual. And it seemed he still craved that accessibility.

If he needed any more proof of that, he need note that he was sitting in the rutted gravel driveway of Lucky's residence.

The first thing that registered was how beaten down the structure looked. Not just the house itself but everything around it. A free-standing garage was off to the right at the end of the gravel driveway, the windows in the doors broken and cracked and grimy, half the shingles missing, and the roof itself leaning in a way that indicated it wasn't going to be standing much longer.

The same description could fit the one-story house. Putrid green, the peeling paint barely covered the warped wood exterior and he could make out where an addition had been poorly built on, the newer half covered in oxidized white aluminum siding. The small front porch was filled with stuffed black garbage bags, while a simple, faded American flag sticker was attached to the inside of one of the windows. Abandoned tires and car parts littered the overgrown grass of the lawn, the wildflowers sprinkled throughout doing precious little to improve the appearance.

Colin slowly climbed from his SUV, squinting against the evening sun. Not even the golden rays associated with this magic hour could soften the harshness of the living quarters.

He cautiously navigated the three broken cement steps and the creaking wood slats of the porch and then rang the doorbell. He didn't hear anything, so he pushed it again then followed up with a rap on the old screen door that held no screen.

Inside he heard what sounded like either three dogs bark, or one really big one.

He stepped back from the door and waited.

A tattered curtain moved in the window to his left. He was debating whether or not to wave when the door opened up and he was staring at an older woman wearing a flowered housecoat and a black hairnet, a cigarette dangling from the side of her mouth with an ash on it an inch long. "Whatever you're selling, we ain't buying."

Colin tried to make a physical connection

between the woman in front of him and Lucky, but fell way short of the mark. "Apologies, ma'am, but I'm not a salesman," he said when she moved to close the door in his face. "I'm looking for Miss Clayborn?"

Dark eyes squinted out at him as she removed the cigarette from her lips, mindless of the ash that fell to the floor next to the three dogs yapping at her feet and pawing at the screen door. "What do you want with Lucky?"

Colin didn't realize he was hoping that he'd gotten the address wrong until that moment. "I'm a...friend."

The woman gave him a long once-over then gave a doubtful grunt. "She lives in the apartment in the back."

The door slammed in his face, leaving Colin standing staring dumbly at the chipped wood.

He made his way back down the stairs and around the side of the house. He could just make out the grille of Lucky's old Chevy parked in the back. His throat grew tight at the knowledge that she was home and he would soon be face-to-face with her. Suddenly it didn't matter that he had to watch where he stepped. Or that this house should have been on somebody's demolition list years ago. All that mattered was that he was going to see Lucky for the first time in a week.

He had to round the house entirely before he finally saw the door to what had to be the back apartment. At one time it had probably been the back door leading to the house's kitchen. The window next to the door was cracked open and he made out the sounds of the same oldies station he listened to and the scent of strawberries. He heard a clang then a soft, "damn."

Colin swallowed hard then lifted his hand to knock.

More sounds from inside, then the door opened, "I told you I'd have the rent…"

Her words stopped as she stared into Colin's face. A kitchen towel was wrapped around her left hand and she wore a black cotton sundress that seemed to emphasis the deep red of her hair and the paleness of her skin.

"Colin," she breathed more than said.

Realizing he should probably say something, he stuffed his hands inside his pockets to keep from reaching out for her and said, "You didn't make your appointment today."

She blinked at him. "Oh, God. Is it Monday already?"

He looked both ways, feeling awkward standing outside. "May I come in?"

She squinted at him, pulling the towel tighter around her hand. "No."

Colin looked over her shoulder, wondering if someone else was with her. But unless the person had gone to the bathroom, he couldn't see anyone else inside her apartment, a room no larger than his living room. A single mattress was on the floor in one corner, the faded flowery sheets rumpled as if she'd just crawled from it. A small battered table with two mismatched chairs sat beside that, and then there was a sink, a microwave and a two-burner hotplate on the opposite side of the room. In the sink he made out a stainless-steel colander filled with fresh strawberries. Behind the sink sat five or six bottles of alcohol in various states of emptiness.

Lucky caught the direction of his gaze then stepped out next to him and closed the door. "Look, tell Dr. Szymanski I'm sorry I missed my appointment. I worked closing last night at my new job after working the morning shift at my other job and I…" She stared at the blood staining the towel. "And I guess I slept late this morning."

Colin held his hands out. "Let me have a look."

"I didn't think you were that kind of doctor."

His gaze flicked to her smiling face. His relief to see her looking more like herself was complete and startling. "Shut up and give me your hand."

She raised a brow. "Ah, the prominent doctor goes native."

Instead of waiting for her to offer, Colin took her hand gently in his and began unwrapping the towel. He marveled at how small and delicate her fingers were in contrast to his larger ones as he ferreted out the source of the blood. There was a small cut on the outer edge of her index finger, likely made by a knife.

"I was cutting strawberries."

He nodded, thinking about how cool her skin felt against his warmer fingers.

"We should rinse this out with water and bandage it properly."

He didn't miss her shifting her weight back and forth on her bare feet. Feet that were as small and delicate as her hands. And that were attached to the sexiest legs he'd seen in a good long while.

He caught her tugging on the hem of her sundress. A dress that was easily six inches longer than some of the miniskirts he'd seen her in. Why would she be self-conscious about the way she looked now?

She was nervous, he realized. But why? She glanced over her shoulder at the closed door.

"Look, is that all you wanted?" she asked, running her free hand through her tousled red hair.

"No," he said, realizing he'd meant it. "I thought you and I might have a talk."

She narrowed her green eyes at him. Eyes devoid of makeup and doubly intoxicating. "Talk?"

He grinned. "Yes. You know that thing that two people do when they have something to say to each other."

She glanced over her shoulder again.

"Lucky?"

"Hmm? Oh. Okay. I guess it wouldn't hurt to talk. There's a restaurant down the street there. Meet me there in, say, fifteen?"

She wanted him to meet her somewhere else.

It didn't make sense to Colin. But he wasn't about to argue the point. She'd agreed to talk to him. That should be enough.

Strangely, though, it wasn't.

"Okay. I'll see you in fifteen."

CHAPTER SIX

LUCKY CLOSED the door then leaned against it for support, her heart beating a million miles a minute. An upbeat oldies tune filled the small, shabby apartment. She reached for the radio and switched it off then absently wrapped the towel back around her finger.

Colin had come to her apartment.

Colin had seen where she lived.

She rushed to her bed and began straightening the sheets, then she reached for the clothes left on the floor when she'd taken them off early that morning. She started to shove them into the full laundry basket in the corner, then stopped and fished out the white blouse she needed to wear for work again that night.

Next she returned to the fresh strawberries she'd been cleaning in the sink, her movements manic, her mind racing with what he'd seen…and more importantly, what he must have thought of it.

She realized she hadn't cleaned her cut so she unwound the towel then thrust her hand under running water and closed her eyes.

The only person other than herself who had seen where she lived was her landlady, and that was only because she owned the joint. There was something…intimate about being inside someone's place. It left you vulnerable in ways that were hard to explain. And she was very guarded about letting anyone inside her apartment. She'd learned that lesson the hard way when she was seventeen and had rented a room in a downtown flophouse. She'd brought her boyfriend home only to wake up to find everything but the bedsheets she lay on gone. He'd even taken her clothes, which she'd later found out he'd given to his other girlfriend, who had thought he'd bought them.

She'd immediately moved out of the room and into another and had never made the mistake of inviting anyone to where she lived again.

She opened her eyes and her gaze settled on the bottles of liquor sitting on the back of the sink. Had he seen them? She swallowed hard then grabbed the two with only an ounce or two left in them and threw them away. But she hesitated when she reached for the others. The bottles and their contents were sometimes all that stood between her and insanity.

She switched the water off, realizing she should be getting ready to meet Colin. She had little doubt that he'd come back here if she didn't show. He'd come this far already, it likely wouldn't take much to make him return.

The thought motivated her into action.

COLIN GLANCED DOWN at his watch. Twenty-five minutes since he'd agreed to meet Lucky at the restaurant in fifteen. He nudged his watched around his wrist then straightened it. Was she standing him up? Had her agreeing to meet him only been a ruse to get him to leave her place so she could disappear?

He accepted a refill on his coffee and thanked the waitress then sat back in his chair. Tonight he'd seen a different Lucky. She hadn't been the seductress who had thrown herself at him twice at his office. Nor had she been the sassy waitress who had gotten fired from her last job. No, this Lucky… this Lucky had been somehow more exposed. As if he'd caught her off guard and she hadn't been able to recover from the surprise of finding him outside her door.

He sipped at his black coffee without really tasting it. And she'd been so damn sexy it had taken everything that he had not to sweep her up in his arms and carry her to that mattress on the floor.

Sure, he'd seen places similar to hers. But usually they belonged to college kids who were just scraping by until they graduated. And Lucky was no college kid. She was a full-grown woman who obviously was having a hard time making the rent.

That, he wasn't used to.

"That coffee strong?"

Colin blinked up to find Lucky taking the seat across from him.

At the sight of her, his every muscle relaxed at the same time a simmering heat worked its way under his skin.

She'd put on a pair of snug jeans and a clingy black T-shirt, strappy leather sandals rounding out her casual appearance. She'd applied makeup, but not much. And her hair was pulled back into a neat ponytail, making him want to pull off the rubber band and let the sensual waves fall over her shoulders.

"It's good," he said in response to her question, motioning for the waitress to bring her a cup.

There was a simple black leather tie around her left wrist. For some reason he couldn't quite explain, Colin was fascinated with the piece of jewelry. Perhaps because it seemed to mirror the qualities of its owner. Or perhaps because it brought to mind leather bonds and soft moans.

"You said you wanted to talk?" she asked, adding cream and sugar to her coffee, then using both hands to lift it and take a sip.

He narrowed his gaze. "Morgan nearly reported your absence to the court."

"Nearly. That means she didn't."

He nodded. "I talked her out of it. Promised I'd look into it."

Lucky's shoulders seem to loosen. "Thanks." She smoothed back her already smooth hair. "I really don't need that hassle on top of everything else."

"You're late on your rent?"

She refused to meet his gaze. While she might have forgotten about what she'd said when she'd opened the door and thought he was someone else, he hadn't.

But her stance told him that didn't mean she had any intention of answering his question.

Anyway, what did it matter to him whether or not she could make her rent? Was he prepared to pull his money out and loan her the amount to tide her over until her next paycheck? Was she even working a steady job, or did she move from place to place without ever managing to save a dime?

These were all questions he wanted answers to, but questions he didn't dare ask.

Instead he said, "I guess you don't get very many visitors."

She finally lifted her eyes to him, the expression on her face downright sexy. "You guess correctly."

"Why?"

"Playing therapist again, Dr. McKenna?"

"No. I'm trying to be your friend."

He watched as she shifted uncomfortably. "I don't need any friends."

About to sip his coffee, Colin froze. "Everyone needs friends, Lucky."

"What I meant is that I don't need any more friends."

Why did he get the impression that's not what she meant at all and that her first comment was the more honest one?

Was it possible that the woman across from him didn't have a single friend? Not even one person, forget a whole network of people, she could count on when the clouds obscured the sun and when she needed help in making the rent every now and again?

"Then accept me as your big brother," he said, closely watching her pretty face. "Or don't you need any more family, either?"

Her smile was decidedly provocative. "Why brother? Why not Sugar Daddy?"

"Is that what you want me to be?"

"I don't want you to be anything. You came to see me, remember?"

Oh, yes, he remembered.

He felt something touch his ankle under the table and realized it was her toes. He glanced to find she'd slipped out of her sandal and was working his sock down until her skin touched his. Heat sure and swift swept through his groin.

He cleared his throat.

He got the distinct feeling that she was trying to distract him with sex. And he'd be damned if he was willing to allow her to do it. The truth was he'd been wanting her for so long now that his desire was taking on a life of its own.

"I take it going back to your place is not an option," he said quietly.

She shook her head, keeping her gaze even with his.

He peeled off money to cover the coffee and a generous tip. "Well, then, my place it is."

IF IT WAS TRUE that a place said a lot about the person, then what did Colin's apartment say about him?

Lucky stood just inside the door of the penthouse

apartment, taking in the rich leather furniture, the paintings, the brass lamps, and thought that it said that he was wealthy.

"Having second thoughts?" he asked, shrugging out of his suit jacket then loosening his tie as he headed toward what she guessed was his bedroom.

She watched his backside, the tension she'd felt as she followed him to the downtown building reaching a pressure point. She thought about following him but found it impossible to move from the spot where she stood.

"There's some wine in the fridge if you want some."

"How about a beer?"

A pause then, "There may be one or two in there. Why don't you check?"

Lucky craned her neck to look down the hallway where he'd disappeared, then the other way, which she guessed led to the kitchen. She switched on the light inside a cavernous room with terra cotta floor tiles and a woodblock island, thinking it looked better than some of the nicer restaurants she'd worked in.

And it revealed absolutely zero about the man who owned it.

She moved toward the industrial-sized refrigerator. She spotted four or five bottles of imported beer immediately, but as she pulled out two she paused to examine the remainder of the fridge's contents. She smiled at the box of pizza and the half-empty container of chip dip, then opened the freezer to find it well stocked with gourmet-style frozen dinners, vegetables and chocolate-almond ice-cream bars.

She put the beers down on the island, found a plate, then filled it with the leftover pizza, after sniffing it to make sure it was all right. She nuked it, then went back out into the living room at the same time Colin re-entered the room from the other side.

Lucky froze at the sight of him looking like an average guy.

She swallowed hard. Not that she thought him a super stud or anything. But she'd never seen him wear anything but suits, so catching him in jeans and a navy-blue T-shirt and bare feet caught her off guard.

"Hungry?" he asked.

She blinked at the plate of pizza.

He crossed to her, took the plate and the beers from her then carried them to a gaming table against the far wall where he put them down. Lucky followed, running her fingertip along the inlaid wood chessboard that was part of the table and trying not to notice the way the soft denim molded to his backside. Colin pulled a cord and the white curtains opened.

She caught her breath for a second time, staring at another view she'd never seen from this angle before. That of downtown Toledo and the Maumee River at dusk.

"Yeah. That was pretty much my reaction when I saw it. It's the reason I bought the place."

He owned, not rented, the apartment.

But of course he would. Renting was for people like her who lived from hand to mouth.

"Do you want to go outside?" he asked, motioning toward the French doors and the wrought-iron furniture on the balcony beyond.

She shook her head, glanced at her hands, which she was wringing, and found something else to do with them. More specifically, entwine them in Colin's thick, dark blond hair while she kissed him.

ONE MINUTE COLIN had been wondering what to say to Lucky, the next he was kissing her as if it wasn't the pizza he was hungry for but her.

As she launched a breathless attack on his mouth, she pressed her breasts tightly against his chest, her hips bumping his as she sought a closer meeting. He worked his fingers up under the hem of her shirt at the same time she unbuttoned the fly of the jeans he'd just buttoned up. Within seconds she held his rock-hard length in her hands. Colin broke contact with her mouth, groaning aloud. Her touch was gentle yet bold. Her strokes stoked the flames licking through his groin into a full-fledged fire.

Giving up trying to work his own hands under her tight shirt, he instead pulled the stretchy fabric over her head, momentarily pausing their kissing. The instant the fabric was free, her mouth sought his and her hands rested against his throbbing length again.

Never had Colin wanted anyone with the intensity he wanted Lucky. He popped the catch on her bra, then cupped her breasts and greedily licked the swollen mounds of flesh, sucking her right nipple deep into his mouth before switching his attention to her other breast. He heard her low whimper and the sound sent his desire level soaring through the roof.

"I want you so bad I hurt," she whispered, kissing the side of his mouth then moving to his neck.

That was all the incentive Colin needed as he swept her up into his arms.

"No…no," she said, grasping his shoulders tightly. "Not the bedroom."

His steps faltered as he gazed into her passion-filled green eyes.

She smiled. "The couch. I don't think I can wait for the bedroom."

He practically launched her toward his overstuffed black leather couch where she went to work slipping out of her sandals then shimmying out of her tight jeans. Colin was rooted to the spot, watching as she revealed the skimpiest pair of black underwear he'd ever seen up close and personal. The panties matched her open bra and both matched his couch. She looked as though someone had poured fresh cream over his sofa.

She reached out and yanked him toward her by the pocket of his jeans, reminding him that he had yet to disrobe. He'd begun pulling off his T-shirt when he felt her hot, hot mouth on his straining member.

Dear Lord…

Colin's knees nearly buckled underneath him as he somehow managed to get the shirt off and toss it aside. He stared at Lucky's wild red hair escaping her ponytail and followed the movements of her decadent mouth as she took in as much of his length as she could, then pulled back again. Her hand replaced her mouth and then she went down on him again, nearly draining him as her tongue cradled the sensitive underside of his penis.

As much as he hated to stop her, he wanted their first time to be about mutual sharing. He gently squeezed her shoulders, using every ounce of will-power he had to tug her skillful mouth away from his sensitive flesh. She blinked up at him, obviously confused.

"When I come, I want it to be with you," he murmured, kneeling down in front of her.

Something flickered in her eyes, but he couldn't be sure what it was. Surprise? Maybe.

She automatically spread her legs, welcoming him between her slender thighs. He grasped her near the knees then ran his fingers up her supple skin, denting her soft flesh, until his thumbs reached the crotch of her panties. He watched as she sank back into the cushions, giving him full access to her engorged womanhood just beneath the satiny fabric. He lightly stroked the growing wet spot then moved just to the north of it. Her hips bucked involuntarily and he knew he'd hit the target area. Increasing the pressure of his thumb, he started making small circles, listening as her breathing grew more ragged as she tried to fill her lungs with air.

He grabbed the string that made up the side of the panties with his other hand and pulled, satisfied when the material gave, finally baring her to his hungry gaze.

So swollen…so wet…so luscious.

The fabric no longer impeding his progress, he

tunneled his thumb through her springy curls and found her fleshy core. Her back came up off the couch and she bore down as if seeking something only he could give her.

He grabbed for his jeans and pulled out the condom he'd put in there not five minutes ago, then quickly sheathed himself, his frantic movements not stopping until he slid into Lucky's sweet flesh to the hilt.

Then everything seemed to stop.

His movements.

His breathing.

His heartbeat.

He met Lucky's gaze, and in the back of his mind he heard what sounded like a low click.

Slowly everything started working again. Double time.

Lucky stared into Colin's dark eyes, mesmerized by the sight of him as he filled her to overflowing. Her heart beat thickly, as if weighed down by a pound of honey. Honey that coated her insides and melted low in her belly, spreading, spreading until she nearly couldn't bear the sheer pleasure it brought.

She sought purchase on the edge of the sofa but found none on the slick leather. So she grasped Colin's shoulders instead, thrusting up to meet him as he withdrew then stroked her again. An agonizing pressure seemed to build up in her very veins and she moaned as his hard arousal slid inside her tight, wet flesh. And, throughout, her gaze was locked with Colin's.

Most men closed their eyes when they had sex. Not Colin. His brown eyes appeared almost black as he watched her watching him. She felt connected to him in a way she hadn't felt connected to anyone before him. Connected by shared pleasure. Ecstasy.

Colin grasped her hips and hauled her down farther so her bottom rested against the edge of the sofa cushion. Then he re-entered her, sending her spiraling ever higher and higher. He withdrew then stroked her again…and again, each thrust faster and deeper than the one before. She felt her breasts sway. Her stomach tremble. Her fingers sink into his shoulders as she rode wave after wave of pure sensation.

Then she felt him stiffen. She bore down on him hard, tilting her hips up then down again, rubbing her pelvis against his.

He groaned, and she joined him in the shared orgasm he'd desired.

CHAPTER SEVEN

HOURS LATER Colin lay in his bed next to Lucky, feeling like the luckiest man in the world. He couldn't remember a time when he'd enjoyed sex more. Enjoyed? The word didn't come near to describing his insatiable want of the naked woman curved against him. His fingers still stroked her breast even though she'd fallen into a deep, exhausted sleep a little while before.

He knew if he were to part her swollen flesh and enter her from behind, she'd respond welcomingly. But no matter how much he wanted to do that, to continue what he never wanted to end, he let her rest.

In the dim light filtering in through the floor-to-ceiling windows, her thick hair looked black and her skin seemed to glow eerily white. So beautiful. So responsive. So sensual.

So guarded.

He shifted his hand off her breast and to her flat stomach, pleased by her unconscious shiver. She was so open to him sexually, yet she'd blocked him from entering her place the night before. What had she been hiding? What hadn't she wanted him to see? It seemed odd that the shameless woman would be ashamed of her own apartment. But what other explanation was there?

He rolled onto his back. Lucky murmured then turned and snuggled up to his side. Colin stared into her sleeping face and finger-combed her hair from her temple. Normally he was the one used to sleeping like the dead after a night of great sex. But somewhere within him he knew that what had happened in the past few hours hadn't just been about sex. It had been great, yes. But it had also been something more.

He squinted at the woman in his arms. She was a sexy enigma to him. So much he didn't know about her. And yet he had invited her into his apartment, his bed, with few reservations, and even those were professional. On a fundamental level he knew he could trust her not to steal the silver. Knew he could count on her not to go through his things while he slept. He wasn't sure how he knew, but he did.

Of course he knew the reason why he couldn't sleep. Beyond his continued and unquenchable want of Lucky was his concern about what would happen in the morning. Would she still be there when he got up? Would she want to share breakfast? Come out and run with him?

He thought of her jeans and sandals and ruled that out. Unless she went back to her place and picked up running gear.

And if she did? Was he ready for things to go so far so fast?

He didn't realize she was watching him until he heard her deep swallow. "You're awake."

The sheets rustled as he covered them both. "So are you."

She flattened her palm against his chest as if wondering at the sight of her skin against his. "What's on your mind?"

He smiled into her hair then kissed her head. "I thought that was my line."

She rubbed her nose against his nipple. "When you're at work it's your line. When you're here…"

Her words seemed to imply she planned to stick around longer than tonight.

She rolled away from him and sat up, her feet over the side of the bed.

Colin resisted the urge to reach for her. "Where are you going?"

"Home."

Home. Back to that ramshackle room on the opposite side of town.

"I was supposed to go in to work tonight."

Colin raised his brows then ran his fingers through his tousled hair. He hadn't even thought to ask what her schedule was. Then again, she hadn't mentioned anything, either.

He watched as she plucked the sheet off her lap and got up. "I guess I have to pound the pavement again in the morning to find another job."

Colin lifted to his elbows, watching as she went into the bathroom. Moments later he heard the sound of the shower. He lay there in the dark, considering what she'd said. He was still there when she emerged from the bathroom smelling like his shampoo and soap then padded out into the living room where he watched her put on her clothes. Moments later she was standing fully dressed in the open doorway.

"Thanks," she said quietly.

"For what?"

"For the great night."

He would have been insulted had he not recognized the humor in her voice.

She began to turn away.

"Lucky?"

She stopped. "What?"

He couldn't make out her beautiful face in

the dark. "How much do you need to make your rent?"

She didn't say anything for long moments but he detected a change in her posture. A slight stiffening. "Why? Are you offering to pay it?"

"Yes."

Again, silence.

Then, "No. But thanks for thinking of it."

Colin threw the sheet off and followed her out into the living room. "Then think of it as a loan. You know, until you can get back on your feet."

He caught the flash of her smile. "This is as good as it gets, doc. As much on my feet as I ever am."

He watched as she crossed her arms over her chest.

"Tell me, Colin. Is this where the rich guy feels guilty about banging the poor girl from the wrong side of the tracks and offers to save her from herself?"

Colin felt suddenly, totally exposed standing there in the nude facing her.

"I don't need saving."

She regarded him for a moment, then sighed softly and crossed to stand directly in front of him. She gave him a lingering kiss.

"Thanks, anyway. It was sweet."

He called her a cab, insisting he at least pay for

that, then watched as she gathered her purse and let herself out of his apartment.

Colin stood there for long moments, listening as the elevator in the hall dinged open then closed, whooshing Lucky away into the dark night.

Then a thought occurred to him: Maybe it wasn't her he was offering to save.

THE MIDDAY SUN glared against the windshield of Lucky's old Chevy, making the interior of the car almost unbearably hot when it wasn't moving. She adjusted her sunglasses and stared at the red light, wishing it green. The radio issued a burst of static and she reached out to switch it off, leaving nothing but the rumbling sound of the old car vibrating beneath her.

She'd hit no fewer than twenty bars and restaurants in the area and all of them had told her the same thing: they didn't have any openings but if she'd like to fill out an application they'd keep it on file in case something came up.

Lucky blew a long breath out between her lips. She could count the times she'd been contacted that way on one finger. Unless she had an in by knowing someone else who worked at the place or she happened upon a bar where a waiter or waitress had just quit, her chances of landing a position lay somewhere between slim to none. Especially given her spotty work record as of late. While she'd been employed at the pancake house for over a year, her job at Harry's had lasted four months. And her latest gig at the new country-and-western bar and grill near her house had lasted a grand total of six days.

Of course, she wasn't going to tell a prospective boss that the reason for that was she'd chosen sex over a paycheck, so she chose not to mention that job on her applications.

The light finally turned green and she pulled into a strip mall that held several adult dancing clubs. No, she had never danced, and never planned to, but she had worked at one or two as stop gaps until she found something she liked better. The tips were good even if the last time she'd had to wear a string bikini, leather chaps and a cowboy hat when she served the oversexed clientele their expensive drinks.

Dr. Colin McKenna would never be caught dead in a joint like that.

And, she suspected, under normal circumstances neither would he have been caught dead seeing a woman like her.

She pulled into a parking spot facing a strip club and cut the engine. She knew that if she hadn't been assigned to attend counseling at his office the likelihood of their paths crossing would have been low. And even though they had slept together she knew they were about as different as two people could get.

Put simply, she was a twenty-five-year-old Chevy, and he was a brand-spanking new Lincoln Navigator. And while her old muscle car could give his a run for its money any day of the week, at the end of that day it was still an old Chevy.

And she was still the same old Lucky.

Still, the possibility of never seeing him again sent a knife-sharp pain shooting through her chest.

Five minutes later she was still sitting in the car staring at the doors to the strip joint, her hands clenched against the hot steering wheel, her mind firmly on Colin McKenna, when sunlight reflected off a nearby door, snagging her attnetion. Lucky squinted at a customer exiting a shop two doors up from the strip club. A brunette about her age propped open the door then began sweeping the sidewalk. She took in the sign above the store.

Women Only.

Lucky cracked a grin, finding the name apropos given its location. What else would you name a shop next to a gentlemen's only club?

A Help Wanted sign caught her attention.

She hadn't worked in retail much. She'd found the hours weren't as flexible and the pay without tips not nearly as much as she made as a waitress.

She got out of the car and headed for the strip joint.

Halfway there she switched courses and turned toward the other shop.

The woman cleaning the sidewalk stopped sweeping and looked up at her. Lucky pushed her sunglasses to the top of her head and asked, "You looking to hire somebody?"

Tsk, tsk. Bad Dr. McKenna.

COLIN STARED at the note he'd found under his windshield wiper outside his apartment building this morning. He didn't have to wonder who had left it. Obviously Jamie was still avidly stalking him.

He resisted the urge to crumple the paper and instead tucked it into the band under his sun visor so he could hand it over to his attorney in his ever-hopeful bid to press stalking charges against his former patient. As he waited for the light to change, he gripped and released the steering wheel.

Obviously last night Jamie had spotted him going back to his place with Lucky. And obviously Jamie thought Lucky might still be one of his patients.

At any rate, he couldn't afford to make any more mistakes like that, as his attorney kept reminding him. "Play it low-key, Colin. We'll just have to hope that Jamie will back off, move on to someone else, and this will all be over with."

Only Jamie wasn't backing off. And he was getting tired of living his life constantly looking over his shoulder.

The traffic in front of him moved forward and he followed suit, turning off into a parking lot a half mile up the road. Will had asked him to meet him for lunch at a rib joint and while he'd rather follow up on what was happening with Lucky, he'd decided a few ribs and some straight talk might be just what the doctor ordered.

Twenty minutes later, well into his second rib, he said to Will, point-blank, "I slept with her last night."

His British friend gave him one of his best poker-faced stares. "Slept with whom?"

Colin put the rib down and wiped his hands on a napkin.

"So," Will said, apparently realizing Colin wasn't going to rise to the bait, "was it everything you imagined it would be?"

Colin met his friend's gaze head-on. "And more."

Will forgot nonchalance and raised his brows. "I was expecting a 'no.'"

Colin grinned. "I know you were. But sorry, mate, I can't give it to you," he said, mimicking his friend's accent.

They ate in silence for a few moments. "That good, huh?" Will asked.

"Mmm. And better."

One night, right after Amanda had left Colin, the two men had finished off a twelve pack of beer and discussed how women might find these male exchanges. Will had surmised that since women romanticized everything, they'd be horrified to hear themselves being referred to by a rating system. Colin had liked to think women were more open-minded than that and had even been privy to a few female conversations where size had definitely been mentioned.

Will finished off his ribs then washed them down with the rest of his pint of beer. "So when do you take her home to meet the parents?"

Colin's light mood took a dark nosedive.

"Uh-oh. I don't know if I like the looks of that expression."

"You can be such an arrogant ass, do you know that, Will?"

His friend crossed his arms on top of the table.

"I daresay my irreverence is one of the things you love about me."

Which was true.

Except his jibe this time had definitely hit the wrong chord.

"So you're not taking her home to meet the parents, then?"

Colin gave up on the rest of his ribs. "We slept together, I didn't propose to her."

"Well, that's good then."

Colin stared at the bubbles lining the walls of his glass of club soda.

"It is good, isn't it?"

"I don't even know if I'm going to see her again."

"Why not? Obviously you enjoyed the sex." Will leaned back and allowed their server to take his plate. Colin bristled at the open way his friend eyed the pretty young waitress, because it made him wonder how often Lucky got the same attention. "Don't tell me. She's making serious noises already." He sighed. "And why not? A doctor like yourself should be a good catch for someone of her station."

He tamped down his irritation at Will's continued underhanded jabs at Lucky. "To the contrary, she didn't indicate one way or another that she wanted to see me again, either."

"But she enjoyed the sex."

"She very definitely enjoyed the sex."

"So what's the problem, mate? By all means have more of it, then."

The problem was that he feared he was hearing his own brand of serious noises in his head.

"So, tell me," he said, deciding he needed to change the subject, "how did everything go with pink ribbon number thirty-two?"

Will gave an exaggerated sigh. "I haven't been half as lucky as you in that department, unfortunately. Get it? Lucky?"

Colin chuckled quietly and listened as his friend told him about his trials and tribulations with a woman who had decided she wasn't going to have sex again until the day she was married.

CHAPTER EIGHT

AT TEN O'CLOCK that evening Colin sat on the same sofa he and Lucky had had sex on the night before, a psychology magazine open on his lap, the large-screen television flashing muted pictures of a newsmagazine show.

But his mind was on none of it. Instead his hand absently caressed the rich leather against which Lucky and her flawless skin had lain. And his mind focused on all that she'd said, all that she'd done up until she'd kissed him goodbye and left.

While Will's words at lunch had made him a little hot under the collar, the fact remained that there were some real issues surrounding his connection to Lucky Clayborn.

But none of them stopped him from wanting her with a physical intensity that was foreign to him.

He'd called her number earlier, only to find it was out of service. A casualty of her unstable lifestyle? More than likely. Although he guessed Lucky was the type of person who would change her number just to keep people guessing. Just as she had prevented him from entering her place the night before, so she barred everyone from learning too much about her.

And for that reason he'd restrained himself from stopping by her place again. If he were to be truthful, he was half afraid he'd find she'd already moved on. Or might if he continued to invade her private sanctum.

He wondered how much those bottles behind the sink had to do with finding her peace of mind.

Colin picked up the remote, surfed through a few satellite channels, then he switched off the television altogether. He was all too familiar with addictive personality disorders. And while it was on record that Lucky had claimed her second D.U.I. offense had been the result of cold medication, he couldn't help wondering how often she turned to those myriad bottles at her apartment to help chase away the monsters that were known to come out at night. He glanced toward the chess table set up to his left, recalling that they'd never gotten around to drinking those beers she'd brought them from the kitchen along with the pizza the night before. Also, he'd never detected a hint of liquor on her breath. But that didn't necessarily mean she didn't go back to her place at night and drink herself into a stupor.

He rubbed his face and sighed deeply, pondering what it was about this one woman that fascinated him so. She was prickly to a painful extent, yet soft and sexy and vulnerable. She needed help yet refused it. And she could take him to soaring heights of ecstasy with one little flick of her tongue or tilt of her lush hips.

The downstairs bell rang. He glanced at his watch, then put the magazine down on the coffee table and stepped toward the intercom. "Yes?"

"Colin? It's Lucky. Hope you like chicken balls."

He stood for a long moment grinning, then pressed the button that would allow her access to the lobby and the elevator.

He opened the door and leaned against the jamb. He was still standing there waiting when the elevator finally dinged and the doors opened to reveal her holding up take-out cartons.

"Ah, you were talking about Chinese food," he said dryly.

She snorted inelegantly and brushed past him into his apartment.

Colin briefly closed his eyes, enjoying the scent of her as she passed. He hadn't truly known how much he was looking forward to seeing her until that moment. Though he'd been darkly contemplating his connection to her only a short time before, now he wore a grin that didn't seem to want to budge. And rather than dreading the rest of the evening he was now looking forward to it.

He turned to find her standing in the middle of the room.

"Where do you want it?" she asked.

Colin considered the provocative way she stood, her legs spaced slightly apart, her weight on one foot, calling attention to the shortness of her skirt and the tightness of her shirt.

"Hmm...I think the bedroom would work."

TWO HOURS LATER Lucky straddled a sitting Colin in the middle of his gigantic bed. She was hot and sticky and she couldn't seem to draw a full breath to save her life as he fondled her breasts, her womb still contracting from her latest climax.

She propped her elbows on his shoulders and entangled her fingers in his hair. "What you do to me," she murmured as she placed open-mouthed kisses all over his face then lingered on his delectable lips.

"What *do* I do to you?" he asked, nipping at the skin over her collarbone.

She managed to consider his question even as she reveled in the feel of him still filling her, the ache of her muscles from their second night of fantastic sex, and the hot proof of her passion for him wetting her thighs.

"You make me feel like I don't know myself anymore. Like my body doesn't belong to me."

He chuckled softly and brushed her damp hair back from her face. "I think that's the first time you've answered a question without challenging it."

She searched his dark eyes, realizing he was right.

She rolled off him and groaned when her muscles pulled in protest. "I don't know how much of this I can stand."

Colin stretched out next to her, idly plucking her closest nipple. "I can't remember having so much fun in the sack."

She smiled as she stroked the hand that stroked her. "Then you've been missing out, doc."

The bedding rustled as he shifted next to her. "No, it's not that, Lucky. It's…"

His words trailed off, causing her heartbeat to thicken.

"I don't know about you, but that Chinese is looking awfully good to me right now."

She climbed from the bed, put on her panties and her tank, then padded into the other room where she'd left the food cartons. The dim apartment's only illumination was golden pools of light from the moon that loomed large outside the windows. She wasn't surprised when she felt Colin's mouth against her shoulder and his ever-present arousal against her bottom.

"Here," she said, handing him a carton over her shoulder along with chopsticks. "I hope you like Kung Pao chicken."

"Mmm." He seemed to like her flesh even more as he continued to nibble and lick. "I'd die for some Kung Pao chicken."

He finally took the carton and they sat down across from each other at the gaming table against the window. As Lucky opened a carton of shrimp-fried rice and took a bite, she considered the view that lay ten floors below. The lights from the High Level Bridge twinkled, though she suspected it was more a trick of the wind. The waters of the Maumee River glistened darkly, sailboats anchored on this side of it, large ocean-going tankers on the opposite side. Spotlighted flags flapped lazily in the light breeze at International Park across the way, and it seemed every other window was still lit in the thirty-floor Owens-Illinois Building to the right of the Cherry Street Bridge.

She'd never really seen the city she'd grown up in from this vantage point. Shadows and cracked asphalt and roaring traffic was more a part of the vista outside her apartment window. But at least there were crickets and lightning bugs. Here she suspected there would be none.

"So what happened with your job?"

She blinked Colin's handsome face into view. The pale light from the moon gave it a bluish cast, making him look even more striking, with his hair sloping over his brow, twelve o'clock shadow darkening his jaw.

She took another bite of rice then shrugged. "They fired me."

His silence spoke volumes.

It seemed she'd taken great pleasure in shocking people for so much of her life that she was having a hard time with talking straight.

"But that's all right. I landed a day job this afternoon."

She wasn't sure why she'd offered up the information. Normally she would have left her end of the conversation at "they fired me." After all, it was nobody's business but her own where she worked, how she survived. And it had been so long since someone had actually worried about her that it was...strange that Colin was now.

"Another bar?"

She smiled. "Do you want something to drink?"

She made her way to the kitchen, then came

back with a couple of cans of sodas. She took note of his raised brow as she handed him one.

"What?"

He popped the top of his can and took a sip. "I don't know. I guess I was expecting beer."

She sat back down and picked up her rice again. "No beer tonight. I want to be fresh when I start tomorrow morning at Women Only."

"Sounds like a strip joint."

She laughed quietly. "It's a...actually, I'm not really sure what it is. But it's definitely not a strip joint."

She thought about how close she'd come to by-passing the small business and actually going to a strip joint and sighed.

"The pay's not much, but the girl who manages the place...I don't know. I liked her."

"That's good."

Lucky looked across the small table to find Colin staring at her in a way that made the tiny hairs on her arms stand on end. "What?"

His grin made her stomach tremble. "Nothing. I was just thinking about how beautiful you are."

Lucky returned her attention to her rice. She'd never been called beautiful before. Pretty, maybe once or twice. Sexy, definitely. But never beautiful.

But when Colin said it, she almost felt beautiful.

She reached across the table for the package of egg rolls, startled when he grasped her wrist.

"I think it's time for dessert," he whispered.

Before she knew it, she was being tugged into his lap back first.

Lucky gasped as she felt his rock-hard arousal press against her aching womanhood.

"Has anyone ever told you you're insatiable?" she asked thickly.

His hands sought and found her breasts, then dove under the hem of her tank and cupped them tightly. "Has anyone ever told you you're irresistible?"

He shifted them and the chair so that they were facing the window and the vista outside. She shuddered as one of his hands made a beeline for her crotch and stroked her through the material of her panties. Then the hand disappeared from her breast and a floor lamp flicked on next to them. She inhaled sharply when she discovered that the scene outside the window disappeared, the dark glass instead throwing back at her the image of herself straddling Colin. She hadn't realized he hadn't put anything on until that moment. His dark-hair-covered legs were spread, his manhood magnificently displayed beneath her own spread thighs. One of his hands tunneled inside her tank top and cupped her breast and the other worked its way inside her panties, boldly stroking her.

The sight was so powerfully erotic Lucky shuddered from head to foot. She found his hands with hers, covering them as he caressed and fondled her, until it was not only his hands doing the stroking, but her own as well.

An unbearable pressure built up low, low in her abdomen as he bit into her shoulder then pushed aside the crotch of her panties to reveal the dark-auburn thatch of hair there. He parted her damp flesh, showing her the core of her womanhood as his rigid shaft slid against it.

Lucky moved her hands to his knees and arched her back, her movements placing the knob of his arousal against her slick portal. A simple shift of her hips and he would breach the barrier. But rather than reaching for the condoms she noticed he'd put on the table, she worked her flesh down the length of him and back, avoiding penetration, reveling in the feel of her juices sluicing over his turgid flesh.

His left hand disappeared from between her legs and he was reaching around her to sheath himself. Then, finally, he thrust deep inside her. Lucky instantly climaxed, shuddering all around him as she clutched his legs for balance. He stayed still, his gaze connected to hers in the glass. As soon as her spasms abated, he began to thrust again, his length entering and withdrawing.

A low, primal moan escaped from Lucky's throat as she tilted her hips to meet his hungry lunges. His hands tightly gripped her waist, bringing her down harder and faster, making it impossible for her to catch her breath. In the glass her breasts bounced, her hair tumbled, and her mouth bowed open as flesh slapped against flesh, hard disappeared into soft, and she tumbled into a land she had never dared imagine existed.

She watched as Colin threw his head back and clenched his teeth, on the brink of orgasm. The moment his body stiffened, she bore tightly down against him and ground her hips, hitting spots that guaranteed she would chase right after him with a second climax.

For long minutes afterward, neither of them moved but for their ragged breathing. Then Colin was touching her again, his fingers branding her breast and her clit.

"I love to touch you," he whispered harshly, kissing and licking her shoulder.

"I love it when you touch me."

He grasped her hips and slowly withdrew, then tugged her so she straddled him from the front, putting them face-to-face. Lucky could no longer see their reflection in the glass. But she knew he could. She made the maneuvers necessary to strip herself of her shirt and panties, exchange Colin's condom for a fresh one, then climb back on top of him. She tossed her hair so that it fell in long waves down the middle of her bare back, then pushed out her bottom so that all was revealed in the glass behind her.

She heard Colin's deep groan then felt his fingers on her bottom where he parted her even further from behind so he could get a better look. She positioned herself directly over his rigid shaft then sank slowly down, well aware of the show she was providing for him. She was determined to create an experience he would never forget... and in turn earn herself an orgasm that she would always remember.

CHAPTER NINE

THREE DAYS LATER the manager of Women Only said to Lucky, "You have the look of a woman well sexed."

Renae Truesdale was a few inches shorter than Lucky, but that didn't detract from her dynamic presence. Around the same age as Lucky, Renae seemed to vibrate with a vivid vitality and sexuality most women would envy. Lucky had taken an immediate liking to her that first day when she'd approached her on the sidewalk. And three days later she felt the same.

Renae twisted her lips. "If we could bottle what put that look on your face, we'd be very rich women."

Normally Lucky might have offered up a sarcastic comeback. Maybe something along the lines of "who needs rich when there's great sex to be had?"

Now she merely smiled. Though her mind provided the jibe, something held her back from making light of what was happening between her and Colin. She didn't dare delve into what exactly that something was. She'd learned long ago that today, the moment, was all that mattered. What sense was there in looking down the road when that same road might narrow into a dark and cruel dead end?

Renae began to help Lucky fold the thick, Turkish terry-cloth robes that had come in that morning and put them on the display shelves against the far wall of the shop. From bath and lingerie stuffs to massage oils and aromatherapy candles, Women Only was packed full of everything a woman could want, and many things only a woman could understand. Lucky had yet to see one man come through the door. Not that she could blame the opposite sex. They'd probably feel as lost as she would at a sports supply store.

One of the many fringe benefits of her new job was that yesterday Renae had packed a boxful of things for her to use at home. As she'd put it, "You can't recommend a product unless you've used and liked it."

In Lucky's case, Colin had enjoyed the products as much, if not more, than she had last night.

"You're doing a good job, Lucky," Renae said,

leaning into her in a way that might have made Lucky a little wary a short time ago but that she found herself welcoming now. "I'm impressed with your work so far. Even a couple of customers have commented on how much they like you."

Lucky had never really received compliments on her work and she hadn't expected to. Generally she was only spoken to when a table needed waiting, drinks needed serving and when she wasn't keeping up with the hectic pace.

She didn't know quite how to respond. "I like it here," she said, and found that was the truth.

To her, a job had always been a job, judged by the tips she brought home rather than how she passed the time. She'd chosen the places where she'd worked by how busy they'd keep her, because when she was busy she didn't have time to think. It was hard to think about the landlady wanting the rent or the phone company threatening to shut off your line when you were occupied with serving food before it got cold or refilling a customer's drink.

The front-door bell rang and a woman came in, issued a brief greeting to Renae, then headed straight for the back where a room decorated in white with red candles was separated from the rest of the shop.

Renae put the last robe on the pile in front of her. "Time for my eleven o'clock."

Lucky knew that was her cue to hold down the shop. Renae waited a moment to give the woman time to change into a robe and stretch out on the massage table, then she joined her, striking up a conversation as she pulled the thick, red velvet curtain closed behind her, blocking the two from view.

A massage sounded really good right now. Sex with Colin was introducing her to all sorts of muscles she hadn't known she had.

The bell on the door rang again. Lucky gathered the empty box, stashed it behind the counter then turned toward the customer. "May I help you?" she asked.

A pretty blonde wearing a trendy red sleeveless mock turtleneck and white pants smiled at her.

"You must be Lucky. Hi, I'm Leah Bur—um, West." She laughed. "Sorry, I'm not quite used to my married name yet."

Leah. Now that rang a bell. She realized it was because Leah was the owner of the Women Only satellite shop on the opposite end of town. A place she'd heard described as putting the *P* in posh that was already garnering a lot of attention in the local media.

"Nice to meet you. You're right, I'm Lucky. But

not enough to win the lottery," she said with a wry smile at her lame joke.

Leah laughed and Lucky took the unguarded moment to examine the other woman's features. Renae was right. You could tell when a woman was well sexed.

Huh.

"I called Renae to tell her I'd be stopping by to stock up on a few supplies until I receive replacement shipments." She picked up a jasmine-scented candle, put it down, then lifted a vanilla one. "I shouldn't be long so don't worry about having to entertain me."

Lucky smiled. "Okay. Just wave if you need anything."

She went to work on collapsing the empty box, dusting the glass display case and marking down some of the items of inventory they might need to replenish soon.

The bell rang again. She turned to find Colin standing inside the door looking about as comfortable as a pup in a lion's den. A very handsome and sexy pup.

Lucky's heart skipped a beat. She'd never had anyone visit her on the job before.

Colin's gaze moved to her and she smiled widely at him. He seemed to relax instantly.

"Yes, sir, is there something I can do to help

you?" she said in a tone teasing enough for him to understand she was glad to see him, yet benign enough in case Renae was listening.

Leah West had spotted the new visitor. "Dr. McKenna? Colin, is that you?"

COLIN WAS HELPLESS to explain what happened to him every time his sight was filled with Lucky's beautiful face. His breathing seemed to grow shallower, his libido leapt to attention, and his chest tightened in an unfamiliar way. He recognized that the symptoms weren't a simple matter of sex. While he knew indescribable pleasure when their limbs were intertwined, his want of her was beginning to surpass that surface, physical need. He wanted to be with her, hear her laugh, listen to her opinion on issues that mattered to her, and just plain look at her.

"It is you! Imagine that."

Colin finally glanced at the woman who had said his name. He smiled. "Leah. It's good to see you."

She extended her hand and he shook it, noticing that there was something different about the woman he had counseled along with her ex-husband a couple of short months ago.

"I received your wedding invitation. I'm sorry I couldn't make it."

Leah's brown eyes sparkled. "I take it you noticed the name of the husband had changed."

He nodded. "I not only noticed, I expected it, Leah. And I'm happy for you."

He remembered Leah and her ex-husband, Dan Burger, well, if only because they had been the only couple he'd counseled recently who'd stood a chance of true reconciliation. Not because they'd been a love match. That much had been obvious even to him. But because for whatever reasons each of them held, they'd wanted it to work.

Still, he was secretly glad it hadn't. Settling was no way to go into a union that was supposed to last a lifetime.

On that thought his gaze drifted to Lucky. She was watching the exchange with interest, but made it clear she didn't want to interfere.

"Leah, have you met Lucky?" he said.

LUCKY WASN'T SURE what surprised her more, that Colin was introducing her to Leah, or that she was happy that he was.

"Yes, we've met," Lucky said. "Mrs. West happens to own the sister shop of Women Only."

She watched as Colin's brow rose and he congratulated the other woman on her recent accomplishments, indicating she'd undergone quite a change since he'd last seen her and that the changes suited her.

Lucky covertly watched Colin. Aside from her first group session at his office, she hadn't observed him much around other people. She decided she liked what she saw. A lot. He exuded a commanding presence, and not only because of his size. There was something about him that made you feel welcome and safe and happy all at once. Or at least that's how he made her feel.

Leah looked at her. "I think I have everything I need for now." She held out a slip of paper and Lucky took it. "This is a list of the items I took. Tell Renae I'll replace them by the end of the week at the latest."

Lucky nodded, they exchanged pleasantries, and then the doorbell clanged as Leah left.

Suddenly she and Colin were completely, totally, utterly alone.

Well, except for Renae and her client in the back.

Colin cleared his throat. The telltale sign of nervousness made Lucky smile.

"Nice place," he said.

Lucky looked around. "Yes, it is, isn't it?"

"I came by to see if you have time to catch a bite with me. I'm on my way downtown for a couple of meetings and had a little free time on my hands."

The way his gaze raked over her face and body, she had the feeling that he'd like to have his hands full of much more than free time.

Lucky shivered. "Sorry, my lunch break isn't until two."

He nodded, then shook his head. "Shame."

She agreed. "Damn shame."

"Okay, then, I'll see you later?" he asked.

She nodded.

He began walking toward the door, then hesitated. Taking something out of his pocket, he came back to stand in front of her. He grasped her hand and placed something in the middle of her palm. "I may run a little a late. Why don't you let yourself in?"

Lucky stared down at the key resting against her skin. But she didn't have a chance to respond as he kissed her then left her standing in the middle of the room to make of the exchange what she would.

ONCE A MONTH for the past three years Colin had sat in on group sessions at a local shelter for teenage runaways. His original commitment with Crossroads had been for a year, but when the period had been up, he'd found he couldn't turn away from the nonprofit agency or its boarders. While the stories of abuse and neglect often made him feel sick to his stomach, the resiliency and determination of the teens never failed to awe and inspire him.

This month, as every month, there were at least five new additions to the group, and he noticed that three others were missing, likely having moved back home, in with relatives, or having been placed with foster families. In some sad cases, a few emotionally damaged teens exchanged life at the home for life on the streets.

There were a few mandatory requirements that the boarders met, and one of them was attending these sessions. Considering the members, Colin always left his jacket and tie in his car and folded up the sleeves and unbuttoned the collar of his shirt. Today's session was beginning to wind down.

As he listened to a thirteen-year-old named Melissa talk of her absent, uncaring father and her physically abusive stepmother, who had thrown out all the sentimental items that meant something to the girl, Colin found his mind drifting to Lucky.

A shadow skittered around on the outer edges of his thoughts but he couldn't quite hold on to it long enough to get a better look.

Melissa finished and the housemother cleared her throat, then called the session to an end.

Colin looked down at the notes he'd written. He generally stayed over in case any of the teens wanted to talk to him one-on-one with the house-mother present, and also to consult with the house-mother on others' progress. The group sessions were designed to allow the teens to air their problems, work through them, and understand that they weren't alone, that there were not only others like them, there were others who had it worse.

That realization alone was often enough to help the teens move beyond the past and begin working toward a better future. A future they were in control of.

Again that sensation of missing something haunted him.

"Dr. McKenna, can I talk to you for a minute?"

He blinked up at Melissa, the last teen to speak, and smiled. Some of the others left to see to house chores, go to jobs outside the home, but most of them lingered on, gathering into smaller groups and continuing the rap session on a smaller scale.

Colin patted the spot next to him on the couch he sat on in the room set up to be comfortable rather than utilitarian. There were no hardback chairs here. Only cozy armchairs and sofas arranged in a circle.

"What's on your mind, Melissa?" he asked, determined to fully dedicate the next few minutes to the thirteen-year-old with the eyes of a thirty-year-old.

LATER THAT NIGHT Colin returned to his place, not realizing how much he'd been looking forward to seeing Lucky until he opened the door to a dark apartment. He flicked on a light and glanced around, but found no sign that Lucky was either there or had been there. He tossed his keys to the hall table then looked at his watch. Just after nine.

Over the past few days they had settled into a routine of sorts. Lucky knocked off at the shop at around six and by six-thirty she was at his place. They usually ordered in food and spent the night indulging in all sorts of wicked pleasures. That's why it had seemed natural for him to give her his key earlier.

Why, then, wasn't she there?

He absently rubbed the back of his neck and checked his home voice mail. A message from his car insurance company following up a small claim he'd made recently, a hello from his mother who just wanted to catch up with him and then... nothing.

A brief knock sounded on the door behind him. He glanced toward it then moved to open it.

Lucky stood in the hall holding up his key. "I think this belongs to you."

He hesitantly accepted the key back, noticing

the wary expression on her face. She came inside and he closed the door after her.

It struck him that if given the same type of access to his place, another woman would have put an extra toothbrush next to his. Put a change of clothes and underwear in his drawers. Somehow stamped her presence subtly but meaningfully all over the place, much as a cat marked its territory.

But not Lucky.

Of course he'd already known that she wasn't like most women. It was just taking him a while to figure out how unlike them she was.

"I placed an order for a large pizza before I came over so it should be here any minute," she said, putting her purse on the hall table and walking toward the kitchen, much as she had the past few nights. "Soda?"

No mention of why she had knocked on the door instead of letting herself in with the key. No reference to why she happened to show up at the same time he had instead of letting herself in earlier.

He watched as her shapely bottom disappeared into the kitchen, and then her delectable front faced him as she handed him a can of soda.

"There's a new show on Fox. Do you mind if we catch a little of it?"

Colin shook his head.

But before she could completely turn away from him again, he said quietly, "Lucky, we need to talk."

CHAPTER TEN

IF THERE WERE any four words in the English language Lucky hated, it was those four.

"We need to talk."

Usually when she heard them it meant she was about to be fired or let go or laid off.

Only Colin wasn't her boss.

Still, the graveness of his tone told her she probably wasn't going to like what he had to say.

"About what?" she asked, trying to play it off while knowing her chances of getting away with it with the sexy doc lay between slim and none.

He held up the key in his hand.

Lucky looked from it to him. "What about it?"

"Why didn't you use it?"

She popped the tab on her soda and took a long swallow, somehow managing to get the liquid past her tight throat. "There was no need to. You were already home."

His eyes narrowed. "Convenient."

She smiled and turned toward the couch. "Wasn't it though?"

She found the remote tucked in between the seat cushions and switched on the large-screen television that was probably worth more than she brought home in a month. She found the station she was looking for then crossed her legs in front of her, her short shorts short but enough to cover her decently.

Depending on your definition of decent.

Colin sat down next to her. Peripherally she watched as he put the extra house key down on the coffee table in front of them and fought not to stare at her shorts.

He quietly cleared his throat. "Did you stay past closing time at the shop?"

"Hmm?" she asked, pretending an interest in the show that had just started.

He gestured with his hand. "Work. Did you work overtime today?"

"No."

They sat like that for long minutes, neither of them saying anything, Lucky feeling his gaze on her profile while she stared at the television.

Then he picked up the remote and switched off the show.

"Hey, I was watching that," she said.

The expression on his face was far too serious. She decided it needed to be kissed off.

"Looks like somebody had a rough day," she murmured. Climbing to her knees, she wrapped her arms around his neck, placed her forehead against his, then leisurely pressed her lips against his. When he didn't immediately respond, she ran her tongue along the length of his bottom lip, then slowly slipped it inside his mouth, teasing him, tempting his tongue to come out and play.

He groaned, his hand finding the back of her neck and pulling her forward as he gave in to her attentions and kissed her back. In no time at all, they were both going at it hot and heavy, Lucky grateful for the surge of sensual need snaking through her.

Then Colin's grip increased on the back of her neck and he hauled his mouth from hers, his breath hot on her cheek. "Distracting me with sex, no matter how tempting, is not going to work this time, Lucky."

She pulled slightly back and stared deep into his eyes.

"Why didn't you use the key?"

Desire still throbbed with a life of its own

through her body, even though his words served as a bucket of cold water over her intentions.

She reluctantly sat back across the sofa from him. "Because this isn't my place."

"No, it's mine. And I gave you a key so you could come over early."

Too soon, an inner voice said.

Only that wasn't true, either, was it? Unless her subconscious was alerting her that it was too soon to end her relationship with Colin.

Her heart gave such a hard squeeze she nearly gasped.

"Don't treat me like a child, Colin."

"I'm not treating you like a child. I'm a man who would like to have an issue addressed and I'm calmly asking you to address it. Why didn't you use the key?"

She stared at him, realizing he wasn't going to give up until he got an answer.

So she gave him the only one she had.

"I didn't want to use the damn key, that's why. Is that enough for you?"

She shifted uncomfortably on the sofa, curving one of her legs under herself.

"And the reasoning behind that…?"

"Because I didn't feel comfortable coming in here when you weren't home, Colin. Isn't that enough?"

"Why? What could you do while I wasn't here that you couldn't while I am?"

She made a scoffing sound. "You'd be surprised."

He didn't say anything for a few moments, then asked, "What are you saying? That you might be tempted into doing something I wouldn't like if I left you here by yourself?"

"Now you're putting words into my mouth."

Frustration bracketed his sexy mouth. "Well, somebody has to, because you're not offering any up."

Lucky looked at him long and hard. Colin McKenna touched her in ways she couldn't begin to describe. Along with being the sexiest guy she'd ever met, he didn't pass judgment on her because of their differences. He was generous to a fault.

And he'd given her the key to his place—even if it was for a single use—mere days after they'd first slept together.

But she could do without the third degree. She liked having to worry only about herself. And she didn't particularly like when others started butting into her business.

She fidgeted, feeling more than a little agitated. "What is it with shrinks and their habit of talking everything to death?"

He didn't even blink in the face of the criticism.

"What is it with beautiful stubborn women afraid to share how they're feeling?"

She held his straight gaze for a long moment, and then a smile began working its way up from her heart to her mouth. "Touché. I guess I deserved that one."

His return grin eased her ruffled feathers. "While I, on the other hand, didn't deserve the shrink jibe." He put his hand on her knee.

The movement was so natural, so unaffected, that her stomach pitched to somewhere in the vicinity of her feet.

It made her want to coax the skillful limb a little farther to the north. If only to chase away the unwanted thoughts clouding her mind and help her focus on something else.

She briefly closed her eyes. "What if I told you I didn't use your key today because…because it… this…is moving too fast for me?"

The fingers on her knee tightened.

He didn't answer so she cracked open her eyes, half expecting him to call her a liar.

Instead, he nodded, appearing unhappy with the question but open to it. "Then I'd have to accept that's how you feel."

Lucky maneuvered herself on the sofa until she was curved against his side. Both of them stared at the opposite wall, their fingers intertwined on her knee.

She wasn't sure how he knew, but she was fully aware that he realized her answer wasn't the true reason why she hadn't used his key earlier, why she had waited until now to come over so she wouldn't have to use it.

But she was grateful that he didn't pursue the matter.

Maybe it was because he sensed that to pursue it would be to end it.

"You know," he said quietly, rubbing his temple against her hair, "I've been looking forward to this moment all this day. This time when I could see you again...touch you."

Lucky took a deep breath and smiled into the side of his neck.

"Me, too," she admitted, surprised by how easily the admission came...and how outside the norm it was for her.

And how very much she wanted to have this man inside her again, stroking her until the outside world no longer existed.

She got up and held her hand out to him.

He hesitated, then put his into it, allowing her to lead him to the bedroom, the imminent pizza delivery, and the key momentarily forgotten.

Momentarily...

COLIN AWOKE to the smell of bacon frying.

Sure he was imagining things, he rolled over and groaned into his pillow, only then realizing something was missing from the bed.

Lucky.

He reached for the alarm clock that sat face down on his nightstand and squinted at the time. Just after nine.

Just after nine?

He pushed up to his elbow then ran his hand over his hair and face several times. He couldn't remember the last time he'd slept past seven, even on a Saturday morning. By now he would have been out for his morning run, had his breakfast, read the *Toledo Blade* and *The Wall Street Journal,* and would have been on his way to whatever he had on tap for this morning.

Which happened to be tennis with Will.

He reached for the cordless receiver on the bedside table and pressed the speed dial for his friend.

"You're late," Will said without preamble.

Colin grinned as he swung his feet over the side of the bed. "Actually, I'm not late yet."

"'Yet' being code for you're not on your way here, I take it?"

"Mmm. Let me call you back in a half hour."

"Well, what in the hell does that mean?"

"It means what it means."

"Well, holy hell, Colin, how long do you expect me to wait?"

He sensed he was no longer alone and looked toward the door to find Lucky standing in it wearing nothing but the barbecue apron his ex-fiancée had bought for him as a housewarming gift. It said, Master Of All Things Hot.

Colin suddenly had a hard time getting his thoughts together as he followed the white shoulder straps to where they just covered Lucky's bare breasts. Her fiery red hair was slightly damp and framed her face in a riot of sexy curls.

She held a large metal spatula in her right hand and seemed to indicate, if the need arose, she could use it for something other than turning food.

"Will, I'll, um, call you back."

"Jesus, Colin, don't you dare hang up—"

Colin hung up on him then replaced the receiver on the night table.

"Will, as in Dr. Will, your obnoxious friend with the British accent from Harry's?"

Colin's throat tightened as she leaned against the doorjamb, causing one of the straps to move slightly right of center allowing her nipple to peek out. "That would, um, be him." He stared intently into her face. "Come here."

Her green eyes twinkled at him naughtily. "I would but I'm afraid I might burn something."

"Baby, the only thing burning is me sitting here looking at you looking like that."

She laughed, the throaty sound filling the room, the apartment and Colin's heart with the sweet sound. "Cheesy. Definitely cheesy."

"What matters is the end result."

She seemed to consider his words, slapping the spatula into her opposite palm, her gaze traveling leisurely over his nude body where he sat on the bed. The word *Master* printed on the apron made him entertain all sorts of ideas on what he might allow her to be the master of.

"Over easy or sunny-side up?"

Colin allowed his mouth to curve into a slow, suggestive smile. "Any which way I can get you."

She pointed the spatula at him. "You have a very dirty mind, Dr. McKenna."

"That's because you bring out the best in me." He waggled his brows, completely aware that another part of his anatomy was making its thoughts known on the subject and that Lucky hadn't missed that fact. "Or should I say beast?"

He started to get up, to pull her back into bed and the hell with breakfast, but she quickly turned around, laughing as she ran for the kitchen.

Colin chuckled then sat back down, watching as

her delectable bare ass disappeared back into the kitchen.

He shook his head, having a hard time reconciling the playful, provocative woman of this morning with the closed-off, defensive woman from the night before.

Ignoring how badly he needed to use the bathroom, and how badly he wanted to follow after Lucky, he lay back on the bed and stared at the ceiling, trying to superimpose the latest picture of Lucky on top of the one she'd presented last night when he'd repeatedly prompted her for the reason why she hadn't used his key.

He hadn't received the answer; she'd given him a reason.

He absently rubbed the stubble covering his chin. He couldn't help feeling that there were a few things Lucky wasn't sharing with him, and not just because she wouldn't use his key.

He forced himself up and off the bed, stepped into the connecting master bath, then braced himself against the wall with one hand as he aimed his stiff member toward the toilet with the other.

It had been a long, long time since he'd spent this much time with a woman. Since Amanda, actually. He grinned, thinking his ex-fiancée wouldn't have been caught dead wearing the apron and nothing else, and wondering what she would make of another woman wearing it.

Lucky...

Lucky's mere presence seemed to brighten everything she touched. A man given to routine, he gladly interrupted his schedule in order to accommodate her.

But was she giving him the same consideration? Or was he, as he was coming to expect, a momentary distraction for her?

Ten minutes later, showered, shaved and dressed in his tennis whites, he found Lucky in the kitchen. He frowned when he discovered she'd changed from the apron into her clothes. She buttered whole wheat toast, her sensual expression making him think of everything but food.

Finishing up, she brushed the crumbs from her hands then pointed toward one of the two chairs at the island. "Sit."

Colin raised a brow as he did. "Who knew you were so bossy?"

She brushed against his back as she put a plate of eggs, bacon and homemade hash browns in front of him. "Are you interested in seeing how bossy I can be?"

Colin always seemed to be in various stages of arousal whenever he was around Lucky—hell, even when he thought about her—and right now an erection tented the front of his shorts.

He heard her soft laughter in his ear before he felt her tongue along the outer shell. "Looks like you're not the only one who's hungry."

He reached for her and she easily stepped out of range, smiling as she filled a glass with orange juice then added it to the place setting in front of him.

Only then did he notice there was only one setting.

She leaned in and kissed him on the cheek. "I've got to run."

Colin knew a disappointment so complete that he felt like a kid whose favorite toy had just been taken away.

"Where?" he found himself asking, wincing at the slight whine he heard in his voice.

She hugged him from behind and laughed softly. "To work, of course."

She kissed the back of his neck then released him.

"I'll see you later?" he asked, again sounding a little too needy for his liking.

"You'll see me later."

And just like that his apron angel left him sitting alone in the kitchen, his hard-on rivaling the dried Italian sausage hanging in its casing over the island.

CHAPTER ELEVEN

"OH, YOU'VE got it bad."

Colin sat back in the lounge chair on Will's first-floor balcony and stretched his feet out to rest on top of the stone railing. He folded his hands behind his neck and grinned at his unhappy friend across the glass table from him.

"You've got it real bad," Will concluded.

"No, buddy," Colin disagreed. "I think what you meant to say is that I've got it good. Real good."

And he did. Mostly because when he had finished breakfast and walked back through the living room he'd noticed his apartment key was gone from the coffee table. At first he'd thought Lucky had moved it. But a brief look around had told him it wasn't just gone from the table, it was gone.

And he liked that.

Something resembling a growl came from his friend's direction.

Colin chuckled. "I take it that means your new girl from the hospital is sticking to her no-nookie-until-her-wedding-night promise?"

"You take correctly. In fact, I wish you could take it literally."

Will had played like a man dealing with plenty of pent-up sexual frustration on the tennis court today, growing further frustrated still when Colin refused to rise to the challenge.

"Your Lucky wouldn't happen to have any friends, now, would she?"

"And what would your girl have to say?"

"She's not my girl," Will said vehemently. "She won't be my girl until we sleep together. *Sleep* not being the operative word." He flopped back in his chair. "I mean, this is such a load of horse crap. It's not like she's a virgin. She freely admits that she's slept with her share of guys before."

"Ah, a born-again virgin. Dangerous, those types."

"What do you know of it?"

Colin held his hands up in surrender. "Whoa, buddy, looks like you could do with a bottle of oil and a porn mag. The sooner the better."

Will cursed under his breath, something Colin always found amusing when combined with his proper accent. "I haven't masturbated since I was fifteen years old, for Christ's sake."

Colin cocked a brow. "Really?"

"Yes, really. Since then there's always been one willing female or another to take care of those needs for me."

The midday summer sun was beginning to hit the edge of the balcony. Colin took his feet down from the railing. "And you say I'm the one who's got it bad. Sounds like *bad* is exactly the word for what you've got."

Will shook his head, then began nodding, as if torn between which expression was the right one. "I swear, if I don't get some soon, I'm going to explode."

Colin heard the main door of the building open and close, then he idly watched two young women in skimpy bikinis walk by on the path below the balcony, likely heading for the complex pool.

Will grumbled again. "Then you have her and the other one…"

"Who?"

Will jerked an arm toward the women. "The one in the green swimsuit. I've been going crazy thinking about her and her roommate in bed together right above me every night." He was heartily shaking his head. "This morning I think my sheets were wet."

Colin made a face. "That's something I could have gone without knowing."

"Tough. I've got to put up with you being late for our tennis date because of some floozy who's good in bed—"

"Lucky is not a floozy."

"You're missing my point."

"That's because I don't think you have one."

"My point is," Will said, sitting forward as if getting ready to tell a patient he had a progressive, malignant form of cancer and had no more than a week to live, "you're getting some and I'm not."

"And you don't like that."

Will pointed at him. "Exactly!"

Colin picked up a towel from the table and tossed it at his friend. "Come on, Casanova, let's go get cleaned up and get something in your stomach before you melt into a puddle of quivering hormones."

"What? It's only eleven."

"And I have an appointment at twelve-thirty."

"Oh, you're just full of all kinds of good news today, aren't you?" Will glowered. "I take it it's with her."

"I wish. But, no. This appointment is with my attorney."

"Your attorney? I don't know of any attorneys who keep weekend hours."

"Yes, well, my attorney does."

"Bully for you."

Colin walked back inside the apartment and waited for his friend to follow.

COLIN FOUND himself whistling an hour and a half later as he left his place after a shower and a change of clothes. He glanced at his watch. He had five minutes to get to his attorney's office in the nearby Spitzer Building. He thought about walking the distance then remembered his workouts this morning—and last night—and decided he needed to conserve his energy for Lucky later.

Earlier he'd parked at the curb for easier access, so when he now exited the front of the building he pressed the button for the door lock release. He was shrugging into the suit jacket he was holding when he got a look at his car.

Not so much at his car but at what somebody had done to it.

On the side facing him, he saw a long key mark engraved from the back bumper to the front. His gaze dropped down to the tires to find them slashed down to the rims. Colin's adrenaline level kicked up a notch as he looked around, spotting nothing and no one out of place. He crouched down to inspect the damage to the front tire, then looked under the car to find the same attention had been given to the other side.

Jamie.

It had to be.

He stood up and fished his cell phone out of his pants pocket. "Jack?" he said when his attorney picked up. "You're not going to believe this…"

ACROSS TOWN Lucky was walking back to work after making a run for lunch munchies. She was crunching chips from an open bag she held when she spotted something wrong with her car. The strip mall parking lot was crammed full of cars and hers was caught between a large SUV and a customized van. Across the back in red spray paint was written the word *Whore.*

Her mouth dried up, making it a chore to swallow the potato chips she'd barely chewed. Dropping the remainder of the chips into the grocery bag, she neared the old Chevy, the smell of fresh paint assaulting her nose. She couldn't remember if she'd looked at the car when she'd gone on the store run.

Rounding to the driver's side, she read more words. *He's my man.*

Her heart started pounding in her chest as she backed up and rounded the other side. *Stay home!*

Lucky rubbed her finger against the *S* in *Stay* and it came back with her paint-covered skin.

Her gaze shot to the mirrored windows of the

van next to her. Could the person who had done this be in there watching her?

A woman holding shopping bags stepped between the two vehicles without acknowledging her then got into the van and drove away.

Lucky stood stunned for several minutes, then made her way back to the driver's side. She realized that the words hadn't been placed randomly. Rather she guessed they were meant to be read as a sentence.

He's my man, whore, stay home!

"Lucky?"

She heard Renae's voice but really didn't register it.

"What's the…holy shit."

Renae stopped next to her, taking in the graffiti that stood out like a police siren on a dark night.

"Jesus, who the hell would do something like this?"

Renae fished her cell phone out of her pocket and dialed 911, then disconnected. She picked up Lucky's right hand. "Are you hurt?"

Lucky shook her head. "It's from the paint."

"It's still wet? Good. Maybe we can rub out the worst of it before it dries. Here, give me your bag. I'm going to go get some towels. You stand here and wait for the police."

Lucky nodded, feeling as if her tongue had grown to twice its normal size in her mouth.

Who would do something like this? She tried to remember if Colin had mentioned anything about another woman. An old girlfriend. Any trouble he'd had in the past. Then her mind homed in on what had happened during their second encounter in his office. She'd been a breath away from finding out how well he would fill her when he'd grabbed her jaw and demanded to know whether someone named Jamie had put her up to the seduction.

She hadn't questioned him then. There really hadn't been any reason to. They hadn't had a relationship and she'd barely known him.

But she knew him now, didn't she? And he had never told her who Jamie was.

It seemed she wasn't the only one keeping secrets.

"JAMIE ISN'T an old girlfriend, Lucky. He's an ex-patient."

Hours later, back at Colin's place, after he'd told her his car had also been targeted at around the same time as hers, Colin answered her questions as directly as he could.

"He?" Lucky repeated. "The person who did this is a guy?"

"Yes. An ex-patient is suing me in civil court for sexual indecency."

She was looking at him closely. He knew the instant she put two and two together because her beautiful green eyes widened. "That's why you were so careful with me in the beginning."

Colin felt as if his grimace went all the way down to his bones. "Yes, that's why. Although by all rights I should have been anyway."

The apartment was quiet, both of them sitting in the kitchen at the island counter drinking coffee.

"Did you have an affair with him?" Lucky asked.

Colin squinted at her. "What?"

She shrugged. "It's a legitimate question."

"Maybe to you. But not to me." He was suddenly agitated. If he couldn't convince Lucky that he'd made no improper advances toward Jamie, what were his chances in convincing a judge if it came down to that.

"Look, Colin, you don't have to be gay to be curious."

"Trust me, if something had happened between Jamie and me, I would be the first to own up to it."

She smiled and reached out to cover his hand with hers. "I know."

Colin felt some of the tension drain from him.

"So what do the police say?"

Therein lay the rub, didn't it? "They said there's no evidence the two incidents are connected."

"Oh, both our cars just happened to be randomly vandalized?"

"That's about the thrust of it."

She was shaking her head.

"Look, Lucky, I'd like to pay to replace your car."

She stared at him as if he'd just told her he'd been the one to paint the offensive words on her car. "You're joking, right?"

He shook his head. "No, I'm not. It's my fault this happened. I want to do the right thing."

"And the right thing would be to buy me a new car?"

He grinned at her. "Yes."

She laughed, although there was something a little dark in her eyes. "It was spray paint, Colin. Not a wrecking ball."

He shrugged. "You need a new car anyway so—"

"I don't need a new car. There's nothing wrong with the one I've got. As for the paint, Renae and I rubbed off a lot of it. And I called a repair shop and they said they could probably spot-paint over the rest." She reached for the cream, her movements a little jerky. "I think you should be more worried about your own car. Those key marks are deep."

"My insurance will take care of those."

A tense silence settled over the room. Colin opened his mouth to continue making his case when Lucky held her hand up.

"Drop it, doc. I'm not letting you get me a car."

Colin sat back, his sails effectively deflated. He watched her tap her short, unpainted fingernails against her mug in an angry staccato then saw her knuckles whiten as she gripped the handlc.

"You know I don't mean any harm, don't you?" he asked quietly, not understanding why she was getting so worked up.

"Do I?"

She immediately looked regretful so he knew her response had been a knee-jerk reaction.

He also realized she had just revealed something very important about herself.

"I'm sorry. Of course I know you don't mean any harm," she said quietly.

Colin knew she'd been sorry for her harsh comment but was surprised by her one-eighty.

"But I don't want your help, Colin. Really, I don't."

"But what if I want to help you?"

She smiled at him. "Every time you want to help

me, put an extra few dollars into the cup of the next homeless guy you come across." She stared into her mug. "Trust me, that'll be much easier for you than bringing this subject up with me again."

He narrowed his eyes. "You know, I don't get you," he thought aloud.

She reached out for his mug then pushed both of them off to the side of the counter. She scooted to sit on top and he leaned back so she could settle in front of him with her legs on either side. "Trust me, doc, it's all by design."

Colin's blood began a slow simmer that turned into a quick flash fire when she hiked up her skirt to reveal she wasn't wearing panties.

He swallowed hard as he laid his hands on her supple thighs, his thumbs pointed toward home base. "Have I ever told you that you have a hell of a way of changing the topic?"

She smiled and linked her hands together behind his neck, tugging him forward so she could kiss him. "Mmm. All the time." She leaned her head to the right, then the left, leisurely kissing him. "And I keep telling you that no topic is more important than this."

Colin wholeheartedly disagreed, but he wasn't up to telling her that just now. Not when his thumbs hit home and he found her hot and slick and ready for him.

But rather than looking for penetration, he pushed her so she was lying back down on the counter, then bent to taste the evidence of her need of him.

Five minutes, involving heated panting and a screaming orgasm, later he was about to pick her up to take her back to his room and his supply of condoms when he paused and stared down into her face.

"Why?" he asked, his fingers cupping her bare bottom almost roughly. "Why won't you let me see the real you, Lucky?"

A shadow so dark, so enormous, appeared in her vivid green eyes it nearly stole the air from his lungs. "Nothing personal, Colin, but it's been so long that I don't even know who the real me is anymore." She leaned her head against his shoulder then kissed his neck. "Just let it rest, okay? And trust me."

As Colin picked her up and walked toward his bedroom at the other side of the apartment, he didn't know what to think. The simple truth of the matter was he didn't think Lucky trusted herself. And if she couldn't trust herself, how could he trust her?

CHAPTER TWELVE

THE FOLLOWING Monday, Colin sat back and listened as his attorney laid out the facts for him.

"Look, Colin, I wish there was some way to connect the events happening around you lately. But we have no solid proof to say Jamie is behind anything."

Colin fisted his hand where it lay in his lap. After the car incidents on Saturday, Don Maddox had agreed to move their appointment to that morning before he was due in court. But given that the prominent attorney was distracted at best, irritated with him at worst, the meeting was not going exactly as Colin had hoped it would. As an old friend of his father, Don was the first person he'd thought to turn to when Jamie Polson had sent him the original intent to sue. Don had managed to convince him that this was better than Jamie filing a formal complaint with the police, because that would have opened the case up to the public.

He was beginning to wonder if he shouldn't look elsewhere for an attorney.

"But you believe he is," he asked Maddox. "Behind what's happening, that is."

"What I believe or don't believe bears no relevance here." Don sighed heavily then looked at his watch. "I have to be in court in a little over an hour, so let's go over what I wanted to talk to you about."

He opened a file on his desk, then turned it so Colin could view the contents. An eight-by-ten-inch glossy photograph of him and Lucky at the restaurant last week leapt out at him.

He picked it up, shocked to see the moment caught on film. In the shot he was leaning forward talking to her while under the table she was rubbing her bare toes against his ankle.

"I thought we agreed you'd keep a low profile when it came to your, um, social activities," Maddox said, his chair squeaking as he reached for his coffee cup.

Anger, sure and swift, roared through Colin as he thumbed through the remainder of the shots. Him at Women Only. Lucky entering the outer doors of his apartment building. Lucky sitting in the waiting room of his office. "Where did you get these?" he demanded.

"They were couriered over last Friday. Thus the reason I asked on Saturday to meet with you today." He stared at Colin over the edge of his coffee cup. "So you understand my concern?"

"I understand that I'm being held hostage by a egomaniacal ex-patient who feels spurned because I didn't return his feelings."

Don shook his head. "You're still not getting it, are you?" The older man leaned forward, folding his hands on his desktop. "Colin, in cases like these the truth is a secondary consideration. We've talked about this. The damage to your career, your reputation, if this suit goes public…it will be irreparable."

"I don't care. File the countersuit." He closed the file and pushed it back across the desk.

One of the options all along was to answer Jamie's claims with a countersuit alleging libel and willful tort. Don had managed to talk him out of it so far, mostly with a lot of counseling from Colin's own father. But it was long past time for him to make a stand. Take some kind of action.

"I haven't been able to live my life since Jamie started all this bullshit and I'm tired of it," he told Don.

The seasoned attorney didn't blink. "And you

think countersuing and taking this into the courts is going to end it quickly? Or how about your being tried in the court of public opinion? Even if criminal charges aren't brought, and you win your suit, do you think your partners want to be associated with someone who's been accused of improper sexual conduct against not only a patient, but a male patient?"

Colin winced. The older attorney's reasoning had managed to sand off the sharp edge of his anger.

But the anger was still there.

And, damn it, he intended to do something about it.

LUCKY SAT in the reception area of Colin's office waiting for his associate Dr. Morgan Szymanski to welcome in her and the other three members of her group for their session. She leafed through the few pages she'd written in her journal. Mostly she'd recorded random thoughts, things the therapist might want to see, like her feelings on alcohol and the consumption of it before getting behind the wheel of a car.

But on a couple of occasions she'd actually begun to write about those items of the most concern to her. First and foremost Colin McKenna.

She'd had enough forethought not to include his

name in the writings. But even she could tell the difference in her handwriting when she'd begun sharing her relationship with Colin, for example, thoughts about his offering up the key to his apartment. While the loops and swirls were neat in other areas, they all but disappeared when the topic turned to Colin, her mind no longer on how she was writing but rather on what she was writing.

She wished the passages were limited to a page or two so she might tear them out, but the thoughts were interspersed with the other entries and would take extensive rewriting, something she didn't have time for right now, even if she was moved to try.

She glanced at the closed door, wondering if she should take the journal out to her car and leave it there, then pretend she'd forgotten to bring it.

The problem lay in that there was already enough friction between her and the female psychologist. She didn't want to invite more. Not when her driver's license and possible probation hung in the balance.

"Good morning, Dr. McKenna."

Lucky's heart hiccupped in her chest as the receptionist greeted Colin. He was entering from the outer door, obviously just arriving at the office or perhaps returning from an appointment.

And looking none too happy to be there.

He hadn't spotted her yet and she took the

opportunity to note the deep grooves on either side of his mouth and his stern expression.

When she'd left him a few hours ago he'd been grinning and happy and oh so sexily disheveled. What had happened since then?

He accepted a handful of messages from the receptionist then turned toward his office, his gaze immediately falling on her. He blinked and she smiled, expecting him to return it.

Instead his grimace deepened further as if she was not only the last person he expected to see, but the last one he wanted to see.

"Okay, I think we're a go."

Lucky glanced at where Dr. Szymanski had opened her office door. She began getting up along with her other three group members.

Colin briefly closed his eyes and she thought she heard him utter a mild curse. "Miss Clayborn?" he asked before she disappeared into the other office. "If you have a few moments after your appointment, I'd like to have a word with you in my office."

She smiled at him, but the expression somehow didn't make it below the surface. "Sorry, Dr. McKenna, but I have to get to work straight after."

His eyes narrowed then he nodded. "Very well then."

Lucky glanced at the receptionist, who was

listening to the exchange with open interest, then followed the rest of her group mates into the office and closed the door behind her.

LATER THAT AFTERNOON Colin had his elbows planted on his desktop and the telephone receiver held to his ear. He absently rubbed his closed eyelids, wondering how one day could seem so endlessly long.

Lucky hadn't stopped by his office following her session with Morgan earlier, just as she'd said she wouldn't. He had hoped she would change her mind and duck in for a moment, if only so he could apologize to her. Although he supposed he couldn't blame her. Had she looked at him the way he was sure he had looked at her when he'd first spotted her in the reception area, he wouldn't have wanted to see her so soon afterward, either.

He blew out the long breath that filled his cheeks and sat back hard in his chair, the memory of the photographs his attorney had shown him shifting through his mind. It seemed that not only was Jamie not giving up, as he and Don had hoped he would, he was upping the ante.

Were he and Lucky at physical risk? He couldn't be sure. But he wasn't about to sit back and wait to see if there was even a chance that spray-painted cars and slashed tires might turn into something more serious, something more dangerous.

"Mr. McKenna? I can do it," Jenny Mathena came back on the line. "But you have to know that given the accelerated time frame you've given me it's going to take cash and lots of it—"

"Money's no object."

Barely a pause, then, "Very good then. I'll be in touch. Possibly as soon as tomorrow."

"Thanks, Miss Mathena."

"It's Jenny, please."

Colin broke the connection soon afterward, then sat staring at the wall displaying his license to practice and his diplomas. Finally he got up and collected his briefcase and jacket, feeling more hopeful now than he had all day—in fact, than he had in a good long while.

During the drive home he opened his windows instead of switching on the air-conditioning, embracing the signs of summer rather than rejecting them. He didn't know how Don Maddox would feel about what he was doing, but the older attorney wasn't going to find out unless and until Colin got results.

He parked his repaired car in the underground garage of the building then rode the elevator up to his apartment. Immediately the elevator door opened, the smell of something cooking assaulted his nose. Usually he couldn't tell what the other tenants were having for dinner. He unlocked the apartment door and discovered that the scent wasn't emanating from another apartment but rather from his own.

Lucky had used his key.

He stood reflecting on the many implications of her actions. She'd so vehemently and mysteriously rejected the idea when he'd originally suggested it. Now she'd gone ahead and used it on her own. Did it mean something more than that she'd wanted to cook him dinner? Or was it a simple matter of control and that she needed to be the one to decide when to use the key?

Either way, he was glad she was here.

He quietly put his briefcase down on the floor and hung up his jacket then rounded the corner to peer into the kitchen. Lucky was wearing a pair of snug white shorts and a clingy black tank, which softly emphasized her provocative curves. Colin leaned against the jamb and crossed his arms, enjoying the sight she made from behind as she stirred something in one pan then added spaghetti to another. Her feet were gloriously bare and her hair was tied into a loose knot at her shoulders. She was summer and its sultry heat wrapped up into one irresistible package.

Something warm made its way through Colin's

bloodstream. Something that had nothing to do with sex and everything to do with...love.

He swallowed hard. The sound must have been loud enough for Lucky to hear because she swiveled around to face him, the wooden spoon she held dripping red sauce on the black-and-white tile of the floor.

"Oh!" she said, quickly putting her other hand under the spoon. "I didn't hear you come in."

He grinned, watching as she moved the spoon to the sink then rinsed the sauce from her hands. Colin grabbed a paper towel and crouched to the floor at the same time she did to wipe up the spot. The position put him exactly where he wanted to be: face-to-face with Lucky.

He looked into her flushed face, his gaze taking in every familiar feature. Then he kissed her, nearly knocking her back on her heels. She smiled at him. "Where did that come from?"

"Hmm...I don't know. But there's lots more if you want it."

She smiled at him in that way that made his stomach tighten and his arousal stir. "Mmm. A man with a one-track mind. I like that."

Colin kissed her again, lingering there against her lush lips. Rather than a man with a one-track mind, the train in his head had come into the station a while ago and was now facing myriad other tracks. And he wanted to explore all of them with this amazing woman.

She pulled away and laughed. "You sure know how to sweep a girl off her feet."

"Then let me help you back onto your feet." He easily got up and held his hand out, helping her to stand in front of him.

"I hope you like spaghetti," she said, turning back to the stove.

"I love spaghetti."

Was it him or was there a stiffness about her?

"There's a bottle of wine breathing on the counter over there. Pour us a couple of glasses?"

He did and handed her one.

"Thanks," she said, taking a sip.

She seemed to be extraordinarily interested in what she was doing on the stove.

Of course. Kissing her nearly had made him forget their run-in outside his office.

Colin leaned against the counter next to the stove. "About this morning," he said quietly. "I'm sorry I reacted the way I did when I saw you. I'd just met with my attorney and was distracted. I'd forgotten it was your day with Morgan."

She stirred the spaghetti with a fork. "So you thought I'd stopped by to see how I could heat things up?"

He reached for a lock of her hair, rubbing the silken strands against his skin. "Mmm."

He debated telling her what had happened at Maddox's, but felt that doing so would be akin to offering up an excuse for his bad behavior. And he was never one for excuses. An apology was better.

"So how did everything go?" she asked, taking the spaghetti from the burner and turning the contents into a colander.

"With my attorney? Not so good."

She glanced at him while she ran cold water. "What happened?"

Colin ran his hand over his face.

She shut off the water and leaned her hips against his. "Now look what I've gone and done. I've chased the grin from your face."

He smiled down at her and grasped her rounded hips.

"That bad, huh?" she asked.

He nodded.

"Let's not talk about it, then. It always makes things worse to talk about bad news."

Colin blinked at the classic signs of avoidance as she turned off the last burner then picked up a plate and began piling spaghetti on top. "Tell me when."

He did, only he found himself wishing he could say "when" to her.

This cat-and-mouse game they were playing with their relationship was beginning to wear on his nerves. He didn't like not knowing what was going on in her head. He didn't like not knowing what resided in her heart.

Within moments they were both seated at the kitchen island instead of the formal dining-room table in the other room. Lucky opened the foil-wrapped garlic bread she'd taken out of the oven.

"Lucky...tell me something about yourself," he asked quietly. "Your hopes, your dreams. What you were like growing up. Tell me something no one else knows about you."

He watched as she seemed to have a hard time swallowing.

"Did you want to talk about what happened with your attorney?" she asked.

"No. This isn't about me. This is about you."

That casual atmosphere took a very chilly nosedive and there was nothing Colin could do to change that.

"So we're back to that again," Lucky whispered, pushing spaghetti around her plate without eating it. "Look, Colin, I don't come here to delve into the past, to examine every aspect of my life under the light of a microscope trying to figure out why this happened or how I might have been able to circumvent that. I come here to forget."

"But you can't, can you?"

She grasped her wineglass and took a long sip.

"Whatever you're running from...it's starting to find you here, too, isn't it?"

CHAPTER THIRTEEN

MUCH LATER that night Colin jerked awake and pushed up to lean his weight against his elbows. What was that? He glanced around his darkened bedroom, not sure if it was something in his dream that had awakened him or a sound in the apartment.

He glanced at the empty spot next to him, then tossed the top sheet from his waist and sat up.

Tonight had not gone the way he'd planned. In fact the entire day had seemed to play out slightly off-kilter. But he'd counted it as a good sign that Lucky hadn't left when he'd pressed her for answers during dinner earlier that night. He hadn't made any headway into understanding what made her tick, but perhaps he'd made a small dent in her armor.

And armor was exactly what it was, wasn't it? Not just one simple reason why she welcomed him between her thighs yet kept him away from her heart. Whatever was behind Lucky's behavior ran deep and had damaged her to an extent he could only guess at.

He rubbed the sleep from his face. Sometimes it sucked being a psychiatrist. He couldn't look at someone without wanting to know what had made them into the person they were.

He couldn't look at Lucky without wanting to possess her fully, heart, mind and soul.

He glanced toward the empty bathroom then put on his boxers and stepped into the living room. A sweep of the kitchen and the rest of the large penthouse showed no sign of her. It was only when he walked back into the living room that he spotted one of the French doors slightly open, the sheer curtains billowing in the light breeze.

He pulled back the gauzy fabric and opened the door farther, immediately spotting Lucky sitting on the marble tile of the balcony, her back against the wall of glass, the remainder of the bottle of wine from dinner next to her along with a single glass. She didn't seem to be aware that he'd joined her. She merely sat staring sightlessly out across the Maumee River.

But she was still here.

As he took her in, from the way her shoulders

slumped, to the sadness on her face, he grabbed onto that thought and held it close.

She was still here.…

LUCKY KNEW the moment Colin had joined her. But she was slightly foggy from the wine and the enormity of her thoughts and couldn't seem to make herself respond. Not to sit up straighter. Not to greet him in some way. Not even to acknowledge his presence.

He pulled a chair out from the large glass table positioned a short distance away and sat down, his body angled toward hers. He didn't say anything. And she was glad for that.

Lucky closed her eyes and stretched her neck to accommodate her hard swallow. She was thirty years old and had long ago gotten used to the cycles of her life. Despite what the court thought, liquor was not her drug of choice, sex was. And the better the sex, the more successful she was at keeping her many demons at bay.

But the instant the excitement associated with sex began to wane, when she either grew bored or the guy started asking too many questions, started making commitment noises, she was out the door, the latest cycle complete.

And that's when liquor entered in. A little something to tide her over until she met the next guy.

Only this time the cycle had come full circle sooner than it ever had before.

And it wasn't because the sex had lost its appeal—if anything, the heights she achieved with Colin were higher than she'd ever reached before. It wasn't because she was bored—Colin fascinated her on so many levels that he emerged somewhat like a Christmas present with an infinite number of smaller presents wrapped inside.

And it wasn't even because he had started making commitment noises.

No, this time the cycle was different.

Because this time she'd fallen in love.

She reached for the wine bottle and poured the last bit into her empty glass. But she didn't drink it. Instead she nudged the glass around by the base on the tile, watching the contents swirl around. She was as numb as she was going to get, which was not numb at all. She had the sneaking suspicion that no amount of alcohol was going to make her all right this time around.

"I can't have children," she said into the dark night.

She blinked, unaware that she'd said the words aloud until she heard them.

There was no response for a long time, making her wonder if her mind was playing tricks on her, if the wine was making her imagine things.

"I'm sorry," finally came Colin's soft response.

She slowly turned to look at him, her head still resting against the glass door behind her. "Why are you sorry? I made the conscious decision not ever to have children."

He squinted at her. "So what you're saying is that you don't want kids."

"No. What I'm saying is that I can't have kids. I paid for a tubal ligation when I was nineteen."

Any other man might have looked at her strangely. But not Colin. While curiosity and concern painted his handsome features, he didn't judge her for her actions. He merely accepted her.

And, curiously enough, didn't question her.

She gave a small, sad smile. After all the questioning he'd done in the past week, it was ironic that he wasn't asking any questions now. Was it because he knew she was ready to tell him herself? Or having caught a glimpse of what she'd kept hidden for so long, was he afraid of what she might reveal?

"I've never known you to drink," he said quietly.

She looked at the glass she was still toying with. "Funny, don't you think, considering that's the entire reason we met?" She cleared her throat. "The reason you haven't seen me drink until now is that I haven't needed to drink."

"But you need to now."

She looked at him. "Yes."

DESPITE HER WORDS, Colin had yet to watch Lucky take a sip from the glass since he'd joined her on the balcony. Oh, he was aware that the bottle was empty. But he felt a burst of gratitude that she wasn't chugging down what remained in her glass then going in search of something else inside the penthouse to blur her pain with.

And pain is exactly what he saw written all over her. From her beautiful face and the uncaring way she held her body to the dark shadow in her eyes, it was obvious this woman had been hurt and hurt deeply in the past. And that hurt had never gone away.

He clasped his hands tightly between his knees, considering her surprising desire never to have children and the actions she'd taken to make sure she never would. He knew of few doctors who would agree to perform the surgery on a nineteen-year-old. Which further emphasized the severity of her reasons for having done it.

Children. Yes, he admitted, he wanted them. At least two. As an only child, he'd always wondered what it would have been like to have a sibling. And depending on the soundness of his career after Jamie got done with him, he might like to have three or four mini McKennas running around the place.

The thought that there was no chance of having them with Lucky twisted his stomach in a way that went beyond physical pain.

It was then he realized that despite the appearance of their relationship being strictly sexual, he'd secretly begun imagining a future with Lucky, a future that included weddings and baptisms and Christmases spent in front of a roaring fire.

An undetermined future Lucky had the power to give him...or take away from him.

The chair he sat in squeaked as he leaned back. He'd never been this close emotionally to somebody this damaged before. No, he didn't know the details behind her pain, but he'd suspected from the beginning that Lucky was different. He'd kidded himself into thinking she was just more of a free spirit, more sexual. And while almost everyone had his or her neuroses, Lucky didn't have a fear of heights or of commitment or of touching objects like doorknobs that somebody else might have put their germs on or anything like that.

Rather he sensed her problems were not ones that could be fixed with a year's worth of therapy. No. Hers would take an entire lifetime to address, and still she might not ever come close to fixing them.

"Do you want to know why I became a psychiatrist?" he said quietly into the dark.

She didn't say anything and he was afraid either she hadn't heard him or had decided not to respond. Then, finally, she looked at him, her glorious long hair shifting on the smooth glass behind her. "Because you grew up in a dysfunctional family and wanted to save the world?"

He smiled faintly at that. "Because I couldn't stand the sight of blood."

She blinked at him.

"That's right. The very first day of my residency at St. V's, a patient with an arterial wound was wheeled into emergency—the type of wound that if not immediately addressed can cause death in less than fifteen minutes. Essentially the patient bleeds to death." He looked out at the waters of the Maumee. "When I released the tourniquet and blood spurted across my neck and the front of my smock, I choked. I couldn't move."

He remembered standing there completely frozen as the other staff moved efficiently and quickly around him, unaware of his dilemma. Will, who was doing his residency at the same hospital and happened to be on with him that day, had caught onto what was happening and stepped in to see to the patient. His friend had been completely unaffected by the thick, red substance coating his arms and gloves.

Colin hated to think of what might have happened if Will hadn't taken charge.

"It was your first day," Lucky said quietly.

He looked at her. "It only got worse from there." He rubbed the heel of his hand against his brow. "So what becomes of a doctor who can't hack it in the emergency room?"

"He becomes a shrink?"

He laughed softly, marveling at her attempt at humor given her precarious emotional state. "That's exactly what he does."

The sound of a plane passing overhead, moving in the direction of the Toledo Airport some twenty miles outside of town, caught his attention. Colin watched the blinking lights as it passed, then stared at the sliver of moon seemingly suspended in the sky by a string.

"My father was a doctor. A surgeon."

Lucky's words surprised him. Given what he'd seen of her, the jobs she held, the way she lived, he'd guessed she'd come from simpler means.

Of course she'd never offered up information to dispel that image. But he still felt chagrin at his incorrect snap judgment of her.

"And your mother?"

She finally picked up the glass, stared into it,

then swallowed the contents. "She died of pancreatic cancer when I was fourteen."

Colin stiffened. She'd revealed more about herself in the past half hour than she had in the past three weeks. And while he was grateful for the insight into her past, he couldn't help the feeling that it was just a glimpse. That the wounds she bore went deeper still.

"I'm sorry," he said.

Such ineffectual words. But the only words he had.

She nodded.

And just like that Colin felt the connection between them snap.

Lucky pushed to her feet, picked up the bottle and glass and turned to face him. If she hadn't needed him to move in order to pass, he suspected she would already have been inside.

"Excuse me," she said quietly.

Colin looked up at her shadowy face from where he still sat in the chair. Considered the even larger shadows that resided within her.

"No."

The word was simple but meaningful. Whatever had started tonight had to continue tonight. He wasn't going to give up that easily.

Lucky began to try to pass and he gently grasped her wrists, forbidding her passage.

"Please, Lucky," he pleaded with her softly. "Tell me what's causing you so much pain."

The unmistakable glisten of tears in her eyes made his chest tighten.

"Let me go," she whispered, her body going rigid. "Please."

The problem with her request was that Colin feared she didn't mean just let her go now...but let her go for good.

And he couldn't do that.

"Please," she said again.

She jerked her arms to free herself and he strengthened his grasp. The wineglass slipped from her grip, breaking into scattered shards on the tile beneath their bare feet, shattering the silence of the night.

Colin swept her up into his lap, holding her so tightly he couldn't breathe. He took the bottle from her hands and put it on the table behind him.

"Please, please don't walk away from this, Lucky," he murmured into her ear through the fragrant cloud of her hair. "Please don't walk away from us."

She pushed against him, fighting hard. Fighting for everything she was worth.

And he held on just as tightly.

"There is no us," she said vehemently. "There's you...and there's me...and I'm done."

He grasped her chin and held her face in front of his, wildly searching her face. "You can't be. Because I won't let you."

She stared at him, the tears in her eyes sliding down over her dark lashes and streaking her cheeks.

"I love you, Lucky."

CHAPTER FOURTEEN

LUCKY WANTED to put her hands over her ears. Block out Colin's softly spoken words. Close her eyes and deny herself the luxury of seeing his handsome face. So full of warmth…so full of emotion… so full of love.

"No!" she whispered. "No, no, no!"

She pushed at him, battling as much against a primal something emerging from inside her, slashing at her heart, thundering through her veins, as she was struggling against him.

But the harder she fought, the tighter Colin held her in his arms.

"I love you, Lucky. I love you."

The words were what so many little girls dreamed about hearing from the man they would some day love. But they inspired nothing but darkness inside her. "Stop it! Stop saying that!"

Love you…love you…love you…

"Why, Lucky? Why should I stop saying it?" Colin pressed his lips against her wet cheek, the gentle gesture in sharp contrast to the way he restrained her. "It's how I feel."

Her throat was raw and tight. "What do you know about what you feel? What do any of us know about what we feel? Love is…love is just a word. A ridiculous, stupid little word we all pack so much meaning into, but in the end that's all it is. A word."

"A word that's caused you pain."

She stared at him, filled with the desire to kiss him and battle against him all at once. "Yes," she breathed, giving brief vent to the conflicting emotions roiling within her.

"Is it your mother, Lucky? Is it her death that hurt you?"

Her muscles tensed further. "My mother loved me. And I knew that, up to, including and even after the day that she died."

"Then someone else…"

Yes, very definitely someone else…

She continued struggling, but to no avail. Colin merely waited her out until exhaustion settled over her strained muscles like a heavy shadow. She was so tired of fighting. Not only Colin, but the demons she warred with every day. She went still, completely still, in the circle of his arms. But she didn't draw comfort from his embrace. Instead his arms were a makeshift prison cell designed to keep her from doing what she most wanted to do. Run.

"You know, I once thought it was written somewhere that parents are supposed to love their children," she heard a woman's voice say, a voice that sounded remarkably like hers. "A man, a woman, they get married. They set up house. A loving house in which to bring up a baby, maybe two or three." She swallowed hard, the thick gulp sounding loud in the quiet night. "And that was my life."

Silence for a long moment, then, "Until your mother died."

She stared at him, wishing it were lighter so she could see him better. "You think you know everything, don't you, Dr. McKenna?" she asked him softly. "You think you know how it feels to live in a house that was a warm and loving home one day, then overnight turned into nothing more than a collection of empty rooms devoid of laughter, of sunshine…of love. Rooms full of fear and unspoken threat."

"Your father didn't love you."

She trapped his gaze with hers, her eyes narrowing. "The problem wasn't that my father didn't love me. The problem was that after my mother died, my father loved me the wrong way."

Her breath hitched in her throat as she dared

him to say the words she couldn't. Dared him to try to take the conversation in another direction.

Instead he said, "Oh, Jesus."

Lucky had expected any response. Any response but the grief-filled, loving reaction Colin showed her.

He tightened his arms around her.

And she fought him.

Only she was no longer fighting against only him. She was battling against the barrage of acid memories from her past. Memories of coming home after school at fourteen, determined to keep her family together in the wake of her mother's death, and realizing that her father was looking at her in a different way. Staring at her in a strange, unsettling way that made her skin crawl and made her feel…dirty.

He was watching her in a way that a father shouldn't watch his own flesh and blood.

But still she plowed forward, hoping beyond hope that she was imagining the cause for the uneasiness she felt with each passing day. With the help of a housekeeper, she made sure dinner was on the table every night by six. That her father's newspaper was laid out on his home office desk, his slippers and remote by his easy chair.

And every night she'd bid him goodnight from the living-room doorway and hurry off to her room where she would lock herself inside until she would hear the housekeeper come in the following morning.

Still she couldn't help the foreboding that followed her like a dark shadow. She'd open the shower curtain after taking a shower and find her father standing there. Not offering her a towel and a loving smile as he had so many times when she was a child, but openly staring at her nude body, the expression on his face not one of fatherly love, but of twisted physical need. She'd wake in the middle of the night and hear him knocking on her door begging to talk to her and she would cower under the covers and pretend she didn't hear him, hot tears scalding her cheeks, waiting for him to go away.

She'd felt so terribly, utterly alone. The happy life and memories she'd once had crumbled in her hands the tighter she tried to hold on to them. The only person she had left in the world was the only one she couldn't turn to. One desperate afternoon she'd tried talking to the one person she thought she could trust, the only one who might be able to help. She reached out to her mother's sister, her aunt. And she'd received a stinging slap across the face for her efforts that still branded her heart. Her father was an important surgeon. He'd just lost his wife. How dare she utter such vile lies about him, her aunt had told her.

Devastated, she'd had little other choice but to go back and continue living in fear of her own father. And she had. For three long years. Keeping busy with school activities during the day, and hiding in the prison cell that was her bedroom at night, counting off the days until she left for college…and praying that tonight would be the night that he wouldn't come to her door and plead for her to let him in.

Then came the day where she was seventeen and she'd arrived home from school and found the locks removed from her bedroom door.

"Love," she whispered now, her heart pounding so hard against her ribcage she was afraid it might punch straight through. "My father said he loved me. Kept saying he loved me. Especially when he…he violated me in my childhood bed…across the hall from the room he used to share with my mother…in the house that had once been a beautiful home."

She stared at Colin.

"So don't you ever talk to me about love again, do you hear me? Because it doesn't exist. Not in any way that matters."

COLIN GAZED into Lucky's tear-streaked, pain-filled face, feeling as if she'd just told him night was day. That the moon had just been ripped from the sky.

He pulled her closer and she fought him, although not half as hard as she had earlier. Telling him what she had, baring herself so completely, had drained her.

And had spilled a permanent stain across his own heart.

He pressed his chin against the side of her head and said fervently, "What your father did to you, that was not love, Lucky."

A bitter, black fury filled him to overflowing toward the man who had hurt this unique and stunning creature. He knew a desire to inflict physical pain in a way he had never felt before. To do damage, to lash out on Lucky's behalf, to right what was so horribly, terribly wrong.

As he sat there holding her tightly, he felt so overwhelmingly helpless in the face of such pain that he didn't know what to say. What to do. Was incapable of doing anything more than merely hold her.

"I left the next day and I never went back," Lucky whispered, continuing with a story he no longer wanted to hear. That he wanted to block out as surely as she had tried to block it out for so many years.

Maybe she was right. Maybe talking about bad things sometimes only made them worse.

Fourteen years old. Still a child in so many ways. A girl who had lost her mother. Who needed the support of her father.

Professionally he'd dealt with countless cases similar to Lucky's. Heard the stories from the girls and guys at Crossroads. Knew the cold hard facts: one out of three girls and one out of five boys would not reach eighteen without being sexually molested in some way by a relative, neighbor or family friend.

But knowing about it and hearing about it from others was far different from learning it had happened to the one you loved.

His kneejerk reaction was visceral. All-encompassing. Vicious.

"Where is he now?" he asked, his jaw clenched so tight he heard it pop.

He tried to keep his expression neutral as Lucky searched his face.

"Why, Colin? So you can track him down? Make him pay for what he did to me?" She looked into his eyes then tried to free herself. Not in a jerky, overly emotional way as she had before. No, she seemed to have regained control over her emotions somewhat.

So he released her.

She got up and carefully stepped well to the left of the broken glass and to the wrought-iron railing.

"He's dead."

Colin stared at her back.

"He died almost a year to the day after I left. Suicide."

He felt as if he'd been physically slapped. All that anger. That pain. And no outlet for it. No closure. Because the man who could have given her that had taken it with him to his grave.

"I don't know how many times when I was out there by myself, working crappy part-time jobs and living in flophouses that I…that I wished him dead. Then just like that…he was."

"That's not your fault, Lucky." Neither was her father's twisted need for her.

She turned to face him, looking so somber, so serious, so injured that he had a hard time reconciling her with the fun-loving woman he'd first met. The devil-may-care woman who had so easily destroyed all of his barriers while keeping her own carefully intact.

"I know that," she whispered. "But that doesn't make living with myself any easier." He noticed the way she tightly gripped the iron railing with her hands. "Despite everything, for the fourteen years before my mother died, he was my father. And I loved him."

He heard the grief in her voice. Grief for the mother she had lost. The father who had betrayed himself and her. Grief for the little girl who'd had to grow up too fast.

"There's that damn word again. *Love*."

"Lucky, I…"

When he fell silent and didn't finish his sentence, she looked up at him. "You what?"

"I'm…I'm sorry."

Those horribly inadequate words again.

"I'm sorry that the solid, loving foundation that had formed so much of your early life was jerked out from underneath you. I'm sorry that you were denied the love and the security that every child born on this earth deserves." He got up and went to stand in front of her, not continuing until he knew she was looking at him. Really looking at him. "I'm sorry that you've never known what real love is. Real adult love between a man and a woman."

She moved to pass him.

One last time he grasped her wrist. She stopped and he forced himself to release her, no matter the risk of flight.

He gazed at her, feeling love warm him to the core…and wishing he could pass it on to her like some sort of virus. "I can't erase your past, Lucky.

I can't wave a magic wand and make it all go away, as much as I'd like to try." His heart pounded. "And I can't make you stay."

She didn't move.

"But I do want you to stay. If just for tonight. If just so I can hold you one more time."

She looked up at him, gratitude and, yes, love shining from her eyes, even if she didn't realize that's what she felt.

This time it was she who did the touching. She reached out and slid her fingers into his, then she kissed him, saying with her actions what her words denied.

LUCKY LAY against the soft sheets of Colin's bed, watching him as he gazed at her. The only sounds were the thick beating of her heart and the rustle of bedclothes as Colin moved. His touch as he stroked her body was so gentle, so tender, she felt tears collect in the back of her throat all over again.

He'd been wrong when he'd said he couldn't wave a magic wand and make it all go away. Because being with him made her think of nothing else but him. Of this. Of the thought of their bodies connecting in a way she'd never experienced with another man. Oh, sure, she might have been able to forget for a few precious moments before. And the pursuit of those diversions might have engaged her mind for brief periods.

But no one had ever touched her heart before.

And as Colin ran his hands slowly, almost reverently, down the sides of her arms and waist and thighs, he made her feel as if he was stroking her heart.

By design, she liked her sex fast and hard and spontaneous so she wouldn't have the chance to think about what she was doing. So she couldn't consider who she was, where she'd come from and where she was going from there. The moment of release was what she sought single-mindedly.

But as Colin set a slow, leisurely pace now, she found that while a restless energy filled her, it neither frightened her nor compelled her to speed things up. She was content to lie there, concentrate on her breathing, and process the ways his touch affected her.

His fingertips skimmed over her right nipple and shooting stars of sensation arced toward her sex. His light stubble rasped against her belly and she melted against the mattress, trembling with sweet awareness. He kissed her and she no longer felt like one individual person but rather a part of a union that not only felt right, but felt natural. Something bigger than her. Bigger than both of them.

He'd said he loved her. And while shadowy

demons had crept out of the dark places in her heart to deny that love, now she allowed herself to feel it as surely as if the sentiment were a thick, velvety cloak that he'd gently tucked around her. Something tangible. Something that refused to be denied.

When his fingers would have touched the damp curls between her thighs, he hesitated, then pulled away, instead curving her body against his from behind and holding her. Merely holding her.

Lucky opened her mouth to protest, but he made a soft shushing sound.

"Lie still," he murmured. "Tonight I just want to hold you."

Unreleased sexual energy seemed to fill her to overflowing, but rather than act on it, she lay still, listening to the beat of her heart, his heart, and reveling in the feel of his skin against hers.

And before she knew it she was asleep.

CHAPTER FIFTEEN

THREE DAYS LATER, Colin sat at a stool at his kitchen island, alone, sipping coffee and pretending to read the paper. He'd gone for his morning run. He'd showered and changed. He'd eaten breakfast. And it was still only 7:00 a.m., the minutes on his watch seeming to pass with torturous slowness, a good hour to go before he had to be at the office.

He'd known when Lucky had left his apartment Tuesday morning that he might not see her again. But knowing that and living it were two completely different things. He'd worked on automatic pilot for the past few days, consulting clients, meeting with his attorney and running until his feet ached from pounding relentlessly against the cement walkway rimming the Maumee River, then in through the city, running not until he ran out of road, but until he couldn't physically take another step.

Despite his best efforts, still Lucky was with

him, the secret she had revealed clinging to him to like an unshakable shadow that refused to retreat even in the brightest light. He needed to see her, but held to the promise he'd made when she'd sweetly kissed him goodbye.

"Please," she'd said, searching his face. "Please give me some time alone to work through all this."

He'd wanted to tell her no. To try to convince her that he could help her. But he was afraid that the harder he tried to make things work, the more they wouldn't.

So he'd promised to give her the space that she needed.

If only he wasn't afraid that space would take her away from him forever.

Throughout his entire career he'd worked at helping others solve their problems, but with a great deal of remorse in the days since Lucky had shared her secret, he realized he'd never been *dedicated* to those same patients. Had never gone beyond the approaches he'd been taught, had never tried to implement new treatments or strategies. He'd gone with the flow, no more than a nine-to-five worker who looked forward to the end of the day, and planned what he would do outside work when he received his paycheck. Even when it came to the kids at Crossroads, the runaways who needed the most help, he never visited more than once a month. He'd convinced himself that his being there, free of charge, every thirty days was enough. Patted himself on the back for being such a caring person, a humanitarian, not merely a therapist. But when all was said and done, his actions were small, merely a single cinder block against the overwhelming tide of need that would swell toward him if he reached out and unlocked the flood gates.

Of course now that he saw that, understood that, now that he was inspired to do more, do better, he couldn't help the person he wanted to help most in the world: He couldn't help Lucky.

Or could he?

He closed the paper, finally giving up on making any sense out of it, his mind catching on to the patterns that made up his own life.

In medical school, professional detachment had been drummed into him and his fellow students from day one. Words like *limitations* and *boundaries* had seen more emphasis than the words *compassion* and *dedication* and *do no harm,* which were outlined in the Hippocratic oath. After all, he had to protect and maintain and recognize his own personal borders. So when he faced patients like the Hansens, listened to their marital problems, and looked at his watch to tick off the minutes until the session was over, he excused himself for his indifference, telling himself there was only so much he could do.

His pattern of behavior was just as damning as Lucky's was. Possibly worse, because hers had been born of tragedy and pain while his stemmed from the detachment he'd been taught and had taken literally.

No, it was no longer detachment now, was it? Instead it had morphed into passivity and ignorance.

The people who sought his attention were at the ends of their ropes. If he didn't go the extra mile to help them hold on to it and give them the tools they needed to climb back up, what was he really doing but playing the role of sounding board?

The more he thought about the situation, the more agitated he became, and the greater the temptation to excuse himself grew.

But not this time. No. This time he was going to do something about it, one step at a time, one foot in front of the other. His wasn't a job that could be forgotten about the moment he walked out of the office at 5:00 p.m. He didn't work at a textile plant; he was being entrusted with people's lives. And it was long past time he began giving them the attention they not only needed, but deserved.

And maybe, just maybe, through them, through

correcting his own ugly patterns, he would learn
how to get through to Lucky.

LUCKY SPRAYED foam cleaner on the glass then
in slow, lethargic circles ran a cloth over the front
window of Women Only, her mind a million miles
away. Her heart was across town, held tightly by a
man she had resolved to pack away into the past,
the way she had packed so much of her life.

Only Colin refused to be packed away. Not physically. Physically he hadn't contacted her, hadn't
sought her out. And, she told herself, she was glad
he hadn't. Happy he was staying true to his promise
not to pursue her.

But still he was always there, lingering on the
fringes of every thought, present with every beat
of her heart.

Something significant had happened to her
Monday night. Something she couldn't begin
to explain. Something she feared she wouldn't
completely understand even with twenty years of
thought. But when she'd opened up the battered,
weathered door to her past and let out the contents
for Colin to see, the ghosts hadn't gone back into
the closet. Instead they stood right in front of her,
no longer looming as the undefeatable enemies she
combated with sex and drink. Rather they seem

to coalesce into one giant, oversized, ugly puppet, staring at her, waiting for her to tell it what to do.

And she had no idea what to instruct it.

And since that Monday night when she'd sat on Colin's balcony and drunk herself into a stupor before going stone-cold sober in the light of his refusal to let her run, she hadn't had a drop of alcohol. In fact, last night she'd thrown every last bottle hidden around her apartment into the garbage bin, then hauled it all out to the curbside where she'd stood and watched the city refuse collectors pick it up this morning.

She'd expected to feel panic at the sight. To be assailed with the desire to run out and replenish her supply.

Instead she'd felt...relief. Something akin to freedom. Or maybe not so much freedom. Instead it felt as if she'd ascended to a step from which the world looked slightly different from the reality she'd known for so long.

"Uh oh. Trouble in Lover Land."

Lucky blinked at the square foot of glass she had been rubbing for the past five minutes, then looked at Renae standing in the open doorway, her arms crossed, her smile bright as the morning sun.

Lucky offered up a genuine smile. Over the past week and a half, she'd become attached to Women Only, Renae and owner Ginger Wasserman and the other employees in a way she'd never allowed herself to before. She'd even quit her second job at the pancake house across town despite the hole it would mean in her income, and she found she looked forward to coming to work, chatting with the others, talking to the customers. And instead of knocking off directly at closing time, she more often than not lingered on, doing work that could be left to morning, so she could prolong her contact with Renae, brainstorming ideas for new products and displays and services.

And she'd been immensely thankful that although Renae seemed to sense something was wrong, she hadn't said anything.

Until now. Until this morning.

"Renae, I think I've screwed up the best thing that's ever happened to me because of a past I haven't been able to get over."

Lucky thought she should feel surprised that she'd revealed something of such a deeply personal nature, but she didn't. And she wasn't shocked, either, when Renae didn't blink at her, change the subject or turn the other way.

"Pretty screwed-up childhood, huh?"

Renae's words, however, did shock her.

She didn't know what to say so she said nothing.

Renae smiled. "Lucky, I can spot another damaged

soul at fifty paces. It's part of the reason I hired you without any solid previous retail experience." She glanced at a car pulling up into a space in front of the store next door. "We lost souls have to look out for each other, you know?"

Lucky felt such a burst of gratitude and warmth toward the other woman she was incapable of speech.

Renae turned her gaze back on her. "You mind if I share a bit of advice I learned a little while ago?"

Lucky stared at her, unsure if she wanted to hear what her friend had to say. "Please," she managed to squeeze out of her tight throat, her hands clutching the cloth.

"You know all the bad stuff you have no control over when you're a kid? I believe that anything that happens before you're eighteen, you're a victim of." She seemed to search Lucky's face, as if checking to see if she was really listening. "Everything that happens after that? Well, it makes you a volunteer." She seemed to reflect on something Lucky wasn't privy to, then said, "Hell, girl, we're all screwed up in some way or another as a result of our childhoods. All you have to do is look at the guys who drink at the strip joint down the way—and the girls who strip there—for an easy example. It's what you do after you grow up that separates those who can take the experience and use it to make them stronger from those who allow the tragedies to destroy them."

Words so easily said. And so difficult to implement. "How do you do that? How do you use them to make you stronger?"

"How?" Renae asked, moving toward her and gently grasping her arms. She turned her to face the lot and the world beyond. "By looking forward."

"And forgetting the past?"

Renae briefly tightened the arm over her shoulders. "No. By accepting it. By knowing it's there and there's nothing you can do to change it, but acknowledging that it doesn't hold power over you anymore. That you are in charge of your life, your future. By moving forward, step by step, breath by breath."

Lucky's gratitude toward the woman next to her ballooned exponentially.

She lifted her arm, linking it around Renae's slender waist, touching her in a way that she hadn't touched another woman since her mother had died. Then she stared out at the future Renae painted. A future that she was determined to look forward to with a new mind-set and a full heart.

COLIN CONSIDERED the day of work he'd put in so far and felt oddly good about what he'd done.

While he didn't expect changes overnight, recognizing that things had to change, that he had to change, was enough for now. As long as he knew there was more work to be done tomorrow.

He glanced at his watch. His couples session with the Hansens was set to begin in five minutes. They'd cancelled their appointment last Monday, and requested to move their weekly sessions to Friday. Something Colin didn't have a problem with.

He leaned forward in his chair and opened their case file. He was disappointed to discover his notes on their sessions were so sparse, horrified to find that he'd passed judgment on them during their first meeting and hadn't done anything really to help them since.

He pulled a fresh notepad from his drawer and began writing.

He was still writing when Jocelyn and Larry Hansen entered and started to take the seats across the room where Colin usually accepted his patients.

Instead he motioned them to sit in the two chairs positioned in front of his desk.

He'd come to the realization today that sitting face to face in a more relaxed environment was preferable when dealing one on one with a single patient. But in the case of couples and groups, sitting close to them, becoming one of them, made it too easy to take on the group mentality, too tempting to tune out.

Also the participants looked upon him as one of them and it was easy for them to disregard his advice and guidance.

Sitting across a desk from them in a position of authority, much like a teacher with students, created a more serious atmosphere.

He noticed the changes in Jocelyn and Larry immediately. Usually Jocelyn would already be tearing her husband down, telling him she'd been waiting all week to tell Colin something, and thus launch into the Jocelyn hour, dominating the conversation and the session.

Now she was uncharacteristically quiet, and she had her feet crossed at the ankles and her hands clasped in her lap, much like a child sent to the principal's office.

Colin made a few more notes, then he put his pen down on top of the pad.

"Larry," he said, sitting back in his chair. "Do you love your wife?"

There was a heartbeat of silence while Colin waited for an answer. He knew it was risky, asking a question this personal. Normally he would be inquiring about what progress and setbacks the couples had experienced over the seven days since their last session.

But he'd decided that remaining impersonal in what were very personal cases wasn't going to get him—or the Hansens—anywhere.

"Of…course I do," Larry finally uttered after looking back and forth between Colin and his wife several times.

Colin nodded, giving a mental sigh of relief. The session would have gone very differently indeed if Larry had answered in the negative.

"When's the last time you told her?"

Silence. Larry didn't appear to know what to say, and Colin wasn't going to help him out.

"He tells me every day," Jocelyn said.

Colin looked at her. "I don't mean at the end of a brief phone call when you two aren't together and you're distracted." He glanced back at Larry. "I'm talking about when you're both at home, perhaps the kids are in bed, and it's just the two of you. Maybe you're sitting in front of the television and you look at your wife and remember the first time you ever set eyes on her. Or think about that moment when you realized this was the woman for you out of all the other women in the world, the one that you wanted to spend the rest of your life with, the one you wanted to create a family with."

Larry blinked at him and Jocelyn's silence spoke volumes.

"I don't know."

"Would you agree it's been a long time?" Colin prompted.

Larry nodded. "Yes. Yes, I would agree."

The other man seemed to look at his wife in a way that didn't speak of frustration or impatience or exasperation. Rather he appeared to be remembering exactly what Colin had asked him to remember.

And Jocelyn's open, questioning expression in response made even Colin sit up and take notice.

"No," Colin said, writing something down on his notepad. "I don't want you to tell her now, Larry."

"Why not?" Jocelyn wanted to know.

Colin held his hand up and smiled. "Because it wouldn't count. Instead, Larry, I want you to remember this moment. I want you to think about it throughout today, into tomorrow and over the next week. And then, when you're really feeling it, you know, when it seems even your toes are bursting with the love you feel for this woman, your wife, I want you to tell her. Then and only then."

In the reflective silence that followed his suggestion, Colin considered that maybe Lucky's secret wasn't what had precipitated this change in him;

perhaps his love for Lucky was the true catalyst. Because in order to understand love you had to experience it.

And at that moment he felt he understood it completely.

CHAPTER SIXTEEN

THE SATURDAY-MORNING sunshine spotlighted Colin as he sat on his living-room sofa going over the materials private investigator Jenny Mathena had couriered over to him that morning. Following his last visit with his attorney, he'd decided that he could no longer wait to see what Jamie Polson would do next. He had to take action. He had to protect himself and Lucky from Jamie's escalating obsession with him.

And Jenny Mathena had provided him with the means to do so.

He sat back, thumbing through the photos she'd provided. She'd had one of her people cover Lucky, as well. Colin's eyes lingered on a shot of her standing outside Women Only, her gaze far away. As far away as she was from him right now. As far away as she'd always been from him…and from herself.

He traced his finger down the side of her

hauntingly beautiful face, wondering if there would ever be a time he could approach her again. Wondering if she'd welcome him if she saw him at her door or if she'd turn him away.

Had she grouped him with the clutter of men that littered her past? Was she even now using their sad parting as another reason to barricade herself from the world, to continue on being an unhappy soul?

He yearned for her so intensely it was a physical, constant ache. Not merely in his chest, but his stomach. He hadn't known what love was until she'd unwittingly shown him.

It seemed ironical, then, that she would turn that love away when he revealed it.

Colin put the photograph down with the others and closed his eyes, missing Lucky with every molecule of his being.

Lucky...

It seemed incongruous to him that someone named Lucky should have had such an unlucky life. But what remained was that while he could see her pain, analyze it, he could never truly understand it. Know what it was like to have lived in her shoes.

What he did understand was that until she was ready to open up, to seek help with her journey, he was helpless to do anything but stand back and watch her let the bitter sadness of her past destroy her. Destroy any chance they had for a future.

Destroy their love.

He glanced at his watch. He'd contacted the housemother at Crossroads and asked if it was possible for him to stop by and visit Melissa. She'd been surprised by his call, but welcomed his visit. It meant forgoing his weekly tennis match with Will, but he felt this was more important to him right now. More important to him and to Melissa.

Besides, Will had his own problems to work out now with his young resident and the impasse they'd reached in their sex life. Colin couldn't begin to help him with those problems.

He slid the photographs and the information back into the envelope in which they'd been delivered, then grabbed the small bag of items he'd bought for Melissa—the latest best-selling young adult novel, cosmetics designed to make any girl her age feel pretty, and a small, white stuffed bear wearing a T-shirt that said Princess. Personal items she'd unfairly never gotten and that he wanted to help her start to re-accumulate, if just to learn they weren't important in the overall scheme of things.

No, he might not be able to help Lucky and, by extension, them as a couple.

But maybe he would be just in time to help Melissa.

THE ONLY sounds in Lucky's apartment that night came from the small transistor radio tuned to her favorite oldies station—the tinny rendition of "Sitting on the Dock of the Bay" seemed to characterize the hot, humid June night—and the cadence of crickets outside her open window. Around her the meager items that constituted the whole of her life were packed away into bags and boxes, ready to move, although she didn't know where she would be moving to yet.

Lucky sat at the chipped linoleum-covered table, a single box the size of a crate in front of her. She hadn't opened the box in over five years, but it had moved with her from place to place, apartment to apartment, the first thing in, the last thing out when she came and went. She slowly moved her hands over the top and sides, considering what it held, the significance of what she was about to do. The box and its contents represented the past that she'd left behind. The box was the last bruise against her heart.

She took a deep breath and lifted the top, allowing it to slide off to the side. She didn't realize she'd closed her eyes until she opened them to stare at the contents within.

The first thing that caught her eye was a small pillow covered in eyelet lace that was as familiar to her as her own reflection. Her mother had made it for her when she was five and she had had a hand in decorating her room for the first time. Every morning when she'd made her bed it had been the last thing she'd put on top. Every night before she'd gone to bed, it had been the first thing she'd taken off.

The ghost of a smile played along her lips as she lifted the heart-shaped pillow to her face then pressed it to her nose, breathing in the scent of lavender and rosemary, the smells of her childhood, flooding her mind with happy memories of her mother, of her family, before everything fell apart.

It had been so long since she'd thought about that time in her life. The laughter, the holiday meals, so many milestones that she'd blocked out in favor of clutching the blackness that had fallen over her.

Was Renae right? Was she now a volunteer rather than a victim? Was she to blame for the stark state of her life, holding on to old hurts when she might have been able to move beyond them?

It seemed improbable, but not impossible.

More and more she seemed to be open to other ideas, to be willing to take a look at her life from a different direction. And while nothing had been capable of erasing the pain she'd felt almost every day for the past sixteen years, she no longer winced away from it.

Lucky put the pillow in her lap then reached in for the next item. The eight-by-ten frame was cheap, but the degree in business in her name it held wasn't.

Right behind the frame was a savings passbook. Still holding the frame, she opened the check-sized plastic holder. The bulk of the money she'd inherited upon her father's death was still there, the only withdrawals had been to cover her college tuition. She hadn't even relied on the money to pay for room and board but had instead worked throughout college to support herself, the money seeming tainted somehow. The degree she'd used the money to achieve had seemed dirtied, as well.

She'd wished for her father's death and he had died. Which made her reluctance to touch anything connected to her inheritance doubly intense.

The next item in the box was the family photo album.

She paused, not knowing if she was up to opening it. She smoothed her fingers over the faded, dark leather. She hadn't looked at it since the day of her mother's funeral. She had been unable to gaze at the other life she had once known, for it made what had come after doubly painful.

Now she opened it, the smell of old paper and photographs filling her senses.

The pages were filled with memories her mother

had so carefully catalogued of smiling faces, her first steps, her first bike…and the three of them as a family.

She caught herself staring at her father's face, back then happy and handsome and full of the right kind of love for her.

Accept…move forward.

Renae's words echoed in her mind. She'd lived so long with one foot firmly planted in the dark shadow of her teenage years that she didn't know how to pull it out. But she vowed that she would learn. And she would not only bring the foot parallel with the other, she would edge it forward, finally taking a step toward the future.

She would one day be able to look at the past and not feel as though it had happened yesterday. Would remember the good along with the bad.

She closed the album and hugged it to her chest, a mental photograph of another man filling her mind and her heart.

Colin…

Her heart gave a tender squeeze.

As for Colin, he deserved better than what she could give him just then. He deserved more than the shattered soul she had to offer.

And she vowed one day to give it to him if he'd still have her.

COLIN STOOD at the double doors to the mammoth house that bore the address in the file Jenny Mathena had given him. He'd wanted to come earlier, but his brief visit with Melissa had turned into a day-long event at Crossroads, ending in him sticking around for dinner with the house mates on the premises and Kathy Oberon, the housemother. He'd even kicked in with clean-up.

When he'd finally left a half hour ago, Kathy had thanked him for coming, for helping the teens.

He'd told her that they were helping him more than he could ever help them. And after spending casual time in their company, drinking in their unflappable spirit, that's exactly the way he felt.

While he'd gotten to know them to a certain degree during the group sessions he'd sat in on monthly, he'd never seen their other sides. He'd marveled at how…normal they'd appeared. They'd looked and acted just like the houseful of teenagers that they were. While he'd read about the resiliency of the human spirit, he had never viewed it firsthand.

Today, he had.

And that gave him even more hope for what he was about to do.

Clutching the envelope from the private investigator under his left arm, he knocked on the door in front of him with his right.

Jamie Polson, aka James Randolph Polson, IV. Only son of wealthy Toledo industrialist James Randolph Polson, III. Twenty-nine years of age, unemployed, five years of college with a degree in nothing.

And another member of the walking wounded Colin was beginning to realize comprised a good deal of the regular population.

The door opened on a housekeeper who blinked at him before saying, "May I help you?"

"Yes. I'd like to speak with Jamie, please."

"Is he expecting you?"

No, Colin thought. He probably wasn't.

But he should be.

"Yes," he lied.

The housekeeper led him into what looked like a library, replete with floor-to-ceiling bookcases. Everywhere he looked reeked of money and privilege.

Everywhere he looked reeked of isolation and loneliness.

He knew this was Jamie's father's house. And that James Randall Polson, III, for all intents and purposes didn't live there anymore, but rather home was his Myrtle Beach estate home where he lived with his fourth wife, a woman half his age.

Jamie lived all by himself in this hulking, dark

manor, with nothing but the staff to keep him company.

It occurred to Colin that perhaps in some patients' cases a house visit would be in order. In two minutes he'd learned more about Jamie than in six months of one-on-one sessions.

Of course, having a private investigator look into a patient's past was bad form, and was very likely illegal. But Jamie had crossed the line from patient months ago and there was no turning back.

Except for this one last session.

"What are you doing here?"

Colin slowly turned to face Jamie where he stood in the open doorway. Though the same height as Colin, Jamie had a much thinner frame, the polo shirt and shorts he wore ill-fitting, too big, as if they weren't his clothes at all but somebody else's.

His father's?

"I've come to convince you to call this whole thing to a halt."

Jamie lifted a brow. "Why ever would I want to do that?"

Colin had been afraid he'd say that. And was prepared for it.

"Why did you never tell me you were homosexual?" Colin asked, rather than answering Jamie's question.

Jamie's grin was one-hundred-percent malevolent. "Well, Dr. McKenna, why do you think my father, the king of heterosexual males, runs a tab with nearly every shrink in town? Because I'm straight?"

"Then I think your father might be interested in learning that his gay son bedded his young stepmother on the chaise lounge in their backyard in Myrtle Beach a little over a year ago."

Jamie appeared prepared to deny the charges, but Colin held up the envelope in his hands to stop him. He didn't need to show the proof. Just knowing he had it was enough for him. And apparently for Jamie.

"What better way to prove to dear old dad that you're not gay?" Jamie said quietly, the bitter challenge in his voice gone.

"But once you did it you couldn't bring yourself to confront your father with it, could you?"

Jamie didn't say anything, merely stared at him as if he'd like nothing more in that moment than to see him gone. "*Now* you play therapist. Isn't that special?"

Colin mentally winced but kept himself from visibly reacting, Jamie's comment hit a little too close to home. "If you'll remember, I suggested you consult with someone else because it was obvious we were just wasting each other's time."

Jamie's smile was nothing short of malicious. "I'd have loved to have seen your face when you were served the initial intent to sue papers."

Colin narrowed his eyes. Even after everything that had happened, all that Jamie had done, he'd been woefully unprepared for the malice dripping from the other man's voice. "My guess is that if you didn't see my face, you had someone get a picture of it for you."

Jamie didn't say anything.

"Is that how you occupy your time nowadays, Jamie? No dad around to bully and poke for a reaction, so you've transferred your immature, juvenile play for attention on to others."

"You don't know anything about me."

"On the contrary, Jamie, I think I know more than even you know about yourself."

He put the series of photos on the nearby desk.

I stopped by to see if we could work this out, Jamie. Despite everything, I don't want to add more hurt to what you've already experienced from other people in your life." He shook his head. "But since that's not going to happen, I thought I'd let you know that I'm planning on leveling the playing field a little. In that envelope you'll not only find shots of you taking liberties with your father's wife, you'll find photos of you gaining access to my apartment, following me around. I'd have to check with my attorney, but I'm pretty sure what you've been doing falls solidly into stalker category."

Jamie stood completely still, apparently unsure what to do now that his bluff had been called.

"So know that if you continue to pursue this fraudulent case against me, I'm going to countersue for libel. And given your past record of bringing false suits against a number of others…well, guess who the courts and Daddy are going to believe?"

Colin stepped toward the hall, but before he left he stopped alongside Jamie and said, "My advice to you would be to get out of this house…now. The sooner the better. You need to get out there and find out what life is really about, kid. Accept your homosexuality, embrace it even, and push aside whatever issues remain between you and your dad until after you get to know yourself a little better. Learn to support yourself. See that there's more to life than trying to make everybody else's as miserable as yours."

Jamie had kept his gaze forward and Colin watched as he swallowed hard.

Colin softened his voice. "And if you want a referral to a good therapist who just might be able to help you if you let her, here's her card."

When Jamie didn't reach out for it, Colin slid it into the other man's breast pocket.

He crossed the cavernous foyer, opened the door, then looked back to see Jamie holding the card and reading it.

CHAPTER SEVENTEEN

THE LETTER was delivered in care of Women Only.

Lucky stood at the counter and froze midway through sorting the mail. In the upper left-hand corner of the plain white envelope Colin had written his name and address.

Her heart did a triple beat as she turned away from Renae.

"I'm going to go straighten up in back," Lucky whispered, unsure if Renae had heard her but too preoccupied to care. She walked into the massage therapy room and pulled the curtain shut behind her, unaware that it was still half open as she stared at the envelope she held.

Shakily, she tore open the end.

Inside was a simple square sheet of personal notepaper.

Meet me at this address on Thursday
at 7:00 p.m.

It was signed simply Colin.

She absently pushed her hair back from her face as she turned the paper over then back again, rereading the words. The address, though near downtown, wasn't that of his apartment. She didn't recognize it at all.

"What is it?"

Lucky looked up to find Renae watching her through the partially open curtain. "Um, nothing. Colin wants me to meet him somewhere."

Renae came to stand next to her, reading the note over her shoulder. Such familiarity would have made Lucky bristle a week or so ago. Now she welcomed it as she tilted the note so Renae could read it.

"Cryptic. Are you going to go?"

Lucky swallowed thickly. "I don't know."

She felt Renae's hand on her shoulder. "If you go, you don't have to stay, you know that, don't you?"

Lucky nodded.

"But even I'm curious to see what the sexy doc has up his sleeve."

Lucky stared at her. "How did you know he was a doctor?"

Renae shrugged and smiled at her. "When I first saw him come in here I knew I'd recognized him from somewhere. His friend owns the condo downstairs from mine."

"Will?"

"You know him?"

"We've met once or twice."

"Now talk about your sexy docs. I wouldn't mind getting the tongue depressors and anal thermometers out for that one."

Lucky burst out laughing, recognizing the sound of happiness in her own voice.

"Now that's something I haven't heard in a while," Renae remarked. "I think you should go, Lucky. Hear what he has to say."

"I don't know if I'm ready yet."

"Sweetie, if any of us waited for when we were ready, well, we'd be waiting forever."

COLIN COULDN'T REMEMBER a time when he'd been more nervous. He paced the floor in front of the door to Crossroads, pushing his watch around his wrist and staring out the front window at any cars that might be entering the parking lot.

It was five after seven and upstairs the group was already gathering, waiting for him to join them before beginning the rap session.

He absently rubbed the back of his neck. He

hadn't really considered what he'd do if Lucky didn't come. Sure, he'd realized the possibility existed, but once he'd put his plans in motion he'd moved full steam ahead, not allowing for variations.

Such as her not showing.

Damn.

He stared at the face of his watch again, trying to work out a cut-off point. If she didn't show within the next five minutes, he'd have to admit that she probably wasn't going to show.

The door beside him opened, startling him. He looked up to find Lucky standing there, her vivid green eyes wide, her face pale.

"Hi," he said, silently cursing himself for the lame greeting. But he couldn't help himself. It seemed a lifetime since he'd last seen her, heard her voice, enjoyed being in her presence. And just looking at her made his longing for her multiply exponentially.

"Hi, yourself." She offered up a shaky smile. "What is this place?"

His plan. Standing there gaping at her, Colin had nearly forgotten where they were and what he'd planned to do.

"I'm glad you came," he said quietly.

She searched his eyes for a long moment. "I'm glad I came, too."

He held out his hand for hers, hoping that he was doing the right thing. Praying that he wasn't rushing things. But he'd sensed on a fundamental level that calling her up and asking her out on a date wouldn't have brought her to him. So he'd determined that while he couldn't help her, he could maybe help her to help herself.

"They're waiting for us," he said.

She slowly looked around the quiet first floor of the old house, craning her neck to peer into the rooms branching off from the foyer.

"This is a shelter," he said as he began leading her up the narrow staircase.

"A shelter? For whom? Homeless people?" A shadow of wariness backlit her eyes.

"Of a sort, yes," he said, purposely being cagey.

He was afraid if she knew it was a shelter for runaway teens she'd turn and walk straight out the door.

His hope was that the instant she saw the kids face to face, she wouldn't be able to turn away. Just as he hadn't been able to so many years before.

"Everybody, I'd like you to meet Lucky," Colin said as he drew her into the room.

"Hi, Lucky," the eighteen teenagers greeted loudly.

LUCKY FELT like the section of wooden flooring she was standing on had just been cut out from under her.

A shelter...the age of the kids in the room... She realized that the house wasn't a place for homeless adults, but homeless children. Children the same age she'd been when she'd needed help. When she'd run away.

Her hand felt ice-cold in Colin's warm grasp. She was helpless to do anything but follow as he led her to a loveseat grouped in with the other sofas and chairs. She sat down, her legs feeling as substantial as water.

Why had Colin invited her there? She looked at him, her heart pounding in her chest.

As a woman slightly older than her on the other side of the room directed the teenagers to introduce and tell a little about themselves, he seemed to tune into her need to know more. "I volunteer here," Colin whispered to her, "And I thought it was something you might like to see."

Across from her, a girl of about thirteen began speaking, and Lucky's gaze riveted on her young face. Miranda. Her alcoholic mother had abandoned her when she was ten, her father had left her home by herself most of the time, and she'd been a full-fledged alcoholic and drug user by age eleven.

Lucky's chest felt so tight she nearly couldn't breathe.

"My name's Jason," the teenage boy next to Miranda said. "I'm sixteen, have been through twenty homes in the foster-care system since I was five, and I...I tried to commit suicide last month."

Lucky's gaze dropped to where red, puckered scars were plainly visible on his wrists.

She tried to tug her hand from Colin's, but he held tight.

The next teen spoke. Then the next. And with each, Lucky felt both overwhelmed and awed. Not only by what they had endured and were continuing to endure, but by the calm, reflective way they were able to tell their stories. A couple of them ended their introductions with "and I'm going to be all right." And she couldn't help believing that with the faith and friendship they were surrounded by they would not only be all right, they would flourish.

What had Renae called her? A damaged soul. Every last one of these teens was a damaged soul. And though she'd once closed off her heart in order to deal with her own past, now it opened up so wide it seemed impossible to stop the love that poured out.

She realized it was Colin's turn to speak and

she turned to look at him, her gaze feasting on everything that was him.

"I'm Dr. Colin McKenna and I've been volunteering here at Crossroads for the past three years. I've seen many teens come and go, some onto better things, some to seek out the rock bottom they need to hit in order to make the journey back. But this group here…this group has to be the most impressive yet."

The teens laughed.

"On a more serious note…"

Lucky blinked when he looked at her.

"I used to fool myself into thinking I was doing a good deed by coming here once a month. It made me sleep a little easier at night knowing I was doing something. Until I realized that I didn't have a clue as to what was truly going on, and that my efforts didn't amount to a drop in the bucket compared to what I could be doing. So now I'm here two to three times a week for however long I'm needed." He quietly cleared his throat. "And I'm always shocked to discover that I learn more from each of you about love and life and the beauty of the human spirit than I could ever teach you."

Hot tears burned Lucky's eyes as she searched his handsome face. Whereas he'd been merely sexy before, a man she could spend the rest of her life looking at and never tire of his features, now he emerged so breathtakingly beautiful she was spellbound.

After long moments she became aware of the silence in the room around her. She glanced at the participants, finding them looking at her warmly.

She realized they were waiting for her to speak.

Panic rose up from her stomach and she searched her mind for some wise-ass crack to make, something that would diffuse the somber atmosphere in the room, deflect the attention away from her.

Instead she squeezed Colin's hand and said, "Hi, my name's Lucky Clayborn. And I'm going to be all right."

And in that one moment she knew that she would be.

"IT WAS NICE MEETING YOU," the last of the teens said to Lucky at the door. "Come back and visit anytime."

Her answer was a smile as she returned a hug, her gaze glued to Colin's face over the girl's shoulder.

Colin shifted his feet. While it appeared that Lucky had responded well to his surprise, he knew that he couldn't fully know what was going on inside her mind, inside her heart. All he knew was that he'd had to try to help her move on somehow, and regular therapy sessions weren't doing it for her. She'd thrown up a giant roadblock the first time she'd come to her session with him. And he understood from his partner that she wasn't having much luck making any major breakthroughs with her, either.

So he'd thought that if he approached from a reversion-type position, put her in a room with kids the age she had been when she'd gone through what she had, he might be able to reach her somehow.

And his heart had contracted when he'd seen her connect with the kids, seeming to have gained some sort of acceptance about her situation. He didn't kid himself into thinking he was responsible for it. But he'd like to think he'd played a small role in her progress.

He'd liked to think he could continue playing a larger role in her life.

Finally they were alone. Or as alone as two people could get with so many teenagers in one house. Sounds of laughter came from the kitchen. The television was on in the room to their right. And upstairs a girl was upset that someone had borrowed her shirt without telling her.

But all Colin could see was Lucky.

She avoided his gaze and quietly cleared her throat. "They're a great bunch of kids."

"That they are."

She lifted her face to look at him, her eyes filled with curiosity. "Thank you for inviting me."

He nodded. "Thanks for coming."

Colin wanted to invite her out. Offer to drive her home. Ask her to come back to his place with him. But he knew it was too soon for any of that. He'd already decided that he wasn't going to pursue anything more with her. Not now. Not tonight. His invitation had been but the first of many steps he had planned to work Lucky back into his life. Not just now, but forever.

She appeared uncomfortable. "Um, I guess I'll be going now."

Colin nodded again, thrusting his hands deep into his pants pockets to keep from reaching out for her. Touching her. "Good night."

She looked a little confused and his resolve nearly snapped. Then she turned and with a final wave to the teens looking on from the other room, she walked out the door.

CHAPTER EIGHTEEN

COLIN HAD NEVER KNOWN a week could be so long. Seven days that seemed a lifetime, simply because he'd gone that time without seeing Lucky. He hadn't feasted on her lovely face, looked into her remarkable eyes, kissed her lush, provocative lips.

But if his plan had a chance in hell of working, he'd have to take things one slow step at a time. And if he needed any reminder of that, the fact that Lucky hadn't tried to contact him since the Crossroads session shouted it at him.

One good thing happening in his life just then was that ever since his visit to Jamie, he hadn't received any peculiar notes or threats or suffered any damage to his property. And private investigator Jenny Mathena assured him that nothing was being done to Lucky, either. Which, of course, might have something to do with Colin's no longer seeing her.

He sat back in his office chair, making a few final notes on the addictive personality session he'd just led, then closed the file. He was easily doing double the work he had before, but curiously his activity seemed to fill him with twice the energy rather than draining his emotional and physical resources. He still jogged every morning, but no longer maintained the punishing pace he'd set for himself before.

Of course, life would be a whole hell of a lot easier if Will could have some luck in his efforts to bed the young resident he'd been dating. What had been weekly tennis matches were now twice a week, only because Colin didn't have time for more due to his commitment to Crossroads and his plan to win back Lucky.

Anyway, he didn't think he could handle the brutal matches into which Will channeled all of his sexual frustration more than twice a week. He was even toying with the idea of buying his friend an inflatable "date," his argument being that if the girl wasn't real it wasn't really cheating.

The telephone at his elbow rang and he picked it up after the first ring.

"Mr. Maddox on the line for you, Dr. McKenna," Annette said.

He thanked the secretary as he scratched the back of his neck. What could Don want? He grimaced, hoping it wasn't bad news. Maybe he'd pushed Jamie straight into filing official charges against him with the county prosecutor's office.

"Colin!" Don Maddox's voice boomed over the receiver. "Good news, buddy. James Randolph Polson, IV, dropped the case."

Colin's relief was immediate and complete. "I can't tell you how glad I am to hear that."

"Not any happier than I am, dear boy. Not any happier than I am. This whole debacle had the makings of a real mess."

He was telling him. "What happens if Jamie wakes up tomorrow and changes his mind?"

"Thankfully, the chances of that are slim to none. Polson's attorney, whom I also happen to golf with once a week at Inverness, tells me James is in the process of moving to San Francisco where he's going to open an art gallery."

Colin smiled. *Good for you, Jamie. Good for you.* "I'm happy to hear it."

And he was. Because it might mean that Jamie would stop taking his misery out on others and start concentrating on making himself happy.

Don sighed. "I won't keep you. I just thought you'd want to hear the news the instant I got it."

"Thanks, Don. It's very good news indeed."

He slowly replaced the receiver then got up and went to the filing cabinets behind him. Opening the

one marked *P* he thumbed through the files until
he found Jamie's, stamped Closed across it with
the stamp in his middle desk drawer, then put the
file in his out box for Annette to put away in the
archives.

Then he grabbed his jacket and headed out the
back way, his only thought to get home and continuing his plans for winning back Lucky.

TRAFFIC WAS LIGHT and the weather was perfect,
making the drive from Sylvania to downtown
Toledo almost a pleasure rather than a trial of patience. Colin parked his car on the street, relieved
that he no longer had anything to worry about in
that regard, then took the elevator upstairs and unlocked his door.

The instant he entered his apartment, he noticed
something different.

He stood stock-still for a long moment, trying
to put his finger on it. Then he identified the difference. Not so much a difference, really, but an
addition. A scent. More specifically the smell of
ginger, the scent Lucky always wore.

His heart pitched to sit on the marble floor next
to his feet.

Of course, he knew she still had his key. And
secretly he was glad she hadn't felt the need to

return it. As for her using it, he hadn't dared to entertain such high hopes.

He put down his keys and his jacket and walked into the kitchen to find everything exactly the way he'd left it, and then he crossed the living room to the master suite where, again, everything was in order.

Then he spotted it. The piece of white notepaper in the middle of the coffee table...along with a single key.

His stomach clenched so tightly he nearly doubled over with the pain of it.

She had returned his key.

He slowly crossed the living room toward the table, hardly daring to hope he was wrong. Praying he was seeing things. But he wasn't.

He slid the folded note out from under the key then opened it.

Dear Colin—I figure it's only fair.
Meet me at...

He went on to read an unfamiliar address in the nearby Old West End section of Toledo.

He reached down to pick up the key. It was then he realized that it wasn't his key.

LUCKY STOOD IN THE KITCHEN of her new one-bedroom apartment—easily four times the size of her old apartment—and forced herself to stop looking at the clock every two seconds. Colin would come.

Wouldn't he?

She burned herself as she took lasagna from the oven, waving her hand to cool it before sticking it under cold running water. Ever since she'd seen him last week she'd known it was time to invite him back in. When she'd gazed into his eyes right before she'd left Crossroads, she'd known down to her bones that she loved the man, and that he not only loved her, he…well, he got her. He'd obviously done some soul-searching of his own while they'd been apart and it looked good on him.

Good? It had been all she could do not to use her key to his place that first night.

But considering all she'd gone through already that night, and on so many nights before and since, she'd thought it a good idea to take things a little slower. For a decade she'd rushed into relationships then just as quickly rushed back out.

But this one…Colin…well, he deserved special consideration. And not just because she owed him.

And she did owe him. More than any human being on the face of the earth. That night on his balcony he'd forced her not only to share the ghosts of her past but face them down. And while initially she'd hated him for it, she was coming to see that the showdown was long overdue. She'd wasted too many years living in self-imposed isolation. She'd lived in squalor because she couldn't bring herself to touch money that was rightfully hers. Couldn't bring herself to use her education because to do so would require more commitment than she'd been prepared to give to any job.

She'd begun meeting Dr. Morgan Szymanski for one-on-one sessions instead of group sessions this past week. And during the very first appointment Morgan had helped her realize that all these years she'd blamed herself for her father's behavior. That maybe if she'd dressed differently, acted differently, she could have made him not want her. Morgan had helped her understand that while nothing could excuse her father's behavior, it was well documented that after a family tragedy—such as the death of her mother, the anchor of their family—the male parent often mixed up familial roles. It didn't mean he hadn't loved her as his daughter. But without help and intervention, his mental illness had worsened until he'd believed the only just punishment for his actions was taking his own life.

Lucky didn't kid herself into thinking she was all right. But she did take comfort in the belief that one day she would be, just as she'd told the kids at Crossroads.

Not only had she moved from her dilapidated apartment into this larger, airier one in the charming older section of Toledo, she'd put together a proposal for Renae to open another satellite shop of Women Only downtown, using her inheritance to fund the project. Renae had been ecstatic with the prospect and they were already shopping for a home for the new place.

Still with everything she'd been doing lately, she realized one thing was glaringly missing. Or rather someone: Colin.

Merely thinking about him made her heart beat faster and her palms dampen.

Dear, sweet, sexy Colin.

She turned to put the dish of lasagna on the old oak table she'd positioned in the middle of the kitchen and spotted him standing in the kitchen doorway. She didn't know how long he'd been there, but she suspected it was a while, given his relaxed stance and the way he leaned against the jamb.

Her mouth watered with the intense desire to kiss him.

Her heart squeezed with the intense desire to love him.

"Hi," she said, giving him what could only be classified as a goofy smile.

"Hi, yourself." His smile made her toes curl inside her sandals.

Though he had never been inside the new place, it felt as if he'd been there forever. It felt as if he belonged there. They belonged there. Together.

Then again, it really didn't matter where he was, or she was. So long as they were there together.

"I have to warn you up front. I need to take this slow," she said.

He nodded, his dark eyes serious. "We'll go as slow as you like."

She realized she still held the lasagna dish and put it down in the middle of the table. With shaking hands, she took off her oven mitts.

Then, before she knew that's what she was going to do, she rushed to the opposite side of the room and threw herself into Colin's arms, her fingers bunching into his thick, soft hair, her mouth finding his cheek…and his eyebrow…and his forehead…then finally his mouth.

Oh, how she'd missed this. How she'd missed him. He made her feel beautiful and special and safe and loved. He made her feel like there wasn't a thing in the world she couldn't do if she put her mind to it. And that was a very precious gift, indeed.

Morgan had told her that she'd need to retrain herself sexually. That jumping into bed was never a good idea. But already Lucky realized a difference in her physical reaction to Colin. Yes, she wanted him with a desperation that took her breath away. But she also felt her heart swell in her chest. She felt the warmth of love swirl through her veins, the sense of completeness, of coming home that came with merely being in his arms.

And surely that couldn't be wrong.

Reluctantly, she hauled her mouth away, then rested her forehead against his, laughing into his eyes.

"Is that your idea of slow?" he asked, his voice thick with desire, his eyes brimming with love.

"I think it's a better idea if we maybe make things up as we go along," she whispered.

"That's the best idea I've heard in a long, long time...."

EPILOGUE

One month later...

COLIN FOUND IT IMPOSSIBLE to believe that just a
short time ago he'd had to run to combat his sexual
frustration. Now he was running to keep up his
stamina so that he could keep up with Lucky, both
in and out of the bedroom.

His feet slapped against the cement path through
Promenade Park, the Maumee River catching the
first rays of the rising summer sun. It never ceased
to amaze him how everything looked the same.
He'd undergone so many changes in the past couple
of months that surely the world around him should
have changed as well.

Instead the summer grew hotter. The days grew
longer.

And his love for Lucky grew more and more.

"You're a sadist," she said beside him, her

tennis shoes having a difficult time keeping up with his.

Colin slowed the pace, reminding himself that she wasn't used to running. At least not physically. Emotionally…well, she'd done enough of that to last a lifetime.

He drew to a stop, watching as she doubled over, trying to catch her breath.

He grinned at her. "You're not supposed to do that."

Her damp red ponytail shifted to the side of her face as she considered him from the corner of her eyes. "It works for me."

Hc shook his head and stepped to the railing overlooking the muddy depths of the Maumee. Moments later she stepped next to him, automatically tucking her hand inside his. Colin marveled at the simple yet meaningful movement as he lifted the back of her hand to his mouth and kissed it. She smiled, then kissed the back of his hand. Then both of them turned to take in the view, their heads together, staring out at a future that promised to be as bright and golden as the sunrise bathing them in its summer warmth.

* * * * *

WICKED

We dedicate this book to
Cissy Hartley, Sara Reyes, Celeste Faurie,
Debra Evans, Helena Beasley, Lee Hyatt,
Janice Bennett, Kathy Boswell
and the entire gang at Writerspace.com.
Thank you for providing a warm and
wonderful forum that lets us be fans as well as authors.

CHAPTER ONE

SIZE DOES MATTER.

Emergency Room Surgeon Will Sexton had always believed that to be the case. But being British, he liked that Americans actually understood that. There was no such thing as the size of the ship doesn't matter, it's the motion of the ocean. As he dragged himself home after twelve straight hours on duty at St. Vincent Mercy Medical Center in Toledo, in a mammoth SUV that could comfortably hold three families, he brightened at the thought that once inside his large condo, set back on a large piece of land, he could collapse on his large king-size bed. It all added up to a vastness he'd never come across anywhere in working-class Southwark, England, just south of the Thames outside London.

Will parked his car in the large lot, which was designed to hold other large cars and was never without a free space, and climbed out onto the hot asphalt. The hazy August sun was beginning to peek over the horizon as he made his way down the long walk that led to his large condo and thus to his large bed. Okay, so yes, occasionally he did miss his bangers and mash. And it very rarely got this hot in jolly old England. But ever since skipping over the pond that was the Atlantic in order to earn his degree at the Medical College of Ohio nine years ago, he hadn't been back home for more than a week's stay. Fact was he'd grown comfortable, liked it here with the Yanks. Not only was everything around him bigger, but the citizens themselves seemed to think bigger. Well, maybe not all of them, but if one were inclined to take his life into his own hands, one could make a run of it here a lot easier than he could make it back home. Work hard, and you were rewarded well. Seemed like a good, solid philosophy to him.

And if William Charles Sexton, middle son of Dorothy and Simon Sexton, housewife and meat factory worker, respectively, had done anything throughout his life, it was work hard.

And he'd been well rewarded.

Will hiked his duffel a little higher on his shoulder. Still, somehow he thought he'd never get used to the hot summer weather here in the midwestern U.S. Heat and lots of it seemed to be the name of the game as of late. Actually that applied both literally and figuratively when it came to his life.

His good, if exhausted, mood took an immediate nosedive at the reminder.

Five months. That's how long he'd gone without sex. And not because of a size issue, thank you very much. Rather he'd been dating senior resident Janet Nealon for the past five months. And it was just his luck that Janet had decided the month before they'd started going out that she was going to wait for her wedding night before she had sex again.

Again.

Will hiked his duffel up again and scowled.

"Ah, one of those born-again virgin types."

He recalled his best mate Colin's words when Will had complained about the state of his sex life a few months back.

"Those are the worst kinds."

Will had made the mistake of asking him how so.

"Well, because you know they've given it up—they're just not giving it up to you."

Will eyed the six-unit building that held his apartment, his gaze immediately drawn to the condo on the third floor, directly above his. Of course, it didn't help that the female neighbors in 3B had cast themselves in starring roles in his growing sexual fantasies. It seemed not a night went by that he didn't think of the two hot lesbians in bed together, sweaty and naked. Crikey, he'd had to change his sheets just last week after a particularly steamy dream in which both women had taken a great deal of pleasure from working on *him*.

Of course, he knew that if Janet finally gave in, his fantasy life would vanish. Well, maybe not disappear entirely—after all, the two women fantasy was a popular one among men his age and he didn't see that changing anytime soon—but at least he wouldn't have to rely on those same fantasies to give him the physical release he needed.

And he wasn't going to take things "in hand" himself, as Colin had suggested he do.

The problem was he was getting nowhere fast with Janet. The night before last, before she'd left for a ten-day medical seminar in L.A., he'd pulled out all the stops during their hot and heavy petting session, taking great satisfaction in bringing her to orgasm. But when he'd convinced himself she was going to return the favor with some primo, long overdue sex, she'd buttoned up her blouse, kissed him lightly on the mouth, then thanked him before handing him his coat, so to speak.

Will's teeth had been set so tightly together his jaw had hurt.

It was a good thing Janet seemed to meet some internal criteria that he'd set up long ago with her fresh good looks and her bubbly disposition. Still, he didn't know how long he could stand it.

He pulled the door to the building open and froze. Considering the sad state of affairs, this would happen to him, only to him.

On the stairwell coming down stood the number one billed star of his fantasies from 3B, Renae Truesdale. Will squinted at her. And if he wasn't mistaken, she was wearing what looked like… what appeared to be… He swallowed hard. She was wearing a bloody belly-dancer outfit. At eight o'clock in the morning.

Oh, he really didn't know how long he was going to be able to stand it.…

RENAE TRUESDALE KNEW two things for sure: that sexy doctor Will Sexton from 2B thought she was hot, and that sexy doctor Will Sexton thought she was a lesbian.

She slowed her steps on the staircase from her third-floor condo, the gold disks that made up her top and the low waist of her belly-dancer costume giving an enticing jingle. Of course, it went without saying that she'd had the hots for the doc since she'd moved in six months ago. Who wouldn't, what with all that wavy, slightly disheveled light brown hair, bedroom-blue eyes and lopsided naughty grin? Oh, and then there was that irresistible British accent and his hesitant mannerisms that made it seem that he was thinking bad, bad thoughts every time she ran into him.

And now was no exception.

Of course, she wasn't a lesbian. Her roommate, Tabitha, was, but she wasn't. But she had come to enjoy playing up Will's misperception to delicious perfection. There were few things more satisfying than watching a man as attractive as he was treading foreign waters. No matter how acceptable the alternative lifestyle was becoming on television and in the media, the simple truth was that not very many people actually knew someone gay or lesbian, much less could call one a friend.

From personal experience Renae also knew that certain men were turned on by the thought of two attractive women living together, whether or not they were homosexual. Will, with his throat clearing and hot gazes, definitely fell into that category.

"'Morning, Will," she said, purposely swaying her hips as she descended the remainder of the stairs with suggestive jingles and shakes until she stood in front of him.

She watched a swallow make its way down his throat, past his Adam's apple even as his gaze plastered to her breasts, then lower to her bare stomach and the red crystal navel ring she wore.

"Um, yes. 'Morning."

At some point she really should put the poor guy out of his misery and tell him that she wasn't a lesbian. Her smile widened. But not this morning. Not when he looked about a breath away from climaxing on the spot.

As the only daughter of a stripper, she'd learned long ago that it wasn't so much what you said that mattered, but the time you chose to say it. No one had to know of her challenging upbringing unless and until she decided to share it with them. The same went with her friendship with Tabitha. She and Tabby had been best friends ever since high school, well before Tabitha's coming out of the closet, and when her friend had said she'd needed help with the condo payments six months ago when she'd been laid off, Renae hadn't hesitated to move in and share the financial burden, no matter what everyone thought.

Especially no matter what handsome doc Will Sexton and countless others believed.

He cleared his throat again and gestured toward her apparel, the back of his hand nearly grazing the tips of her breasts. "Um, going to work, are we?"

Renae couldn't help a small laugh. He looked so uncomfortable, so damn sexy. "Yes, I am."

Oh, she knew full well that he had no idea what "work" for her constituted. Seeing what she was wearing at 8:00 a.m. on a Saturday morning, she could only guess what he was thinking. And shoot her if she was wrong, but she was pretty sure his idea didn't include the Women Only shop where she did retail work along with teaching belly-dancing classes. While she normally didn't wear her costume to work, she'd been running late this morning and had discovered that she hadn't any acceptable clean clothes to wear. So she'd improvised.

Besides, she'd reasoned, who was going to see her that early on a Saturday morning?

She'd forgotten that was the time Will usually came home.

She pulled the side of her bottom lip into her mouth. Then again, maybe she hadn't forgotten at all.

"Do you, um, you know, give private shows?" he asked.

Renae raised her brows. While she normally enjoyed teasing Will, this was the first time he'd come out and said something so blatantly and directly sexual to her. She'd figured it was because he couldn't quite wrap his mind around the whole lesbian angle. That he was coming on to her now marked a change of sorts. A change she wouldn't mind encouraging.

"Mmm," she said evasively, a shiver running over her exposed skin at his continued visual interest in her and her costume. "It all depends on who wants the performance."

Something about the way he stood gave her the distinct impression that he was about to grab his wallet out of his back pocket and offer her any amount she wanted to perform for him.

Little did he know she'd do it free of charge.

"I see," he said, clearing his throat again.

Renae gave a wicked shimmy. "Don't you just love the costume?"

His gaze flew to hers. "Love...yes. I daresay it is an intriguing bit of apparel." He gestured again, his hand brushing against her breasts this time before he quickly drew it back. "There do seem to be parts of it missing though."

"Do you think?"

She swayed her hips, the metal disks clinking together again, drawing his gaze there.

While Renae didn't fool herself into thinking she was a perfect female specimen, she did know she was attractive, despite her shorter stature and her fuller curves. The ample size of her breasts alone was known to stretch a few necks. And giving belly-dancing classes over the past four months had honed the muscles of her stomach until they were defined, firm and supple. Her skin was tanned warm gold from the swims she took in the community pool every morning and afternoon when she knocked off of work.

Will's quiet chuckle surprised her.

"You're a tease, do you know that, Miss Truesdale?"

She considered him leisurely, suggestively. "Who said I was teasing, Dr. Sexton?"

His blue eyes darkened as he looked at her, plunging them both farther into uncharted territory.

Renae blinked, caught off guard by the rush of hormones through her system. What had been harmless flirting before had just moved into more serious, more sensual terrain. And, she was surprised to find, she wanted to explore it. If just for a little while.

And Will appeared equally willing. "Then what is it you would call what you do every time our paths cross?"

"Oh, I don't know," she said ambiguously. "Issuing you an invitation?"

"An invitation?" he echoed.

"Mmm-hmm." She stepped closer, smoothing down the collar of his crisp white shirt, the sleeves of which were rolled up to reveal his strong, hair-covered forearms. She'd meant to put him on alert, but found her own palms sensitized as she stroked the Egyptian broadcloth, feeling the heat of his body just below the material.

"An invitation to what, might I ask?"

She stepped closer, increasingly aware that she wasn't only arousing Will, she was arousing herself. Her nipples tingled in sweet anticipation, her stomach tightened, and her thighs squeezed slightly together. "What do you think?"

Her hips skimmed against his, and she instantly detected his very obvious physical reaction to her come-on. Oh boy. Suddenly she was having just as much difficulty swallowing as he was.

Who would have thought? While she'd always gotten a little thrill at flirting with Will, she'd never seriously considered pursuing anything with him. But as she stood there, well aware of the signals he was giving off, the signals her own body was sending her, she realized they'd reached a fork in the road. She had one of two choices: either laugh off the current sexual tension radiating from them both and walk away, or kiss him and let nature take its course.

Funny, but she didn't seem to be in a hurry to make either decision. Instead she allowed her gaze to drop leisurely to his mouth. His lips were so well defined. So sexy. So naughty. And she had little doubt he'd know what to do with them.

Liquid awareness swirled in her stomach then

gathered at the center of her sex. She shivered slightly in response. How long had it been since she'd had sex? Gone out on a date, even? Too long, her body instantly responded. At least eight or so months. And even then the experience hadn't been anything to remember.

"You, um, should probably get going," Will said quietly.

Even as he said the words, Renae got the distinct impression that he didn't want her to go anywhere but up to his condo with him.

"Otherwise, you might be late," he continued.

Renae recognized the sexual tension that seemed to emanate from him and wind around her. She decided she liked the feeling. Liked knowing that Will wanted her but appeared to have his own reasons for not laying claim to her. Reasons that went beyond his misperception of her relationship with her roommate.

"Mmm," she finally agreed. "Yes, I probably should be going."

She said the words even as she knew she wasn't going anywhere.

DAMN IT ALL TO HELL, he was going to kiss her.

Will looked down into Renae's provocative face, suffering a need so consuming, so overwhelming it loomed outside anything he'd experienced before.

Oh, he was a normal male with normal male urges. But considering what he knew about the woman looking up at him like the answer to his sexual prayers, the only thing he should be doing was heading for the door.

Instead he said, "What would you do right now if I kissed you?"

Her full, luscious lips curved slightly upward in a sexy smile. "Oh, I don't know. Kiss you back?"

That was all the answer Will needed. He curved his hands around her gloriously bare back and hauled her to him, noisy costume and all, not stopping until he'd molded her mouth to his.

Damn. He'd been hoping that her lips would be dry, her skill lacking. But kissing Renae Truesdale was nothing short of sweet heaven. Squared.

Or, rather, burning, seductive hell. Because surely that's where he was heading by kissing a woman who was definitely not Janet. A woman who led her life differently from the majority of society.

A woman who was making him not care a lick about any of it with every delectable flick of her tongue.

Will moved his hands against her back, growing all too aware of the softness of her skin, the suppleness of her warm flesh. Heavy breathing filled his ears and with a start he realized it was his own.

He groaned and caught her pert bottom in his palms, crowding her even tighter against his almost painful arousal. How easy it would be to carry her up the flight of steps to his condo. Lay her across his unmade king-size bed. Act out every last wicked fantasy he'd had about her ever since she'd moved in.

But to do so would be to tempt fate in a way he wasn't sure he should just then.

Unfortunately he wasn't having much luck convincing his hormone-ravaged body that it should care.

Renae's fingers had pulled his shirt from his trousers and were even now flattening against the taut skin of his stomach, her moves bold and mesmerizing. She slid her touch lower and cupped the length of him in her hand.

Will's answering shudder was so all encompassing that he feared if she suggested they do the deed right then, right there, he would be helpless to stop himself from pressing her against the wall of mailboxes and curving her legs around his waist.

The hand disappeared from the front of his trousers at the same time her mouth moved from his.

Will blinked at the sexy vixen, his brain little more than scattered gray matter turned to lustful mush.

"Well, I'd better get going," Renae said, her color high, the pitch of her raspy voice even higher.

He found himself nodding stupidly, his mind knowing she was right but his body screaming otherwise. "Yes, you'd better."

She smiled, skimming her luscious body against his in order to gain access to the outer door. It was all Will could do to stop himself from collapsing against the wall of mailboxes. Thankfully he was still standing upright when she turned toward him.

"That was definitely interesting," she said, as if surprised and pleased at the events of the past few moments.

"Interesting...yes. That it was," he agreed.

And Will had the feeling that things were only going to get a lot more interesting from there.

CHAPTER TWO

RENAE LOVED WORKING at Women Only. The shop that sat on the Ohio-Michigan border was more than a job to her that provided a check at the end of the week. Ever since owner Ginger Wasserman had opened the place and hired her on the spot five years ago, she'd felt invested in the shop's success. Responsible for making the clientele happy. Dedicated not only to coming up with new ideas for services and supplies women might be interested in, but to seeing them through.

That was why it seemed strange that the shop was the last thing on her mind when she arrived there fifteen minutes after her intimate encounter with Will Sexton next to the mailboxes.

"Boy, you must really be looking forward to this class."

Renae blinked Lucky Clayborn's pretty face into focus. More than her co-worker, she and Lucky shared similar pasts that had aided in their growing close over the past two months. And now that Lucky was opening up a satellite Women Only shop downtown, Renae saw more of her than ever. Which made coming to work doubly enjoyable.

"The costume," Lucky said by way of an explanation.

Renae stared down at the belly-dancer outfit she wore, almost surprised to discover she still had it on.

It had been a long time since a guy had driven her to the point of distraction.

Longer still since one had made her forget what she was wearing.

Very interesting, indeed.

"Your class awaits," Lucky said, motioning toward the curtained-off room to the right.

What had once begun as a traditional one-showroom retail shop had slowly expanded to take up four units in the strip mall that had once been Strip Joint Central. While a couple of men's clubs remained, Women Only was quickly growing to crowd them out and the area was becoming better known for catering to the positive needs of women rather than the baser needs of men.

To the left of the showroom were the cushy massage rooms and a comfortable class area designed to look like a large, inviting sitting room where everything, from how to give a blow-his-mind blow job to educating women on their G-spot, was discussed. To the right was the open studio room lined with mirrors where Renae and others taught belly dancing and, yes, even the art of stripping. But rather than for dollars, they taught them the skills to perform in private for their mates.

"Renae?" Lucky moved her hand in front of her eyes. "Are you all right?"

She considered the way her blood still thrummed through her veins, and the dampness of her thighs, and smiled. Oh, yes. Everything was more than all right. It was great.

"Fine. I'm just fine. Have you seen Ginger?"

Lucky wrote something down on a pad she held, seeming more than a little distracted herself. Which was normal, Renae thought. If she had a guy like Colin McKenna waiting at home for her every day, she'd spend the rest of her life with her head in the clouds.

"She was in and out already. Said she might be back after lunch." Lucky looked at her. "Did you want something in particular? You could always call her cell."

Renae made a face as she adjusted the top of her costume. What she had to discuss with Ginger couldn't be done over the phone. And she didn't want to make an appointment, either. Because to do so would indicate something was on her mind.

No, she wanted to catch Ginger when she had a free moment.

"No. I just wanted to ask her about some new stock, that's all," Renae fudged.

"Hmm." Lucky didn't appear to believe her. Which was odd, because there was no real reason why her friend should think her motives were other than what she professed. Were they that tuned in to each other?

She heard music from the other room and looked in that direction.

"The natives are getting restless. I'd better get in there."

She moved toward the curtained-off area, then paused at the door. "By the way, what do you know about Colin's friend Will?"

Lucky's pen stopped moving where she'd returned to writing something on her clipboard. "That he's a doctor."

"Very funny. I meant what specifically?"

Lucky squinted at her and smiled. "Like what is his favorite color?"

Renae gave her an eye roll. "As in is he seeing anybody?"

Lucky's eyes widened. "Oh." She put the clipboard down on the counter as the sound of Middle

Eastern music grew louder in the other room. "I think he's dating a resident at the hospital."

Damn.

Of course, it was just her luck that the instant the dynamic between her and the sexy doc changed, he'd already be involved with somebody.

Then again, she wasn't looking for involvement with him. She was looking for sex.

But she also didn't relish the idea of being the other woman, no matter how briefly.

Well, first things first, she had to decide if she really wanted more of those fireworks that had shot off between them that morning.

She blinked to find Lucky still staring at her. "What happened?" she asked.

Renae merely grinned. "Nothing. And everything. Remind me to tell you later."

She stepped into the room and drew the curtain closed behind her, ignoring Lucky's, "You can bet I will!"

THE BALCONY DOORS and heavy white vertical blinds were drawn tightly against the late-morning sun, casting the room in shadow, nothing but the ticktock of the clock his mother had sent him from England last Christmas and the central air-conditioning unit breaking the silence. At this time on a Saturday the complex was quiet, and now was no exception. Will knew from experience that the usual weekly hubbub of grocery shopping and errand running had yet to begin, and those seeking the community pool had yet to rouse from sleep.

Still half asleep, he dragged his wrist across his damp brow wondering if he should turn down the temperature of the thermostat. But he was all too aware that the summer heat wasn't to blame for his sweaty condition. Rather Renae Truesdale and the naughty dream he'd just had about her was responsible.

He rolled over then groaned when he nearly permanently injured himself. Holding up the top sheet, he stared at his erection, a hard-on that could rival Big Ben.

"At ease," he muttered, letting the sheet settle back down.

This wasn't going to do at all. Five months of waking to pulsing hard-ons. Dreams filled with images of women he shouldn't be lusting after. Hell, he was plowing through his supply of sheets because no matter what chilly temperature he kept the room at, he woke up soaked with sweat. For a short time, vigorous tennis matches with his mate Colin worked out much of the frustration. But lately not even that was working.

Especially since Colin had called the brutal matches to an end a couple of weeks ago claiming

Will's unrelieved frustration was making the games too intense. Worse, Colin had tried to hand him money to buy a little female company. Five minutes, Colin had told him. That's all it would take.

But just as Will hadn't masturbated since he was twelve, he'd never paid for it. And he wasn't going to start now.

He stared at the face of his alarm clock, surprised to find that he'd managed a few hours rest and that the buzzer was about to go off to wake him for his lunch date with Colin. He switched off the alarm, tossed off the top sheet then headed for the shower, turning on the water full blast and as cold as he could stand it. He climbed inside and gritted his teeth, waiting for the punishing spray to weaken his erection. After a few long moments, he cracked his eyelids open to find that the water was having absolutely zero effect on Ben.

Well, Christ. What was he supposed to do? Walk around all day trying to hide a hard-on the size of a baseball bat?

Unable to take the cold water anymore, he adjusted the knobs until the spray warmed, then leaned his hands against the ceramic tile and took a deep breath. Damn Renae Truesdale and her wicked belly-dancer costume. He put his face into the spray, remembering the soft globes of her breasts, the sleek smoothness of her skin, the defined muscles of her abdomen. Then there was her kiss…

His erection twitched and he groaned. It wasn't fair, being offered up a temptation of Renae's caliber while he lay in wait for the woman who was supposed to end up the love of his life. Then again, he'd learned pretty early on that life was anything but fair. After all, what was the difference between him and Prince Charles but for the legs they'd popped out from between? While his mother had been trying to rub the ever-present mud from his face, Charles had been photographed on the finest of thoroughbred horses in his chaps, mud everywhere but on his elite person.

But when all was said and done, he and Charles weren't really all that different, now, were they? After all, Chuck had ditched a perfectly good princess in order to shag a woman he hadn't been able to exorcise from his system.

And Will was obsessed with the idea of banging the hell out of Renae Truesdale when the only woman he should be wanting was presently on the other side of the country.

He grabbed the soap and lathered up his hands, thinking even as he did so that no amount of soap would be able to cleanse the mud from his mind.

"Face it, you're not going to get her out of your head until you sleep with her."

That was another thing that life had taught him. That no matter how much you wanted a woman sexually, the instant you had her, it was a whole new ball game. He couldn't count the number of times he'd woken up to find himself staring at a woman whom he'd wanted within an inch of his life the night before but whom he wanted nothing more than to run from the next morning. That's why he'd decided five months ago that in the future he would conduct his relationships with his head rather than with his Johnson.

Or in this case his Ben.

He stared down at the traitorous body part that was just begging to be touched. The problem was, it didn't want his attention. Rather it was more interested in seeing if the oral talent Renae had demonstrated with her kissing extended to oral sex. He ran his soapy hands over his stomach and arms, then lathered up again. He reached for his rock-hard arousal at the same time he imagined Renae's decadent mouth closing over the tip…and he came with the power of a twelve-year-old experiencing his first orgasm.

Oh…oh…oh.

When the spasms finally subsided, Will instantly released his erection and stared down at it with all the disgust of a man at war. This was not happening. He had not just masturbated. He'd merely been washing himself and...well, Ben had taken over from there.

"You and me," Will said to the faithless organ that even now seemed to be grinning at him in sated bliss. "We have to have a chat. A nice long one."

And not once, he decided, would the name of Renae Truesdale come up.

"YOU LOOK LIKE HELL."

Just what Will needed to be told in that moment.

He stared at Colin McKenna across the table from him even as he took a deep slug of a cold draught of beer. Harry's Bar was their usual hangout of late. It was where, if he remembered correctly, he'd met Colin's friend Lucky Clayborn for the first time. Well, right before she was fired as a waitress from the bar, became a patient of one of Colin's colleagues, then became the love of Colin's life.

"Right o," he commented dryly. "Thanks for that astute observation, friend."

Colin chuckled and pushed aside the menu neither of them needed. "Dare I ask what's behind this morning's scowl? Or is it the same battle that's been raging for the past five months?"

"Same old battle," Will confirmed, downing half the ale and stretching his neck.

"Still not getting any from the new girl-friend?"

Will waved him away as he made room for the waitress to put down his fish-and-chips. Harry's was the only restaurant that came close to offering up something akin to what he'd grown up on at home. Fast food British-style. "No, it's not that."

Colin raised his brows. "So you are getting some?"

Will scowled. "No, no. Unfortunately."

"Then what is it if it's not that?"

Will tried to pick up a piece of fish, found it too hot, and shook his fingers to cool them. "It's just that…well, since my sex life is not quite up to par as of late, my fantasy life has geared up to take up the slack."

"Ah. The lesbians upstairs." Colin nodded.

"Actually, it's not both of them, but just one, as luck would have it." He chewed thoughtfully on a chip. "I had the most delicious encounter with Miss Renae Truesdale in the hall next to the mailboxes this morning."

Colin hesitated where he had just picked up his own chicken burger. "Define 'encounter.'"

"Oh, nothing out of the ordinary, mind you. Just some harmless flirting." The fish was finally cool enough to eat and he bit into it. "Oh, and the most phenomenal kiss," he said around a full mouth.

"You kissed her? Who initiated it?"

Will thought about it a minute. "I don't know. It was more of a mutual thing, I guess."

Colin's grin was altogether too self-satisfying for Will. "I thought lesbians were considered lesbians because they weren't interested in men."

Will made a face and dragged his napkin across his chin. "Yes, well, maybe she's one of those new-fangled lesbians. You know, bisexual instead of homosexual."

He supposed he found the fact that Renae had kissed him a bit odd himself. While she'd played a starring role in his fantasy life, given her sexual status, he'd had no idea that she might be interested in him, no matter her playful flirting up until now.

"So what do you think I should do?" he asked.

"About what?"

The waitress supplied them with fresh draughts and made off with their empty glasses. "What do you mean 'about what'? What should I do about the intriguing Miss Truesdale, of course?"

"Oh, no." Colin put his burger down. "There's no way I'm getting involved in this. Lucky works with Renae, you know."

Will nodded, then shrugged. "Anyway, it's quite possibly a nonissue already. The instant she walked away this morning she probably realized her mistake."

"Mmm. Because it's easy to mistake you for a woman, you mean."

Will remembered the way she'd gripped his manhood. "No, I mean maybe she just…slipped or something." He shrugged as he downed another half a draught. "At any rate, it should be relatively easy to avoid her."

"If that's what you want to do."

"Are you saying it isn't what I should want to do?"

"I didn't say anything of the kind." Colin opened the ketchup bottle and created a red puddle next to his perfectly good chips. "But I am getting a little tired of hearing about your empty bed."

Will squinted at him. "So you think I should force the issue with Janet then?"

Colin took a deep breath then chuckled. "I think you should do whatever it is you need to do, Will."

"A whole lot of help you are."

Yes, he thought. He'd avoid Renae. Shouldn't be too difficult. When he returned home from work in the mornings at the same time she normally left for work, he'd simply park in the far corner of the lot and wait until she left before going inside.

Yes. That should work out just fine.

And it wouldn't have to be for long. After all, Janet would be home in a little over a week's time.

"Now, how about we start up those tennis matches again?" he asked Colin, who was already shaking his head.

CHAPTER THREE

OKAY, SO SHE WOULD avoid Will.

When Renae knocked off work, she was happy with her plan, and decided it should be easy to implement. After all, they kept very different schedules, and if it came down to it, she could always park in an adjacent lot on the other side of the apartment building to avoid running into him coming or going.

Truth was, she hadn't expected to feel so…attracted to Dr. Will Sexton that morning. Hadn't anticipated that the light, flirty tone that had always existed between them would dive into something more palpable and solid. When they'd kissed, no one had been more surprised than her. Pleasantly— no, blissfully—surprised, but surprised. After all, she wasn't in the market for a man just now, even for sex, no matter what her body was telling her— and what her growing budget for batteries to use with her private toys was telling her. It wasn't that she was antiman; it was that right now she needed to concentrate on her career. More specifically, she needed to convince Ginger Wasserman to let her buy into Women Only. Become a more solid part of the venture, and as a result take home a bigger piece of the pie.

Not that she wasn't being paid well for her work. She was. She shifted on the cracked white leather seat of her 1971 pink Cadillac Eldorado convertible. It was just that she wanted to feel more… connected somehow.

She was perfectly aware that she might not feel that way had it not been for Leah Westwood opening a Women Only shop in the west end of the city, then Lucky doing the same downtown. Had neither woman come into her and Ginger's lives, she would very likely still be operating the way she had for the past five years.

But they had and as a result she felt different. Wanted more. Her mind was functioning with more of an eye on the future, her future, and the bottom line.

Truth was, she wanted a place of her own to hang her hat at night. Sure, she might be able to afford a comfortable if small condo, or even a house, but she'd like something a little bigger, a little nicer, maybe. And while she was happy living with Tabitha, her roommate's girlfriend, Nina, made it clear she was very unhappy with the arrangement. Nina wanted Renae to move on, even though Nina had moved in three months ago while Renae had been there six.

She pulled her T-shirt away from her damp back, questioning the wisdom of driving with the top down when the August temperatures easily soared into the nineties at this time of day. Of course, Tabitha had no clue about the animosity that existed between the two women. And Renae didn't think it a good idea to point it out to her. Male-female, female-female, the gender of those involved didn't matter; a threat from the outside, from a friend or neighbor, perceived or otherwise, did.

She took a corner, the disks on the belly-dancer costume, wrapped in plastic in the back seat, jingling as she did so. She glanced down at the jeans, T-shirt and flip-flops she'd changed into at work, then back at the costume, a slow, easy smile turning up her mouth.

Will…

For a few sweet moments the tensions that littered her life melted away, leaving nothing in its wake but the memory of his skillful mouth and his hard, welcoming body.

Blame it on the heat, but she couldn't remember wanting a man as powerfully as she'd wanted Will that morning. Given the way she was raised, men and relationships had always been something to question rather than to surrender to. That's what she'd liked about Ginger Wasserman on the spot. Ginger understood her in a way that a Suzie Home-maker type never could.

And it's why she'd instantly understood that dark, lost look in Lucky Clayborn's eyes when she'd walked into the shop months back.

Renae pushed up her large, dark sunglasses on her nose and turned up the volume on the radio, hoping to edge the heavy thoughts out of her mind with a little rock 'n' roll. Heart's "Crazy on You" filled the humid air and she nudged the volume level up even farther.

Of course, it was just her luck that the tune would make her think of Dr. Will Sexton again.

She sighed. That's all right. She knew that a little time and effort and avoidance would put him right back where he belonged, which was solidly in flirt territory. Whenever her heart or her hormones threatened to lead her in the wrong direction— which, granted, wasn't often—she knew that as quickly as the emotions surfaced, they could as easily die away. And if she ever questioned the philosophy, she needed only to remember the pil-low-shock syndrome that nearly every red-blooded human being had gone through at one time or another. Namely that moment when you opened your eyes the following morning to find the person who had seemed perfectly suitable and lust-worthy a few hours earlier had turned into the person you wouldn't be caught dead with on a deserted island overnight.

And experience had taught her that the sudden, unexpected change in her playful connection to Will bore all the earmarks of pillow-shock syndrome.

Great sex material one day.

The date from hell the next.

She smiled to herself as the radio station launched into another Heart tune, this one more befitting her mood: "Even It Up." Forgetting she hadn't meant to, she began turning into the regular parking lot at the building, then at the last minute swerved back into traffic, earning her irritated honks from the drivers behind her. She waved her apologies then swung around to the back lot and claimed the last open parking space. She glanced at the SUV to her right, thinking it looked an awful lot like Will's....

Then he climbed out.

ALL RIGHT THEN, some sort of higher power had it in for him.

That was Will's deduction as he stood next to his

SUV and stared at Renae, her long, tangled sun-kissed hair, her clingy white T-shirt that did little to hide the lacy bra she wore underneath and her big, black glasses that made her look like the one-hundred-percent luscious, hot American woman that she was.

He flinched when the radio station she was tuned in to launched into the opening strains of the old The Guess Who song "American Woman" before she switched the ignition off and plunged them both into a shocked kind of silence.

"Come here often, do you?" he asked with a raised brow, accepting that avoiding her now was out of the question.

She gave him a leisurely once-over then pushed her sunglasses onto the top of her head, her smile decidedly decadent. "Funny, I parked over here to avoid you."

He chuckled at her refreshing honesty. "Ironically, I was doing the same thing."

The way he saw it, the only thing to do now would be to walk with her to their building. To give her a brief wave then take off would be so appallingly rude as to make him shudder. So he waited as she pushed a button that put the top up on the hideous pink contraption she called a car, gathered what he could see was the costume she'd been almost wearing that morning from the back seat, then joined him next to his SUV.

"I know why I want to avoid you," she said as they began walking together down the path that would take them to their building. "But why are you avoiding me?"

Will was amazed by the myriad emotions pulsing through his bloodstream caused by merely walking next to the woman. For one, he couldn't seem to keep his gaze off her pretty tanned face, even though it was currently devoid of makeup. And the way he kept eyeing her T-shirt and jeans, one would think he hadn't seen a woman dressed in that way before. But it was the fact that he was inordinately interested in her feet, wrapped in her hot-pink flip-flops, that was the cause for the most concern.

"Are your feet actually tanned?" he found himself asking.

Renae looked down, appearing as caught off guard by his inane question as he was. The problem was he'd never before really noticed a woman's feet and whether or not they were tanned. And it was more than just the neon-pink toenail polish she wore. There was just something wickedly attractive about her feet that made him fantasize about seeing them sticking out of a tub full of frothy bubbles... while she sat gloriously naked on top of him.

"Why yes, I guess they are," she finally responded, throwing him a sexy little smile. "And you're avoiding my question."

Will stiffened a bit. "Well, it's not that I'm avoiding your question, actually. It's just that…" He couldn't help grinning. "It's just that I can't recall it."

"Why are you avoiding me?"

"Ah, yes. That question." Will eyed their building that seemed to loom outrageously far away. He felt the urge to pull at his collar, although he wasn't wearing a tie but rather a white open-throat polo shirt. And a pair of stonewashed jeans and sports shoes he couldn't wait to get out of.

What was the question again? Oh, yes. Why was he avoiding Renae?

"Well, you see," he said carefully, "there's this little issue of another woman that I'm seeing—"

"The resident."

He squinted at her although the sun was behind him. "You know about her?"

"Lucky filled me in."

"Ah, yes. Lucky. Colin's Lucky, I presume?"

Renae seemed interested in his mouth as he spoke. "One in the same."

"And she would have shared this information because…"

"I asked for it."

"I see."

Will shoved his hands deep into the front pockets of his jeans despite the abominable heat. Partly because he was filled with the almost irresistible urge to tuck a windblown strand of her dark blond hair back behind her ear. But mostly because he was afraid where the itchy appendage might roam from there. More specifically down the line of her intriguing back to her nicely rounded bottom, which might make it necessary for him to usher her straight into his condo and the bed therein.

But while he couldn't touch her, he could look at her. And what a feast for the eyes she provided, too.

He cleared his throat. "And your reason for wanting to avoid me?"

She smiled. "Oh, pretty much the same. The resident."

He chuckled softly at that one. "You're avoiding me because I'm dating someone else?"

"Mmm-hmm. Why do you sound so surprised?"

"Because that doesn't strike me as something you'd do."

The pathway wasn't disappearing under his feet at the quick rate he'd like it to. But the building was finally coming up. Thank God. He honestly didn't know how long he could withstand such a strong dose of temptation incarnate without succumbing to it.

"How so?" she asked.

He shrugged. "I don't know. You seem like the type that when she wants something, she takes it."

"Funny," she said for the second time in so many minutes. "You strike me as the same."

He looked at her. Really looked at her. At the appealing shape of her mouth. The openness of her attractive face. The wanton invitation right there in her creamy-green eyes and said, "Your place or mine?"

Without batting an eye she said, "Yours, definitely."

IF THE HUNGER RAGING through Renae's body had been for food, she would have devoured an entire buffet.

No sooner had the door to Will's condo closed behind them than they were going at it like a couple of sex-starved teenagers, all groping hands and wild hormones. Her plastic-protected costume dropped to the floor along with her purse even as Will yanked up the hem of her T-shirt and cupped her breasts.

"Ouch," she said when he squeezed a little too tightly.

"Sorry."

The pressure quickly turned pleasurable. Meanwhile, she tugged his shirt out of the waist of his jeans and flattened her palms against the rock-hard length of his abs. When she suddenly shifted her head to the right, she made solid contact with his nose.

"Ouch," he said.

"Sorry."

Quickly their clothes dropped away to the sound of zippers being undone and fabric seams being ripped. Renae couldn't seem to get enough of him. From his arms to his back to his hotly throbbing erection, her fingers moved, her blood surging through her veins, her breath coming in rapid gasps.

Finally his fingers found her heat, burrowing through her tight curls then coming to rest against her swollen folds. She shivered, so close to climax that she surprised even herself. She bit down on her bottom lip as he parted her engorged flesh then slid a finger up her dripping channel then drew it back out. She started trembling so badly she nearly couldn't hold herself upright.

Oh, yes. This was everything and more than she'd hoped—she'd feared—it would be with the sexy doc.

"The bedroom's this way," he said unnecessarily

as he turned her while barely breaking the contact of their mouths, bumping her nose in much the same way she'd bumped his moments earlier. Walking backward was awkward at best, especially given the liquid consistency of her knees just then. She bumped into a couch—white leather—then nearly toppled over a plant stand—white lacquer—before her back hit the doorjamb that led to the bedroom beyond.

They fell to the bed in a jumble of elbows and knees. Renae's breath rushed from her lungs at the feel of Will's elbow in her stomach and he made a low sound of warning and she looked down to find her knee a millimeter away from not only ruining the moment, but the entire lifespan of Will's sex life.

"Hold on…a sec," she whispered, working her leg out from in between his and bending it instead around his thigh. Then she removed his elbow from her stomach and lay back, licking her lips in anticipation. "Now, where were we?"

She watched his blue eyes darken and heard an almost animal-like growl emit from his throat as he launched a fresh attack on her mouth. Renae curved up into him, relishing the rasp of his lightly hair-covered chest against her smooth breasts. It had been a long time since she'd felt so out of her mind with need that she burned from the inside out. And Will was the only one with enough hose to put out the fire.

She kissed him several times then drew away so she could look at where his erection was pressed against her lower belly. She swallowed hard. And oh what a hose it was, too.

"Condom," she whispered urgently, taking his impressive length in her hands and stroking him.

He shuddered. "In the drawer to your right. Yes, right there."

Renae pulled out a matchbook promoting a nearby bar, a pen, then found what she was looking for. She opened the foil package with her teeth then rolled the cool, lubricated latex down his length, hoping it wouldn't roll right back off because of his considerable girth. The scent of rubber and of hot arousal filled her senses as her fingers finally met with his scrotum. She gave the hair-covered globes a leisurely, explorative squeeze then spread her legs farther and positioned him against her waiting flesh.

Yes…oh, yes.

He bent down and kissed her and she restlessly moved against him, trying to force penetration even as his tongue swirled around in her mouth. She rubbed her breasts against his chest, reveling in the flames seeming to lick along her skin to join the inferno between her legs. Will pulled her right nipple deep into his mouth and she moaned, throwing her head back against the white comforter—was everything in his place white?—and jutting her hips up hungrily toward his.

"Please," she pleaded, seeking the connection he was slow in giving to her.

Finally he parted her slick flesh, positioned himself against her portal, then sank in to the hilt, filling her beyond capacity. Filling her beyond her wildest imagination.

And finishing before they had even begun.

CHAPTER FOUR

SWEET GOD IN HEAVEN...

Will's body finally stopped twitching and convulsing and he froze above Renae feeling a mortification he had never encountered before in his life.

There was no playing off what had happened. No pretending that the instant he had entered her he'd climaxed as fast as a thirteen-year-old who'd paid for the pleasure. Even as he called on every ounce of willpower he possessed to prevent it from happening, Big Ben quickly turned into Little Willy.

And Renae was making movements for him to get off.

Will rolled to the side and lay on his back staring at the ceiling. "Well, that was certainly unfortunate now, wasn't it?"

He saw it as a good sign that she hadn't immediately gotten up, put on her clothes and left without a word. He heard her head turn against the bedding as she looked at him. "Anticlimactic would have been my choice of words."

He looked at her, unable to stop the grin that threatened. "Well, for one of us anyway."

She began getting up and he gently grasped her arm and held her in place.

"Sorry. Bad attempt at humor." He fought to catch the last of his breath. "Give me a moment, will you? I can't possibly let you leave after putting in the worst performance of my life." He swallowed hard. "God, I haven't come that quickly since... well, never." He looked at her. "At least not since I was six and first discovered my penis was capable of providing pleasure."

"Six?" she asked with a raised brow.

"Mmm. I was a young starter."

She rolled to her side and propped her head up on her hand. "And a quick finisher."

He chuckled. "Very funny."

She lightly shrugged her shoulders, causing her delectable breasts to bounce. "Until you prove differently, that's going to be my story."

"Your story?"

"Mmm-hmm. You'll go down in my personal sexual history as Quick Withdraw McGraw."

"Ouch."

"You're telling me."

Despite the humiliation that threatened, Will found her easy banter putting him at ease. "What would be the female equivalent to what just happened?" he asked.

"Oh, I don't know," she said quietly. "My reading a newspaper while you went about your business."

"Now that would be downright rude."

"Do you see a newspaper anywhere?"

Will considered the shadows playing against his bedroom ceiling. He hadn't opened the vertical blinds from the morning and the room was dim and cool.

And the woman beside him was sexy and hot.

"Be a good bird and hand me another condom, won't you?"

Renae blinked at him, then down at his growing erection. She lay back and reached into the drawer to get another square packet. "Are you sure you want to subject yourself to this again?"

He took the condom from her. "I think the question is are you game for another round?"

"Seeing as I can barely remember—oh!"

Freshly resheathed, Will rolled quickly back on top of her, pinning her arms above her head and allowing his gaze to roam over her deliciously shapely body. He spread her thighs with his knees then positioned the tip of his fully throbbing arousal against her once again. This time when he filled her, he took his time about it, absorbing her every shiver and quake…and keeping his own control tightly in check.

Finally he was into her to the hilt and she moaned. He kissed her mouth then pressed his nose against hers. "What was that you were about to say?"

Renae restlessly licked her parched lips, her heart thudding hard in her chest, her womb contracting to the point that she believed she might be on the verge of climaxing.

Considering that moments before she'd firmly believed that pillow-shock syndrome had struck hours too soon, the rush of physical need that suffused her muscles, and the sensational chaos Will was so easily re-creating in her, was…well…shocking.

And oh so nice.

He began stroking her with his manhood in a way few men knew how to, expertly skimming the head of his erection against her G-spot then withdrawing before plunging in and tilting his hips to hit her pleasure spot head-on again. Oh, nice was so not the word for the way she was feeling. Orgasmic was closer to the mark. Out of her mind with pleasure would also fill the bill. She curved her hands around his tight posterior and squeezed, holding him deep inside her for a moment longer and grinding her pelvis against his, cherishing the friction of his hair against hers.

Oh, yes. That was so much closer to what she'd expected. She moaned as he stroked her again. In fact, it was quickly surpassing it.

His hips stilled and she cracked open her eyelids, afraid he might have bailed before her again. Instead she found he wasn't climaxing. Rather he was cupping her right breast then bending to run his tongue slowly along her distended nipple. Renae swallowed hard, unable to blink as she watched him swirl the tip of his tongue around and around then pull her nipple deep into his mouth, seeming to tug on some sort of invisible chord that linked her breasts to her throbbing sex. Without his having moved his hips she felt ridiculously on the verge of orgasm.

She stretched her neck and closed her eyes, trying to regain control. She wanted this to last. Wanted him to deliver on his promise to perform better the second time around.

She wanted to make the risk she'd taken by coming into his condo with him worth it.

He withdrew halfway then plunged almost roughly back in to the hilt. Renae's back came up off the bed and a long moan escaped her throat.

Then before she knew it he was rolling so he lay on his back, her on top.

Considering she'd been on the verge of climax, she wasn't sure she liked this change in position. At least not until he thrust upward and chased all coherent thought from her mind.

Bracing herself against his shoulders, she tilted her hips forward, then back. Oh, yes. That was so, so good. Will's size practically guaranteed a girl a good time. Of course on the condition that he could actually maintain an erection. What good was a big member if you couldn't keep it that way? But despite his unpromising beginning, the sexy E.R. doc was delivering everything and more than she had spent all day imagining.

Her stomach began trembling and hot, liquid fire exploded through her body. She gripped his shoulders tightly and threw her head back, riding the exquisite waves crashing through her like a trained surfer. Only not even she was prepared for the length and the power of her orgasm. As her muscles began to calm, she tried to calm her surprise at her incredible reaction. After all, when she'd handed him the second condom, she'd been devoid of any expectation.

Now...

Well, now that she'd just experienced what could

possibly be the best orgasm of her life, she didn't quite know how to respond.

"And?" Will asked, fondling her breasts.

Another shudder worked its way through her body and she smiled down at him.

"And that was definitely worth the risk of giving you a second chance."

Damn, he was sexy. His hair always had a kind of just-got-out-of-bed look about it, but now that it had really been tousled, he looked like the worst kind of devil, grinning up at her with his lopsided, British grin.

She began to roll off him.

He stayed her with his hands on her legs. "Where do you think you're going?"

She blinked at him. It was three in the afternoon and she hadn't been back to her apartment yet.

"Oh, Miss Truesdale, I'm nowhere near through with you."

She playfully widened her eyes. She'd been so enthralled by her own climax she hadn't noticed whether or not he'd come again. "Oh?"

"Mmm. I figure since we've gone this far, we might as well go all the way."

Renae found herself licking her lips in sweet anticipation. "Excuse me, but isn't all the way what we just did?"

"Uh-uh." He shook his head, his fingers drifting

from her outer thighs so he could press the pads of his thumbs against the magic button between her legs.

Renae moaned.

"That was just the appetizer. And I fully plan for this to be at least a five-course meal."

Renae gasped when he lifted her from his hips then coaxed her in the other direction so she still sat astride him, but facing his feet.

"Be a good bird and get me another one of those condoms, won't you?"

Renae reached back and took out a handful of condoms. She let them rain down on his chest as she grinned in naked challenge. "Now make this bird sing."

HUMPH. Seemed ironic somehow that while he was having such a hard time getting one woman in his bed, he couldn't seem to get the other one out.

Will stood drinking an extra-large glass of orange juice from the doorway to his bedroom. It was past 6:00 a.m. Sunday morning and, a part of him told him, time for his bed partner to make a graceful departure. In the hopes of rousing Renae from the sleep of the dead, he'd already made about as much noise as he possibly could with absolutely no luck at all. Of course, his being halfhearted about actually wanting her to leave was something he preferred not to think about just then.

Instead he idly considered other ways he might go about chasing her from his condo even as he leisurely leaned against the jamb and took in her silhouette under the white top sheet. Damn, but she was beautiful. Most women didn't fare a fraction as well within a few hours of him bringing them back to his place. But Renae... Well, Renae looked somehow even sexier after the hours and hours of great sex they'd shared. Her dark blond long hair was tangled, sure, but rather than looking like a nest where bats might consider taking up residence, it appeared soft and appealing, framing her tanned face just so. And while she hadn't been wearing lipstick when he'd run into her in the parking lot yesterday, her lips still somehow managed to look seductively pink and wet, as if awaiting his kiss.

His gaze slid down her shapely body, which he knew was naked under the sheet. From the curve of her exposed arm, to the soft swell of material against her breasts, down to her curvy hip, he visually roamed. He glanced down at the front of his own shorts, surprised to find Big Ben chiming the hour once again.

He raised his brows. It had been a good long time since he'd spent so many unbroken hours having sex. And he couldn't recall the last time he'd still wanted a woman this much after having had her myriad ways over more than twelve hours.

He moved his half-empty glass from one hand to the other then knocked loudly on the open door.

Renae smiled, cooed, then turned in the other direction, completely oblivious to his attempts to wake her.

Which had been the case for the last hour.

Will couldn't resist stepping closer and peering over her shoulder at her completely contented expression.

Intriguing…

Especially when she blinked her eyes open, reminding him of how vividly green they were, and looked up at him. Her smile widened even farther as she rolled to her back and yawned. "Good morning," she said, her voice husky.

"Yes, um, good morning to you, as well." Will stiffened and absently rubbed his chin. "You weren't planning on moving in here, were you?"

Renae turned her head to stare at him.

"Because, you know, if you are, I'd have to set some ground rules. Like no sleeping later than me. And—"

She grabbed a belt loop on his cargo shorts and tugged him forward. "No fear there."

Will's first reaction was to ask why. Then he

remembered that he wasn't supposed to want her in his apartment for reasons other than sex.

"Ah, yes, that's right," he said. "You already have a roommate."

He remembered the other woman who lived directly upstairs. She had some kind of cat name. Tabby or Spot or something like that.

Then again, she wasn't just a roommate, was she? She was Renae's live-in lover.

Somehow over the past fifteen hours he'd forgotten about that.

Intriguing, indeed.

He blinked at Renae's purely teasing smile. "Jealous?" she asked.

"Who me?" He pressed his lips together then shook his head. "No. Not in the slightest." He handed her his glass of orange juice then jabbed a thumb toward the ceiling. "But someone else might be."

She pushed up to a sitting position, causing the sheet to drape around her waist and baring her full and delectable breasts. Breasts that bore red patches from his considerable attentions the night before. He rubbed his freshly shaven chin and imagined himself slathering lotion all over her delicious skin.

"Are you talking about Tabitha?" she asked after she finished off the juice and handed him back the empty glass. He wasn't sure he liked the secretive smile she wore. Well, okay, he liked it—a little too much if you asked his opinion—he just didn't like that he didn't know what had caused it. "That's so not what our relationship is about."

He bit back his instant query for her to explain what it was about, then reminded himself that he didn't want to know.

This...Renae...them...this was a one-shot deal. As soon as she walked out the door, she wasn't going to walk back through it again.

She lay back in the bed again and crossed her arms behind her head, her bare breasts jiggling in an all too enticing manner.

In order for that plan to work, however, he actually had to get her out the door.

She looked at him from head to foot. "You didn't have plans this morning, did you?"

Will found his tongue suddenly altogether too big for his mouth. "No. You?" he fairly croaked, unable to pry his gaze from the engorged tips of her breasts.

She slowly pulled the sheet from the rest of her body, offering up even more delectable vistas as she smiled at him wickedly. "Oh, I think I can come up with one or two."

Funny, but Will no longer wanted her to leave....

CHAPTER FIVE

FOUR HOURS LATER Renae was in the kitchen of the condo she shared with Tabitha, washing the dishes that had been left in the sink—dishes she hadn't dirtied—and humming to herself. She was idly surprised that the tune she couldn't seem to shake was the Heart song "Crazy on You."

She smiled, recalling the near look of panic Will had worn after they'd wrapped up their last sack session and he'd gotten a look at the time. They'd been just a few hours short of spending an entire day in bed together. And he hadn't looked too pleased at that realization. In fact, he'd looked two breaths away from piling her clothes into her arms and shoving her through his door butt naked just to finally get rid of her. No matter that certain areas of his anatomy had other ideas.

The only reason she'd left at all was that they'd

run out of condoms, both from his drawer and her
purse.

And even now she was wondering if she had one
or two stashed away somewhere in other purses.

She laughed at what Will's reaction might be if
she showed up at his door holding the foil packets.
He'd been surprised enough that she, a so-called
lesbian, had carried condoms with her. He'd probably look adorably shocked initially. Then he'd
likely yank her inside his apartment where they
could put the rubbers to good use. After all, as Will
himself had said when she'd been about to leave
and found another in her purse, "A good condom
is a terrible thing to waste."

"Now that's one look I haven't seen on your face
for a good long time."

Renae glanced over her shoulder at Tabitha who
was placing a shopping bag down on the glass-top
kitchen table.

"What? The look of getting properly laid?"

Tabitha smiled at her as she unloaded the grocery bag. "Yes, that would be it."

Renae tried to control her smile and failed. She
finished up the dishes and dried her hands.

"Anybody I know?" Tabitha asked. She finished
emptying the bag and then folded it up and put it
in the recycling bin in the pantry.

"Uh-huh."

Tabitha raised a brow as Renae helped her put the food items in the refrigerator and the cupboards. "May I ask who?" Tabitha took two cans of iced tea from the fridge, handed one to Renae, then they sat down across from each other in the wrought-iron chairs around the glass table.

"Sure." Renae pointed to the floor below them with her thumb.

"Disappointing?"

Renae realized she was giving the thumbs-down sign and laughed. "No, silly. I'm referring to our downstairs neighbor."

Tabitha nearly spewed her drink all over the glass tabletop. "Oh, God, say it isn't so."

Renae enjoyed her friend's reaction.

Truth was, both of them had gotten a kick out of teasing Dr. Will Sexton all through the summer. Had enjoyed putting on their skimpy bikinis and heading for the pool, making extra sure when they ran into him to fertilize his belief that they were lesbians and causing it to grow even further.

Of course, it wasn't the first time the two friends had done something of that nature. The two of them had quickly become close friends their freshman year at Start High School, and had remained friends since. They'd gone through Tabitha's hesitant coming out their junior year. But even before Tabitha had told her of her orientation, Renae had always guessed at her friend's sexual preferences. When they went to football games Renae always commented on the players' tight buns, while Tabitha had always been more interested in the cheerleaders. Not because she'd wanted to be one, but rather because she'd wanted to date one.

And ever since they'd both hit puberty, they'd been aware that whenever two hot women were together, men were wired to fantasize about them being together in a sexual sense. And they'd learned how to work the weakness to perfection. Beginning with their senior prom where they'd been each other's dates. Up until now with Will.

"You explained that we aren't lovers, of course," Tabitha asked now, jerking Renae out of her reverie.

"Of course not."

"And he still slept with you?"

"Oh boy did he ever."

Tabitha's frown barely detracted from her brunette beauty.

Of the two of them, Tab had always been the more attractive. The one guys went after, obviously with little success.

"Did he…has he…"

"What?" Renae asked, knowing exactly what her friend was thinking. "Did he ask me to give you a call and invite you over?" She shook her head. "Interestingly enough, he didn't."

"But you expected he might."

Renae tilted her head. "Yeah, I guess I did. But somewhere after the first five minutes I completely forgot and I think he did, too." She looked at her friend suggestively. "Until this morning, anyway, when he asked if you might be jealous."

Tabitha shook her head. "One of these days you're going to get yourself into trouble."

"Nah. I think I'm a little too smart for that." She looked around, peering into the hall and the living room beyond. "Speaking of jealous partners, where's Nina?"

"Nina's not jealous."

Renae laughed. "Now look who's heading for trouble. Nina was born jealous."

"She was not." Tabitha waved her away. "Anyway, tell me more about Dr. Will. Will you be seeing him again?"

Renae twisted her can around and around on top of the table then wiped away the condensation. "I don't know. Maybe."

"So last night was purely about sex."

"Oh, was it ever."

"So you have no designs on him beyond that?"

"I don't think so. After all, he does have a girlfriend."

"Well, that's interesting." Tabitha reached across the table and stopped her from fiddling with her can. "You just be careful, you hear? You wouldn't be the first woman to mistake great sex for a relationship."

"Mmm," Renae admitted. "And I think you would do well to listen to your own advice." She gave her friend a wink.

"What's that supposed to—"

"Tabby, I was waiting for you outside. I can't believe..." Nina's words trailed off when she spotted Renae and Tabitha sitting with their hands joined. "Oh. Hi, Renae."

She said the words with all the friendliness a snake might give a field mouse.

Renae returned the greeting with a little more warmth then patted Tabitha's hands before releasing them. "That's what that means."

"YOU SLEPT WITH HER."

Colin's words startled Will to the point that he missed his serve on point. When he tried to retrieve the bouncing tennis ball, he lost his grip on his racket.

"What?"

Colin pointed his own racket at him from across

the court at the private club. Colin had insisted they play here, despite the perfectly good courts at Will's condominium complex. "You know perfectly well what I'm saying. That belly-dancing lesbian that lives upstairs from you. You've slept with her, haven't you?"

Will grimaced wondering if he was that transparent to everyone. Because if he was, then he was going to have one hell of a problem on his hands when Janet returned from California next weekend. "You couldn't be further from the truth," he lied, concentrating all his efforts on making a killer serve.

The ball went slightly out and he reached for another ball.

Colin squinted at him. "Come on, Will. The look on your face doesn't come from taking things in hand."

"So to speak."

"So to speak."

"And why wouldn't it?" He served again, happy this time just to get in bounds.

Colin easily returned it. "Because you wouldn't look like you've just been screwed within an inch of your life, that's why. You wouldn't be so relaxed, and grinning all the time. And I swore I heard you whistling when you walked up. Masturbation does not a whistler make."

The sound of a racket being dropped. Will returned the volley and glanced at the next court, which was occupied by a couple of hot young women. One must have overheard Colin and had dropped her racket midreturn. The two women looked at each other and laughed.

"Oh, bravo, Colin," Will said, putting some extra elbow into the next return and taking some satisfaction in Colin's having to hustle to hit it. "I think I recognize one of those girls from the hospital. That's all I need, for rumors like that one to start making the rounds. 'Willing Will, who's not afraid to take matters into his own hands.'"

Colin chuckled and didn't even try to get the next volley Will fired over the net.

"Point, game and match."

"Good." Colin gathered the errant tennis balls then met Will at the net where they shook hands. "I don't think I could have withstood another half-assed match. I think I liked you better when you wore frustrated."

Another round of giggles from the next court.

"Will you stop," Will said under his breath. "Just think what Janet's reaction would be if word of this circled back to her."

Colin stared at him as they left the court. "You should be more concerned about what she'd think if she found out you banged your upstairs neighbor."

His eyes widened. "You didn't sleep with both of them, did you?"

Will waved his hand. "No, no. Just the one."

Colin moved a couple of steps ahead of him and prodded him in the chest with his covered racket. "Aha! I knew it."

Will cringed, catching on to the mistake he'd made.

Colin moved to walk beside him. "So how was it?" he asked quietly.

"Do I enquire about what goes on between you and Lucky after the sun sets?"

"All the time."

"And do you tell me?"

"Never."

"Well, then."

"Yes, but Lucky and I are a couple. You and…"

"Yes," he confirmed, refusing to actually state Renae's name.

"Your experience was a one-nighter. Strictly sex. It doesn't count."

"How do you rationalize that?"

Colin stared at him a little too closely. "Unless it wasn't just about sex."

They'd reached the parking lot and Will opened the back of his SUV and tossed his racket inside along with his gym bag. "Of course it was just about the sex, man. What, have you gone daft in the head?"

Colin had parked next to him and loaded his own equipment. "Well, then, that marks last night as sharing material." He closed the back of his own SUV. "So how was it?"

Will stared at him long and hard, then grinned. "Great."

"I knew it!"

"More than great—it was incredible. I mean, I don't know if it's because I'd gone without for so long, but we went at it for a good twenty hours straight. Well, I mean, with time-out for catnaps and showers and the like."

Colin blinked at him, the humor wiped from his face. "Twenty hours?"

Will nodded, thinking he'd need a crowbar to pry the grin from his face. "Uh-huh. Twenty hours. And even then we stopped only because we ran out of bloody rubbers."

Colin didn't say anything.

And Will decided he didn't like the thoughtful expression he wore. "What? Oh, for Christ's sake, what are you thinking now?"

"Oh, I don't know. I'm thinking last night might not have been about just sex."

"Are you insane? Of course it was. Whatever else might it have been about?"

Colin continued staring at him for a long moment, then shook his head and walked toward the driver's side of his SUV. "You forget, I'm a couples counselor."

"Oh, God, here it comes." Will wiped his face on a towel he'd taken from his bag then threw it back into the truck and closed the door. "I knew I'd regret covering for you back in med school."

Colin chuckled. "It's just that in my professional opinion when a relationship is just about sex, any sexual encounters last no longer than a half hour— an hour max."

Will pointed at him over the hood of his car. "Those are the key words. 'In your experience.'"

"In my professional experience."

Will scowled as he opened his car door. "Yeah, well, who asked for your opinion, professional or otherwise? I don't recall doing it."

He looked over to find Colin grinning at him. "Harry's?" he asked.

Will was half tempted to tell him to bugger off. "Harry's," he said, then closed his door and started the engine, pointing his SUV in the direction of the sports bar a short distance away.

Not about sex.

What a ridiculous notion.

THE FOLLOWING MORNING Renae was still smiling.

And still hadn't gotten around to doing her laundry.

She closed and locked the condo door after herself then turned toward the stairs, trying to keep from making too much noise in her belly-dancer costume.

Well, at least she'd gotten some sleep. After Tabitha and Nina had gone out to the movies at around six last night, she'd curled up on her bed with the latest yummy Stephanie Plum offering and had immediately fallen asleep, not to awaken again until her alarm went off an hour ago at six.

She supposed her body had needed the rest considering the workout she'd given it at Will's place Saturday night. But still, it had been a long time since she'd needed more than eight hours.

She began descending the stairs, her gaze automatically going to the door of 2B and a grin the size of Ohio took hold of her face. Just thinking about what she and Will had done...

Wow.

Of course, she had no intention of seeing him again. Well, aside from running into him in the hall. Their repeating what had happened was not in the cards.

A little voice asked her why.

And she answered. First, there was no way in the world they could possibly better what had happened between them. That night…that night easily ranked up there with the best sex she'd ever had.

She gave a little shiver.

Second, there was the matter of Will's girlfriend. There was no mistaking that he was seriously involved or else he wouldn't have brought her up before they'd headed to his place. And if there was one thing Renae wasn't interested in, it was becoming the other woman. She'd never been that stupid and certainly wasn't about to start now, no matter how good the sex.

And the sex had been good, hadn't it?

She rounded the staircase and began heading down the last leg toward the door, then stopped, much as she had two mornings ago.

There just entering through the door was Will, looking at her in the same stunned way she was looking at him.

"Um, hi," she said, forcing herself to descend the remainder of the stairs and ignore the watery condition of her knees.

He didn't immediately respond and she knew a moment of disappointment. Oh, don't tell her this was going to turn into one of those awkward morning-afters. A twist on the pillow-shock syndrome, awkward morning-afters were worse, mostly because, when you suffered from PSS, neither of you cared what the other one thought—your mutual goal was only to get out the door quick.

But with AMA, one of the parties remembered the tryst favorably while the other ran as far as they could as fast as they could in the opposite direction.

"Um, hi, yourself," Will finally said.

Renae made a face. Definitely AMA. And Will was the one doing the running.

All right. That was okay. She could deal with that. It wasn't like she was looking to repeat what had happened between them the other night anyway.

She began to pass Will, trying to come up with something casual, light to say before diving for the door, when he finally lifted his gaze from the floor, skimmed her costume, then said with a grin that nearly made her cream herself, "What would you say if I requested a repeat of the other night... costume included?"

Renae suddenly had a hard time swallowing. "I'd ask you when and where."

Will stared at her mouth. "How about here and now."

Renae smiled. "Supplies?"

He held up a bag and shook it. "Replenished."

"Then I'd say lead the way."

CHAPTER SIX

SOMEWHERE IN THE BACK of Will's mind he knew a moment of pause. A part of him that he didn't want to give voice to understood that he shouldn't be doing what he was doing. When he'd stopped at the pharmacy on the way home from the hospital that morning to stock up on condoms, he'd convinced himself that he'd been doing it because he and Janet might finally be knee deep in some sex when she returned from California at the end of the week.

But a wicked little voice told him he'd known what he'd been doing all along. That's why he'd sped home, hoping he wouldn't miss Renae when she left for work.

He unlocked his condo door and hustled her inside, liking the way the metal disks on her costume chimed with her every move. Liking the way she looked all soft and hot and sexy in the decadent clothes. And liking that he'd be getting her out of the garments as soon as humanly possible.

And if he doubted she felt the same, the thought was banished when she launched herself into his arms, metal disks and all, kissing him as hungrily as if he were breakfast and she hadn't eaten for days.

The bare skin of her back was silky soft as he sought a release for the top, gave up then dove for the back of the waist.

She laughed and moved out of reach with a clang of disks. "Wait a sec. I have to call into the shop and let them know I'm going to be a little late."

Will raised a brow. "A little?"

He took her hand and pressed it against his rock-hard arousal through the thin material of his scrubs. He watched her pupils grow large in her green eyes.

"Okay," she said slowly, "a lot late."

He reached out and dipped a fingertip inside the top of her bra cup. "Tell them you'll be out the whole day."

He watched her swallow with some difficulty. "The whole day?" A slow, sultry smile spread across her lips. "You really are looking to repeat the other night, then."

He nodded. "And then some."

RENAE'S FINGERS trembled so badly it took three attempts for her to extract her cell phone from her purse. Will had worked her right breast up and out of the top of the costume and was even now pressing his tongue against her distended nipple.

She suppressed a moan and gave him a slight shove. "Give me a minute."

He made a show of looking at his watch. "I'll give you twenty seconds."

Renae pressed the button on her cell for her phone book and received the message that there were no entries.

She stared at the color display, pressed the phone book button again with the same result.

That's odd. She had no fewer than fifty entries in there, the one for the shop the most important.

Will began to advance on her and she backed away, laughing. "You'd better behave or I won't give you a show."

"A show?"

She wondered if all Brits were as sexily handsome as Will was. If they were, she'd have to arrange a visit to London posthaste. "Uh-uh."

She shut off the wireless phone, then powered it back up, only to receive the same message that there were no entries in her phone book.

That was strange....

Will pulled off his green scrub top, revealing

every inch of his honed and toned arms and stomach. Renae's mouth watered and for the life of her she couldn't recall the number for the shop.

Finally she was able to enter it, and then she was shutting off the cell and bunching her fingers in Will's hair. He was down on his knees in front of her, his face buried against her bare stomach.

"I love these belly ring things," he said, dipping the tip of his tongue inside her navel then through the thin ring that bore a red stone.

A shiver washed over Renae's body, the air-conditioning vent above her partially to blame.

Will's hot and wet attentions more to blame.

"Do you want me to give you a private demonstration or not?" she whispered.

"Hmm. Definitely yes."

"Do you have music?"

He blinked at her as if she'd asked him if he had lobster in the fridge.

"Something Greek would be nice. Or Middle Eastern."

Will seemed cemented to the spot on his knees in front of her.

It was all Renae could do not to pull down the tight, elastic waist of the costume bottoms and let him continue what he was doing.

A light seemed to brighten his eyes. "Sting."

Renae frowned. The pop singer Sting was

not exactly what she had in mind when it came to belly-dancing music. But Will was already in front of his stereo console, searching through an extensive collection of CDs then feeding one into the player.

Immediately the sound of Middle Eastern music filled the condo, along with the voice of an Arabic singer.

"Desert Rose by Sting," Will elaborated.

While it wasn't the exact belly-dancing beat she'd been looking for, she determined that she could make it work. Hell, at this point, with Will looking at her like he wanted to swallow her whole, she probably could have shaken her hips to Barbra Streisand, and Will and she would have been satisfied.

Shaking out her arms, she stretched them in front of her. Then she joined her index fingers and lifted her hands above her head. She found the stretch helped loosen up her muscles and get her into the mood. She slowly swung her left hip forward and began a tiny gyration, the disks sewn into the costume clinking.

She watched Will's eyes darken as she caught her rhythm. Slow at first. Concentrating on one hip, then the next. Rippling her stomach in a way that made it impossible for him to look anywhere but there. She shimmied her shoulders, threading her hands out in open invitation even as she gently threw her head back. She drew on the experience that teaching the classes had given her but which she seldom got to use in its intended way. Heat curled deep in her belly, making her hot. Too hot.

She leveled the tilt of her head, looking at him from under the fringe of her lashes as she increased the rhythm of her suggestive movements, making the disks clink faster.

"Fuck me."

Renae nearly burst out laughing. She knew the expletive was the British equivalent of "shit" or "what the hell," not meant to be taken literally. But she wasn't so sure if that's the meaning Will had intended as he practically dove at her. He pinned her to the overstuffed cushions of his sofa in a tangle of limbs and noisy disks.

"Wait," she whispered breathlessly after fighting to keep up with his kisses and batting his hands away from her costume. "Do you know how much this thing cost? Ginger would kill me if I ruined it."

"I'll buy you ten."

She laughed and bit his bottom lip.

"Ow. What did you go and do that for?"

"Give me a minute."

"Another one? But I just gave you one."

"You gave me twenty seconds."

He reluctantly pulled back. "Fine. I'll give you the other forty. But only if you promise not to take them all."

Renae got up and got out of the costume as quickly as she could. Before she could finish draping the top over a nearby chair, Will was tackling her back to the sofa. She caught herself on all fours just as he positioned himself behind her.

She thought about making a crack about his impatience for all of a nanosecond, but found she didn't have the time to voice anything as his hands curved around her waist then dove for her sex. She gasped as he parted her flesh with one hand, then skillfully stroked her bared feminine folds with the fingers of his other one.

"Oh, you're good," she whispered, every inch of her shivering in instant response to his attentions.

"You have no idea."

Renae leaned back, bearing against him. "Oh, I think I have an idea. But if it's all the same to you, I think I could do without repeating the beginning of the last time."

He chuckled against her back then thrust two fingers deep inside her slick opening. Renae gasped, the chaos swirling inside her gaining momentum.

Her eyelids drifted closed and she felt a peculiar type of heat suffuse her muscles.

"Mmm…so tight…so wet."

Will twisted his fingers as he withdrew them then thrust them back up, stretching her muscles, readying her for him.

It was eight o'clock on a Monday morning and Renae was about to have sex with Will on his couch. The total sinfulness of the act set her nerve endings on fire and made her take a look at life through slightly askew glasses. She was normally so responsible, so focused. But one depraved grin from Will and she was calling in sick and stripping naked so he could have his way with her.

So she could have her way with him.

Reaching between her legs, she decided she'd had enough foreplay. She wanted to feel him inside her now. This instant.

She was slightly surprised to find him already sheathed as she grasped his hard girth and guided the knob of his arousal to her dripping entrance. He slid his fingers from her and replaced them with his erection, nearly driving her straight over the edge with the first thrust.

Oh, yes… This was definitely better than work. Better than being a responsible adult living a responsible life. The utter recklessness of her actions left her feeling powerful and different and…alive, for the first time in so very long that she wanted it to last and last.

Will seemed to tune in to her needs as he slowly withdrew, drawing out the action so that she was aware of every beat of her heart, every wash of blood through her veins, every molecule of oxygen she pulled into her lungs. He placed one hand at the small of her back and the other on her hip, holding her still when she might have bore back on him. Then he entered her again just as slowly, torturously, filling her to overflowing, making her feel as substantial as a puddle of melting hormones.

She heard a long, low moan and realized it was her own as sweet, unbearable pressure built up in her lower abdomen. A pressure that spiked with each of Will's skillful strokes. The feel of his white leather sofa was soft under her knees and palms, the heat of his flesh hot against her backside. She wanted—needed—him to increase the pace, her mind suspended between sensation and a desire for release so intense she lost track of time and place. Will moved so that his right foot was on the floor and he continued his slow strokes…in…out…in…out.

Renae's breath hitched high in her throat, making her think she might never take another normal breath again. Then the hand at the small of her back slid to her other hip and his grip increased enough for her to be aware of it. Just as she registered the change, he thrust into her to the hilt, his rhythm not only increasing, but his strokes growing more powerful, demanding. She arched her back and bore back against him. He held her still as he thrust deeply again and again, creating a kaleidoscope of color on the back of her eyelids, launching her into a parallel world that was pure sensation and fundamental human need. With each of his thrusts, her breasts swayed and the slap of his flesh against hers grew louder, challenging the volume of her low moans.

"Christ, what you do to me."

Will's words foretold his crisis and precipitated hers, the tension in her exploding, the chaos taking over her body and swirling and swirling around, her stomach convulsing, her lungs straining to take in a breath. But rather than stop his movements, Will increased the tempo of his strokes, his groan mingling with her moan.

And making Renae wish he would never stop.

THREE HOURS LATER Will lay with the back of his head hanging over the foot of his bed while Renae lay crosswise across the mattress, her legs entangled with his. He'd barely had any sleep for a good twenty hours, and then he'd put in a grueling twelve-hour shift at the hospital during which he'd treated no fewer than seven teenagers apparently involved in some sort of gang dispute, and four car accident victims, one of whom had been life-flighted in. But damned if he felt tired. Sated, maybe. Horny, definitely. But not tired.

Even as he grinned like a fool, he thought there was something wrong there. While sex had always been important to him, he'd never felt such an insatiable need to have it with one woman for long, uninterrupted hours without a break. But he'd be damned if even after three hours and countless orgasms he didn't want to roll Renae over and have at her again.

He lifted his head and zoned in on her pert, supple backside. The hell with turning her over. He'd take her like that.

The bedding rustled as she turned her head to look in his direction, her flushed, smiling face mirroring what he felt.

"Wow," she said.

Will had a hard time swallowing as he let his head loll back over the side of the bed. "Quite definitely wow."

He was aware that Renae was trying to free her right leg from where it was pinned under his, but she wasn't making much of an effort and he couldn't seem to scare up the energy to allow her the freedom. Instead she rolled over and he watched through half-lidded eyes as she pushed herself up into a sitting position.

"You know I'm not a lesbian, don't you?"

Will's brows rose. "Pardon me?"

She made two attempts before she was able to both balance herself and push her hair from her face. "Tabitha and I are just roommates. We're not a couple in the romantic sense. In fact, I guess you didn't realize it but Tabitha has a girlfriend named Nina, who lives with us, too."

Will made a face and shifted until his head was supported by the mattress. "Well, there goes my favorite fantasy."

She smiled in his general direction.

Will pulled in a deep breath then let it out slowly. "I sort of guessed as much. I mean, if you were a true lesbian, you wouldn't have slept with me, much less stuck around following our...unfortunate beginning."

The mattress began to shake although Will heard no sound. He realized she was laughing. "What's that supposed to mean?"

He shrugged and folded his arms under the back of his head. "Oh, I don't know. I suppose every now and again even homosexuals desire sex with those they normally wouldn't. But if you were truly gay, after my...Quick Withdraw McGraw routine, as you so rudely put it, well, a true homosexual probably would have shaken her head and left, her belief in the opposite sex's inability to perform confirmed."

Renae's laughing presumably took so much of her sapped energy she could no longer support her upright position. She fell solidly back to the bed, making Will's head bounce. When her laughter finally subsided, she repositioned herself until she was stretched out next to him. They weren't touching, but for some odd reason Will felt closer to the woman next to him than he'd felt to another person in a long, long time. He almost finished that thought with the words "if ever," but ignored them, not about to go there.

"Has anyone ever told you you're narrow-minded?" she asked, reaching for a pillow off the floor and bunching it under her head.

Will tried to steal the pillow. "I'm not narrow-minded. I'm subjective."

Renae swatted his hand away from her pillow. "Which means?"

Will finally gave up on the pillow and, using his feet and hands, grabbed his own from the other side of the bed. "Meaning I see things the way I want to see them. If I chose to see things the way you see them, then, well, my lesbian fantasy wouldn't hold any water now, would it? Because a true lesbian wouldn't be attracted to the opposite sex no matter how sexy." He waggled his brows at her. "Which brings me back to my sensing that you weren't truly a lesbian."

He watched as she twisted her lips. "You have a convoluted way of thinking. But at least it takes you where you need to be." She turned her head to look at him. "Tabitha *is* a lesbian, however."

Will found the energy to turn to his side and prop his head on his hand. "Do tell."

Her green eyes sparkled at him.

"Maybe my lesbian fantasy doesn't have to die a slow and torturous death after all."

She pulled the pillow from behind her head and whacked him with it. After she was settled again, she fell silent for a long moment, apparently mapping out the tiny lines in the ceiling.

Then she finally said, "So...tell me about the resident."

CHAPTER SEVEN

ONE MINUTE WILL FELT like he was drifting on a warm ocean wave with nothing more important to do than stay afloat, the next a big white shark had come out of nowhere and made a beeline for his privates.

"Uh-oh. Wrong question?"

Will suddenly found it difficult to swallow. "No…no. Not so much a wrong question, really, as the wrong time."

Renae rolled to her side to face him. "Well, seeing as whenever we're together we're in bed, when would be the right time?"

Will couldn't bring himself to look directly into her eyes. "Oh, I don't know. Never?"

And just like that all the humor was drained out of the moment for him.

Oh, he didn't mistake himself for an angel by any stretch, but it had been a good long time since he'd viewed cheating on a girlfriend as acceptable behavior. Well, maybe not so much acceptable as understandable. There had been the time in med school when the hot anatomy teacher had offered to give him a tour of her own private anatomy and to demonstrate her considerable knowledge of the male anatomy, and Will had been loath to refuse the offer, despite that he was dating a fellow student at the time. And another occasion when a close friend of another girl he'd been dating had let spill her fantasies about him, and he'd found recreating them in reality momentarily irresistible.

But all that had transpired years ago when he'd been young and brash and a slave to his libido. Surely even he had grown up a little since.

He drew in a deep breath and slowly released it. Explain then how he'd been able to talk to Janet on the phone for a good half hour the night before, offering a sympathetic ear to her complaints about the hotel staff and the loss of her notes. Renae and their shenanigans had not even entered on the fringes of his mind, just as when he was with Renae, Janet didn't even rate a passing thought.

He grimaced at the thought.

The bedding rustled and he looked at where Renae was lying on her stomach, her chin buried in the middle of her pillow while she considered the wall-to-wall carpeting. Will couldn't resist a visual sweep of her gloriously bare body, from her tanned feet to her rounded rump to her smooth shoulders and dark blond hair.

"You and the resident have a good sex life?" she asked.

Now there was a question. "Actually we don't have a sex life. At least not one to speak of…yet." Curious how the "yet" almost didn't seem connected to the rest of his sentence. It was more of an afterthought than a given.

He watched her brows raise then she turned her head on the pillow and smiled at him. "None?"

He shook his head.

Her smile widened and he had the feeling he was going to regret letting that particular cat out of the bag. "Well, then, there's really no need for the guilt written across your face now, is there?"

Will blinked at her, as if bringing her into sharper focus would have the same effect on her words. "Pardon me?"

She shifted until she lay on her side again, wonderfully unconcerned with her nakedness. "There's a point in there somewhere. Would you like me to explain it to you?"

There were a lot of other things he wanted her to do but he supposed he really should start with that. "Mmm. Yes, I would."

"Well, you're feeling bad because you're in bed with me while we discuss the resident."

"Go on."

"My point is that if you're not sleeping with her, then you're not being unfaithful to her."

"Interesting point." That did absolutely nothing to erase his feeling of guilt.

"No, really. Think about it. Until the both of you commit physically, well, then it's impossible for you to be physically unfaithful."

"So following your reasoning, a man about to go to the altar is free to do what he wants until he utters the words 'I do.'"

She laughed. "No, silly. An agreement is implied then. An engagement." Her eyes widened. "There's no ring involved with you and the resident, is there?"

"No."

"Whew. Thank God. You scared me for a minute there."

"Yes, well, consider what you're doing to me."

She pushed up onto her elbow and looked at him. "This is really bothering you, isn't it?"

"No," he lied. "The fact that I'm discussing it with you is a cause of some concern, though."

Her eyes danced with light. "Because I'm the other woman."

"Because you're lying naked in my bed."

"Ah."

"Yes, very definitely 'ah.'"

She twisted her lips, emphasizing how very full and kissable they were. "Would you like me to leave?"

Surprisingly their conversation had momentarily impacted Big Ben's control over Will. But as he looked at the pert tips of Renae's breasts, the smooth skin of her stomach, the neat triangle of hair between her legs, Ben was quickly reasserting his dominance.

"No."

"So you want me to stay then?"

"No," he said just as quickly.

She laughed. "Well, since I'm not about to hide in your closet if, when and until you decide, maybe I'd better go."

"No," he said again, gripping her arm when she might have rolled off the other side of the bed.

He gazed into her face, thinking of how incredibly sexy she was. How inappropriately irresistible. While he may have been unfaithful to women before, even the anatomy teacher and the friend of his ex hadn't managed to keep his attention for longer than a couple of hours.

But Renae...

It was going on the fourth hour of his second sexual tryst with her and not only wasn't he tiring of Renae Truesdale's company, he wanted more of it. Of her.

"I've got an interesting question for you," he said quietly.

"Oh?"

"Don't you think it a bit odd that you're not jealous of…the resident?" He winced at following Renae's lead and calling Janet "the resident" rather than referring to her by name. But Janet wasn't the topic of conversation right now. Rather Renae and her curious behavior were what interested him.

"Jealous?"

"Mmm. I mean, for all intents and purposes I'm dating someone else. And while I might not have had sex with her…yet," he forced himself to add, "I've wanted to."

"And because of that I should be jealous?"

"Well…yes. Wouldn't that be the normal human reaction to the situation?"

"Depends on your definition of normal."

He conceded the point. "So yours differs from most everyone else's then?"

"Maybe it isn't the definition so much as the circumstances. And the circumstances in this particular situation—"

"Our situation."

"—are that I knew you were involved with someone when we began having sex."

"Mmm. But that doesn't explain why you're not jealous now that we've surpassed one-night stand territory."

Her laughter, which usually inspired in him lustful thoughts, now seemed to rub him the wrong way. "I wouldn't classify what's going on as a long-term relationship, Will."

"No, I don't suppose you would."

She remained silent for long moments, the smile slipping from her face as she openly considered him. "Would you? Classify this as a relationship?"

"Well, there lies the dilemma, doesn't it?"

"I'm not following you."

He sighed heavily and ran his hand over his face. He needed a shave, a shower. But he couldn't seem to scare up the energy for either.

He looked at where Renae's belly ring glinted up at him, calling his attention to her supple abdomen, her smooth flesh. He idly wondered how he even had the energy to think about taking up where they'd left off.

"Of course you're not following me," he offered up. "Simply because I don't know where in the hell I'm going with this, either."

The uncomfortable feeling in the pit of his gut had him worried. He supposed it was only natural considering the situation he'd put himself in. It was guilt, plain and simple.

He glanced at the woman next to him. Then again, it could be something else entirely.

"Are you seeing anybody?" he asked.

RENAE FELT LAUGHTER bubble up from her chest. Will and his obvious struggle with morality was nothing if not the cutest thing she'd ever witnessed.

"Excuse me?" she asked.

He waved his hand. "I mean, I know we've already established that you're not involved with your roommate. But is there…a man anywhere in the picture?"

"Hmm. A man."

He really was having trouble with this, wasn't he?

Renae propped her head on her hand. When she'd agreed to play hooky from work—something she'd never even thought about doing before, much less did— to spend the day in bed with Will, the last thing she would have expected was this peculiar conversation.

"If you're asking if I'm dating anyone, my answer would have to be no."

"Engaged in a harmless flirtation?"

She laughed. "No."

"Talking to an old flame on the phone?"

"No."

"Fixed some poor sap in your sights?"

"No."

He looked strangely relieved and disappointed by the news simultaneously.

"I'm currently man-free." She reached out and smoothed his hair back from his forehead. "Present company excepted, of course."

"Mmm. Of course." He turned his head to look at her. "And you're truly not jealous. Not in the least."

Renae's hand hesitated at his temple. Then she smiled, drew her finger along the line of his cheek then down to his jawline and kissed him. "Not in the least."

Now had he been sleeping with the resident…

Renae caught her mind traveling down the unwanted avenue and tried to draw it to a halt.

But the truth was that the instant he admitted that he and the woman he was dating weren't engaging in any sack sessions, that the resident hadn't spent the night in the bed they were currently in while she had spent a nice-size chunk of the past three days there…well, gave her a bit of satisfaction, however wicked.

Not that she'd ever let Will know that. Oh, no.

No matter how deliciously tortured he looked, she wouldn't feed that tidbit to his enormous ego.

Speaking of enormous…her gaze dropped to his semierect male member that was large even in slumber. And a part of her was glad that she knew that over the resident. Liked that when she reached out, she could touch the warm flesh, watching as it grew thicker, more erect. Reveled in the feel of its hardness in her palm, a hardness caused by her and her actions.

"So tell me more about these fantasies you used to have about me and Tabitha," she coaxed, her mouth watering with the desire to taste him against her tongue.

Will groaned as she completely encircled his girth and gave a calculated squeeze. "'Used to have' being the key words," he said, dipping his chin into his chest so he could watch her. "But of course you shot all that down by revealing you weren't a lesbian. Or at least bi. Bi would have been nice. Because it means you—"

Renae scooted closer to him and pressed her tongue against the head of his need. She looked up at him. "Has anyone ever told you you talk too much?"

"No. Never. Perhaps it's nerves. Or guilt. Guilt does the strangest things to—"

Renae moved her mouth over the head of his

arousal and swirled her tongue along the sensitive rim, satisfied when his sentence ended in a low, needy groan.

She slid her mouth farther down his length and applied suction, then released him. "You were saying?"

"I was saying?" His eyes had a faraway look in them. "To hell with what I was saying. Just continue."

She gave a quiet chuckle and did just that.

CHAPTER EIGHT

THE FOLLOWING NIGHT Will was no closer to making sense out of what was going on inside his head than he'd been the morning before—with or without Renae's decadent mouth on his person.

He swept through the waiting area of St. Vincent Mercy Medical Center, not willing any ill fortune on the general population but wishing things were a little busier so he could occupy his mind with something other than the dilemma he was currently facing. He'd been on the job for an hour and it felt like he'd been there at least ten.

He ran into first-year resident Evan Hadley coming out of one of the examining rooms. "Hey," Will said. "Anything interesting happening?"

Evan had everything going for him: good-looking, clever, with the type of all-American football-hero grin that made the nurses swoon. Will would have hated him on sight if he hadn't been instrumental in bringing the resident on board as a favor to one of his college professors.

Besides, the nurses had swooned over Will in the beginning, too. But once someone on the staff reached the one-year point, and fresh blood came in, the previous object of the nurses' affection was cast aside.

Evan was shaking his head. "Nope. Nose-bleed."

Will made a face. "That's about as exciting as it gets tonight."

Evan nodded as he made a notation on the chart he held. "Makes me wish I was still in L.A. Even a boring medical convention is more interesting than this."

Will pointed at him. "That's right. You attended the first weekend, didn't you? Did you run into Janet?"

"Once or twice in the hall." He shrugged. "What's it look like today from your side of the center?"

"Even more dead than on your side."

Evan began walking toward the nurses' station. "I guess we should hope it stays that way."

"I guess."

Will glanced at his watch, conversed with a couple of the nurses about ongoing cases, then walked back toward the locker room, his thoughts circling back to Renae. He tried to convince himself that it was the void that allowed her entrance, but the truth was he couldn't seem to shake her from his mind no matter how hard he tried.

Despite his strange conversation with her the day before, precipitated by her asking about Janet, they'd gone on to spend not only the remainder of that morning in bed having phenomenal sex, but the rest of the day, getting up only to raid the fridge and place a call for Chinese delivery. And they'd ordered lots of it, because not only did everyone know that you were hungry again a half hour after eating Chinese food, but at the rate he and Renae were burning calories, they'd needed the sustenance.

Funny, he'd never factored in pure exhaustion as a reason to stop having sex.

At somewhere around four in the afternoon he'd fallen into a dead sleep only to wake to the sound of the alarm at seven-thirty…alone. No note. No panties left behind on his bedside lamp. No sign that Renae had been there at all.

Well, except for his memories, his tired muscles and her scent, which seemed to be everywhere.

The maddening woman was out to drive him insane. He could feel it in his bones.

And the idea that she was in it only for the sex

bothered him on some level he was reluctant to pursue.

"Bugger."

That didn't make any sense, now, did it, it bothering him that she was after him just for the sex? After all, he was only in it for the sex, so why shouldn't Renae feel the same way? His judging her actions as somehow…questionable emerged as downright sexist. The whole what's good for the goose is not good for the gander argument. The man was a stud, the woman a slut syndrome.

He slapped the chart he was carrying down on the round table then sat in one of the five chairs, the locker room blessedly empty at the beginning of the shift. In an hour or so the opposite would be true as the night staff began coming and going, restlessness settling in.

Only Will's restlessness seemed to be a constant presence these days.

He didn't find it the least bit amusing that it had been his restlessness, his sexual frustration, that had chased him into Renae's arms to begin with. Now it was Renae's arms—and his not wanting to leave them—that were the cause of his restlessness.

Colin had been right to stay out of this one. Hell, if *he* could find a way out, he'd take it.

If only Renae had been the least bit clingy…

asked him to stop seeing Janet…displayed just a hint of jealousy, he suspected everything would be different.

And there lay the quandary.

Will had never believed himself to be shallow. But he couldn't help thinking if he was—if men in general were—it was because of the women they dated. He'd faced his share of scornful women who had willingly shared his bed one night, knowing there would be nothing beyond that and then had hated him when he didn't call them the next day anyway.

Was the reason why he'd sought Renae out after the first time because she hadn't expected him to call? Hadn't expected anything from him, period?

Will rested his head against his hand and scratched his temple. If that was the case then there was more than a little merit to those books on dating rules and the whole Mars-Venus angle that he'd scoffed at such a short time ago. Could it be true that all women had to do was play hard to get? Make the man feel like he had to work to get her attention, and—bam!—the man in question was a goner?

Another curious question began forming in the back of his mind. Would he even still be dating

Janet had she slept with him early on in their relationship?

He glanced at his watch again. Oh, boy, this was certainly getting him nowhere fast.

Of course, the mind-set of the woman in question would actually have to be for real. Janet genuinely wanted to wait for her wedding night. Renae was genuinely in it just for the sex. He didn't think he'd be struggling with thoughts of either of them—or thinking about them at all—had he sensed that they were playing games. Like if Renae showed even a hint of "I'm pretending I don't care, but I'm just playing with you, but could you call tomorrow anyway?" Or if he saw in Janet anything that equaled, "I'm not giving you sex because it's my way of manipulating you into paying for the most expensive wedding this side of the Atlantic."

Then there was another question: Was it possible to want two different women for two completely different reasons?

He glanced toward the sealed window at the dark night beyond. Was it possible for him to be in any worse shape?

There was a brief knock on the door and then it opened inward, revealing Janet's father, Dr. Stuart Nealon, who also just happened to be the head of staff at the hospital.

Will swallowed hard as he scrambled to a standing position.

"Will, there you are," Stuart said, his face looking stern. "I was hoping we could have a talk, you and I. Man to man."

Oh, yeah, he realized with growing dread, it was very possible for things to get worse. And they just had.

RENAE FOLDED thick Turkish terry cloth robes and stacked them on the display shelf at Women Only, her thoughts as far away as where the robes had come from. Before she knew it, she reached the bottom of the shipping box and stood for long moments blinking as if unsure what to do with it.

"The robes are nice, but they're not that nice."

She looked up to find Lucky coming into the main showroom from the dance room. Lately the pretty redhead had been coming in after-hours to do some stretching and simple calisthenics, claiming she needed to wind down after a long day of trying to get her shop together downtown and before she went home to Colin.

Renae smiled and shook her head. "Sorry, what did you say? I just can't seem to concentrate on anything lately."

Lucky came to lean against the checkout counter, her gaze homing in on Renae's face. "I was just commenting on your distractedness." She took the box from her and began collapsing it so it would fit in the Dumpster out back.

"I was hoping Ginger would come by tonight. She's barely been in the shop all week and…" And Renae had been hoping to talk to her.

Lucky squinted at her. "Look, Renae, there's obviously something going on that I don't know about, something you've been reluctant to talk about."

Was it that obvious? Renae picked up some packing material from the floor.

"I just wanted to let you know that if you need an ear, I'm here, you know?"

She stood up and took in the genuine affection on Lucky's face. "I know," she said quietly.

And that's exactly when she decided to talk.

But it wasn't about Will and their…strange but exciting rendezvous, even though he seemed to be taking up more and more of her thought space recently. Rather for the first time since the idea had taken root, she poured out to Lucky all her professional hopes, all her dreams.

"I don't know where to start," she said, deciding the beginning would be best. "When Ginger took me on five years ago, I never thought beyond the next minute. You know, stock the shelves, come up with new ideas that women might be interested in—"

"Give massages, teach belly-dancing classes," Lucky added with a warm smile.

"Exactly. Everything was going fine. I mean, I was happy with my job. Happy working with Ginger."

"But..."

Renae hadn't realized she'd fallen silent until Lucky prompted her. "But...no, not but. I'm still very happy here. I can't think of any place else I'd like to work. It's just that...my interest has evolved."

"Interest in the shop?"

Renae nodded, stared at where she still held the packing material in her hands then rounded the counter to throw it away. "First Leah Westwood announces plans to open a sister shop near Sylvania. I mean, I knew she was part owner here, but..."

"Then you hired me on...." Lucky lead on.

Renae smiled at her. "You know where I'm going with this, don't you?"

"Mmm. I suspect I've known since before even you realized it." She drew up beside her and slung an arm around her. "You don't want to merely work here anymore, you want to buy into Women Only. Or maybe even open a sister shop of your own."

Renae stared at her.

Lucky smiled. "What's say we go into the parlor and talk about this over a cup of ginseng tea?"

Despite the added weight to her shoulders caused by Lucky's arm, Renae felt like a hundred pounds had been lifted from her. Now that she'd spoken the words aloud, her hopes and her dreams didn't seem like some sort of wispy, insubstantial fog, but a solid ladder leading to heights unknown.

And as Renae followed Lucky into the other room, she discovered her heart was pounding with the desire to climb as high as she could go.

"WHERE DO THINGS STAND between you and my daughter?"

Will blinked at the elder Nealon. Upon hunting Will down, er, finding him in the staff locker room, he'd suggested they go to the cafeteria for coffee and a doughnut. Will had skipped the doughnut, and wished he'd gone for the decaffeinated coffee because his nerves were already stretched taut, his hand nearly shaking when he lifted the paper cup to his lips.

"Pardon me?" he very nearly croaked.

Stuart grinned. "Did you think you'd be able to keep your dating Janet from me for long?"

Will put his cup down and shook his head, trying for a casual grin of his own. "No, sir, I didn't. I just didn't think you'd find out about us so soon."

In all honesty, he hadn't been thinking at all when it came to Janet's connection to the hospital chief of staff. It had been two weeks into their dating that he'd even learned of the connection. And by then he'd already been knee-deep into his plan to seduce the pretty resident.

"Yes, well, I've actually known for some time. Since the beginning, in fact. You see, my daughter and I don't have many secrets."

Will was glad he hadn't been sipping coffee just then or else he might have spewed it all over the other man.

"She made me promise not to say anything to you, though."

Then why was he telling him now?

Will absently rubbed his chin. "Yes, well…I've grown very…fond of your daughter, sir."

Stuart waved his hand. "Enough with the 'sir' bit, Sexton. You've worked here for how long now?"

"Nearly six years, sir." And two years ago Stuart Nealon had been elevated to chief of staff.

Stuart's grin widened. "I think that's long enough for us to advance to something more personal. Please call me Stuart."

Will nodded. "Stuart. Yes, right then. Stuart."

Why was he getting the impression that Stuart was going to ask him what his intentions were toward his daughter? And just what "secrets" hadn't the two kept from each other? Did his boss know that he had yet to have sex with his daughter? Or did he think the two of them were going at it at every opportunity?

Stuart's stern face didn't give anything away. Will knew that one didn't rise to Stuart's level without having learned a certain amount of self-control—and a really good poker face.

"Anyway, as luck would have it Janet is not the reason I wanted to speak to you."

Will fought not to blink. "Oh?"

"Yes. You see, I've had my eye on you for some time now, Sexton." He shook his finger at him. "You've made quite an impression on me and on everyone you work with."

Will's ego inflated at the bit of flattery even as a warning alarm went off in the back of his head.

"I seem to recall your being interested in a day position in the trauma center...."

"Um, yes, sir. I mean, Stuart. I was and am still very much interested."

Stuart smiled. "Good. Keep your nose clean, boy, and you just might get what you want."

The older physician stood up and Will followed suit even though he was afraid his knees were knocking together so hard the other man would hear them.

That was it? That's what Stuart had wanted to speak to him about? To tell him he was being considered for the day slot?

Or was his mission to hint, keep his daughter happy and Will would in turn be given a chance at professional happiness?

Oh, what a tangled web we weave, Will thought.

"Pardon?" Stuart asked as he led the way out.

Will blinked at him. "Sir? I didn't say anything."

At least he hoped like hell he hadn't said anything. Because everything he'd been working toward for the past six years hung in the balance.

CHAPTER NINE

THE FOLLOWING DAY was Renae's usual day off and she'd decided to use it to take Lucky up on her advice and come up with a written plan for Ginger to consider. A plan that would give her the option, over time, of buying interest in the shop. A plan that would take her into the future.

The future...

Now that was a concept she hadn't given much consideration to before. Even now—as she lay across Will's bed, spent and sated, one of his legs crossing hers—tomorrow loomed large and mysterious and more than a bit exciting.

"I always wondered what that song 'Afternoon Delight' meant."

Renae chuckled quietly at Will's joke, rolling her ankle to knock it against his. "We've had sex in the afternoon."

"Yes, but until now it usually started at another

point. You know, in the morning...the night before..."

Renae's smile felt plastered to her face.

The last person she'd expected to see at her door an hour earlier had been Will. She'd thought that since he'd worked last night, he'd be asleep. Instead he'd stood at the door looking as irresistible as a double-double chocolate brownie and invited her down to his place for a quickie—he'd said it with an irresistible waggle of his brows that indicated there would be nothing quick about it. Since she'd already put together a lot of what she hoped to present to Ginger, she'd decided she needed the break. The emphasis on break. She intended to be back in her condo by five o'clock in order to put the finishing touches on her proposal.

She felt a hot, meandering hand on her inner thigh and moved her head to watch as Will inched his way toward her throbbing sex.

"I can't believe you. Aren't you tired? You already admitted you haven't gotten any sleep since knocking off work this morning." She glanced at the slender watch still on her wrist, the only thing that remained from what she'd had on an hour earlier. "Seeing as you have to be back at work in four hours..."

"Are you saying you'd rather sleep?"

His fingers reached her swollen womanhood,

the tips following the folds of closed flesh then coaxing them open. A shiver worked its way up from Renae's toes, hitting every spot in between. "I'm saying that maybe you should think about getting some sleep." She swallowed hard as he drew his fingers through her slick channel. "I mean, if I foul up on the job, someone gets a wrong size robe. You screw up, a scalpel shows up on X-ray the next day."

He lightly pinched her hooded flesh. "Very funny."

Renae giggled and moved out of reach, suddenly feeling the desire to talk to him. Just talk. She propped her head on her hand and handed him a pillow, which he took and put under his head. "Did something happen that you want to talk about?"

His brows rose high on his forehead, drawing her attention to his sexily disheveled hair, his naughty eyes. "What makes you ask something like that?"

She shrugged. "I don't know. You seem…a little distracted today, that's all."

He lifted up onto his elbows. "Are you implying that I've been derelict in my sexual duties?"

"No. That's not what I mean at all."

He made a sound of satisfaction. "That's what I thought."

Renae lay back and stared at the ceiling. "Conceited. Definitely conceited."

"Confident. There's a difference, you know."

He reached for her again and she laughed and moved out of touching distance. "You can't possibly want to have sex again."

"Why can't I?"

"Well, for one, I think we finished plowing through every last chapter in the *Kama Sutra* sometime yesterday."

"And your point is?"

"My point is…"

What was her point?

For a moment there, Renae had mistaken Will as someone who was interested in more than sex from her.

And for a moment there, she'd made the mistake of thinking she was interested in more than sex from him.

He rolled to his side. "Uh-oh. What's going on in that pretty little head of yours?"

Renae opened her mouth then snapped it back closed. She realized with a start that she was a breath away from sharing her plans for Women Only with him. Telling him how frustrating it was that she hadn't yet been able to catch up with Ginger. About how Lucky had made her see the light yesterday and she was planning on calling

Ginger later that day to make an actual lunch date so she could pitch her proposal to her flat out. Tell him that spread out upstairs on the kitchen table were her scribbled ideas and plans and all she had to do was put them into some comprehensible order.

"Actually you're right," she said. "I don't have a point."

She began getting up and he curved his fingers around her bare ankle and tugged. "Where are you going?"

"Back to my place. You need some sleep."

"Oh, no, you don't."

He pulled her until she lay alongside him then he pinned her to the bed, hovering above her like some sort of sexy British god. She tried to keep her smile from showing but failed.

"Get off of me right now. You're smooshing me."

He waggled his brows. "You've never complained about my smooshing you before."

"That's because I wanted you to smoosh me then."

"And you don't now?"

Renae caught her bottom lip between her teeth and bit down, his skin against hers making her remember how very much she loved having sex with him. "No."

His expression went suddenly serious. "No?"

He began releasing her.

Renae took the opportunity to trade positions with him and pin him to the bed.

"All that so you could be on top?" he asked as she straddled his hips, putting her sex in direct contact with his. "Completely unnecessary. All you had to do was ask."

Renae leaned in to kiss him.

"Now that's more like it," he said.

The telephone on the bedside table chirped.

They ignored it.

Renae reached toward the opposite bedside table and fished a fresh condom out of the drawer. She ripped it open then held it up above Will's eyes like bait. "Are you sure this is what you want?"

"Give me that rubber."

The telephone continued to ring even as Will grabbed the condom from her fingers.

"Persistent," Renae said, gasping when he suckled on one of her nipples.

"Rejection. They'll get used to it."

The telephone finally stopped its incessant ringing and Renae relaxed, scooting back so Will could put on the condom.

"Now, where were we?"

The telephone instantly began ringing again.

"Bugger," Will cursed.

Renae rolled off him and he took that to mean he should get it.

"Maybe they need you at the hospital," she suggested.

"I have a beeper for that."

"Oh."

Very definitely "oh," Will thought as he sat on the side of the bed and snatched up the receiver.

"This had bloody well better be good," he said into the receiver.

"Will? I'm sorry, did I wake you?"

He shot from the bed so fast you would have thought he'd been catapulted.

Janet.

Jesus Christ and all his Apostles.

"I figured you'd probably be up by now and I had a break between seminars and thought I'd call, you know, to see how you're doing."

He listened to Janet apologize for waking him when he'd been nowhere near asleep but rather about to continue banging the hell out of his up-stairs neighbor. Will stared at where Renae lay across his bed like a siren waiting for him to respond to her tempting song.

He quickly turned from Renae and the bed and paced toward the nearby bathroom.

Shit, shit, shit.

He heard the cradle of the telephone hit the

floor, having inadvertently pulled it from the night table.

"Will? What was that?"

He picked up the cradle, tugged on the line to make sure he had enough give, then headed into the bathroom. "I dropped the phone."

"Hard night?"

Will closed his eyes tightly, remembering that Renae had pretty much asked him the same question a few minutes ago. "No...no, it was fine. I was just a little late getting to sleep after I knocked off this morning, that's all."

"Because you missed me?"

Will met Renae's curious gaze from the bed as if she'd heard the question Janet had asked.

He closed the bathroom door and leaned against it. "Yeah...that must be it."

"Aw, that's sweet. I miss you, too."

How much? was on the tip of his tongue. Where, thankfully, the words stayed.

"Are you still coming to pick me up from the airport this Sunday?" Janet asked.

Sunday. It loomed so far away yet somehow seemed too soon. "Sure, yes."

There was a long pause as Will tried to listen through the wood for what Renae might be doing in the other room.

"Will? Is everything all right?" Janet asked.

He was everything but. "Fine, fine," he said instead. "I just need to hit the toilet and catch a shower is all."

"Okay. I won't keep you then. My seminar starts in a couple of minutes anyway and I want to get a good seat up front."

Good ole Janet, half a country away in California with nothing more serious on her mind than getting a front row seat.

He really was a cad.

"Okay. Have a good seminar, then."

"I will, thanks. Goodbye."

"Bye."

Will began to put the receiver into the cradle of the phone he held in his other hand, then lifted it back to his ear only to change his mind again and finally hang it up.

Well, wasn't that just peachy?

He usually remembered to forward all his calls to voice mail when Renae was over, and if he'd needed a reminder of why, this was it. He'd been hoping to avoid this very incident.

But today he'd forgotten and he'd been caught smack-dab with his pants around his ankles.

He stared at his ankles. Worse, he wasn't even wearing pants. And pretty much hadn't been for the past five days.

He heard a soft knock on the other side of the

bathroom door. He stepped away and opened it. There Renae stood wearing the same clothes she'd had on when he'd gone up to her place to tempt her down here an hour ago. The pink and white striped capris and white tank shouldn't have looked as sexy as they did but, well, there you had it.

"Was it something I said?" he asked, clutching the phone in front of him.

Renae smiled. "I've got to get back to my place."

"Yeah, right. I see."

But did he?

No, he realized, he didn't.

A man who had a firm grip on reality didn't date one woman and not have sex with her, and not date another while having the most incredible sex he'd ever had.

"Would you like me to see you out?"

Renae shook her head as she put on her other sandal, drawing his attention to her incredibly sexy, tanned foot with the neon-pink toenail polish. "Nope. I know the way."

"About tomorrow morning…"

She leaned in and kissed him, then worked her index finger between their lips in order to hold his closed presumably to keep him from finishing his sentence. "Tomorrow morning is tomorrow morning. Let's wait and see what happens then."

"Right. Okay."

He seemed to be saying those inane words a lot lately. But for the life of him, he couldn't seem to rattle another response out of his shell-shocked brain.

And somehow he got the impression that it wasn't going to get any better from there. He'd made—or unmade—his damn bed, and he was just going to have to find a way to either lie in it or get rid of it altogether.

CHAPTER TEN

RENAE LET HERSELF BACK into her condo, puzzled that even though she'd had a great orgasm a few minutes ago, her body was restless, her mind preoccupied with Will and what had just happened.

For a moment there, she had been jealous.

A moment? The instant Will had leapt from the bed, pulled the phone off the nightstand, then disappeared in all his butt-naked glory into the bathroom so he might speak to the resident without Renae overhearing, she'd known an envy so strong it had taken her breath away.

Not good. Not good at all.

Renae closed the door after herself and put her keys on the hall table, looking for a measure of comfort from the familiarity of the condo she'd lived in with Tabitha for the past six months, but oddly not finding it. Part of the reason might have been Nina's having redecorated the entire place.

The soothing earth tones had been "spiced up," as Nina put it, with garish neon-orange pillows and lime-colored throws, making Renae blanch whenever she took a look around the place. But since Tabitha didn't seem to mind the changes, and when all was said and done the condo was hers, Renae had kept her tongue firmly in her mouth.

"Tabby?"

While there was no reason to expect her friend to be home from work yet, she always called out to let whomever was in the apartment know she was there. Since Nina had been laid off a month back, she was the one usually home, but somehow Renae had never warmed to the idea of calling out her name. There was no reason to pretend she liked the other woman. *She* wasn't sleeping with her.

Then again, her own judgment when it came to bed partners might also be a little off-center.

She headed for the kitchen. At least her proposal for Women Only would get her mind off everything. Will, Nina, Tabitha, the fact that if things continued on the way they were she would have to look for a place of her own whether or not Tabby needed financial help. The simple fact was, she felt like a stranger in her own apartment. And that wasn't a good place to be no matter how you viewed it.

Since the afternoon sun had arced to the other

side of the building, she had to switch on the overhead light in the kitchen. And the instant she did, she became aware of something amiss.

The kitchen table was empty, nothing but a fresh bowl of fruit where her notes had been.

Renae's heart did a little flip in her chest.

She rushed to the table, looked around the chairs, then opened the drawer from which she'd gotten the pad and pen. The pad and pen were there, neatly tucked away, as if she'd never used them, the pad not even showing the indents from her words on the top page.

"Nina?" she called out.

As she pulled out the garbage can that held that morning's empty orange juice container and butter wrapper she listened to the silence that greeted her in the condo.

She closed the cabinet door. This wasn't happening.

She turned and took in the room, then systematically made her way through the apartment, beginning with her bedroom where she hoped against hope that Nina had placed her notes on her dresser or bed, somewhere where she might find them. Nothing. She moved on through the dining and living rooms with the same result.

Outside the closed door to Tabitha and Nina's room, she paused. She'd never invaded Tabitha's privacy. If at night the door was open, and Tabitha invited her in, she went without hesitation, often stretching out on the bed next to her friend to catch an episode of *Northern Exposure* or *American Idol*. Of course, that had been before Nina moved in. After that...

Well, after that, Renae barely dared even to look through the open doorway for fear of what she might find. A rational fear since Nina seemed to get a great deal of joy out of moving about the place sans clothes, sometimes with no apparent reason at all. Being comfortable with one's body was one thing. Being an exhibitionist was quite another. And Nina fell solidly in the latter category.

And unfortunately she'd just added thief to the growing list of other names Renae had for her.

Bypassing Tabitha's bedroom, she stepped back into the kitchen and stood there staring at nothing and everything. She gathered the pad and pen from the cabinet drawer, backtracked to her own bedroom, then closed the door, vowing to be more careful about where she placed her things from here on out.

TWO DAYS LATER Renae sat across from Lucky at Coney Island Hot Dog on North Superior—the oldest restaurant in downtown Toledo if you were to believe the words on the window—picking at the contents of her plate, her mind a million miles away. She hadn't seen Will since the phone call incident at his place. Which probably had a lot to do with her going out of her way to avoid him. And his going out of his way to avoid her. Just this morning she'd been at the top of the third-floor stairs and stopped when she'd heard him enter. She'd listened to him check his mailbox—though there would be no mail that early—then climb the steps to his condo. But he must have lingered there in the hall after unlocking his door because she hadn't heard it close. Out of curiosity, she'd backtracked to her condo door, opened it, then shut it. A split second later she'd heard his door close, and he'd been nowhere to be seen when she'd descended the stairs. Obviously he'd wanted no chance meeting.

What had she been thinking, getting involved with someone who lived in the same building?

Correction. She and Will were not involved. They'd had sex. And so long as she could continue to avoid him, and him her, well, there was no worry about any awkward moments.

She caught herself scratching her arm where it was left bare by her black tank top then caught sight of a spot of chili sauce on her white pants. She grimaced. Great, just great.

"You're awfully quiet today," Lucky said, her

appetite apparently healthy as ever as she bit into her hot dog with gusto.

Renae had made an inventory delivery to Lucky's blossoming shop a short ways away an hour ago and after spending some time going over other needs, Lucky had suggested they lunch at the popular hot dog place that, interestingly enough, sat smack-dab next to the swankiest restaurant Toledo had to offer.

"He's Georgio's and I'm Coney Island."

Lucky blinked at her and said around a full mouth, "What?"

Renae hadn't realized she'd said the words aloud until that moment. She waved her hand, picked up one of her own hot dogs, then chose a side and took a bite. "Will and I," she said, the food muffling her words. "He's Georgio's and I'm this hot dog place."

Lucky choked on a laugh and reached for her glass of soda. "You are not a hot dog place."

"Yes, I am. I'm a high school dropout who never even thought about getting her GED much less considered going on to college."

"And that makes you a hot dog place?"

She nodded and pointed her thumb in the direction of the wall that separated the two restaurants. "And Will's the gourmet place next door."

"How do you figure?"

Renae gave an eye roll and leaned forward. "Come on, Lucky, surely I don't have to spell it out to you."

"Indulge me."

"Fine. Will is a fancy restaurant because not only has he finished high school and college and med school, he's a friggin' doctor—a surgeon—for cripe's sake."

Lucky continued eating her hot dog as if they were discussing nothing more important than the weather, which currently happened to be hazy and hot, the restaurant's air-conditioning a draw for those looking to escape the August heat.

"I'm still not following the allegory."

"An analogy, I think." She put down her hot dog and crossed her forearms on top of the table. "You see, there's no skill needed in preparing a hot dog. What's there to do? You boil or broil the dogs, slap them in a bun, offer up a lot of condiments, throw in a bag of chips, and voila, an inexpensive meal is born. While Will…"

She'd done a lot of thinking about him, her and what had happened between them the past couple of days. Not because she'd wanted to. But rather she'd needed to. The other day she'd compared them to a bicycle and a BMW roadster. This morning she'd stared at the contents of the refrigerator and used tuna and salmon to demonstrate how they were different.

Now it was hot dogs and filet mignon.

"Will…well, he's a gourmet dish made up of expensive ingredients, some of which it takes sniffing pigs in France to find, and each item has been carefully cut and prepared just so, taking time and patience and knowledge."

"Mmm. As well as his being delicious," Lucky added.

"What's the matter with hot dogs?" To prove her point, she picked up the one she was working on and filled her mouth with a bite.

Lucky smiled at her then cleared her throat when she realized Renae wasn't amused. "Actually that was going to be my question. What is wrong with a hot dog? Providing, of course, that I'm accepting your comparing yourself to one?"

It took Renae a good minute to chew what was in her mouth then swallow before she could speak. "Man cannot live on hot dogs alone?"

Lucky waggled her finger at her. "Yes, but filet mignon isn't an American classic."

"Will isn't American."

This time Lucky burst out laughing, further deepening Renae's grimace.

"This is not funny."

"I beg to differ. I find this entire conversation

very amusing." She polished off her first hot dog then started on her second. "If I were to buy what you're saying right now, Renae, well, then, I'd have to go home and boot Colin out of my apartment."

"You two are living together?"

Lucky made a face. "Well, we haven't spent a night apart since working everything out two months ago, although neither of us has changed our mailing address." She waved her hand. "Anyway, back to my point. If it's your contention that hot dogs and filet mignon don't mix…well, then I've got a problem on my hands."

"You are so not a hot dog."

"And you are?"

Renae felt the beginnings of a smile take shape. "A really good hot dog. A popular one. What's that brand? The kind that plumps when you cook 'em? Or, no, wait. Maybe I'm a brat. Yeah, I like that better, I think."

"Will would say you were a banger."

"No, Will would say he wanted to bang me, but that's neither here nor there."

Renae felt better after a few minutes with her friend than she'd felt over the past few days. Not so much because of what they were saying, but rather because she was talking to someone at all. She'd been so busy with the shop, helping Lucky get ready for her grand opening in a couple of weeks, and trying to avoid both Will and Nina that she hadn't had an honest to God conversation with anyone during that same time period. And while her and Lucky's exchange didn't change or solve anything, it had allowed her to vent and the mere act of doing so made her feel enormously better.

Lucky shifted in her booth. "So have you called Ginger to invite her to lunch yet?"

Renae shook her head, intrigued by the way Lucky had worded the question. She hadn't asked about her proposal, although, when they'd initially discussed it, she had offered to take a look at it if Renae wanted her to. "I'm still putting the finishing touches on the documentation."

Lucky seemed to be looking at her a little too closely.

Renae considered telling her about the other troublesome person in her life at that moment, but decided there was such a thing as too much venting. Especially to one person.

She got the ridiculous image of Lucky leaving the restaurant with her hair permanently blown back from her face from the impact of Renae's rants, and smiled inwardly.

"You know, you may just be using this whole hot dog versus filet mignon argument as a crutch to keep you from advancing your relationship with Will."

It was Renae's turn to blink at her friend. "What?"

Lucky shrugged, as if it were of no consequence to her, but Renae got the impression that Lucky was sharing more than advice. "Let's just say I've been there. And it's a constant topic of conversation between Colin and me." She put the last half of her hot dog down and brushed her hands on a paper napkin. "Sometimes I feel like I'm in so far over my head I just want to scream."

Renae realized she hadn't even blinked at the odd pairing of Colin the psychologist with one-time bar waitress Lucky. Which further emphasized the holes in her own argument.

"I mean, Colin took me to the opera at the Valentine Theatre a couple of weeks ago. The opera. I didn't have a clue how to dress, what to say when he introduced me to people he's known for years...." She swallowed hard, indicating she still wasn't completely over the experience. "Doing something like that is second nature to Colin but for me—"

"You'd take a smoke-filled bar any day"

Lucky smiled. "Yes. Something like that. Only they're not smoke-filled anymore, are they? What with the new law and all."

"Shame. I was thinking about taking up the habit."

Lucky smiled.

"Did Colin pick up on your feelings?"

"Of course. What kind of psychologist, and lover, would he be if he hadn't?"

"And I suppose he made you talk about it until you were blue in the face afterward." Renae shook her head. "I can't imagine what it would be like being involved with a shrink. I mean, does he have an off switch, or is he basically on all the time?"

Lucky smiled. "We're working on the off switch."

Renae sat for long moments merely enjoying being in Lucky's company. While the details of their past were different, she felt a connection with the other woman that she'd never felt with anyone else. Sure, she and Tabitha were close, but it had taken their friendship several years and many shared memories to be cultivated. In contrast, she and Lucky had clicked the first day Lucky had walked up to Women Only looking for a job.

At any rate, with very few words she knew Lucky would understand where she was coming from in just about any situation, and the same went for her with Lucky. Neither one of them was completely comfortable discussing her feelings. And that mere fact made it easier for both of them to do it.

"You know, it probably wouldn't be easy living with an E.R. surgeon, either."

Renae's gaze snapped to Lucky's face. She pretended an over-interest in dipping the last of her potato chips into the leftover chili topping, but Renae wasn't fooled.

"I mean, there's all that being on call. The long hours. The follow-ups during his down time."

"You seem to know an awful lot about E.R. docs," she said carefully.

Lucky's grin was infectious. "That's because I've been asking Colin a lot about them in case the information might come in handy."

"Hmm. Does he know about me and Will?"

She nodded. "Seems Will told him."

Renae's breath left her lungs. "Will told him?"

"That's what I said."

"What else did he say?" Renae felt ridiculously like she was in grade school talking about a guy she had a crush on.

Lucky shrugged. "I don't know."

"What do you mean you don't know?"

The restaurant owner came up to the table Lucky greeted him.

"You know all that fast food is no good for you. You should let me give you something else next time. Something Greek, maybe," the Cypriot said with a friendly smile.

"Maybe."

"Okay, then. You girls have a nice day, no?"

"Yes," Lucky said.

"Eat here often?" Renae leaned forward. "What else did he say?"

Lucky looked momentarily confused, then she backtracked to what they'd been talking about before the restaurant owner had come up. "I already told you, I don't know. Colin held up his hands and refused to say anything else, you know, while wearing that expression that said he was afraid he'd already said too much."

Renae chewed on that as a waitress took their plates away then gave them each a piece of pie, compliments of Frixos Stylianides.

She picked up her fork, toyed with the flaky top crust, then said, "Will and I are just like this piece of pie—"

Lucky held up a forkful of whipped cream. "Don't even start."

CHAPTER ELEVEN

WILL STOOD BEHIND the partially closed vertical blinds in his living room, watching as Renae parked her Cadillac convertible in the lot. She had the top down despite the heat, her sunglasses perched on the edge of her straight nose, her dark blond hair windblown and sexy, her skin glowing like warm honey in the afternoon sun.

And damn if he didn't want her more now than ever.

He dry-washed his face with his hands. His continued powerful attraction to her didn't make any sense to him. Sure, ever since she'd moved in six months ago, he'd had a thing for her, an intense physical reaction, although it was restricted to his fantasy life and at the time included her roommate, Tabitha.

Then he'd slept with her.

Well, that sentence was sorely lacking, wasn't it?

He hadn't merely slept with her. He'd been lucky if he'd gotten a straight four hours of sleep ever since running into her by the mailboxes nearly a week ago (had it really only been a week?). At first his lack of shut-eye had been the result of their having sex—constantly.

Now, however, his inability to saw some much-needed logs stemmed solely from his *not* having sex with her. If that made any sense. Which, of course, it didn't. Because nothing about his life made much sense of late.

Will watched as Renae went about taking grocery bags from the trunk then headed for the building without bothering to put the top up on her car. She wore a black tank that seemed to emphasize her deep tan, and white slacks that made him squint in case he could catch a glimpse of what she wore underneath. She looked good enough to eat and Will suddenly found himself ravenous.

She pushed her glasses to sit on top of her pretty head and looked up at his window. Will stepped slightly back, although he couldn't really say why. He grimaced as she moved out of sight, likely entering the building. Moments later he heard her footfalls on the steps in the hall. The rustling of her plastic grocery bags stopped just outside his door. Will waited. Would she knock?

He heard the rustling again then shortly thereafter the closing of her condo door upstairs.

Damn.

Behind him the telephone began ringing. He stood for long moments, ignoring it, not up to another conversation with Janet should it happen to be her. But the caller was persistent and somewhere around the tenth ring he stepped into the dining room and picked up the extension.

"Willem?"

Relief suffused Will's muscles when he identified the caller as his mother. Though his name was William, she'd always left out a vowel and changed another.

"Hallo, Mum," he greeted, easily falling back to his native accent. Not that he made an effort otherwise, but his speech pattern naturally blended with those around him when he was in the States. "How's everything?"

"Fine, fine. With you?"

Will paused. And the instant he did so, he knew he'd live to regret it. "Fine. Couldn't be better."

He cringed. Even worse, the overdoing it part.

"Mmm. That's interesting. Because judging from the sound of your voice, it's anything but. Come on. Be a dear and tell your ole mum what's happening in your life."

Dorothy Sexton had five children, of which

he was the middle child. He was the only one to leave England, and each of his siblings had not only stayed close by the family, they now had families of their own, including his youngest sister, Nancy, who had married last year and was due her first child any day now.

"Nothing much, you know. The same old, actually. Has Nancy dropped the bun yet?"

"Nancy's as big as an overstuffed sofa and just as uncomfortable. And quit trying to change the subject."

Will smiled as he sat down at the kitchen table.

Even though they were an ocean apart, and it was two in the afternoon by his watch and 7:00 p.m. in London, the clear sound of her voice made it seem like she was right next door. "It's nothing, really. Just some things happening at work."

"The doctor of the family is having problems, is he?"

While two of his siblings had pursued higher education, he was the only one to go as far as he had, mostly on scholarship and a mountain of student loans he'd just managed to pay off a year or so ago. While he was usually quite proud of what he'd accomplished, it never took more than a few words from his mother to remind him of his roots and his family and how he was still just the middle Sexton child from Southwark to her.

"You see, I've been after this promotion for some time now and I fear I may never achieve it."

He wouldn't go into detail about why. The whole Janet-Renae issue would only confuse her and he was half afraid she'd be on the next plane over if she thought that either of them might be wife material. Which was funny, because none of his family had come to visit him. As far as they were concerned, he was on the other side of the world, not a five-hour plane trip away.

Then again, he hadn't been home more than once a year for a week or two himself. And for some reason the thought suddenly made him sad.

"Hang in there, my boy. If there's one thing I know for sure in this world it's that whatever my Willem wants, my Willem gets."

He grinned at the familiar refrain, sometimes said in exasperation, most often with pride.

"Thanks, Mum. I guess I needed to hear that." He shifted in the chair. "So tell me, what did you have for dinner today?"

"It's Friday so we had shepherd's pie, of course. Your da's favorite."

Will closed his eyes, imagining the cramped Sexton kitchen with its old Formica table and red-plastic covered chairs, the room redolent with the smell of lamb and thick mashed potatoes. Of course, it would be only his mum and his da there now, the kids all gone, but two Sundays a month the whole family still gathered at the small flat for roast beef, Yorkshire pudding and two veg for dinner.

For the first time in his years in America, he genuinely missed home.

"If I recall correctly, shepherd's pie used to be your favorite, as well," his mother said. "But that's probably changed to a Burger Mac and, what do they call chips? Fries. Yes, fries, I think."

Will perked right up, as he suspected his mother knew he would. "On the contrary, I have fish 'n' chips for lunch nearly every other day. And I'll also have you know that I've been known to whip up quite a hotpot every now and again.…"

And so it went, his mother challenging him on forgotten traditions and him defending himself. And for a short little while Will managed to forget about Renae and Janet and work and concentrated solely on his mother and everything he loved about her and England.

RENAE STOOD INSIDE her condo door and took a deep breath. Merely coming home anymore was awkward. She'd known Will was in his apartment, his behemoth of an SUV was parked right up front in the lot. Just knowing he was in the same building, that only a couple of doors separated them, sent her hormones into overdrive.

Or was it her hormones?

"There's someone I haven't seen much of lately."

Renae automatically smiled at Tabitha who had craned her neck from where she sat on the living-room couch to look at her.

"Hey."

"Hey, yourself. Why don't you go put that stuff away and come sit with me? I don't know about you, but I'm going into chat withdrawal."

It took Renae a whole two minutes to put the few items she'd picked up at the market away— milk, juice, eggs, a loaf of bread. She tucked the plastic bags into the recycling bin then grabbed a couple of sodas from the fridge and walked into the living room. The hideous pillows and throws aside, Tabitha had created a room that felt comfortable the instant you entered it. She sank down onto the faux suede couch beside her friend and handed her the other soda. Luckily Nina was nowhere in sight.

Tabby thanked her then said, "So tell me what's going on in Renae's world."

Renae stared at her. It seemed odd that so much

had happened in such a short period of time. Or maybe it hadn't and she was making a big deal out of it.

She thought about the proposal she had tucked away for Women Only. It seemed strange that her best friend, the woman she shared a condo with, didn't know a thing about it.

"You still having sex with the sexy doc downstairs?"

Renae settled deeper into the cushions and crossed her legs. "No. That ended a couple of days ago."

After her and Lucky's conversation today at lunch, she found herself thinking of what her mother's reaction would be to the news that she was sleeping with a surgeon. No doubt, Daisy Truesdale would be overjoyed that her daughter had landed herself a doctor. Then again, she might not even bat an eye at the news. After all, the Truesdale women knew how to bag a man with deep pockets.

She shuddered.

"Wow, that must have been some thought."

Renae blinked Tabitha's face back into focus. "Sorry. I guess I'm not very good company today."

Tabitha leaned her arm against Renae's. "Who said you're good company at any other time?"

Renae smiled. "Our long-standing friendship, maybe?"

"Yes. I guess that would be proof."

They sat that way for long moments, neither of them saying anything as Renae reflected on the many years she'd known Tabitha. And how she might bring up her suspicions about Nina without alienating her friend and jeopardizing their friendship.

Tabitha toyed with the remote, turning down the sound as she settled on a soap opera. The great-looking guy and beyond beautiful girl on the screen loomed surreal and inaccessible to Renae.

"You know, I've always told you that men are more trouble than they're worth," Tabitha said.

Renae laughed. "My mood has nothing to do with Dr. Will."

"Sure it doesn't."

"Speaking of people being more trouble than they're worth, where's Nina?"

Tabitha jabbed her thumb in the direction of the hall. "In the bedroom."

"Oh. I thought maybe she wasn't here."

Her friend looked at her curiously. "You don't like her much, do you?"

Renae thought about how she might fill Tabby in on her missing notes and her messed-up cell phone and the items of clothing that she'd noticed had disappeared, but in the end she bit down hard on her bottom lip. Truth was, she hadn't liked Nina since first meeting her, and while the notes were a little hard to explain away, the rest of it was circumstantial so she feared she'd merely sound catty if she mentioned it.

She put her arm around Tabitha's shoulders. "What matters is that you like her."

"Mmm. And that I do."

They settled into the couch together, Renae's arm around Tabitha, their physical closeness mirroring their emotional connection.

"You know, she only has the best things to say about you," Tabitha said.

Renae nearly choked on her soft drink. "Excuse me?"

Tabby nodded. "She's always talking about how nice you are, how pretty, and how lucky I am to have you as a friend."

"Are you sure we're talking about the same person?"

"Yes."

"Funny, because whenever I'm in the same room with her the air conditioner isn't necessary."

Tabitha laughed. "It's just your imagination."

"No, it's not. It's plain fact. That girl doesn't like me, doesn't like our friendship, and I suspect if I said I was moving out she wouldn't hesitate to help me pack."

"You're being paranoid."

Was she? Renae was positive she wasn't.

"Why would she say such nice things about you to me, then?"

"Because she knows how you feel about me, more than likely. I mean if she were to slam me verbally, what would you do?"

Tabitha thought for a minute. "I don't know. A month ago I would probably have asked her to leave."

Renae searched her face. "And now?"

Her friend remained silent for longer than Renae was comfortable with. She'd sensed a change in the atmosphere for a while now. Watched as Tabitha grew more involved with Nina, their relationship deepening until Renae had begun feeling like a third, very unwanted wheel.

Now she had the proof that she was.

"What do you think of this one?"

Renae and Tabitha turned to where Nina had entered the room wearing a pink and white striped dress, looking more like Suzie Homemaker than Nina the Lesbian.

"Oh, hi, Renae. I didn't hear you come in."

"Hi, yourself." Renae shivered and pretended

an interest in finishing off the contents of her can, sensing Tabitha's gaze on her.

"You didn't answer my question," Nina said in a whiny voice that turned Renae's shiver into a shudder. "Is this better than the last one?"

Tabitha tapped her finger against her lips as she considered her lover. She requested she turn around so she could see the back. "I think I like the first one better."

Nina blew out a long breath. "I like this one."

"So wear that one then."

"You are absolutely no help at all." She swung on her heels and headed back toward the bedroom where she lightly slammed the door.

"Hot date tonight?" Renae asked.

"Mmm. A couple of friends of ours are getting married. You remember Marty and Jo."

That would be Martha and Joann. "Sure, I do. Give them my congratulations, won't you?"

They heard slamming drawers and closet doors come from the other room as Renae settled back into the cushions and enjoyed her friend's company for as long as she had it.

"Talk about people being more trouble than they're worth," she said quietly.

She wasn't sure what Tabitha's response would be, but was grateful when she started laughing so hard Renae couldn't help but join in.

THAT SUNDAY NIGHT Will paced outside the doors of the Toledo Express Airport, wanting to be anywhere but there waiting for Janet to disembark from her plane. He spotted a couple of smokers standing near an ashtray and wished he'd taken up the habit, if only to have something to do with his hands right then.

Hell. Sheer hell. That was his life of late. And unfortunately he didn't see that changing anytime *soon*. Not when the girl he was dating, who had no idea Renae existed much less that he'd been sleeping with her, would be standing in front of him any moment.

Did he look different? Did his infidelity show on his face?

You can't be unfaithful if you're not having sex with her.

Renae's words came back to haunt him. Oh, yeah, that would sound good, wouldn't it? "Janet, honey, it didn't count."

"Will!"

He swiveled around at the same time Janet dropped her bags and threw herself into his arms.

Oh God in heaven, he was going to burn for this one.

He fought more to keep his balance than to return the enthusiastic hug. Had he ever been greeted so warmly by someone before? Even his mother made do with a dry peck to the cheek and a pat on the shoulder.

"God, you don't know how good it is to see you," she said.

He wished he could say the same but the truth was he'd been dreading this moment for so long that, now that it was here, he wanted to run flat-out in the opposite direction.

She finally loosened her grasp and stood back to smile up at him.

Pretty. She was still very pretty. Her soft brown hair was pulled back into an efficient ponytail, her makeup was simple and her polo shirt and cargo shorts looked very California.

"You look good enough to eat," she said.

Will started, trying not to recall that he'd thought the same words a mere five days ago—and that he hadn't thought them about Janet but about Renae.

"How was your trip?" he asked, bending to pick up her bags.

"Thanks. It was fine. Long, but fine. Not a free seat on the plane which is always uncomfortable, but it's all right now that it's over."

Will felt like his smile was so brittle his teeth might shatter. "I'm parked over here."

He led the way and she followed by his side.

Her laugh caught him up short. "Where's the fire?"

Will realized that he was walking fast enough to qualify for a marathon. He forced himself to slow his step.

"Boy, you must really be glad to see me."

Janet tucked her hand into his arm and he nearly jumped out of his skin.

She looked at him curiously.

"Sorry," he said. "I haven't been getting much sleep lately."

She took her hand away. "And I think I know why."

CHAPTER TWELVE

WILL NEARLY SWALLOWED his tongue whole at Janet's quiet statement.

"What?" he practically croaked.

She looked down at the pavement in front of them. "I said I think I know why you haven't been sleeping much lately. Daddy told me."

Will blinked at her, unable to connect the dots. Her father knew about him and Renae?

"He asked me not to say anything, but I couldn't help it." She smiled up at him. "Congratulations on being considered for a promotion."

Will's relief was so complete that he nearly dropped into a puddle right then and there.

"Oh, yes, that," he said, remembering exactly how much he had on the line here. And not liking it one bit. A rock and a hard place had nothing on what he felt caught between that minute.

He realized she was waiting for a response and

said quickly, "It really is quite exciting, isn't it? My finally being considered for that promotion, I mean."

She laughed. "What did you think I meant?"

He shrugged as they finally reached his SUV in the short-term parking section of the airport. One step at a time. That's how he would take this. One step at a time.

And thankfully this step allowed him the freedom of not looking at her. Instead he popped the back door of the SUV and hauled her suitcases inside. "I hadn't the faintest idea what you were talking about."

Will closed the back door and opened the passenger's side. As he helped her up, he felt mercury line his stomach. Her bringing up his bid for promotion was just as disturbing as her accusing him of being a cad while she was away, now, wasn't it? After all, he suspected that his dating her was the sole reason he was being considered for the position at all. Her mentioning it served to remind him of that fact like a brick to his head.

He paused before getting in the driver's side of the car, trying to gather his wits about him. He'd half hoped that the instant he'd seen Janet, everything would have clicked into place. That he'd have remembered why he'd been so interested in her. Why he'd gone five long months without sex when he would never have gone one week without before.

Instead he felt like even a bigger mess than he'd been before.

He climbed into the car and started it, offering up a half-assed smile in her direction.

"So, how was the convention?" he asked, desperately trying to divert the conversation away from him and onto her.

"It was great. So many new techniques and pharmaceutical breakthroughs. I feel like my head is going to burst with all the new information...."

And there she went.

Will instantly relaxed into the buttery-soft leather seat, listening as Janet told him about the latest in cancer research and the other residents and doctors she'd met, and how she looked forward to going to the next convention. And somewhere around her saying something about being amazed by how much had happened since she'd finished med school, he allowed his mind to wander.

How had he not noticed before how much she chattered? Maybe because before it hadn't bothered him. It didn't bother him now, either, he hastened to point out. So he wasn't tuned in to every word she was saying. Surely that was the case with every relationship. You couldn't be "on" every minute of every day. It was unreasonable even to think it.

She's only been back for ten minutes, a small voice in his head said.

Oh, shut up, he told it.

"Did you say something?"

Will blinked several times then looked at Janet. "No, no. Not a word." He tried his best grin. "Please continue. It makes me wish I had gone with you."

Oh, boy, did he ever wish he'd gone to the convention with her. If he had, he wouldn't be marinating in the duck soup he currently sat in the middle of.

She tapped the soft-sided briefcase on the floor next to her feet. "Don't worry. I took plenty of notes for you."

Had he just winced?

Yes, he had.

Of course he had. Because the more Janet talked, the lower he felt. She'd taken notes for him. How thoughtful.

How anal.

His brows shot up on his forehead.

He was getting the very definite impression that there was a war of sorts being played out on the battlefield of his subconscious. But why and from which direction the shots were being fired, he couldn't be sure. And until he found out, he had the sinking sensation he was going to be a mere bystander.

He merged with traffic in the right-hand lane of Airport Highway, hating that the airport was so far from the city. A half hour drive sitting in the hot seat before he could drop Janet off.

A half hour of sheer hell.

He grew aware of Janet's silence next to him and looked over to find her staring out the window. It almost looked as if she were thinking the same thing he was. Which was ridiculous, really. He was merely projecting his emotions onto her.

He cleared his throat. "So, how is L.A., anyway? I've never been, myself."

She glanced at him. "Actually I didn't get much of a sense of the city. There was a tour bus that took us to Anaheim one day, but I met this wonderful resident from Minnesota and she and I talked throughout the entire trip. I can't even remember the color of the bus."

She'd gone to L.A. and hadn't seen any of the city. No Rodeo Drive, no Grauman's Chinese Theatre. How dedicated.

How boring.

Will tightened his grip on the steering wheel.

"It seemed nice enough. Smoggy. Different. In fact, while I…"

Off she went again. Which, Will firmly told

himself, was a far sight better than her silence moments ago. So long as she was talking, everything was all right. He wasn't looking at her too closely. And, more important, she wasn't looking at him too closely.

Finally, in the middle of Janet's description of the hotel she'd stayed in and the convention layout, he pulled up in front of her apartment complex in Sylvania, on the western edge of Toledo. He gazed at the new buildings as if they were the Promised Land.

"Well, here we are," he proclaimed unnecessarily.

Janet looked around her. "Oh! I didn't even register that we were here already."

Will, on the other hand, had mentally been there for the past thirty minutes.

He shut off the engine and climbed out, meeting Janet at the back of the SUV.

He jumped when Janet tucked her hand into his arm as they walked to her building. "You know, I've had a lot of time to think while I've been away," she said.

"Oh?" Will was busy counting the steps left to the door. Thirty, twenty-nine…

"Mmm-hmm."

The tone of her voice snapped his head around even as he quickened his steps.

"I was thinking—"

Will swung the building door open so fast he nearly hit her head-on with it.

"Oh!"

"Sorry," he mumbled. "Are you all right?"

She'd put a hand to her chest then checked out the status of her ponytail…complete with pink ribbon.

Damn him and his childhood obsession with girls in ribbons. Especially shiny pink ones.

"Here, why don't you give me your keys?" he said as they ascended the steps to her second-floor apartment.

She handed him her keys, complete with pom-pom key chain in blue and gold. The reminder that she'd been a football cheerleader jolted him a bit.

"There you go," he said, swinging open her apartment door—thankfully it opened in so there was no risk of bodily harm—and putting her suitcases down inside the door without actually entering. "Home safe and sound."

She hadn't said anything and Will realized that he hadn't really looked at her since midway through their drive from the airport.

He looked at her now and was fairly convinced he'd just swallowed his tongue.

"You know, you haven't kissed me yet," she said in a low voice he had once viewed as sultry.

She hooked her finger inside the flap and between the middle buttons of his oxford shirt.

Oh, boy.

"Sure, I did," he croaked.

Hadn't he?

She shook her head. "Which brings me back to what I thought about when I was in L.A."

Oh, God. She had that look on her face. Not one he'd seen her wear before, but the expression he'd seen on countless women's faces—had seen on Renae's face more times than he could count—right before they were going to make an indecent proposal.

"All this…waiting until my wedding night stuff…" She edged closer to him, but rather than making him hot, it made him want to edge farther away from her. "Well, I've decided it's old-fashioned."

Will swallowed hard, incapable of making a response. Not because he was turned on beyond belief, but because he was occupied with measuring the maneuver it would take him to make it to the stairs.

"I want you, Will," Janet whispered, kissing his chin and smiling up into his eyes. "I want you now. Tonight."

"Sex?" Will blurted.

She gave a quiet giggle. "Yes, sex."

Oh, boy, oh, boy, oh boy…

Janet dislodged her finger from between his buttons and curved her hands around his waist until she had her fingers flat against his rear end. He gave a startled sound of disbelief.

Was this the same woman who for five months had waited for him to make the first move? Who had said no to him so many times that he'd begun to think he'd just have to marry her to get her out of her panties?

A little over a week ago he'd said goodbye to a docile lamb. Now he was facing a she-cat intent on getting what she wanted.

Janet rubbed herself suggestively against his front.

Strangely enough, Big Ben didn't budge.

"Make love to me, Will," Janet breathed, moving even closer to kiss him.

The moment before her mouth would make contact with his, he caught her shoulders and jerked her away. She gasped, nearly losing her balance and falling backward into her apartment. She probably would have had he not had a vise grip on her shoulders. Not to keep her from falling, but to keep her away.

"Actually I've been doing…some thinking of my own while you've been away," he said, his words coming quickly, a trickle of sweat working its way down his forehead. "And I don't happen to think waiting for one's wedding night is old-fashioned at all." He tried for a grin but was afraid he'd ended up with a grimace. "In fact, I was just telling Colin that your impressive self-control and need for tradition are what initially attracted me to you."

Even as he spoke, he stepped backward, his reach growing longer as he continued to hold her at bay.

"And it's what continues to attract me to you.…"

Just two more steps but he couldn't make them without letting her go first.

"In fact, I think I should go before we do something we both might regret."

"Will!"

He was about to release her but instead held tight. "What?"

"You haven't even kissed me yet."

"Oh, yes. Right."

With his feet planted at the top of the stairs, he leaned in, hesitated at the look of submission on her face as she tilted up her chin, then he gave her what had to be the driest, quickest peck on the cheek in history.

"Very well, then. Good night!"

And with that he was down the stairs and out of the building like a shot.

CHAPTER THIRTEEN

RENAE SAT ON THE STEPS outside the condo door, listening as Tabitha and Nina had one of their world-famous arguments. Actually it was more like a fanatical rant. Essentially Tabitha tried to reason with Nina while her irate lover raged on for what sometimes seemed like hours.

Renae stared down longingly at the half gallon of Ben & Jerry's Chunky Monkey she'd run out to get.

The agreement she and Tabitha had come to when Renae had moved in was that if there was a heated situation with one or the other of them with their significant others, they would make themselves scarce.

In this case it meant that rather than going inside and interrupting the scene that was undoubtedly taking place in the living room, Renae was sitting on the hall steps with a carton of melting ice cream, without a spoon. Which seemed to pretty much sum up the whole of her life at that very moment.

She parked her elbows on her knees then dropped her head into her hands. Was it really just over a week ago that everything had been running like clockwork? When she'd been happy with her job at Women Only without yearning for more? When she'd come home with no suspicion of someone sabotaging her personal belongings and tampering with her cell phone? When she'd been happily single without thoughts of a hunky, unavailable surgeon hanging out on the fringes of her mind— whether she was awake or asleep—always present, always tempting her?

Yep, her life was a carton of melting ice cream without a spoon and she wasn't sure what, if anything, she could do with the mess that would surely remain afterward.

And there would be an afterward, wouldn't there?

She puzzled over that one.

If there was one thing life had taught her it was that there was always an afterward. Postchildhood. Postadolescence. Hell, there was even postpartum depression, although she hoped never to run into that one. Then again, judging by the way her life was progressing so far, she'd probably have to suffer through that as well when and if she ever got married and had children.

Now there was a thought....

Her cell phone vibrated in her pocket. She sighed as she fished it out, then stared at the lighted display. Her mother. Oh, great. Just what she needed now.

"Hi, Mom."

"God, I hate caller ID," Daisy Truesdale said with a dramatic sigh. "You can never surprise anyone anymore."

"You never surprise me anyway." Simply because her mother's goal in life was to provide constant surprises, so Renae had come to expect them. "What's up?"

"Why does anything have to be up in order for me to call my daughter, my only child?"

If there was any justice in this world, it was that Daisy had only had one child to screw up. "Because something's always up."

Renae was aware she was being more cynical than usual. Probably had something to do with being locked out of her own apartment while sitting on the steps watching her favorite ice cream melt.

"Okay, in this case, you're right."

Renae closed her eyes, mentally bracing herself.

"I'm moving to Vegas to become a showgirl."

Renae shook her head and grimaced. Her mom, a forty-three-year-old Vegas showgirl. At least it was in line with the remainder of Daisy Truesdale's life. Underage stripper at seventeen who'd gotten pregnant by a customer who'd sworn he'd always take care of her then had burned rubber when he'd found out she was pregnant. Renae had been raised in the back rooms of strip clubs around pasties and G-strings and silicone breasts. And as soon as she was old enough, she'd followed in her mother's footsteps, never really knowing any other kind of life.

Until Ginger.

"So?" her mother said after long moments. "Are you going to say anything?"

"What's there to say?"

"I don't know. Good luck?"

"Good luck."

"Well, that sounded sincere."

Renae's shoulders slumped. She didn't mean to be rude to her mom, she really didn't. It was just that so much of her life was for crap right now that she couldn't sum up much enthusiasm for Daisy's latest escapade. From dancing on cruise ships, going to New York to try her hand at Broadway, this new news wasn't…well, new.

"Look, Mom, are you leaving today?"

"No. Not for another week."

"Good then, we have some time. I've really got to go right now, though."

A few moments later, after promising Daisy she would call by tomorrow, Renae disconnected the call and turned off her phone, resisting the urge to lie back on the floor in a gesture of surrender. She didn't know if anyone was currently controlling the strings of her life, but if they were, she wanted to write them a long, detailed letter of complaint.

Downstairs, she heard the outer door open. She sat up a little straighter, hoping it wasn't anyone who lived on the third floor who might see her sitting outside. Nudging the bag of ice cream aside with her foot, she bent over to look down the stairwell. She made a strangled sound as Will looked right up to stare into her eyes.

And the day just kept getting better and better.

She supposed that's what she got for questioning the great puppeteer of life.

Renae quickly drew back and closed her eyes. Oh, great. What she really needed right now was for Will to think she was sitting there waiting for him.

Her heart thudded against her rib cage as she strained to hear him continue up the stairs to his apartment. Nothing. Which was a good thing, right? Because it meant he wasn't coming up—

Something touched her arm. She shrieked and nearly leapt straight out of her skin.

"Whoa. I mean, I know I have quite an impact on the ladies, but I didn't think I was that good."

Renae stared into Will's face, but rather than finding the grin that normally would have accompanied his words, he wore a grimace. A handsome, irresistible grimace that made her stomach pitch to somewhere in the vicinity of her feet and made her toes curl where they were visible in her flip-flops.

Toes he seemed to be a little preoccupied with presently.

"Um, hi," she said. "In case you're wondering, I'm not sitting here waiting for you."

As if on cue, the sound of something breaking against the apartment door made them both jump, indicating the argument within was not only still going strong, but had escalated.

Will looked from the door to her. "Actually I was going to ask if you'd forgotten your keys."

She held them up and again he seemed inordinately preoccupied with the simple silver icon of her astrological sign of Leo.

Renae tucked the keys half into her pocket, far enough to keep them anchored, then picked up the bag holding the ice cream.

What did he want? Surely he didn't expect her to

buy that he'd been concerned she'd gotten locked out of her condo? Excuse her if she was wrong, but over the past few days she'd gotten the impression that if she'd been lying half dead in need of CPR, he'd have stepped over her and closed his condo door in order to avoid her.

She looked at him again, noticing how nice he looked in the simple white oxford shirt and tan Dockers. All the tennis he played had given him a deep, golden tan, and kissed his forever-tousled hair with sun-bright highlights.

And when he grinned…

She swallowed hard as he did just that, the gesture seeming to call a halt to all rational thought and beckon to her body.

"Your ice cream's melting."

That's not all that was melting, but she wasn't about to tell him that. Especially not when she was getting freezer burn on her fingers from desperately holding the bag in front of her.

"Would you like a spoon?" he asked.

She'd like much more than a spoon from him. She wanted to follow him back to his place, shut off the air-conditioning and throw open the windows and see what imaginative things they could do with the ice cream to keep cool.

She must have looked suspicious because he sighed and looked away. "Hey, I'm not trying to come on to you. Trust me that's, um, the furthest thing from my mind right now." He ran his fingers through his hair. "I just thought that if you wanted to wait at my place, you know, until you can get back into your own, you're more than welcome."

Renae squinted at him. "Wait. At your place."

He nodded.

"Just…wait. Nothing more?"

"Nothing more. Well, unless you want to talk or something while you wait."

"Talk…" she said drawing out the word.

"Right. Bad idea."

Something else broke against the door. Renae stared at it. "That's going to leave a mark." She looked back at Will. "I think I'll take you up on your offer."

FIFTEEN MINUTES LATER Will was ready to have himself committed to the nearest mental health facility. Renae sat cross-legged on his leather sofa, the carton of ice cream in her lap, a spoon in one hand, the remote control in the other. She wore a baggy white sweat suit that had Women Only written across the chest in navy-blue cursive letters, she didn't have on a lick of makeup that he could tell, and her hair was pulled back into what he'd describe as a messy ponytail, with dark blond tendrils curving all over the back of her golden neck.

Definitely not the type of ponytail he was usually drawn to. And nowhere was there a pink ribbon, or a ribbon of any color for that matter.

She found a station she liked and put the remote down on the coffee table.

"Are you sure you don't mind my waiting here?" she asked, glancing at him where he stood in the archway between living and dining room.

"I don't mind."

"It might be awhile."

Bugger. "That's fine."

"Do you like *Sex and the City?*"

Will nearly choked on his own saliva.

Renae didn't miss his reaction if her own momentary pause was any indication. And he'd bet the Queen's royal jewels that it was.

She pointed at the television and he realized she was talking about the show.

Not that it mattered. The idea of watching the provocative sitcom while in the same room as her was a bad one, no matter which way you sliced it.

She appeared to feel the same as she reached for the remote with a trembling hand and switched the channel to a news show.

Better, but only slightly.

He glanced into the kitchen behind him. "I'm,

um, just going to make myself something to eat. Do you want anything?"

She lifted the carton of ice cream without looking at him.

"Right."

She'd offered him some of the cold concoction when he'd originally handed her a spoon, but he thought it better if he passed, especially considering the way she put the spoon first into her mouth to wet it before sticking it into the carton. Renae's licking anything was not something he thought he should be watching now.

He stood with the refrigerator door open for long minutes. He didn't get it. Not a half hour ago he'd had a beautiful woman he'd been lusting after for the past five months practically throwing herself at him and he'd run from her like a bat out of hell. While now...

He began taking items out of the refrigerator without looking at them. He'd figure it all out on the counter. Something, anything, to take his mind off the sexier-than-sin woman sitting in the other room. She laughed at something and Will dropped a green pepper.

The initial plan had been to pick Janet up from the airport, take her to dinner, then drive her home, so he hadn't had anything to eat since a bagel that had served as breakfast-lunch. The problem was, his appetite didn't seem interested in anything he looked at. He went through the cupboards, coming away with the same feeling.

Great. He needed something to do while Renae was inside his apartment, something to keep his hands busy if not his mind, and he couldn't seem to produce a single, solitary idea as to what.

Scooping the food items back up, he dumped them into the refrigerator then closed the door.

Okay, that had burned up an entire thirty seconds.

He turned around and found himself staring at Renae where she stood in the doorway.

Damn.

Damn, damn, damn.

Up this close, in the bright, unflattering light of the kitchen, she looked even better. Her green eyes were a mesmerizing, creamy jade, her skin was clean and inviting, her body soft and tempting even with all that thick cloth on top of it.

"Aren't you…um, hot?" he asked, motioning toward the heavy material and long sleeves.

She either misinterpreted his meaning, or purposely chose to ignore it. "Very."

Will's willpower was quickly deserting him. His palms itched to feel her skin. His very skin seemed to yearn to touch hers.

"This helps," she said, holding out the closed carton of ice cream in front of him.

"I'm not a big fan of ice cream."

"Try it. You might like it."

Will was through with trying things he wasn't supposed to like.

"Then could you hold it in your freezer for me until I can get back into my place?"

"Oh, um, sure."

He took the carton and put it away. When he turned back around, she was on his other side. Not only was she on his other side, she was bending over, her perfectly rounded rump high in the air as she gained access to his dishwasher.

She backed up in order to close the door, putting that same delectable rump in direct contact with Big Ben, who had definitely had a change of heart since dropping Janet off.

"Oh!" Renae swung to face him, her skin wonderfully flushed, mussed tendrils of hair clinging to her cheek. Will caught her by the shoulders to prevent her from falling backward. "I was just, um, putting the spoon in the dishwasher."

"I see that."

"Of course."

Will found it ironic that he was holding Renae in the exact same manner he'd been holding Janet such a short time ago. But rather than using the grip to hold Renae away from him, he was battling with the most incredible desire to pull her closer.

His gaze swept over her features. From her remarkable eyes, to her softly feathered brows, her high forehead and cheekbones, down her smooth jawline to her downright wicked mouth.

Her pink, pink tongue darted out to moisten her lips and fire raged a path down his stomach straight to his groin.

And confusion reigned in his head.

He didn't get it. What was it about this one woman that he couldn't seem to stop wanting her? Couldn't seem to stop thinking about her? The only common bond they shared was sex. They talked about nothing else, did nothing else.

Then why was it that when Dr. Stuart Nealon had told him about his possible promotion the other night, it had been Renae he'd wanted to share the news with? Not only hadn't he thought of telling Janet, he hadn't even felt inclined to discuss it with her when she'd brought it up. Why was it Renae was the first thing he thought about every morning when he woke up, and was the last thing he thought about before he went to sleep?

Why was it he wanted this woman with an intensity that scared the hell out of him?

"Here," she said, her voice low and gravelly. "Let me make this easier on you."

Then she was kissing him, and he was more than letting her—he was kissing her back. And every coherent thought scattered from his mind as he gave himself over to sensation.

CHAPTER FOURTEEN

RENAE FELT as if she'd been trapped in an air-less room for the past four days and that she was just now being allowed to take in a long, fresh breath.

Will's mouth on hers felt so damn good. So right.

The hands that had been on her shoulders moments before now gently cupped her jaw, holding her still as he slowly leaned his head one way and kissed her, then the other, his lips softly massaging hers. Renae's bones melted and she sought support from him. Had she ever been kissed so sweetly? So honestly? So tenderly? She couldn't remember. But what she did know was that she'd never been kissed that way by Will before. And she wasn't sure what to do with this change in him.

His fingers moved from her jaw to her neck, then over her shoulders until his hands finally rested against her bottom. She gasped when he hiked her up to sit on the counter, his mouth barely breaking from its sweet, torturous attentions.

Renae shifted to a more comfortable position on the hard granite then wrapped her calves around his waist, pulling him in until his long, hard sex rested solidly against hers through their clothing. A shiver started somewhere in the vicinity of her toes then spread up and up and up until it was a downright shudder by the time it reached her shoulder blades. Will's fingers found the hem of her sweatshirt and pushed it up, then pressed against her quivering stomach.

Will broke briefly from their kiss and stared deep into her eyes. Renae was helpless to do anything but stare back. He seemed puzzled, as if he was trying to figure something out. In the back of her mind she told him not to bother. That she'd been doing the same thing since the day she'd first given in to her temptation for him and she'd finally accepted that there was no explanation for what she felt for him. It merely…was

Then he was kissing her again

Renae moaned as he unsnapped her bra then stroked her breasts under the soft material. Each of his moves was so slow, so meaningful that she didn't know how to respond, how to react. He tugged the sweatshirt up and over her head then slipped her bra free, both items of clothing hitting the floor at his feet.

"You *are* hot."

Will's quiet words seemed to caress her along with his breath. He drew a finger down the damp skin between her breasts, then slid it inside the waistband of her pants. Renae braced herself against the side of the counter as he stripped the cotton from her burning body, leaving the white lace of her panties in place. He moved away from her and she whimpered in protest.

Moments later he was opening the top of the ice-cream carton and retrieving a fresh spoon from a nearby drawer. For a moment she was afraid he might leave her like that, panting, nearly naked on the counter, as he went off to eat ice cream.

Until he spooned a healthy portion of the sweet concoction from the carton then held the dripping spoon above her right nipple.

Renae gasped, both surprised by his bold move and the cold sensation of the ice cream against her skin. She watched as the white ball started sliding down over her nipple. Will leaned in and caught it in his mouth, then licked her puckered flesh with long, slow stokes.

Her eyes drifted closed at the exquisite combination of hot and cold, inanimate and animate coming together on her right breast. Will finished laving her then drew her nipple deep into his mouth, seeming to pull on a line that went straight down to her clit.

He stepped away again and it was all Renae could do not to melt to the floor in front of him in a mindless puddle. She watched as he duplicated the ice-cream bit with her left nipple, this time allowing the cream to melt further until it pooled in her navel. By the time his tongue lapped around her belly ring, her elbows were trembling so badly she nearly couldn't hold herself upright.

"I...I thought you weren't an ice-cream kind of guy," she whispered so quietly she almost didn't hear herself.

His blue-eyed gaze met hers. "Lately I'm coming to realize that there's a lot about myself I don't understand."

Renae could not only relate to his statement, but she could empathize with Will. Ever since they'd taken things from flirty to dirty her life hadn't been the same. She was no longer content to just bring home a check from Women Only...couldn't ignore the goings-on in her own condo. And Will...

He pressed his mouth against the white cotton crotch of her panties and blew, nearly shooting her physically off the counter, and psychologically into another dimension.

Sex between them before had been about instant

gratification, of seeking an orgasm, then seeking it all over again. They hadn't taken much time to explore each other at leisure. Any rest time had been reserved solely for rest. There'd been no foreplay, no during play, just "get down to the act, thank you very much" play.

His unhurried attention made a completely different kind of chaos accumulate in her belly. It was deeper, somehow, more intense, her heart thudding in a way that would have been scary had she been thinking clearly. Her hips automatically bucked up off the counter as he bared her to his gaze then fastened his lips firmly to her clitoris. Then again, how could she think clearly when he was doing his best to chase all coherent thought from her mind, period?

Will laved and suckled her with a patience and a consideration she'd never experienced before. His long tongue lapped her, meeting with the fleshy hood of her arousal then gently pulling it up until she trembled violently.

The world exploded behind Renae's closed eyelids, her hips jerking, her breathing ragged, but rather than freeing her, Will remained where he was, drawing out her crisis by suckling her, pulling the bud of her center into his mouth and swirling his tongue against it.

Renae ran her hands through his hair again and

again, not wanting the moment to end, yet eager to have him connect with her in an even more intimate way.

As her climax ebbed, she tugged on the coarse strands of his hair until he was once again kissing her. She devoured his mouth much as he had devoured hers moments before, somehow unable to get enough of him. Of the taste of herself on him. She restlessly pulled the hem of his oxford shirt from the waist of his slacks, surprised to find him still fully dressed. Rather than wasting time with all the buttons, she undid the first two then yanked the shirt over his head, barely pausing to let the piece of clothing fall to the floor before diving for the zipper to his slacks.

Will caught her hands in his and broke off the kiss.

Renae knew a moment of panic. Maybe there was a reason why he was still dressed. Maybe he didn't want her.

He leaned his forehead against hers and stared deep into her eyes for long moments. She heard her own deep swallow, words out of her reach. Then he grinned.

"Where's the fire, Renae?"

She wanted to tell him it was everywhere. Running rampant over her skin. Searing through her veins. Causing an inferno between her legs. But she didn't get the chance because as she watched, he slid her panties down her legs then opened his own slacks so that their clothes covered the kitchen floor.

Finally he was naked in front of her.

Renae shivered just looking at his fine masculine form. He was made up of just the right amount of muscle, lean and powerful and so mouthwateringly gorgeous he took her breath away. His skin was golden-brown from doing laps in the pool, the white swatch below his hips down to the tops of his legs like a welcoming beacon. This man and she were different in so many ways, she sometimes wondered how they'd ever come together. He exercised, she sunbathed. He oozed self-discipline and plowed ahead with single-minded intent while up until now she'd bounced off the walls of life, pondering each cut and bruise, unprepared when the next wall went up in front of her.

So different...but in that moment, the same.

She curved her calves around his legs and moaned when his rock-hard length was cradled in her soft, wet folds. He moved away to put on a condom he'd taken from his back pocket, and she watched, entranced, as the latex stretched across his straining member. Then she scooted closer to the edge of the counter so he would have easy access.

He fitted the tip of his erection against her fleshy portal and paused. Renae wanted to groan with impatience, force his entrance. Just when she might have reached down to do just that, he tilted his hips forward, entering her a scant few inches, then withdrawing.

Renae did moan. Too little…too fast.

Restless chaos built and built, her position of no power driving her insane. If they were in bed, she would have slammed him back to the mattress and then saddled and straddled him in two seconds flat.

He stroked her again and she tried to force him in to the hilt. He grasped her hips and held her still, withdrawing again.

Renae's breath came in such ragged gasps she actually heard herself. She wanted him to fill her so badly she throbbed with the power of her need, trembled, her body no longer her own, but his to do with as he pleased.

She frantically searched his face, finding his jaw tense, his expression determined as he entered her again, no doubt intent on withdrawing before hitting all the way home. But as she watched, the pure sensation of it seemed to wash over his face and instead of withdrawing, he was sliding into the hilt, finally filling her in the way she longed to be filled.

Every molecule of air exited from Renae's lungs. Every muscle contracted. She knew a moment of fear that she might not be able to breathe or move again. Then Will pulled slightly out and surged forward again, drawing a moan from her that broke the spell and coaxed her to an even higher plane of pleasure. The cool counter under her bottom was no longer hard. The kitchen itself no longer existed. All she knew was that moment and this man. And somewhere deep down she thought that's all that she really needed.

She tightened her legs around Will's hips, teetering on the edge of orgasm. Seeming to sense her condition, Will lengthened his strokes, each one a little faster than the one before. Renae stiffened as an almost unbearable pressure took hold of her stomach. She tightly gripped his shoulders, subconsciously trying to maintain balance even as she snowboarded off the edge and into a snow-white wilderness.

Somewhere through the clouds of her own climax, she heard Will's low groan, felt him go whipcord straight.

Long moments later they were out of breath and clinging to each other, sweat glistening on their bodies, the ice cream melting on the counter next to them. And Renae looked at Will as if she really didn't know him at all.

The sound of a ringing phone pierced her ears. Renae was reminded of another telephone call a few days earlier that had not only shattered the moment, but splintered her from Will. Was it going to happen again?

Will didn't want to acknowledge the ringing phone. Didn't want to withdraw from Renae's soft body. He wanted to explore the myriad emotions that once he'd relaxed and opened the gate to, had rushed through him like dam waters being set free.

He searched Renae's face and eyes. When he'd looked at her before tonight, he'd seen a sexy woman he couldn't wait to heat up the sheets with. Now...

Damn the ringing phone.

"I...think I should get that."

He watched as Renae dropped her gaze, looking everywhere but at him as he moved away from her. Two steps and he was snatching up the receiver in the dining room. "Sexton."

"Will? Is that you?"

He tried to place the female voice but couldn't. "This is he."

A sigh then, "Good. This is Tabitha, you know, Renae's roommate upstairs. She wouldn't happen to be with you, would she? I've been calling her cell but she's not picking up."

Will looked at where Renae had her back to him. She'd already put her panties and pants back on and was working on the sweatshirt, although he knew she had to be steaming hot in the heavy cotton.

"It's for you," he said, holding out the phone.

Renae turned to face him, her shocked expression touching something deep inside him.

"It's Tabitha," he explained.

She instantly appeared to relax as she took the receiver then walked into the other room. Will used the time to clean up and get dressed himself. When Renae turned back around, he was leaning against the counter watching her.

"Coast is clear," she said, hanging the receiver back up.

Will nodded, feeling he should say something, wanting to say something, but unsure what exactly it was. He knew now wasn't the moment to lay on the table that, wrong or right, he no longer wanted to be with Janet.

After all, where did that leave him with Renae?

"Well, um, thanks for letting me wait here," she said, turning from him.

He followed her into the living room where she gathered her cell phone and her keys from the coffee table, then to the door where she appeared to hesitate for a moment before she closed it behind her.

Will leaned against the wood and dry-washed his face, trying to interpret everything that had happened in the past hour. More than just the sex. What had made him go to her when he'd seen her sitting on the stairs? What had compelled her to agree to wait at his place?

What had made him kiss her in the way he had?

He'd lived a fairly straightforward life. He'd grown up in South London in the working-class area of Southwark. No, he hadn't had the best clothes or the best bike or even the best education, but he'd made do with what he did have, getting strength from his parents whose work ethic was nothing if not stoic. Then he'd come to the States to attend medical school, bringing his sense of what he wanted out of life with him.

Or rather what he'd thought he'd wanted out of life.

Now everything emerged a thick, impenetrable fog, the future unclear and a tad intimidating.

He found himself absently rubbing his chest and looked down at where his heart still throbbed thickly beneath his breastplate. He'd never felt quite this way before, so he had absolutely no frame of reference to compare it to. To say, oh yes, I remember this, and shortly thereafter this, this and that would happen.

Instead he felt like he'd been flung into a vast sea and was navigating the waters without the aid of a chart or even a compass, the shore so far away as to be nonexistent.

The question was, did he allow the current to take him where it willed? Or did he pick up a paddle and make for the closest coast and familiar ground?

Now that was certainly something to think about....

CHAPTER FIFTEEN

RENAE NORMALLY DIDN'T have a problem with Monday mornings. But today…well, she suspected today would go down as her own personal worst. And it was only eleven o'clock. Not even the memory of last night, of her and Will, helped. In fact, considering what had happened since then, it actually hurt.

It hadn't been enough that her alarm hadn't gone off and she'd gotten up late. She hadn't been able to find the clean basket of laundry she'd put just inside her bedroom door the night before and had been forced to look for her belly dancer costume. But when she'd put that on, an important thread had given across her breasts and the sequins had popped from the material like a series of buttons being ripped from a shirt. She'd had little doubt who had been behind the mishap, but she hadn't had the time to confront Nina as she'd rushed from the apartment in a bathing-suit top and belly-dancer bottoms, reaching Women Only with only ten minutes left to go into the class she'd been scheduled to lead.

Thankfully Lucky had stopped by the shop first thing and had not only opened, she had directed the class in her jeans and T-shirt. Renae had checked her cell phone to discover it had been switched off, something she didn't remember doing. In fact, after Tabitha had been forced to call Will's direct line, she distinctly remembered turning her cell back on before returning to her condo.

And now, two hours later, she was in the middle of her sixth interview from hell to fill the position that would be left open by Lucky's pending departure.

"I don't know how my mom would feel about my selling stuff…like this dildo," the fresh-faced nineteen-year-old woman said, picking up an electric massager and staring at it.

Renae wanted to tell the overgrown teen that maybe she should consider growing up and moving out of her parents' house. "I understand completely. I wouldn't want you selling anything you hadn't a clue about, either. This," she said, taking the box from her, "is a massager or a clitoris vibrator, not a dildo. And besides, one of the job requirements is that you not only know your physical self, but that you're an expert on it, you know, should you need to fill in for someone during our popular Clit 101 course."

The teen gasped, turned as red as the curtain to the room where the class in question was conducted, then mumbled an apology as she headed for the door.

Lucky's laugh sounded from the counter where she was comparing inventory sheets. "Don't you think you were a little hard on her?"

Renae gave an eye roll. "Jesus, the girl probably didn't even know where her clitoris was."

"Yes, but when did that become one of the requirements for employment? I mean, a floor salesperson doesn't need to be an expert on the female anatomy."

Renae waved the massager. "No, but she should know that if a woman attempted to insert this she'd probably never get it back out." She shook her head as she restocked the item. "I can see the headlines now: 'The victim of electrocution was told she'd achieve the ultimate orgasm by a worker at Women Only.' And never mind the lawsuits."

Lucky tsked tsked. "Somebody woke up on the wrong side of the bed this morning." She tucked the inventory sheets away. "Actually, lately I've been wondering if you pushed your mattress against the wall so that you're getting up on the wrong side every morning."

Renae grimaced, then drew a deep breath and released it. "You're right. I have been a bit bitchy lately, haven't I?"

Lucky rounded the counter and came to stand in front of her. "Have you spoken to Ginger yet?"

Renae nodded. "Yeah. She can't have lunch with me until later this week."

Lucky smiled. "Well, that's good, isn't it? At least you'll finally get your proposal heard."

"Yeah, I guess. It's just that I couldn't help feeling she was giving me the brush-off. And, trust me, that's not a way I'm used to feeling with Ginger."

"I think she just has other things on her mind."

"Mmm." As did she.

Namely the person she'd seen coming out of Will's apartment this morning.

Lucky was looking at her a little too closely. "Are you sure that's all that's bothering you?"

"Yes," she said quickly. Then she leaned against the counter and sighed more than said, "No."

"Ah. I didn't think so."

"What is that supposed to mean?"

"That's supposed to mean that Colin told me the resident returned from California last night."

"Like I needed to be told that. I saw her coming

out of Will's apartment at nine o'clock this morning."

The words were out before she could swallow them back.

Renae winced and turned toward the counter, going through a small pile of coupons then straightening and putting them back near the register for customers to take.

After last night, she hadn't known what she'd expected. She'd sensed that something had changed in Will...had changed in their strange relationship. But when she'd returned to her condo to find a momentary peace treaty had been signed by Tabitha and Nina, she'd determined to just let whatever was happening happen. It wasn't like she had any control over it anyway. The harder she tried to understand, the more elusive the answer became. She hoped coasting and allowing the road to take her where it may might shine a spotlight on what she was missing.

Upon coming to that conclusion, she had felt like the weight of the world had been lifted from her shoulders and had slept better that night than she'd slept in a long, long time. So well she was grinning when she'd awakened, even though her alarm hadn't gone off and she was late. Not even her missing clothing and her costume mishap had managed to wipe the smile from her face.

So there she was, wearing her bikini top and belly-dancer bottoms, taking Will a couple of bagels smothered with cream cheese and smoked salmon despite how late she was running, when she saw his condo door open…

And the resident come out.

She couldn't have been more shocked had someone scooped her up while sleeping and dumped her into an ice-cold pool.

And if all that hadn't been bad enough, the resident had looked straight at her, took in her mismatched, bizarre apparel, smiled and said good morning.

Good morning.

It was the worst morning in Renae's life.

She chanced a look over her shoulder at where Lucky's brows appeared to be stuck in the middle of her forehead. "Oh?"

Renae pushed her hair back from her face and looked down at the shop sweats she was wearing. "Yeah."

"Have you thought about telling Will how you feel?"

After last night, she didn't think it was necessary to say anything. "What? That I'm jealous?"

Lucky smiled. "No. That you're interested in pursuing something…more with him."

"After the resident stayed at his place last night?" Renae shook her head. "No."

"Why not?"

"Why not?" Renae practically sputtered. "Because…because he slept with her, that's why not."

"So?"

Renae stared at Lucky as if half her marbles had just rolled out onto the floor.

Lucky crossed her arms in challenge. "Ah, so it's perfectly okay for him to sleep with you while seeing Janet, but he sleeps with Janet and it's over."

Renae squelched the ridiculous urge she had to cry. Tears burned the backs of her eyelids and her face grew hot. "No, because last night…before the resident must have come over…"

"You two had sex?"

Renae nodded then shook her head. "But that's not it. What happened between Will and I…"

"What? What happened?"

"I don't know. It was just…different somehow. It wasn't only about the sex. At least not to me."

She felt Lucky's hand on her shoulder and experienced the most incredible desire to lean into her, take her up on the comfort she offered. But she couldn't, simply because she knew she was the fool. That she'd not only allowed something really awful to happen, but she'd welcomed it with both arms wide open.

Quite simply, she'd fallen in love with Will Sexton.

WILL PACED THE FLOOR of his apartment, his mind on everything but the carpet he was currently wearing down.

The last thing he'd expected when he'd opened the door at nine that morning wearing nothing but a towel after finishing a shower was Janet bringing a homemade breakfast in a wicker basket tied with little pink ribbons.

But expected or not, there she had stood in the hall, smiling up at him like he hadn't run flat-out in the other direction from her the night before.

He'd had no choice but to let her in. After five months, certainly she deserved the courtesy of an explanation.

Unfortunately having been caught off guard and standing there in nothing but a towel hadn't exactly provided the right environment for such a conversation.

As he'd watched her set his table, he'd been afraid she was going to try what she had the night before and come on to him. Thankfully when she'd moved away from the table, he'd seen it was set for one, and after sitting him down in the chair she'd given him a kiss on the top of the head and told him she had an appointment at the hospital and left.

Of course, he'd eaten the breakfast.

But he was still berating himself for not leveling with her while he'd had the chance.

Which meant he'd have to see her once more.

The thought made his stomach knot up all over again.

"Look, Janet, I don't love you," he rehearsed, wincing at the sound of the words coming out of his mouth.

Maybe the direct approach wasn't the best one. Maybe he should say something about needing a time-out. Suggest that they see other people.

But that wouldn't work, either, if only because the excuse left the door open.

And it didn't help that it would be a lie.

He stopped pacing and uttered an oath toward the ceiling. Well, he couldn't bloody well tell her that the reason he couldn't see her anymore was that he had banged his upstairs neighbor nonstop while she was away.

An upstairs neighbor he'd watched walk out of the building right behind Janet.

He recalled the expression on Renae's face as she'd glanced up at his windows this morning. She'd look upset and angry and betrayed.

And Janet had practically skipped all the way to the parking lot.

Damn it all to hell, what was he supposed to do?

His phone rang and he snatched it up.

"You rang?" Colin asked.

Will instantly relaxed. "Harry's. Now."

"I'm with a patient."

"Well then just hand them an overdose and meet me at Harry's."

Colin chuckled. "I'll meet you after the session's over in fifteen."

"Fine."

He only hoped his friend would be able to offer up some lifesaving advice. Because the way things were looking, he might end up being the one asking for an overdose if just to stop the incessant war waging in his mind.

"WHAT IN THE HELL does it all mean?" Will asked Colin an hour, two cheeseburger platters and three draught beers later.

Colin had remained quiet during most of Will's speech, occasionally asking him to clarify which event had happened with what woman every now and again. Will had hoped that the mere act of pouring it all out to his friend would prove cathartic.

Instead he felt worse than ever.

"It means you need some serious therapy," Colin said with a grin.

Will gaped at him as if his friend was offering up a tiny bandage after a shark had attacked him. Which in essence he was. "Hell of a lot of help you are."

Colin sat back and thought for a moment then said, "You didn't honestly think I was going to fix this for you with a snap of my fingers, did you?"

"Why not? You're the bleeding psychologist, remember? The one who nearly fainted—no, wait a minute, you did faint—at the sight of blood at med school and decided matters of the head were more your style?"

"You're never going to let me live that down, are you?"

"Not so long as you keep giving me asinine answers like the one you just gave me, I'm not."

His friend sighed. "Look, Will, I told you straight up that I didn't want anything to do with what you were about to involve yourself in. Do you recall that?"

Will muttered under his breath.

"Did you ever think to ask me why?"

He squinted at his friend. "I think you should stop counseling others because their illnesses are beginning to affect you."

Colin chuckled. "Seriously, did you ever wonder why I didn't—don't—want to get involved?"

"No, I honestly can't say as I did."

"Think about it. What advice did you offer up when Lucky first came into my life?"

Will grimaced. What did all this have to do with the price of tea in China? "I suggested it might not be in your best interest to get involved with her."

"And in doing so you gave me the worst advice I'd ever received in my life."

Will sagged against the leather booth. "So you're getting revenge by not giving me any advice now."

Colin chuckled. "No, Will. I'm doing you the greatest favor of all by letting you figure this one out on your own."

CHAPTER SIXTEEN

RENAE'S NERVES were stretched to the breaking
point. There was only so much one woman could
take before she careened over the edge, wasn't
there? Forget that she still hadn't found a replacement for Lucky, which meant she was working
double-duty at Women Only. Her lunch appointment with Ginger was the following day and she
was so nervous her stomach refused any food she'd
tried to feed it since yesterday.

Then there was Will...

Three days since the ice-cream encounter on
the counter. Two days since she'd seen the resident coming out of his condo. One day since she'd
resolved to put him out of her mind altogether,
although chasing him out of her heart was a little
more difficult. More times than she cared to count,
she'd found herself absently rubbing at the ache
that resided in her chest.

Talk to him.

That was Lucky's advice.

Since he'd made no effort to talk to her, she didn't think there was anything left to talk about.

As the sun made its final journey toward the western horizon, smearing the sky with vivid purples and oranges, she parked her convertible in the complex lot and shut off the motor, which in turn switched off the radio that had been playing an old Fleetwood Mac tune. The silence pressed in around her much like the humid air, reminding her that summer was still here. She'd somehow forgotten about that. Summer. While she'd spent most of June and July hanging out at the complex pool, she hadn't even thought of swimming for almost two weeks. Her mind had been occupied with other matters that had launched her into a semitimeless state. While she was acutely aware of every second that ticked by, the passing moments seemed to hold no connection at all to the actual passage of time. So she was surprised to discover that August was quickly racing toward September and that soon autumn would be on its way.

She pushed her sunglasses back on her head, picked up the repaired belly-dancer costume and a small bag of necessities she'd bought from the drugstore then climbed out of the car. She glanced at the sky to check for rain, saw no sign, and decided to leave the top down. She didn't have to worry about anyone stealing anything. The radio was the original push-button that had come standard when the car was initially manufactured. The only items in the glove compartment were the old manuals that came with the car.

She turned toward the apartment building, her heart giving an immediate squeeze as she looked up at Will's closed vertical blinds. As soon as she got this conversation with Ginger out of the way, she should really think about moving out, getting a place of her own. While Tabitha might still need her to make the mortgage payment, she personally no longer needed the hassle that went along with the arrangement. Especially when it came to Nina.

Of course, if Will had anything to do with her need to move, she wasn't going to acknowledge it. She had enough reasons without him being a consideration.

She opened the outer building door and climbed the steps, not even pausing outside Will's door as she usually did on her way to the third floor. She shook her keys out, found her house one, then slipped it into the lock. Only it refused to turn.

She grimaced and tried again, with the same results.

That's funny....

She took the key out, checked to make sure it was the right one, then reinserted it. Nothing.

What was going on?

She switched the drugstore bag from her left hand to her right then knocked on the hard metal. It was nearly 9:00 p.m., which pretty much meant someone should be home.

Nothing.

Renae leaned her forehead against the cool metal and closed her eyes. This wasn't, couldn't, be happening.

The door across the hall opened. "A locksmith was over early this morning to change the lock."

Renae turned to take in the elderly woman who had lived in the condo across from theirs since the places had been built. While they'd traded good-mornings and holiday greetings, it wasn't often their paths crossed, and Renae was slightly surprised she was talking to her now.

"I told her the community committee would need a copy of the key for safety reasons, but she closed the door in my face."

It would probably have been a good idea if the roommates had also been provided with a copy, you know, in case they should want access to their own home.

Renae tried to make sense out of what was happening. Why would Tabitha change the locks?

Hope alit in her chest. Had she finally asked Nina to move out?

"I've never liked that Nina. She's rude and obnoxious and there's something about her I don't trust."

Renae's thoughts exactly.

"That's why I thought it was odd that she was having the locks changed."

Renae's heart stopped. "Nina had the locks changed?"

"Yes, missy, she did. And I feel obligated to inform you that I've already reported the incident to the community committee."

Renae allowed her parcels to drop to the floor where she parked herself soon after. She wondered to whom she should report that she'd been locked out of her own house.

THIS WAS IT. The moment of truth.

Well, it would be, anyway, if Will could just capture Janet's attention for more than two blinks.

He shifted in the chair at the swanky Italian restaurant on the outskirts of Toledo near Sylvania and considered the woman across from him who had the menu held up in front of her face and was ordering what could possibly be everything on it. Will tugged on his tie. Not because he couldn't afford what would undoubtedly be an expensive meal, but because he'd been hoping they wouldn't be there long enough for Janet to eat it.

"And would you like to order dessert now?" the overly polite waiter asked.

Will briefly closed his eyes, sending up a prayer that she wouldn't.

She handed him her menu. "I'll wait and see then."

Thank God for small favors.

Finally he had her attention.

And he no longer wanted it.

"This was a nice surprise," she said with a soft smile. "I was beginning to think you were avoiding me."

Will nearly choked. "Avoiding you? Why ever would I want to avoid you?" He cringed. The truth, man, give her the truth. You *have* been avoiding her.

"I had lunch with Daddy today," Janet said, sipping at what would have been an excellent Chianti if only Will had been able to get anything down his throat.

"Oh?" Will experienced the overwhelming desire to smack his forehead against the table. Because right there, laid out in front of him, had been exactly the reason why he hadn't done what he was planning to do until now.

He squinted at the pretty brunette across from

him. Could it be that Janet was subconsciously aware that her father and his position as head of staff at the hospital were the key to her personal future?

No. His own situation must be making him a little cynical.

As well as making him feel guilty as hell.

"Actually, Janet, regarding the avoidance thing. I think you have a good handle on the situation—" he began.

Two servers placed their salads on the table at the exact same time. Will jumped, not having seen them approach.

Janet made a ceremony out of placing her napkin in her lap. "It sounds as if what you have to say is serious," she said with a smile. "Why don't we wait until a little later? Enjoy the meal first? I'm starving."

And he was going to die if he didn't get the words out right now.

Instead he nodded, stared at the various greens on his plate that looked like weeds and reached for his wineglass. He stopped short of chugging the entire contents, thinking it not a good idea to be blotto when he had this conversation with Janet.

And he was going to have this conversation.

Simply, he could not continue the way he was, wanting one woman while officially attached to another. Especially when the one he was officially attached to seemed to have had a change of heart and was now offering her body up along with her heart.

The waiter topped off his wineglass and Will watched as finally their appetizers were brought, then the entrees. Somehow he managed to smile and nod at Janet's comments on the cuisine and at the tidbits she shared about her day, although how he managed was beyond him.

Maybe he should have taken her to someplace not quite as well known for its food. Like a burger joint. If anything, at least he wouldn't have had to wait through three courses before finally being given the go ahead.

Their plates were collected and Janet folded her hands on top of the table, her smile indicating she was ready. "Shall I order dessert now or wait?"

Will sat up straighter, the thought of sitting watching her eat another course excruciatingly torturous. "No, no. I think you should wait until I've said what I came here to say."

Color suffused her cheeks and her eyes seemed to dance in the flickering candlelight.

Will squinted at her again. He was getting the feeling she didn't have a clue what was on his mind.

But then again, how could she? She'd gone off

to California expecting—reasonably, he added—to come back to a loyal and loving…boyfriend. He winced at the use of the word, but that's what he amounted to, wasn't it? He really never rated as her lover.

At any rate, Janet had no reason to believe he'd been anything but the dutiful boyfriend waiting impatiently for her return.

Instead he was impatiently waiting to end things.

"Look, Janet, what I'm trying to say is…"

He drifted off. There really was no other way to say this than to just come out and say it. But damn if he could get the words out.

"Will, I think I know what you want to say," Janet said softly.

"You do?" he stared at her hopefully.

But before he could gauge the possibility of what he wanted to say being anywhere close to what she thought he wanted to say, she was saying it.

"You want to marry me."

Will nearly fell off his chair he was so shocked by her words.

She thought he wanted to propose?

He frantically looked around the place. Most of the diners were young couples, not unlike him and Janet. The atmosphere was quiet and romantic, the tables softly lit, wine bottles chilling in silver ice buckets. Exactly the type of place a man would come to propose marriage.

Will had chosen it because it was the restaurant most central to both their condos.

"You've been so adorably nervous that I couldn't bear watching you stumble over your words one more minute," she said.

He stared at her as if she had another head growing out of her cheek.

How could she have read his intentions so incorrectly?

Because, fool, she doesn't have a clue what you're all about.

Will sat for long moments, digesting his thought along with the little food he'd eaten. Sure, his agitated state could very well have been misinterpreted as pre-proposal jitters. But coming on the heels of her trip and his ducking of her physical advances…well, was the woman completely daft in the head?

No, not daft. A little naive maybe. Trusting. But not daft. After all, he'd been the one who had played her impeccably mannered date all these months, a date whose sole intention had been to get her into the sack.

"Janet, I—"

"Will, please. Don't say anything more," she interrupted, her gaze cutting away from him as she put her hands in her lap. "While I appreciate the gesture, and I really would have liked to have seen the ring..."

Ring? She thought he had a blasted ring?

"My answer is no."

Will blinked. Then he blinked again. He felt like someone had just dumped the entire contents of an ice bucket over his person.

"No?"

Okay, so he forgot that he had never intended to propose to her and instead focused on her answer, merely because it was so shocking.

Well, that, and it began dawning on him that Janet wasn't the one who was daft, he was.

"The truth is, I've become attracted to someone else."

If Will's eyebrows had been able to fly straight off his face, they would have.

"It's actually been going on for some time now."

"You've been sleeping with someone since we've been dating?"

Oh, some ladies' man he was turning out to be. He couldn't get into her panties when all along some other man had been gaining access.

"No...no. Well, not until a week or so ago anyway."

"In L.A.?"

She nodded, refusing to meet his gaze straight-on.

Not that he could blame her. He'd been unable to look at her when he'd been about to spring news of his infidelity on her.

"But why…why did you try to seduce me the other night?" he asked though there was no reason he needed to know the answer. He just couldn't help wondering.

"I don't know." She finally looked at him. "I hadn't meant to sleep with…well, the other guy. It just kind of happened. And I thought that maybe if we…"

Will couldn't help her as he was completely beyond words at that moment.

She sighed heavily. "We'd been going out for five months and I thought that if we, you and I, slept together, that everything would start making sense again."

Will nodded, then shook his head, her logic making perfect sense yet no sense at all.

"So, you see, it isn't fair for me to accept your marriage proposal."

Fair.

Now there was a word for you.

Fair.

A word that really hadn't played much of a role in recent events. Had it been fair when he'd felt so irresistibly attracted to Renae he'd slept with her before officially breaking things off with Janet? Was it fair that even when he realized that he felt more for Renae than desire that he'd allowed her to continue believing he'd been in it merely for the sex?

Was it fair that Janet had harbored a secret attraction for someone else then had given in to it the moment they were away from each other?

He opened his mouth to tell her they were equally guilty when she patted his hand in an almost motherly way that made him wince.

"I'm sorry to break this to you now, Will, really I am. I probably wouldn't have said anything at all except that you know the man in question."

How could he possibly know the man when she'd had an affair with him in L.A. at the medical convention?

Then it dawned on him. The other man was none other than resident Evan Hadley.

He felt like banging his forehead against the table. How had he missed it?

How? Because he'd been so obsessed with his own wicked deeds that he hadn't stopped to consider that anyone around him could be just as dirty. He realized he'd missed every last sign.

He stared at her. "What if I hadn't refused you

the other night? What if I'd taken you up on your generous offer and slept with you?"

She grimaced. "I don't know. I'd like to think I would have come to my senses at the last minute...."

Well, he'd been dumb enough to ask the question.

"But if we had, I keep thinking of what a mess it would have been all around."

He glimpsed an emotion on her face that he'd grown all too familiar with over the past two weeks. Guilt.

"Well, Janet, there's something I have to tell you...."

And with that, he proceeded to do just that.

He told her that when she'd left, he'd had every intention of staying true to her. That up until that point she was what he thought he wanted. He told her about Renae, about how a one-night stand had turned into a weeklong stand. He shared that he hadn't brought her to the restaurant to propose to her, but rather to come clean.

And all the time he was explaining things, he watched as her face grew redder and redder.

He finally finished the sordid tale, hoping his story would help alleviate a little of the guilt she was feeling.

Instead she picked up her glass of red wine and

tossed it into his face, then got up from the table and stalked out.

Hunh.

CHAPTER SEVENTEEN

RENAE WAS RUNNING LATE for what was probably the most important lunch date of her life.

She opened the door to the bar and grill she'd agreed to meet Ginger at, feeling sweat trickle down the back of her neck and convinced she'd never draw another calm breath again.

She'd waited around outside her locked condo door for two hours last night to no avail. Neither Tabitha nor Nina had returned. And repeated calls to the condo and Tabitha's wireless phone had produced the same results. So she'd bunked with Lucky and had been up until the wee hours of the morning trying to re-create the proposal she'd put together for Ginger. A proposal that had been hidden in the back of her closet inside the locked condo.

Ginger was sitting at a back booth talking on her cell phone. Renae took the seat across from her and smiled her apologies. She picked up a menu and pretended to read it even as she covertly took in the woman who had been more of a friend to her than a boss over the past five years.

Ginger Wasserman sometimes joked that her mother had given her the proper stripper name when she was born. But it wasn't a stage she'd found herself on when she'd been a teenager but rather a street corner because, as she told it, she'd always looked younger than her age, which was bad for someone trying to look older.

Now in her fifties, the pretty brunette could easily pass for forty, her pale skin smooth, her dark eyes clear and friendly despite the rough road she had traveled down.

Renae knew it was no accident that nearly everyone associated with Women Only had had it rough growing up. Not only knew about the shadows of life but had lived in them. There was a kind of scarring that only another person who bore the same psychological scars could spot. A sisterhood that automatically drew them to those who were like them. She'd seen it in Lucky the instant their eyes had met a few months ago. And Ginger had seen it in Renae.

And that's what set them apart from the other members of the walking wounded. When Ginger had offered Renae a hand up, she'd started a chain reaction that added new links nearly every day. She had only to marvel at Lucky's work with a local runaway shelter to understand that.

Ginger ended her call then flipped her phone closed.

Renae put aside the menu she hadn't seen a word of and smiled at her. "Sorry, I'm late. The last interview ran over."

Ginger waved away her apology. "Did you hire her?"

"Unfortunately, no." She grimaced then thanked the waitress for the glass of water she placed on the table in front of her. "She couldn't work the hours we wanted."

"Sorry to hear that."

Renae was grateful that Ginger never questioned her decisions. While she might have her doubts—as she suspected she had now, likely because it was taking Renae so long to fill the position—Ginger merely smiled, reinforcing her confidence in her.

"So what is it you wanted to discuss with me?" Ginger asked.

Renae's tongue suddenly felt like it was cemented to the roof of her mouth. She almost let out a squeal of relief when the waitress came up to take their orders. They both ordered salads and before she knew it they were alone again.

"I've been waiting for the right time to talk

to you about this, but somehow it never seemed to come." Renae knew she was rambling but she couldn't seem to help herself. This meant so much to her. If Ginger didn't like her proposal, if she turned her down, she didn't know what she would do.

Her rambling stopped as did her words. She was almost dizzy with nerves.

"You're not leaving Women Only, are you?" Ginger asked, concern apparent in her gaze.

Renae laughed so hard she nearly cried. Her friend's puzzled expression caught her up short. "Hardly."

"Good. Because I couldn't run Women Only without you, Renae."

She stared at Ginger. That was good, wasn't it? If Ginger really felt she was that much of an integral part of the shop, then she shouldn't mind letting her buy into it.

"I don't know if you've noticed lately, but I've been a little preoccupied," Ginger said.

Renae was surprised by the offering up of the information.

"You see, I've met someone."

Renae sat up straighter. "Really? Who, when, where?"

Ginger smiled and waved her hand, causing the

thin gold bracelets she always wore to slink up her slender forearm. "That's not really important."

"Sure it is!" she disagreed. "If you're serious about this guy, then it's very important."

Ginger cleared her throat. "What I meant to say is that what is important is that he's not from here, Toledo, I mean. He lives in Arizona. And, well, that's where I've been spending a lot of my time lately."

It struck Renae as more than odd that she was just now realizing that Ginger hadn't only been preoccupied with other matters and away from the shop, but she'd been out of town. It was kind of hard to drop by when you were ten states away.

Their salads were delivered and Renae took the opportunity to think about what Ginger had just said. She'd met a man and he lived in Arizona, and apparently it wasn't easy for him to come to Toledo, so she went to him—

Ginger sighed deeply. "You don't know what a relief it is to finally share that with somebody."

"I'm glad it was me you shared it with."

"I am, too."

Then it struck Renae. The way fate was laying the cards out in front of her like a royal flush.

She forced herself to eat at least a bit of her salad, then she pushed her plate aside, pulled her proposal out of her purse and laid it down flat on the table. "Well, then, Ginger, do I ever have the proposition for you...."

RENAE RETURNED from her lunch with Ginger feeling ten times better and ten times worse. While final details had yet to be worked out, Ginger had been intrigued by her idea, first because she felt Renae deserved the buy-in option, and second because the arrangement would free Ginger up to spend more time with her newfound love in Arizona.

Of course, now that the proposal was in and things were officially under way for her new career move, Renae wondered what she'd been thinking. She was nervous, scared and overwhelmed. But in a happy, excited way.

She'd still felt like that when she'd tried yet again to call Tabitha on her cell to tell her she'd been locked out of the condo.

Her friend had finally answered and had been genuinely appalled by the news. She'd had no idea Nina had changed the locks and they'd agreed to meet up at the condo later that day.

Over the remainder of the afternoon at Women Only, Renae had managed to get something of a grip on her nerves, but the instant she pulled into the condo complex parking lot, her heart pounded thickly in her chest. Will's SUV was nearby which meant he was home. But she reminded herself that he wasn't the reason she was there. She needed to find out what the status of her residency was. Did she still live in Tabitha's condo? Or was it long past time for her to move out?

She climbed the stairs to the third floor, wondering what she would do if Will opened up his door and addressed her. A question that went unanswered as she passed his condo without incident. She knew a sharp stab of disappointment, but raised her chin and continued up to the condo. After taking her keys out, she tried her copy one last time. It still didn't work.

So she knocked instead, moments later finding herself face-to-face with a stone-eyed Nina.

"What are you doing here?" the other woman asked coldly.

Renae raised a brow. "The last time I checked I still lived here," she said, carefully rounding the woman lest she should try to close the door on her.

"Tabitha?" she called out.

Her best friend of over a decade came out of the kitchen. "I'm glad we're all three together. Maybe we can clear up this confusion."

Confusion? Nina had changed the locks without giving her a key and just made it abundantly clear she didn't want her in the apartment anymore.

Renae didn't think things could get more cut-and-dried than that.

But rather than saying so, she followed her friend into the kitchen, Nina close behind. She took a seat across from her friend while Nina, of course, took a seat closer to Tabitha.

Tabitha looked tired. More tired than Renae could remember seeing her. "It looks like there's been a misunderstanding and an apology is in order," she said. "It appears Nina lost her keys the night before last and was afraid that someone might be able to gain access to the apartment so she called in a locksmith. But before she could get you a key, we had to go meet some friends we'd arranged to hook up with."

Renae squinted at Tabitha. Certainly she wasn't trying to explain this away? Even if Renae accepted the apology and the reason for the "confusion," why hadn't Tabitha's cell phone been working last night? And why hadn't anyone picked up the phone here all night?

And, more important, why wasn't she being offered a key now?

She looked at Nina for the first time since entering the kitchen. "Then why did you just ask me what I was doing here like I was the last person you'd expect to see at the door?"

Tabitha sighed heavily. "Maybe it's because you usually get home after nine, Renae."

"Or maybe this has all been a ruse since the moment Nina moved in here," she countered.

She remembered her missing notes, her sabotaged cell phone, her missing clothing and felt a disappointment so strong that she could do little more than shrug. "You know what? I'm tired of dealing with this. I'm going to get some of my things now and I'll come back for the rest of my stuff when I find a place."

Tabitha blinked at her while Nina looked on the verge of cheering.

"But just so we don't get in each other's way, why don't you give me a new key now? I'll leave it once I've collected everything."

She looked at Tabitha who in turn looked at Nina.

"What? I didn't have time to make another copy."

Renae gave Tabitha a long, disappointed look. "That's what I thought."

As she got up and went about collecting her clothes from her room, she heard what could only be the beginning of an argument start in the kitchen. But at least she wouldn't be stuck on the steps as the two star-crossed lovers had it out.

"I'M REALLY SORRY you went through what you did tonight." Lucky placed the pillow and blanket Renae had used the night before on the couch then sat down beside her.

Renae could do little more than nod, not only numbed by the day's events, but overwhelmed by everything that had transpired over the past twelve days. Will...Tabitha...Nina...Ginger.

Lucky leaned slightly against her then drew back. "It's been quite a roller-coaster ride, huh?"

Renae hadn't missed her friend's hesitant physical reaching out then retreat. She turned her head and smiled at Lucky then leaned against her arm and stayed there. "Thank God for you."

Lucky didn't appear to know how to respond at first. Then she laughed and leaned into her as well. "You know you have a couch whenever you need one."

"I'm not, um, cramping your love life?"

Lucky's eyes twinkled. "Actually I'm going over to stay at Colin's tonight. That is if you think you can spare me."

Renae's throat tightened, so thankful for Lucky in that one moment she was incapable of speech. "Thank you."

"No need for thanks, Rea. I'm happy to help." She held out a key to her.

Renae slowly took it and sat staring at it for long minutes.

"Funny how life works out, isn't it?" she asked quietly, staring at the opposite wall of the older apartment with its airy rooms and original wood floors. "Just when you think you have everything figured out, bam, life throws a curveball at you that no one could possibly hit."

"Tell me about it." Lucky settled in a little more comfortably. "Do you mind if I share a bit of advice with you?"

Renae looked at her. "Please do."

Lucky cleared her throat. "There are always more pitches and, unlike in baseball, in life you get to take as many swings as you want. And eventually you're going to hit that damn ball."

Renae smiled. "That's nice."

Lucky smiled back. "While the words are different, it's the same advice I received not too long ago from a very, very wise woman. Advice that helped me through one of the toughest times of my life."

Renae's eyes began welling with hot tears as she leaned her head against Lucky's shoulder. Because she knew without her friend telling her so that the woman she was referring to was her.

CHAPTER EIGHTEEN

THE FOLLOWING DAY Will found himself pacing inside his apartment—again. But this time it was for a completely different reason than last time. He glanced at his watch. Half past noon. Renae would be at work....

He rubbed his forehead, just then realizing he didn't even know where she worked. Back when he'd indulged in lesbian fantasies of her with her roommate, he'd allowed himself to imagine she worked someplace seedy and sexy, what with the naughty belly-dancer costume she wore and all.

How was it that in all the times they'd slept together, that he hadn't asked her?

Well, wherever it was, he knew she didn't knock off until after nine. And he wasn't in any condition to wait that long. His mind was clogged full of things he wanted to say to her. Things he wanted to know about her. They'd been there all along, but had somehow been eclipsed by what he'd viewed as the greater problems in his life. Not the least of which was his letter of resignation on the dining-room table behind him.

After the disastrous dinner last night, he'd understood that whatever future he'd thought he had at the hospital was now at an end. The Medical College of Ohio had been after him for years to join their staff. And while they didn't pay nearly as well as the private center where he had worked for the past six years, at least he wouldn't have to sleep with the chief of staff's daughter in order to get a bloody promotion.

Of course, he hadn't begun dating Janet with any such designs. That it had worked out that way—that he'd finally gained Dr. Nealon's attention because he had been dating Janet—had been an unfortunate turn of events.

Without the promotion he was left facing an indeterminate amount of time on the night shift. And right now there was something else he'd much rather be doing with his nights.

More specifically having wicked, marvelous sex with Renae Truesdale.

The mere idea of seeing her again, having her in his bed, sent him heading toward a destination beyond his hall carpet. He hauled open the outside door, climbed the steps to the third floor, then knocked on 3B. He was about to knock again when the newer girl to the apartment—Nina, Renae had said her name was—opened up and stood staring at him.

"What do you want?"

After what Will had been through, her attitude was nothing more than a minor irritation. "I'm looking for Renae."

"She doesn't live here anymore."

Whoa. Now that was something noteworthy, not to mention shocking. "I see. And when did this… parting happen?"

"Yesterday."

She began closing the door and Will caught it with his hand. The woman looked like she would have liked nothing better than to slam his fingers in the door if she'd had the strength. "Forwarding address?"

"None."

Will pushed harder on the door to keep her from closing it in his face. "I was wondering if you might tell me where she works?"

"I don't know. Now if you don't let go of this door I'm going to call 911."

"Mmm. We wouldn't want that to happen now, would we?" Will asked. "You might actually have to answer their questions."

Nina glared at him.

Then it dawned on him. He did know where Renae worked. She worked with Lucky. That's how the two women had met. How could he have forgotten that? Colin talked about Lucky's opening a satellite shop all the time. A satellite of the original where Renae worked.

He released the door, saying, "Have a good day now, won't you?"

The door slammed so hard it shuddered on its hinges.

Will shook his head, grabbed his cell phone out of his pocket and began dialing Colin as he rushed back to his place.

"Where does Lucky work?" he asked his friend without preamble.

"Ah, I was wondering when I was going to hear from you."

"What's that supposed to mean?"

"Oh, I don't know. Just that a certain somebody has spent the last couple of nights on my girlfriend's couch. Don't tell me it took you that long to notice she was gone?"

"Okay, then, I won't."

Colin chuckled. "The name of the shop is Women Only. But which address did you want? To the shop Lucky's opening downtown? Or the original?" he asked in a way-too-innocent voice.

Will said nothing simply because what was on the tip of his tongue wasn't very nice.

His friend finally shared the address to the original location.

"But I wouldn't do anything hasty, friend. She's going through—"

Will hung up on him with nary a thank you.

Will knew where the shop was, if only because he and his college buddies—Colin included—used to frequent the nearby strip joints where they'd get nice and sloshed and empty their pockets of dollar bills every Saturday night.

It seemed ironic that he would be going to the same general location now in order to find the woman he intended to marry.

Marry...

"Now, now, not so fast, man. Get to know the woman a little better," he told himself as he hurriedly collected his wallet and his keys from his kitchen table, then left his condo. "Besides, she may not even want to see your sorry butt again much less marry you."

Marry...

Even during his five months with Janet and her repeated "I'm waiting till my wedding night" speeches, he'd never really given any serious consideration to marrying her. Sure, he'd idly thought she might make good wife material when they began going out. But at no time did he think himself incapable of living without her in his life. At no time did the mere thought of not being able to see her drive him out of his skin.

Renae...

Was it him or was the hair on his arms standing on end?

The change of temperature from the air-conditioned building to the hot outdoors, he explained away, although he fully admitted that Renae Truesdale was enough to make any man stand at attention, literally and figuratively.

Why hadn't he seen it before now? Why hadn't he understood that she offered everything and more than he would ever need in a life mate? Had he been blinded by sex? Distracted by stupid preconceptions? Occupied with the other details of his life?

He climbed into his SUV, summing up every ounce of his willpower not to flatten the gas pedal to the floor in his hurry to drive to Women Only.

Before he knew it, he was pulling into the commercial parking lot. Renae's old pink Cadillac stood out like a neon sign outside the shop. He parked in the first free spot he saw, shut off the engine...then froze, Colin's final words finally registering.

"I wouldn't do anything hasty, friend. She's going through—"

What?

Will realized he'd hung up on his friend without letting him finish his sentence.

There was movement near the shop. He watched as a young woman approached the door to Women Only, clutching her purse to her side as if her life depended on what was about to happen. Will blinked several times as he watched none other than Renae herself greet the new visitor with a welcoming smile.

His heart turned over in his chest.

He fished his cell phone out of his pocket and redialed Colin. "What were you going to say?"

"You do realize I have a life, don't you? In fact, I have an entire career. Which includes patients that don't appreciate these interruptions."

Will gestured impatiently with his free hand. "And?"

"And what I was about to say before you so rudely hung up on me is that I don't think the emotional place Renae is in at this moment is conducive to…well, whatever you have in mind."

"Go on."

"She's just made a very important career step that is causing her a great amount of stress, she's lost her home and is sleeping on Lucky's couch—"

"Then my asking her to move in with me should solve all of her problems then."

Silence.

"Great. Thanks."

"Will?"

He resisted the urge to disconnect the call but kept his hand on the door handle. "What?"

"My advice would be for you to take this slow."

"Like you took it with Lucky?"

"Lucky and I are still not married, not even engaged, even though I want both so bad it hurts."

Will found that a difficult pill to swallow.

"Am I making sense here?"

"Too much," Will grumbled.

"Slow. That's how you want to take this. You go into that shop, guns blazing, and she's liable to shoot back with ammo you're unprepared for."

Will grumbled as he rubbed the back of his neck. "Is this the way you talk to your patients? It's a wonder you even have a practice."

Colin chuckled. "That means you get my point. Good."

"Is that all?"

"Yes, I think that about covers it."

Will moved to disconnect.

"Oh, and one more thing."

Will closed his eyes and cursed.

"Good luck, buddy."

"Luck has nothing to do with it. It's all skill."

And patience.

And unfortunately he'd already demonstrated he wasn't very good with that.

"IS THAT WILL?"

Renae stopped talking to the girl she was interviewing midsentence and froze at Lucky's words. She glanced toward her friend, then followed her gaze through the shop window. Sure enough, an SUV identical to Will's was at the far end of the parking lot.

Her stomach gave a squeeze…then dropped out altogether when the SUV backed up and pulled out of the lot, instantly disappearing into the heavy traffic.

"Sorry."

Renae glared at Lucky.

"Honest mistake. The car looked just like his."

"As do about five percent of the cars in Toledo."

Lucky tried to hide her smile as she wrapped up a customer purchase.

"I said I was sorry."

"Miss Truesdale? Is everything all right?"

Renae blinked, almost having forgotten about the girl she was interviewing.

Jenny Naxos was twenty-one, more than

qualified for the position with a number of retail jobs on her application, and was currently working at a mall store that sold costume jewelry.

But it was the soft look in her dark eyes that won Renae over more than anything on her application.

"Everything's fine," she said, smiling. "In fact, it's more than fine. You're hired."

She'd been talking to the girl for no more than five minutes. But that didn't matter to Renae. She'd gone on gut instinct when taking on Lucky months before. And look what had happened there.

As far as she was concerned, how you felt around a person was more important than anything else.

"What?" Jenny whispered, staring at her.

"I said you're hired. I mean, if you're still interested in the job?"

"Interested? Oh my God!"

She shocked Renae by hugging her, briefly but tightly.

Okay, Renae thought, startled off her heels. They'd have to work on the physical demonstrations. Then again, she thought with a smile, maybe not. Maybe what the shop—and she—needed was someone who not only understood how she felt, but wasn't afraid to show it.

"Welcome to the family," Lucky said to Jenny after the customer she'd helped left the store.

As Lucky and their new employee conversed, Renae felt herself drawn to the shop window and the spot where the SUV similar to Will's had been parked.

If what she'd just thought was true, what were her gut instincts when it came to Will Sexton?

Now that was something that would take a little bit of thinking.

Okay, a lot.

THE HOSPITAL'S TRAUMA center was quieter than it had been all week.

And Will was about to jump out of his skin.

It was more than just this blasted waiting stuff in connection to Renae. He'd personally taken his resignation to the chief of staff's office before clocking in and now it was merely a matter of Nealon officially accepting it and releasing him of his hospital obligations.

He shifted where he stood at the nurses' station then signed off on a resident's opinion, noticing that it was Evan Hadley's opinion he was checking.

Interesting, but he couldn't remember actually seeing the other man in the past two hours. Or the night before, for that matter. This when they were usually bumping into each other all the time as they came and went.

He handed the chart to the attending nurse then

turned to take in the area, halls included. Luckily he didn't have to worry about running into Janet. Although he'd met her when she'd worked nights, she'd been transferred to days a few months ago. But Evan...

He looked into a few of the examining rooms and found Evan in the fourth, alone, making notations on a pad.

Will pushed the door open. "There you are."

Was it his imagination or had the other man jumped?

Definitely not his imagination. In fact, he was a little concerned that the young resident had just swallowed his tongue and might be in need of some medical attention himself shortly. "Will!" he fairly croaked.

Will grimaced and looked into the hall behind him. "Expecting somebody else?"

"N-no. Yes."

At his stuttering, Will had no doubt Evan had been avoiding him because of Janet.

He opened his mouth to say there was nothing to worry about, that he and Janet had parted amicably—well, as far as Will was concerned anyway—but he was suddenly struck with the most devilish desire to draw this out a little.

"So, Janet told me you two ran into each other in L.A."

Evan's eyes were as round as a nearby bedpan. "Yes, we, um, did."

In fact, Evan had told him that himself, but the other man didn't appear to be in any condition to remember small details like that.

"And did you...enjoy each other's company?"

Evan made a small choking noise.

Will chuckled, incapable of making the poor guy suffer any longer. "Oh, forget about it, man. Janet told me what happened."

The resident gaped at him. "And you're not upset?"

Will shook his head. "No, strangely enough, I'm not. In fact, allow me to congratulate you on your great taste in women."

He extended his hand for a handshake but Evan was staring at the appendage like he didn't trust what Will's true intentions might be.

"Dr. Sexton, please report to the nurses' station. Dr. Sexton, please report to the nurses' station. Stat."

Will grimaced at the P.A. announcement as Evan finally put his hand in his and they shook.

Evan looked like he'd just been given a reprieve while strapped into the electric chair. "I can't tell you how relieved I am that you're okay with this."

"Don't mention it," Will said and sighed. "Well, duty calls. Give Janet my best, won't you?"

"Yes...sure."

Will left the examining room shaking his head. What had the man expected him to do? Box him about the ears over a woman?

Of course had the woman been Renae...

He spotted the reason he was being summoned and stopped dead in his tracks. At the nurses' station chatting with the head nurse was none other than Janet's father, Stuart Nealon.

Crikey.

He wondered if the chief of staff would notice if he walked in the opposite direction.

"Will!" Stuart shouted a greeting.

Too late. He was in for this confrontation whether he was ready for it or not.

"I'm glad I caught you during a quiet stretch," Stuart said, meeting him halfway and pretty near knocking him over with a pat on the back. "Come with me to the staff lounge, won't you?"

"Actually I..." Will began.

Stuart looked at him, his face unreadable.

"Never mind. I guess I can spare a few minutes."

He couldn't help registering that he felt the way Evan Hadley had looked a few minutes ago.

Still looked, he corrected, as he spotted Evan

exiting the examining room while they were passing. The resident immediately dropped his gaze and scurried in the opposite direction.

Will reflected that after what he'd just done to the poor guy—making him suffer before setting things straight—that this was exactly what Will deserved.

Truth was, if Nealon wanted to put the brakes on his leaving, he could. There were eight months to go on his contract with the hospital, which meant Nealon could make him stay for at least that amount of time. Then there was the option for the hospital to keep him beyond that.

Nealon opened the door to the staff lounge and allowed Will to go in first. The three staff members currently in the room mumbled greetings then quickly left them alone.

"So…" Nealon drew out.

Will had begun sitting down at one of the tables, but halted when he noticed the other man had chosen to stand, his arms crossed in front of him.

Will gulped.

"I understand things between you and my daughter are a little rocky right now."

Oh, boy. Not exactly an auspicious beginning. "Yes, sir, they are." An image of Evan's purple face emerged in his mind and he wondered if he looked just as ridiculous. "Actually, sir, your daughter and I are no longer dating."

Nealon didn't say anything for a long moment. Merely stood there looking at him as if expecting him to continue.

Will didn't. Instead he squared his shoulders and returned the other man's stare.

To his surprise, Nealon laughed. "Not an easy man to shake up, are you, Sexton?"

Will managed to remain unblinking. "Does that surprise you?"

"Actually, no." He took a piece of folded paper out of his white physician's coat pocket and held it up. "This look familiar to you?"

"Yes, in fact it does. That would be my letter of resignation."

Stuart put it on the table between them. "I'm afraid I can't accept it."

Damn. He was going to make him honor the remaining months on his contract.

"Because I've decided to give you that promotion."

Will did blink then. "Excuse me?"

Nealon chuckled. "You seem surprised. Why? Did you think I was going to give you grief because things ended badly between you and my daughter?" He shook his head. "This is on your merit,

Sexton. And like I said before, I've had my eye on you for a while."

He had? It was?

Will's grin was so wide it nearly hurt his face. He thrust his hand out and animatedly shook Nealon's. "Thank you, sir. You don't know how happy you've just made me."

Stuart chuckled again. "Oh, I don't know," he said, apparently almost losing his balance from Will's enthusiastic hand shaking. "I think I have an idea."

"Oh. Sorry." Will released him.

Stuart turned toward the door and together they walked out into the hall. "Now, about this matter with my daughter..."

Both men laughed while the remainder of the staff looked on with puzzled interest.

CHAPTER NINETEEN

IT WAS HARD TO BELIEVE it was mid-September already. Renae pulled open the door to Women Only at a bit before 8:00 a.m. on a crisp Saturday morning, giving a brief shiver as she hurried into the shop, the clinking of metal disks accompanying her. To her surprise, Lucky had already opened up, the lights were on, and coffee was brewing. Only a week to go before her friend officially opened her own shop downtown, which meant all too soon Renae wouldn't be able to enjoy the other woman's help anymore.

She shrugged out of the jacket she'd been forced to put on over her belly-dancer costume, grimacing as she wished she had thought to get her clothes out of the community dryer at her apartment building last night. But she'd instead fallen asleep while poring over the contracts that Ginger had drawn up. One gave her an opening five percent interest in the shop, and the other allowed for her to buy another forty-six percent controlling interest over the next five years. She'd been so obsessed with the contracts not because she was afraid the legalese was in question, but because the papers represented so many of her dreams realized.

She'd been so engaged she'd woken up that morning with her cheek pressed against the top staple holding the legal documents together and she still sported a dent there. She absently rubbed at it, remembering that when she'd taken her clothes from the dryer that morning they'd been wrinkled beyond repair. In fact, she planned on washing them over completely rather than attempting to iron them.

Which left her wearing her belly-dancer costume to work yet again this morning.

Her steps faltered as she remembered that it had been in a similar situation that the flirtation between her and Will had taken a serious, more intense turn.

Will...

Not a minute ticked by that he wasn't somewhere on the fringes of her thoughts despite that it had been nearly three weeks since she'd last seen him. Through what had gone on during that time— implementing her plans for Women Only, searching for an apartment, moving into her new place, collecting her things from Tabitha's condo, even though Tabitha had since ended it with Nina after discovering she had been every bit as manipulative and psychotic as Renae had warned her—there Will was, indelibly branded into the chambers of her heart. Unforgettable. Lingering. More than just a notch in her headboard, but rather a vital part of her emotional past. Simply because he had shown her, for a brief, precious period of time, what it was like to love.

Some might call her silly. After all, their relationship had been conducted mostly in bed. But she knew her own heart. And she knew with every cell of it that, while she wasn't looking, she'd fallen in love with the infuriatingly handsome British surgeon.

She tucked her jacket behind the counter, wondering where he'd been when she'd collected her things from the condo. She'd tried to argue that she hadn't purposely scheduled her visit to the complex for the same time when they'd met up there all those times. But her attempts failed miserably if only because of the deep regret she'd felt when she'd loaded the last of her belongings into her convertible and neither him nor his SUV had been anywhere to be seen.

"Oh! I didn't hear you come in."

Renae smiled at the latest addition to the Women

Only family, who'd just stepped out of the dance room. "You're here early," she said, "especially considering you weren't scheduled to come in today."

Lucky came out right after Jenny. "I called her in."

Renae was puzzled but didn't question the action. "Are the students all set?"

Lucky and Jenny shared a look then grinned at her. "All ready."

Renae squinted at them. They were acting a little strange this morning.

"Okay. Well, then, I guess I'd better get in there and start the lesson."

Lucky cleared her throat. "Yes…I guess you'd better."

As soon as Renae moved past them, her friend grabbed Jenny's arm and quickly pulled her away from the door.

What was going on? You'd think the two of them were in cahoots or some—

She stopped just inside the mirrored room with its gleaming wood floors, realizing exactly why the two women were acting the way they were. Namely because they *were* in cahoots. Because in place of her regular fifteen or so students stood one person.

And Dr. Will Sexton had never looked so good.

Renae began backing up toward the curtain.

"Oh, no, you don't," Lucky's voice came from behind her as she closed the door, a recent addition to the shop to stop the music from bothering the shop's customers.

Renae's throat grew tight as her gaze flicked everywhere and stayed nowhere. To dozens and dozens of red roses set up throughout the room. To the large red floor pillows at Will's feet that Lucky and Jenny must have taken from the other room and set up in here. To where the stereo played the same Sting CD Will had put on for her such a short time ago so she might dance for him—although if she remembered correctly, she hadn't done a whole lot of dancing.

Then, finally, with nowhere else to go, her gaze rested on Will himself.

God, but the guy was stunning. Even more gorgeous than she remembered, in his dark slacks and tan polo shirt. His light brown hair was neatly combed but it still had that tousled look that had always driven her crazy. Especially when combined with his devil-may-care grin that even now made her toes curl in her sequined sandals.

"Hi," he said, then cleared his throat.

Hi? She hadn't seen him for three long weeks and now he was standing there, the room looking like it was, and all he had to say was "hi?"

Renae suddenly felt dizzy.

"Whoa," he said, stepping forward until he was right in front of her. "I think we've discussed my incredible effect on beautiful women, but you don't have to go demonstrating it for me."

Renae couldn't help the silly smile that emerged. "Sorry. I haven't had anything to eat yet this morning and…" And the lack of food had absolutely nothing to do with her dizziness. "What are you doing here?"

Will straightened his shoulders, attempting to look affronted. "Why I've come for a belly-dancing lesson, of course."

Renae allowed her gaze to skim over his sexy frame, lingering at the width of his shoulders, the narrowness of his hips, and especially on the part of him that was even now tenting the front of his pants. "You're dressed wrong."

"Would you prefer I undress?"

He moved as if to take off his shirt and Renae quickly grasped his arm. "No, no."

She swallowed thickly. She didn't think she was up for this. What was happening? What was he really doing there? What had happened with the resident? And why did she still want him so damn badly she was trembling inside?

"Okay, so I'll remain dressed for what I have to say. That's all right. It's probably better that way, anyway, or else I might end up saying none of what it's taken me weeks to rehearse."

Renae stood frozen. "Weeks?"

He grinned. "Uh-huh."

He'd spent weeks not only thinking about her but putting together something he wanted to say to her?

She heard incidental noises coming from the other side of the door and she looked toward it, wondering if Lucky was regretting closing the thick wooden barrier because she couldn't hear what was being said.

And what was being said? What was Will trying to say? Renae couldn't seem to wrap her mind around the fact that he was there at all much less comprehend what he wanted.

"Well, then," he said, clearing his throat. "I suppose since the girls went to all the trouble, we really should do this right."

Renae drew her brows together, looking at him as if he'd gone insane. "Do what right?"

"Come...I'll show you."

He grasped her hand and Renae was helpless to do anything else but follow him, however warily, across the floor to the pillows positioned in the middle of the room.

Will dropped down to one knee in front of the pillows...and in front of her.

Renae made a strangled sound, her heart thudding so hard in her chest she was afraid it might break through her rib cage.

"Wait, wait…don't say anything yet," Will said, frantically patting his pockets, then appearing to remember something and pulling up a corner on one of the pillows instead. Renae stared at the square ring box, the air rushing from her lungs.

She began backing away.

"Oh, no, you don't," Will said, tugging her toward him again. "You're not going anywhere until I've said what I came here to say."

"Will…I don't—"

"Shh. You don't even know what it is yet."

No…but she was getting the sneaking suspicion of what it might be. And she wasn't anywhere near—

Will popped open the box and held it up to her.

She squeezed her eyes shut without seeing the contents.

Oh God, oh God, oh God.

"Renae Elizabeth Truesdale…would you do me the honor of accompanying me home to meet my parents?"

Renae's eyes flew open. "What did you just say?" She finally registered what the box held.

Rather than a diamond solitaire, she was staring at a diamond navel ring.

The unexpected gift made joy bubble inside her chest.

"May I?" Will said, taking the ring out of the box.

Renae looked at the red crystal navel ring she currently had on. "I'd like that."

After a few fumbled attempts, she decided she should let him off the hook. "Here…maybe it would be better if I do it."

She easily removed the one she had on and inserted the new one. The precious gem flashed in the warm overhead lights.

"Mmm," Will hummed, pressing his mouth against the ring and her stomach. A delicious shiver ran the length of Renae's back as she knelt down in front of him so they could be face-to-face.

"Where's home," she whispered, feeling so much love for the man in front of her that she virtually swam in it.

His gaze swept over her face as if he couldn't quite believe she was there. "London," he said. "Actually it's South London in a place called Southwark on the other side of the Thames."

"And you want me to go because…"

"I want you to meet my family. You know, my

parents, my four brothers and sisters. The whole lot, in fact."

Renae blinked, so overwhelmed with his nearness that she almost couldn't concentrate on what he was saying. "And you want me to do that because…"

He looked at her as if affronted by the question. "Because I love you, of course."

The matter-of-fact way he said the words—as if the state of his heart should have been obvious to her—made her almost burst with the urge to laugh deliriously.

And, she realized, in a twisted kind of way, she *had* known he loved her.

In her life, she had never been wanted so fully, so passionately by a man. During their short time together, he'd made her feel desired and needed in a way that at the time she had mistaken for lust. But lust didn't last.

Now, while she read physical need on Will's face, she also saw love there, shining at her, drawing her in, making her feel warm in places that had nothing to do with sex.

Then he was kissing her. And Renae was kissing him back.

Within seconds they were sprawled across the pillows in a riot of clinking disks.

His elbow caught her in the stomach when he reached for her breast.

"Ouch."

"Apologies."

She accidentally got her fingers tangled in his hair and tried pulling them free.

"Careful."

"Sorry."

Then they got it right, stroking and petting and hungrily kissing each other as if nothing else existed in the world. And in that one moment, nothing else did.

Finally Will drew back, his breathing ragged, his blue eyes almost black with need.

"And the resident?" she asked between attempts to catch her own breath.

"The resident? Oh, Janet, you mean. History, her. The instant you came into my life. Only I didn't realize it until she came back from L.A." He drew a finger along the edge of her top, flicking a couple of the disks so that they clinked. "You seemed surprised to find a belly ring in the box," he said, his gaze lifting to her. "Were you expecting something else?"

Renae found it almost impossible to swallow when her body clamored so loudly for his. "I don't know. Was there a possibility it could have been something else?"

He gave her that lopsided grin she loved so much. Ignoring her question, he asked, "And suppose that it was—something else, I mean?"

She didn't blink as she held his gaze. "Well, then, I would have given you the only answer I could: yes."

He pulled her so close so fast they nearly fell off the pillows.

Renae gasped.

"Then we'll have to go shopping for one together in London. Harrods, maybe. Yes, very definitely Harrods." He pulled back to look at her. "Would you mind if the ceremony actually took place in Southwark? My mother would love that."

Renae twisted her lips, wondering if there was a time when she'd ever felt so complete, so happy, so incredibly aroused. "Oh, I don't know. I guess it depends."

He raised his brows. "On what?"

"On whether or not you still want me to be your wife once you find out I used to be a stripper."

He stared at her for a long, silent moment.

Then he grinned. "A stripper, huh?"

"Uh-huh. It was kind of a family trade."

He kissed her long and hard. "You realize you just gave me a great fantasy?"

She took his hand and placed it solidly between her legs. "Will, I'm giving you the whole package."

"You wicked, wicked woman you…"

* * * * *

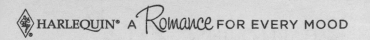

HARLEQUIN® A *Romance* FOR EVERY MOOD

If you enjoyed these passionate reads, then you will love other stories from

HARLEQUIN® *Presents*

Glamorous international settings...
unforgettable men...passionate romances—
Harlequin Presents promises you the world!

HARLEQUIN® *Blaze*™

Fun, flirtatious and steamy books that tell it
like It is, inside and outside the bedroom.

Silhouette® *Desire*

Always Powerful, Passionate and Provocative

Six new titles are available every month from each of these lines

Available wherever books are sold

*If you enjoyed this story from Tori Carrington,
here is an exclusive excerpt from her upcoming book
PRIVATE SESSIONS.
Available October 2010 from Harlequin Blaze.*

CALEB KNEW who Bryna Metaxas was.

They'd met once. And he'd never forgotten her. Bryna was the type of looker who would be right at home sunning herself on a yacht, a white, barely there bikini playing up her physical assets, large sunglasses perched on her petite nose, her long, dark hair combed back while a formally clad waiter served her a dirty martini.

So now, he openly appreciated the pretty young woman who'd stormed his office on a mission after he'd made her wait for half an hour.

"Thanks for taking my appointment," Bryna said, moving her briefcase from one hand to the other and then extending her right.

"No problem." Was her skin really that soft? Caleb shamelessly held on to the feminine digits, rubbing his thumb slowly along the back.

He watched her dark green eyes grow large at the unabashed liberty he claimed.

She cleared her throat and purposely withdrew her hand.

"I have three proposals I'd like to submit to you," she said, sitting down in one of the two high-backed visitor's chairs and putting her case down at her crossed ankles. Slender, shapely ankles that drew his attention. She withdrew documents and held them out to him.

He made no move to take them. Instead, he allowed his gaze to rake up her calves to where the hem of her skirt had hiked up to just above her pleasing knees.

Bryna placed the proposals on his desk. "I'm sure that

once you've had a chance to review them, you'll see that a partnership with Metaxas, Ltd. would be in everyone's best interest."

He liked her spunk. And obviously she'd put a lot of thought into her approach, even though she knew the chances of his taking her up on her offer were remote.

He picked up the folders, glanced at the top one, and then held them out to her.

"While flattered, Miss Metaxas, I'm afraid I'm not interested."

She took the proposals, but the look in her eyes told him that she knew he was interested. If not in what she had to offer professionally, then personally.

"I feel it's only fair to tell you that this won't be the last you hear from me," she said quietly.

Caleb's gaze slid over her face, taking in the hint of heated color and her plump, moist lips before returning to her eyes.

"I certainly hope not, Miss Metaxas."

And the game begins…
To find out who wins this sexy game of cat and mouse,
be sure to pick up PRIVATE SESSIONS, the first book
in Tori Carrington's PRIVATE SCANDALS trilogy,
available in October 2010 only from Harlequin Blaze.

REQUEST YOUR FREE BOOKS!

2 FREE NOVELS PLUS 2 FREE GIFTS!

HARLEQUIN®

Blaze™

Red-hot reads!

SUSPENSE & PARANORMAL

Heartstopping stories of intrigue and mystery—
where true love always triumphs.

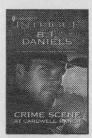

Harlequin Intrigue®

Breathtaking romantic suspense. Crime
stories that will keep you on the edge of
your seat.

Silhouette® Romantic Suspense

Heart-racing sensuality and the promise
of a sweeping romance set against the
backdrop of suspense.

Harlequin® Nocturne™

Dark and sensual paranormal
romance reads that stretch the
boundaries of conflict and desire,
life and death.

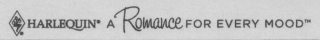